With a mother like this...

Karish was never meant to be the Duke. His older brother had had the title, and, from what I learned, had been thrilled to indulge in the aristocratic lifestyle, but he'd ruined everyone's expectations by dying before marrying or having children. That left it to his mother, the Dowager Duchess, to choose the new titleholder. For some reason, she'd chosen her second son, the Source she'd been happy to send away to the Academy, the son who'd never had a moment of training in the duties of being a titleholder and a landlord, when there were several more qualified cousins clambering to take the title.

Karish hadn't wanted the title, for which I'd be forever grateful. He couldn't be both a Source and a Duke, with all the Duke's responsibilities. If he had taken the title, he wouldn't have been able to work as a Source, which would mean he'd have no use for me. Bonded to him, I wouldn't be able to work with any other Source. I would have been left with nothing to do.

Karish pulled back and straightened his shoulders. "The Empress obviously misunderstands the gravity of the situation and merely needs instruction."

"And the fact that pursuing the title could get you hanged, what about that?"

"That's just the law. What is the law to her?"

Marvelous. The blasted woman was going to get us both killed.

D1012235

The Hero
Strikes Back

Moira J. Moore

ACE BOOKS, NEW YORK

THE BERKLEY PUBLISHING GROUP
Published by the Penguin Group
Penguin Group (USA) Inc.
375 Hudson Street, New York, New York 10014, USA
Penguin Group (Canada), 90 Eglinton Avenue East, Suite 700, Toronto, Ontario M4P 2Y3, Canada
(a division of Pearson Penguin Canada Inc.)
Penguin Books Ltd., 80 Strand, London WC2R 0RL, England
Penguin Group Ireland, 25 St. Stephen's Green, Dublin 2, Ireland (a division of Penguin Books Ltd.)
Penguin Group (Australia), 250 Camberwell Road, Camberwell, Victoria 3124, Australia
(a division of Pearson Australia Group Pty. Ltd.)
Penguin Books India Pvt. Ltd., 11 Community Center, Panchsheel Park, New Delhi—110 017, India
Penguin Group (NZ), Cnr. Airborne and Rosedale Roads, Albany, Auckland 1310, New Zealand
(a division of Pearson New Zealand Ltd.)
Penguin Books (South Africa) (Pty.) Ltd., 24 Sturdee Avenue, Rosebank, Johannesburg 2196,
South Africa

Penguin Books Ltd., Registered Offices: 80 Strand, London WC2R 0RL, England

This is a work of fiction. Names, characters, places, and incidents either are the product of the author's
imagination or are used fictitiously, and any resemblance to actual persons, living or dead, business
establishments, events, or locales is entirely coincidental. The publisher does not have any control over
and does not assume any responsibility for author or third-party websites or their content.

THE HERO STRIKES BACK

An Ace Book / published by arrangement with the author

PRINTING HISTORY
Ace mass-market edition / September 2006

Copyright © 2006 by Moira Moore.
Cover art by Matt Stawicki.
Cover design by Rita Frangie.
Interior text design by Stacy Irwin.

ISBN: 0-441-01440-2

ACE
Ace Books are published by The Berkley Publishing Group,
a division of Penguin Group (USA) Inc.,
375 Hudson Street, New York, New York 10014.
ACE and the "A" design are trademarks belonging to Penguin Group (USA) Inc.

PRINTED IN THE UNITED STATES OF AMERICA

10   9   8   7   6   5   4   3   2   1

To Melissa Stone,
keeper of my sanity

Special thanks to

In addition to the usual suspects . . .

The people of O'Flynn Weese Tausendfreund LLP,
for being the best group of people
I could ever imagine working with,
and for being so supportive of my writing.

And Grecos,
my favourite restaurant in Kingston,
for letting me take over one of their tables
for hours while I wrote.

Chapter One

I was not drunk, but I had every right to be, considering the circumstances. I was on the small side and I'd had little to eat all day. It was cold in the middle of summer. My married mother was on the other side of the room flirting with the new Captain of the Western Runners, and the too-good-looking brother of the hostess was trying to charm me. So, all in all, I deserved a drink or four, and I thought I was doing pretty well. I was still upright, my words weren't slurred, and I hadn't done anything to embarrass myself. Yet.

I couldn't work because my partner, Source Shintaro Karish, was still in Erstwhile, attending the Empress, whatever that meant. I hated not working. I hadn't spent seventeen years of my life in an academy training to be a Shield just to sit around doing nothing. But I couldn't work without my Source, and that was that.

"Can I have another of these?" I asked Erin Demaris, the aforementioned brother of the hostess. I held out my glass, which until a few moments before had held the remnants of a dangerously tasty concoction involving strawberries, rum and crushed ice.

"Certainly," he said, taking the glass and twisting in his chair to hold it out to his sister. "Another berry frost, Risa."

His sister, Risa Demaris, turned from another conversation, her earrings chiming lightly as she moved. I looked at her with envy. Tall, leanly muscled, with tightly braided red hair, she enjoyed an air of power and fierce elegance. Her gorgeous brown skin glowed against her orange and gold sarong. I'd always hated the color orange, but she made it look tasteful and joyous. There was no way she could ever pass unnoticed in a crowd.

I'd met her the previous year, when my Source had gone missing. She'd been one of the Runners assigned to find him. She hadn't, because no one would have ever suspected a Source could be abducted away to another city by another Source. I'd found him myself, but only because I'd been deliberately led to him by one of the abductor's followers.

Many of the Runners I'd encountered upon our return to High Scape had seemed offended by my interference. Runners investigated crimes. Shields protected Sources while said Sources calmed earthquakes and tornadoes and all the other intense natural disasters that constantly threatened our cities. Never the two shall meet.

Risa had invited me over for dinner. She was that sort of person.

She glared at Erin. He grinned back at her, a wide uninhibited display of even white teeth. She snatched the glass from him. She pointed at me as she looked at him. "You're lucky I like her," she informed him before heading off to the kitchen.

I watched him turn back around in his chair. Once upon a time blue eyes had been my preference. Not so long ago, the preference had somehow slid over to black. Erin had just the kind of dark come-drown-in-me eyes that had become so dangerous to me. Short black hair coiled close to the head, creamy brown skin, and that easy white smile. He was, I thought glumly, beautiful. He was also a good deal older than his sister, and he had the comfortable, settled confidence of the mature man. What was he doing talking to me?

He was telling me about the law. He was a solicitor, of all things. But he wasn't boring about it. He'd had me laughing, earlier, telling me about ludicrous obscure laws no one remembered, but for which people could still be prosecuted. Like it was illegal to hang one's laundry outside on sevenday in Darkenwood. Or it was illegal to pretend to practice—though not to actually practice—witchcraft in Red Deer. And my personal favorite, in Gathering Place it was illegal to walk a pig on a leash on the street. Erin couldn't tell me whether it was the pig, the leash, or the city street that was objectionable, though he did claim there were no similar restrictions on any other species of livestock.

"So how long are you staying in High Scape?" I asked him, trying to keep him talking so I wouldn't have to. He was a resident of Erstwhile, the Empress' City. Where Karish was right then.

And could I please stop thinking about Karish? Just for a moment? Please?

Erin shrugged. "However long it takes us to patch together the Bill. There are only eighteen of us." He rolled his eyes. "So it shouldn't take more than a few years."

The Bill. Meant to create a new quota within the Imperial Council. Once it was passed, at least a third of the seats would have to be held by members of the merchant class. Or so said the rumors. Mother was very excited about it, and sometimes I suspected the real reason she was visiting me was to somehow watch the Bill being created. That or Prince Gifford's visit, scheduled for later that summer.

I still didn't understand why the Bill was being drafted in High Scape instead of Erstwhile. High Scape was the economic center, but Erstwhile was the seat of political power. Then again, most of the merchants, the powerful ones, lived in High Scape. Were they actually being consulted?

I'd heard most of the High Landers were spitting nails over the Bill. They had no interest in sharing power, or the

Council's Chambers, with merchants. The Empress was insistent on shoving it through. Her son and heir, Prince Gifford, hated the idea, and had declared his opposition so loudly that even I, generally ignorant of politics as I usually was, had heard of his views.

Risa reappeared, a fresh drink in hand. "Here ya go, kid," she said. "You're lucky I like you, too. Do you have any idea how expensive ice is this year?"

I was sure my stare was quite blank. "Expensive? Ice? It's just frozen water."

Erin chuckled. "Sure, plenty of that in winter. Not so easy to come by in summer. Even one as cold as this one."

I looked at the drink in my hand. "Where does this come from, then?"

Risa shrugged. "I buy it from the ice man, who delivers it in a big cube wrapped in burlap. It's good for only a few days."

"And this costs money?"

"Everything costs money, Dunleavy."

Well, aye, I knew that. Sources and Shields didn't use money, as we were given free goods, services and shelter in exchange for our unpaid labor. Everyone else had to pay for things, though, and I understood the necessity of it.

Still. Ice? Ice was something created by nature. It was like asking people to pay for air.

And this was my third berry frost. I wish I'd known there was a cost associated with it. Because I didn't want it anymore.

But I didn't dare say that. "Thank you, Risa. I really appreciate it."

"No worries," she said with a wink. "Is the music all right for you?"

I'd been too distracted to even hear the music for the past hour or so. I concentrated on the light lyrical strands floating from the flutist stuck in the far corner. "No danger of that making me go berserk," I assured her. "Your furniture is safe. So are your guests."

Risa nodded, then slapped her brother on the shoulder. "Stop monopolizing her."

He raised his eyebrows. "Do you see some kind of barricade around us?" he demanded with amusement. "Anyone is free to join us if they wish."

"Huh," she said, unimpressed. Then she wandered away, her attention caught by someone else.

"But," Erin continued, briefly touching the back of my hand, "whether or not I've been monopolizing you, I have been monopolizing the conversation. So please," he gestured at me, "What's it like to be a Shield?"

Ugh. I hated that question. I heard it so very often. I'd been out of the academy for a little more than a year and I was already sick of trying to describe my calling to people who couldn't possibly understand. There were parts of it I just couldn't explain, because I didn't understand them myself. They just were. Other aspects were, as far as I was concerned, none of their business. But I had to tell them something.

The upside to being asked the same question about eighty thousand times was that I had developed a nice neat answer that usually addressed every element of a regular's curiosity. "I was born with this ability," I said, my voice immediately dropping into the sing-song of a well-worn recital, "and my parents sent me to the academy when I was four years old. I don't remember this happening, but I have been told it was not a traumatic experience for me. It rarely is for Shields. My family was able to visit me often and I feel I know them well." Or as well as I could, under the circumstances. "I enjoyed my classes, mostly. I really do have a little more difficulty feeling things like pain—or the cold—than regulars, and I had to be taught how to feel them when I was a child. I am, however, extremely sensitive to the effects of music, which is why Risa is showing such care. It can make me very emotional, sometimes violent, and it is kind of Risa to invite me to a gathering like this, especially when my Source isn't available to watch

me." I hated, really really hated, that Karish was needed to
keep me under control at times. It was so humiliating. "I
really am bonded to my Source, and no, that does not mean
we are in love or can't bear to be out of each other's company." I knew I was wasting my time there. I'd read enough
novels and seen enough plays to know regulars loved ro-
manticizing the Pair bond. Every Pair in every piece of fiction, tragedy or comedy, ended up lovers. "All it really
means is that I can shield Karish better than I can any other
Source." Well, no it could sometimes mean more than that.
We could make each other feel better with proximity and
touch, easing aches and injuries. I always beat him at cards,
because I could somehow tell how he felt about his hand.
And the big disadvantage: When one partner died, the
other died with them. But I didn't tend to discuss that sort
of thing with regulars. Give them a little bit of information
about the emotional and physical impacts of the bond and
they started weaving weird fantasies. "Shielding is difficult but also exciting. Basically it entails making sure the
forces the Source is handling during an event or disaster
don't crush him and kill him." A simplified version of
events, but it was really hard to explain to people who
couldn't do it.

Erin blinked, looking a little stunned. Then he smiled. I
had a feeling he had realized his question wasn't exactly
original. Smart lad. "And what is it like to be a Shield for
Lord Shintaro Karish?"

Ooh, hated that question even more. "Karish is a thorough professional."

But Erin didn't want to know about that. They never did.
"That's not exactly what I asked," he said, which was kind
of true. "And one hears things about him."

It was my turn to shrug. "No one can help what people
say about him except those that do the talking." And if some
of the rumors were based on fact, well, that was no one's
business. I wasn't going to defend Karish's actions to anyone. He was a good, decent man and an excellent Source

and what he did in his free time with consenting adults was purely his affair.

Another bent smile. "I see."

And that was it. Apparently he was ready to drop it. How unique of him.

Something shattered, the sharp sound exploding across the room, halting music and conversation. "Damn it!" I heard Risa hiss.

Erin was on his feet. "What happened?" he demanded.

"The damned bottle exploded. Just as I was opening it."

"She's sliced her hand up pretty bad," I heard someone say. Bardma stood beside Risa, holding the Runner's hand and peering into the blood. "I can't see any glass," she said, "but it's hard to be sure."

Erin looked down at me. "Excuse me," he said to me. He was off before I nodded. He took Risa by the elbow and led her towards the kitchen. I knew nothing about medical aid, and it didn't appear life threatening, so I decided not to follow him.

Bardma knelt down to pick up the pieces of broken bottle. "Careful," I said, grabbing up some serviettes to mop up the wine. At least the wine was white.

"It's the Spring Vale, too," Bardma muttered. "Too bad. Though it's not like she should be splashing out on that sort of thing."

I had no idea how much money a Runner earned, and if the number of coins were told to me it wouldn't mean much anyway. But it always seemed to me that every time Risa threw a party, she served the best of everything. "Risa is very generous," I said.

"Hmph," was Bardma's response. For some reason this resulted in an uncomfortable silence.

"What was that lovely piece you were just playing?" my mother asked the startled flutist.

She blinked. "Uh, Twilight Sonata," she stuttered.

"Please, start it again. It will soothe my nerves after hearing about poor Lord Greenmist." My mother laid her hand against the base of her throat, as though she were worried about fainting. An oddly fragile gesture from a woman I knew to be robust and calm.

"Oh my yes, can you believe it?" said a young woman named Delia, who worked at the pie shop Risa loved. As far as I knew, that was the only thing the two of them had in common. Delia made pies and Risa loved eating them. Risa could make friends with absolutely anyone.

"Just disappearing like that," Delia continued, snapping her fingers. "It's spooky."

"Oh, no doubt he'll show up in a ditch somewhere," said Samuel, a bailiff. "Probably got drunk and was attacked by robbers."

Shaka, a street artist who thought he knew everything, snorted. "They'd be wasting their time, wouldn't they? Greenmist's pockets have less in them than mine."

It never ceased to amaze me, the kinds of intimate details strangers knew about each other. I'd never heard of Greenmist before he went missing. I certainly didn't know the weight of his purse. But once he disappeared he was famous, and everyone knew how well—or badly—he'd done in school, who he slept with and what he liked to eat for breakfast. Incredible.

"If he looked the part of a lord, they wouldn't know he was broke until after they went after his purse," Captain Wong pointed out.

"And then they would have killed him for raising their hopes."

"Don't say that, Shaka," Delia chided him. "There's no reason to think he's dead."

"No reason to think he isn't," Shaka retorted. "No one's found any of the other High Landers that have gone missing, have they? The Risto Reaper strikes again, and gets away scot free."

Puerile name aside, I had to admit—to myself—that I was feeling uneasy, too. Five disappearances over five months, all of them aristocrats, with no indications of why they were disappearing. No one knew for sure that there was a single person behind it, if the disappearances were even connected at all, but stories of the Risto Reaper, some brilliant, mad villain intent on cleaning out the High Landed class of its least appealing members, were making the rounds. And for that reason, I was willing to let Karish linger in Erstwhile for as long as he liked.

Captain Wong's eyes narrowed at the less than subtle criticism. "We're working on it," he snapped.

"Sure you are, Captain, but nothing's turning up, is it?"

The party had taken a decidedly dark turn.

"He might have merely taken a vacation," said the Captain.

I wanted to smirk. I couldn't believe he'd said that. How weak. Captain Wong knew it, too, if the way he flushed were any indication.

"Without telling anyone about it?" Shaka mocked him.

"Besides," Samuel added, "he didn't have any money either. Where was he going to go?"

Visiting friends and family who had money. I'd heard aristocrats did a lot of leeching.

"What would anyone want with landless High Landers?" the Captain challenged them. "All the High Landers who've gone missing have had no power, no money, no land. There was no reason to take any of them. Or kill any of them. And we have no evidence at all that the disappearances are related to each other. I tell you, it's just a bunch of bad coincidences. Or someone's idea of a joke."

"Oh, who cares?" Zeva piped up, speaking for the first time. She was a prostitute. I found it ironic she had been invited to a Runner's home for a social engagement. "They're High Landers. Useless High Landers. If there is someone picking them off, they're doing us a favor."

"That's a terrible thing to say," Delia scolded her.

"Oh, grow up."

"*If* someone's doing something to these people," said the Captain, "it is a crime, and they will be punished."

"Aye, as soon as you can figure out what is going on and who is doing it," said Shaka, his voice nicely laced with derision.

And they were off. Suddenly the whole room was taken over with competing discussions concerning the uselessness of High Landers and the ineffectiveness of Runners. I folded my collection of sodden serviettes and put them on a table. I made my way through the crowd, sneaking up to my mother's side. "Well done, Mother."

"I thought so," my mother responded without a trace of remorse. "It's certainly more interesting than talking about the most fashionable length of skirts this season."

She had a point there. I didn't know if Risa would appreciate my mother setting her guests at each other's throats, though.

"You seem to be enjoying Erin's company," my mother said.

"You seem to be enjoying the Captain's," I retorted sharply. Ooh, bad. Keep the tone even.

"Yes, he's interesting," she answered, unmoved by my obvious disapproval. "I spend so much time talking to holders and traders, it's nice to meet someone with a completely different perspective on things. I'm sure you understand."

The hell I did. I wasn't laughing coyly and flipping my hair at anyone. "What would Father say if he saw you flirting that way?" And why was I still talking? It had nothing to do with me.

Mother stared at me, surprised. Then she started laughing. Not the reaction I'd been expecting. "My dear sweet cloistered child! That wasn't flirting!"

I was not sweet, cloistered, or a child. "You were fiddling with your hair," I pointed out.

"Yes, well, I wasn't trained out of my natural twitches, dear," my mother said dryly. "Unlike some."

I'd never had any twitches. "I'm serious, Mother."

"Yes, dear, aren't you always."

I had discovered that my mother was never short of

a quick comeback. That could be annoying. "It is not appropriate for you to be making up to another man—"

Mother rolled her eyes. "I was not making up to him, Lee. I was just talking to him, and enjoying it. We are people. People are meant to enjoy each other's attractions."

"Mother!" I couldn't believe what I was hearing.

"I'm not talking about sex, Lee."

Gods. Struck speechless. I was not hearing this. Surely I wasn't too old to stick my fingers in my ears and hum? Surely.

"What is wrong with enjoying another person's wit? Or the timber of their voice? What's wrong with liking the knowledge that they enjoy your company, too?"

I tried again. "When you're married—"

"You swear your loyalty to one person. And your fidelity. It doesn't mean you can't enjoy the company of other people. And it doesn't mean we can't like being attractive to others. Else we'd all be wearing black." She looked me up and down with blatant censure.

I wasn't wearing black. I was wearing a dark blue gown of simple, practical lines. It wasn't the most attractive gown I had, but it was warm. I'd wanted something warm. "Don't start, Mother."

"That dress—"

"I like this dress."

"It's a lovely dress. For someone twice your years."

So? I hadn't noticed a real difference in the fashion of young girls and mature women, more's the pity. "It's fine."

"It does nothing for your complexion or your figure."

Was pale a complexion? And I had, unfortunately, no figure to speak of. I was neither ethereally thin nor sensually voluptuous. The best anyone could say about me was that I was healthy.

There were times when it was appropriate for me to go to the extraordinary effort of looking my pitiful best. An informal party given by a friend was not one of those times. I'd just have to charm people with my winning personality.

But my mother wouldn't accept that. It was the only thing marring her visit. From day one she hadn't stopped harping on my clothes. "Leave it, Mother. I mean it."

"Right then." Mother nodded. "How about we come to an agreement? I won't comment on your way of doing things and you won't comment on mine."

"Fine." My mother was a grown woman. If she wanted to make a duplicitous, unfaithful fool of her . . .

I shook my head, actually shook my head right there in the middle of the room where everyone could see me. It was none of my business. Really. I hadn't lived with the family since I was four years old. I had no idea how they behaved on the day-to-day basis. Maybe my father was a flirt, too.

It was strange, seeing my mother every day, without the rest of my family. I wouldn't have thought of such a visit myself. But I'd barely settled back in to High Scape after returning from Erstwhile before I got a letter from my mother, telling me she was going to visit and teach me how to live in the real world.

She didn't actually write that last bit out, but that was what she meant. I could tell. And I didn't mind. It had been made clear to me, not long after I left the academy, that I didn't understand how regular people lived.

And I didn't really know my mother, despite what I had said to Erin. Despite what I often actually thought. I knew her better than most of the students of the academy had known theirs, for my family had had the means and the inclination to visit me almost annually. But those had been short visits, only a couple of weeks, barely worth the trip. And they had been on academy grounds, where we were all subject to academy rules. And it had been my mother and father and sister and brothers and me.

This was different. Mother was staying for an indefinite time—and with her behavior with the Captain I was beginning to wonder why, if there was something going on with the family that I knew nothing about—and it was just her, with none of the others for distraction. We were both adults, free of anyone's rules but our own. She was staying at an expensive boarding house called the Lion's Den, but she spent most of her days at the Triple S house, occasionally staying the night. Which sort of made me the host, but she was my mother, which meant—didn't it?—that she had some kind of authority over me. It was a logistical mess. Who was supposed to be making the decisions for whom?

I went back to my drink. It had started to melt. It didn't taste as good that way.

Risa and Erin returned from the kitchen, halting the conversations because they were carrying food, which always had that effect. And the food was on fire. Chunks of meat and whatnot on sticks, on fire. Apparently it was supposed to be served that way. I didn't know if serving flaming food to alcohol-filled people was the best idea ever, but it certainly made a good spectacle.

After everyone who cared for some had been served with torched meat and fresh drinks, Erin came back to me. "Sorry about that."

"Is she all right?"

"She seems to be, just washed off the blood and wrapped a bandage around her hand, but with Risa it's always hard to tell. You know these law enforcement types. Can't show any pain unless you're actually dead, and then, well, what's the point?"

He said that as though it were a bad thing.

"Ah hell!" Samuel shouted, disgust blatant in his tone, his words silencing the conversation and music once more. He was staring out a window. "It's snowing!"

Snowing? Was that what he'd said? As in white, frozen precipitation?

A rush to the other windows in the flat, and I was no better than the others. I flipped aside a curtain and, aye, it was snowing. Hard. Pretty.

"But it's summer!" Delia wailed.

"Don't suppose there's anything you can do about this," Samuel said to me.

I was startled by the question. This was snow, not an earthquake. Why would he even think to ask me that? I shook my head. "I can't do anything without Taro. Besides, we can't do anything about snow."

The expression on Samuel's face suggested that might have been one of the stupidest things he'd ever heard. "You don't *do* snow?" he demanded.

That was not what I had said, and I certainly hadn't used a tone that implied mere snow was somehow beneath the efforts of a Triple S Pair. "We can't do anything about snow, rain, overcast days. You know, normal weather. Just cyclones and earthquakes and the like. Big, unnatural events."

"Are you trying to tell me snow in the middle of summer isn't unnatural?"

He had me there, but it didn't change the fact that there was nothing I could do.

I set my drink down. No more alcohol for me. It was depressing me. And really, there was no reason for feeling inadequate. Karish would be back soon; he'd promised in his last letter. Then I'd be back on the roster and back at work and life would feel normal again.

"Damn it," said Zeva. "As if business weren't bad enough this summer. This'll just kill it."

"You're telling me." Delia, who'd been holding up a curtain to stare at the snow, let it slide back into place. She looked at Zeva and smiled wryly. "I'm sure you'll do better then me, though. I have a feeling there are more willing to brave the cold for your product than for mine."

Zeva snorted. "Maybe," she said, "But then I just have to spend more money on frostbite cream, and I have to put it in the most unusual places."

That earned chuckles from everyone, including my mother, so I decided not to be shocked on her behalf.

"If things continue as they are, I'll have to leave town,"

said Shaka. "I'm thinking of heading south. Maybe to Three Keys."

"You're running out of money?" I asked Shaka.

"Aye. Business is real slow."

"But you've always been popular." His shows involved a combination of juggling, sleight of hand and vocal comedy, and every time I'd seen him he'd been surrounded by a throng of spectators.

"No one wants to stand around in this cold."

"But—" I cut myself off. I had no right to ask why, with day after day of huge piles of coins tossed at Shaka's feet, he now found himself without because things had slowed down for a while. While I couldn't understand why someone whose livelihood was so reliant on the weather didn't fortify himself against the event that the weather turned difficult simply by putting aside some money, it wasn't my place to say anything about it. I didn't have to pay for anything. What did I know about budgeting or saving for the future?

"Hey," said Risa, her voice sharp. "That's enough talk about money. I happen to know no one with any class talks about money at parties. Amia, start playing."

The music resumed. Erin fetched more wood and built up the fire until it was roaring. It gave the room a cheery atmosphere, and after a while everyone seemed to forget it was an atmosphere unsuited to the season. More drink, more food, more conversation. All in all, a successful party, despite lacking any outbreak of scandal or a brawl. I had a good time.

But when Mother and I left the warm flat, it was still snowing. That was strange. And I didn't like strange. The last time things were strange, it was because a twisted crazy Source had used his abilities to deliberately create said cyclones and earthquakes and the like. For the fun of it. Because he could. Because he was bored. And crazy. He had chosen toppling cities and causing the deaths of thousands as a sort of hobby.

Strange was bad.

I pulled the collar of my dress closer to my neck. The chill was making even me uncomfortable. And it seemed to me a bad sign. Bad signs put me in a bad mood. And bad moods were just plain unprofessional. .

So I ignored the chill. Problem solved.

Chapter Two

It had been snowing for three days. Big fat flakes that stayed on the ground, and accumulated, and built up, and soaked through boots and caused collisions in the streets and killed crops and generally infuriated everyone. Except the kids, who were having a grand time building snow forts and engaging in snowball fights. But it was winter, in the middle of summer. It was weird and frightening and really, really irritating.

I tapped my boot against the door frame, dislodging the snow that had been caked to the sole. On the second day, when I realized that the snow was going to be around for a while, I had dug out my winter wardrobe, which only gave my mother fresh fodder for eye-rolling and pained expressions. My choice of winter clothing caused her some distress. She claimed it was possible to have clothes that were both practical and stylish. I had begged to differ. It seemed to me one always had to be sacrificed to the other, and I preferred to ditch the style and keep the comfort. Besides, there was a rush on materials that merchants had packed away or left to dwindle for the summer season. The tailors were in a panic and their services were scarce. As a Shield I could be put on the top of any list, my orders given priority over any, even the High Landed, but I'd never felt right about pulling rank like that. Especially when I already had clothes I was perfectly happy with, my mother be damned.

"You're back quick," the bedamned woman called out as I pulled off my boots.

"The stalls weren't out." I'd been sent out by my mother to hunt down bay leaves. Being sent out on errands for my mother was a new experience for me. One I couldn't say I cared for.

"Oh well. I guess I can do without it."

I hung up my cloak on a peg by the door and wandered into the kitchen. "That smells really good."

My mother shrugged. "It's only stew," she said, stirring the pot. "Nothing special. I should teach you how to cook."

I pulled out some cutlery. "Ben usually cooks for us."

"Ben's not here, though, is he?"

There was something censorious about her tone that irked me. "No, Mother, he isn't."

"You shouldn't have to rely on others to cook for you."

I'd often thought so myself. Why did having her say the exact same thing irritate me so much?

We heard the entrance door open and close. A loud thud on the floor, followed by some lighter ones, as of someone stamping their feet.

"Ah, good, one of the others are here," Mother commented. "I've made enough for everyone. I can't believe, with six and a half Pairs living here, how empty this place always is."

I hated being called half a Pair.

I quietly stepped out of the kitchen, into the corridor to the foyer. I wanted to see who it was before calling out an invitation to join us. If it were La Monte or, far worse, Wilberforce, I'd back into the kitchen unnoticed.

There was no chance of that once I saw who was standing at the door, reading a letter. He was shorter and slighter than most men, with golden brown skin and his black hair growing long in lazy curves, and he was most definitely a sight for sore eyes. I smiled. "Taro!"

Lord (former) Shintaro Karish looked up from his letter, the frown between his eyebrows melting away. "Evening, my love!" he said before grabbing me up in a bear hug and lifting me clear off my feet. I rolled my eyes and hugged him back and didn't dwell on the fact that I probably would have felt hurt had he done anything less.

It felt good to hold him. I'd missed him.

"You're back earlier than you'd said," I commented once he'd put me back on my feet. I brushed snow off his shoulder, the one with the black Source braid.

He grinned, the completely carefree grin, the one that made his black eyes crinkle at the corners. "Her Royal Imperial Majesty got bored with me, didn't she?" he announced gaily. "With what she most enjoyed contented least."

I was taking a good look at him, and I was shocked. Karish was a fine-boned, slender man. Right then he looked gaunt, his cheekbones jutting out harshly through his skin. He seemed a little pale, and he was obviously exhausted. "What the hell have you been doing to yourself?" I demanded. "You look awful."

He cocked an eyebrow. "Thank you so much, darling. You always know just what to say to make me feel good about myself."

"Were you revelling every night or what?"

"So I must have been."

"Zaire, Taro. You're not ill, are you?"

He was starting to look annoyed. "I've just gotten off the road, Lee. I pushed myself hard to get here. Give over."

All right. Fine. The solution was not to nag but to get him back into decent shape. "Of course. You're just in time for supper."

His eyes widened in panic he manfully attempted to hide. "Uh—"

I could practically see the wheels turning in his head as

he desperately searched for a graceful way to back out. I thought about letting him hang in torment but decided to take pity on him. I hadn't seen him in months, after all. There would be plenty of opportunities to torture him later. "My mother's cooking, you snob."

"Oi, your mother! I forgot she was here. I'm sorry." He looked up the stairs and bent to pick up his bags, with the obvious intention of heading up to his suite.

I grabbed his arm. "Don't be ridiculous. She'll be thrilled to see you again. It's probably the real reason she came." She'd been disappointed, when she'd first arrived in High Scape, to learn he was still in Erstwhile. "Your cloak, sir. Mother!" He winced at the shout. "Taro's joining us for dinner."

"Good!" she shouted back. "There's plenty."

I raised my eyebrows at him. See? I took his cloak and hung it on a peg, then led him into the kitchen. "I don't know if you remember meeting my mother—"

"Holder Mallorough," he interrupted me smoothly. He just as smoothly took her hand and kissed the back of it. "My memory is indeed faulty. I'd forgotten you were so lovely."

"No flirting with my mother, Karish," I growled at him.

"Mind your own business, dear," my mother chided me in a preoccupied tone, her eyes never leaving Karish's face.

He laughed.

I went back to the cutlery drawer. Perhaps reintroducing my mother and my Source wasn't the best idea after all. They were both impossible.

"Most people who aren't my children call me Teshia, Lord Shintaro."

"Ah." A flicker of discomfort crossed his face. "It's just Shintaro, now. Taro, preferably."

"I told you that, Mother." I let an edge develop in my voice. This was a sensitive subject for Karish, and I had warned her about it. She should have known better.

But my mother was unapologetic. "Some things transcend officialdom."

"Sit down, Taro." I returned the bottle of white wine to the icebox and pulled a bottle of red from the cupboard next to it.

"Yes, do," said my mother, moving back to the stove. "And tell us what the Empress' court is like." She poured the stew from the pot to a bowl and set it on the table.

Karish snickered as he sat. "They'll be breaking their necks any time now."

I thought about that for a moment, then shook my head. Context wasn't going to help with that one. "Huh?" I said.

Karish picked up a serviette and refolded it. "Prince Gifford came to a party wearing gold. All gold clothes and some kind of gold cosmetic all over his skin, and gold glittery stuff in his hair. People went crazy for it. And at the next party, at least half the guests were entirely in blue, or entirely in red, and so forth. No gold, of course. That belonged to the Prince. Yellow was as close as anyone dared to go." He jeered. "Looked ridiculous."

"Oh, and what color did you prefer?" I asked him, filling up his wine glass.

He looked at me with scorn. "I did not wear paint," he sniffed.

"Ah, that's why only half the guests wore it," I teased him. "It must have been a horrible quandary for them, poor nobles. Do they follow the illustrious example of their prince, or that of the dazzling . . . Shintaro Karish." Oops. I'd almost said 'lord.'

He stuck his tongue out at me.

Mother looked a little shocked at that. I was, too, really. Karish was usually a bit more reserved—uh, maybe the more appropriate word was adult—around people he didn't know well. But perhaps he was tired.

Mother placed a bowl of salad and a platter of sliced bread on the table and took her seat. "Certainly after all those months at court you saw more than absurd fashions?" She ladled some stew onto his plate.

"Oh, of course. Lots of drama. Lots of intrigue. Who

was friends with whom. Who was sleeping with whom. Who had fallen out with whom." He smiled, a wry expression. "It reminded me a lot of the academy, actually. Only with harder edges and more serious consequences."

I suddenly had a vision of growing up at the Source academy. It wasn't pretty. Just imagine, day after day surrounded by hyper-emotional Sources. While they were children. And adolescents. What a nightmare.

Karish tasted the stew. "Teshia, this is delicious."

"Thank you," my mother answered, her tone pensive as her mind was clearly on other matters. "What do you think of the movement to put members of the merchant class on the council?"

Karish shrugged. "The general answer is that it's a good idea. They no doubt have a better understanding of economics than your average risto, which will make for a better budget plan, if nothing else. Er, maybe. But I do hope the merchant class isn't expecting some kind of revolution should their members make it to council. They'll just likely take on the opinions of their aristocratic colleagues."

Mother pursed her lips. "That's a cynical attitude."

"Wands are evil."

Mother cocked her head to one side. "I'm afraid I don't understand," she admitted.

Karish's expression was one of untrustworthy innocence. "Understand what?" he asked.

"Why I'm talking politics when you must be sick of dealing with them," said my mother, though I knew that wasn't what she had been thinking about.

"Well, I am happy to be getting away from it," Karish said. "There's too much ritual involved in everything the courtiers do, from saying good morning to asking someone to dance." And all of a sudden, a look of dismay blossomed over his face.

Oh no. "What's wrong?" I asked him in alarm.

He grimaced. "I have to go to that ball party thing Yellows is throwing for Gifford," he said sourly. "There was an invitation waiting for me in the hall."

I started laughing.

"It's not funny."

"It's hilarious." I could think of nothing more boring than a party thrown by aristocrats. Oh, I'd heard of the twisted things some of them got to, when they indulged in private house parties, but this sort of affair, widely known and with the very proper Prince in attendance, would no doubt be as dull as cricket.

"Cruel, evil woman."

"Are you going to let him speak that way to me, Mother?"

Mother wasn't listening to us. She appeared to be studying Karish. "I don't suppose you're wearing a wig."

Karish appeared startled. He wasn't the only one. My head was hurting with all the leaps in subject. "No. Why?"

"That hair is wasted on a man."

He grinned. "Shall I shave it off?"

"Do I want to win the acrimony of every woman in High Scape?"

"And every man," I muttered into my wine.

"Please don't encourage her," said Karish, but I wasn't sure who he was talking to.

"But you might want to trim it a little."

"Mother!" How Karish wore his hair was absolutely none of her business. How could she?

Again, she knew no shame. "And you," she said to me. "You have this beautiful red hair that you insist on wearing scraped back from your face in that unappealing fashion."

So I didn't like my hair hanging in my face. Who cared for fashion?

"Not always," said Karish, spearing his last morsel of meat. Mother gave him more stew. "She dresses it nicely for parties and whatnot."

No no, it wasn't at all irritating to be spoken about in that way.

"She had it scraped back like that for Risa's party the other night."

Hey, with all that flaming food being flung about I was the safest person in the room.

"And this horrible—"

"It was not horrible!"

"—shapeless—"

"It wasn't shapeless."

"—drab sack of a gown."

"I thought you were going to give this a rest?" Because surely it wasn't right to criticize my appearance like that. Surely it was rude.

"I lied."

Karish snickered.

"I will dress in the way that makes me comfortable, Mother." Especially after hearing her go on about it. Yes, I was that obstinate, contrary and petty. I was not going to let her shoehorn me into anything now. Not even if I liked it.

"Yes, that's all very upfront, this is me, take it or leave it brutally honest," my mother said dismissively. "And while Erin demonstrated his maturity and depth of character by being able to see beyond the bland exterior, don't you think you should reward his remarkable skills of perception by giving him something pretty to look at next time?"

No. Start as you mean to go on, I always say. Besides, expecting me to be pretty was unrealistic.

Karish straightened in his chair. "Who is this?" he asked.

Thank you, Mother. Like he doesn't tease me enough. "Risa's brother."

"Lee's new conquest," my mother added with an impish smile.

More wine. Definitely needed more wine. "You can cease and desist with the wedding plans, Mother. I'm not interested."

Mother looked stunned. "Why not?" she demanded, and

to my ear it sounded like there was an edge of actual anger in her voice. "He's perfectly charming."

"He's too good looking," I announced, and immediately wished I hadn't. When did my tongue get so loose? It would have been fine had I said that when there wasn't an astonishingly good-looking man in the room. I could have explained why gorgeous men tended to be dangerous and unreliable and a little lacking in the personality department. Of course, Karish had personality, and he wasn't dangerous or unreliable as long as I didn't sleep with him, but how could I say all that in front of him without sounding like an idiot? "Besides, he's a solicitor."

"What's wrong with him being a solicitor?" my mother asked, her voice rising very high in her exasperation.

I shrugged. "They're too slick. And too quick with their words. I'd never win an argument."

"Zaire, girl, you're getting ridiculous." Mother wrenched a slice of bread apart with unnecessary enthusiasm. "No doctors because they're all quacks. No moneylenders because their priorities are skewed. No sailors because they're at sea most of the time."

Though, to think about it, that was probably an asset. Really. Keep the romance alive by not seeing each other too often.

"No one in the Triple S because that's *too* incestuous. No one involved in politics or city planning because they're too boring. And now no solicitors because they can outtalk you. Seriously, child, the way you're going, there aren't going to be any professions left."

Karish was watching me. And hey, the return of the expressionless mask. I hadn't seen that for a while. Of course, he'd been away.

"What's next?" my mother asked. "The color of their eyes?"

I sighed, rested my chin in the palm of my hand, and watched my mother. Sometimes it was best just to let things slide.

"Well, Teshia," Karish drawled, "While I agree Lee's list of restrictions wanders some into the ludicrous—" let it slide "—I can't be surprised that she's being so severe with herself. She has appalling taste in men."

I didn't glare at him. Really, I didn't. I just looked at him kind of hard. "One word," I said. "Amanda."

He glared, though. "She was not—" He cut himself off.

What, one of his lovers? Perhaps not anymore, but she had been at one time. If my mother weren't there I would have had a field day with him. His sex life resembled a parade. Lots of material for snappy retorts. But not in front of my mother.

The corner of his mouth quirked up in a familiar sly smile that was never good news for me. "Teshia," he said, his voice low and silky. "Lee is always so reserved, so much in control. It's hard to imagine what she was like as a little girl."

Oh bloody hell.

But my mother didn't light up with glee, as I would have expected. She did smile, but it was a sad expression. "Shield children aren't like other children, Taro," she told him. "Lee was always a little . . . serious. Not so inclined to get into anything foolish. I wish I had some embarrassing stories to tell you, but those kinds of incidents are usually the result of impulse. As I understand it, Shields don't have much in the way of impulse. Besides, she was very young when we had to send her away. We didn't have a lot of time with her."

The awkward moment didn't last long, because Karish reached across the table and tweaked my hair. "*I* can get her to embarrass herself," he promised. "And then I'll tell you all about it."

My mother's smile brightened. "Thank you, Taro. I would really appreciate it."

Aye, thank you, Taro.

Once we had all eaten our fill, my mother covered a small fake yawn with a delicate hand. Subtle as a snowstorm. The only part of the act that wasn't blatantly obvious was the motive. "I should be getting back to the Lion."

"I'll take care of the dishes, Mother. Thank you for the excellent meal."

"Yes, thank you," Karish added hastily. "It was wonderful."

"I'm glad you enjoyed it." Mother leaned in to kiss my cheek. "Good night, love."

" 'Night, Mother."

Mother looked at Karish, reaching out to push back a lock of black hair from his forehead. He didn't flinch back, as I probably would have. He was used to people touching him. "I like you," my mother said. "I'm glad my daughter is working with a person like you."

His eyes widened. I heard him swallow. "Thank you." His voice had a bit of a rasp to it.

What was that about?

Mother left. Karish looked down at the table, tapping his plate with his finger.

I stacked the plates and carried them to the sink. Karish followed me. "Where's Ben?"

"He's been ill. We're not sure what it is. He claims old age."

"Ah." Then he shocked me by searching for the dish towel.

I raised an eyebrow. The idea of Lord Shintaro Karish, whether he actually had a title or not, doing domestic chores was just wrong.

My mother was brilliant. She had boiled water as she cooked and left it on the stove. It was still hot but not painfully so when I poured it into the sink. I never thought of doing that myself.

"Her Grace is coming to High Scape," Karish said quietly.

I scraped some soap from the bar into the sink. "Who?"

"The Dowager Duchess of Westsea."

I hesitated a moment. His mother. "Well, it's been a good while since you've seen her." I handed him a soapy dish.

He snorted. "I've gone a good seventeen years without seeing her."

What could I say to that? "Oh."

"Apparently she had been on some kind of retreat in the country—"

"Flown Raven *is* the country," I muttered.

"City slave," he said.

"Farm boy," I shot back.

"I've never even seen a farm."

"Don't trifle me with details."

"Anyway," he continued, but he looked a little less grim, which had been the point of the interruption. "The gossip failed to catch up with her at the rustic chalet where she was meditating or whatever," he sneered at the word 'meditating,' "and she only recently learned that I had abjured the title."

"Ah." I could see where this was going. "Displeased, was she?"

The sound he made might have been a breathy laugh. "Furious. Enraged. Maddened. I fear for the life of the poor servant who handed the letter to her." He opened a cabinet—the correct one, as it happened—and placed the dish inside. "She has informed me that my behavior is nothing more than rebellious nonsense. She is coming here to give me the code and drag me back to Flown Raven—only she used the word escort—to deliver said code to Archword. The solicitor. Who must be at least a thousand years old."

Damn it. Not this again. I'd thought that was all settled. "Would it matter if you did give it to him?" I asked, dumping the last of the cutlery into the dish basket. "He can't give you the title now."

He was never meant to be the Duke. His older brother had had the title, and from what I learned had been thrilled to indulge in all the aristocratic lifestyle implied, but he'd ruined everyone's expectations by dying before marrying or having children. That left it to his mother, the Dowager Duchess, to choose the new titleholder. For some reason she'd chosen her second son, the Source she'd been happy to send away to the academy, the son who'd never had a moment of training in the duties of being a titleholder and a landlord, when there were several more qualified cousins clambering to take the title.

The title didn't automatically devolve on Karish. Heirs were supposed to be chosen according to suitability, and while there was the dominant trend of passing the title to the next available sibling, lateral devolutions were not uncommon. The Dowager must have had her reasons for setting her sights on Karish, but damned if I knew what they were. The Westsea estate was reputed to be wealthy and powerful. Wouldn't she want someone competent at the head of it?

Different families had different ways of determining who was competent. Some demanded feats of strength, others feats of cunning. The Karish family had cut all of that out, and decided that the current titleholder would give a code—that's what Karish called it, and I knew nothing more about it than that—to the person they deemed worthy. At the appropriate time, when the current titleholder died or stepped down, the new heir would go to the family's solicitor and recite the code, and the title became seized on the heir and, consequently, the new titleholder.

The Karish family history was littered with occasions when the titleholder hadn't handed down the code before dying, and there had been no one else in the family who'd known it. But the blood feuds and the assassination attempts weren't enough to sway the family from their time-honored traditions. Apparently they'd been forced to develop new codes a few times.

Karish hadn't wanted the title, for which I would be forever grateful. He couldn't be both a Source and a duke, with all the duke's responsibilities. If he had taken the title, he wouldn't have been able to work as a Source, which would mean he'd have no use for me. Bonded to him, I wouldn't be able to work with any other Source. I would have been left with nothing to do.

Karish had petitioned the Empress to relieve him of any possibility of ever inheriting the title, and right up until he'd actually said the words, I'd been unable to believe he would really do it. Because to give up all that wealth and power and respect had to be next to impossible. And yet he had. And it had taken all my willpower to not hug him in gratitude the moment he did it.

"According to Her Grace, the Empress has no business meddling in our family's affairs." As though reporting her opinion called the presence of the Dowager Duchess into the room, Karish pulled back his shoulders and straightened his shoulders, a posture of formal attention. "And the very idea of the title going to a collateral line is unthinkable. The Empress obviously misunderstands the gravity of her mistake, and merely needs instruction on the proper way of things." Just as suddenly, he relaxed. A wry smile. "Never say the Karish family is lacking in arrogance."

"And the fact that the very act of pursuing the title could get you hanged, what about that?"

"That's just the law. What is the law to her?"

Marvellous. The blasted woman was going to get us both killed. "Will she know you're back in High Scape, or does she think you're still in Erstwhile?"

"The letter said she was coming here."

This was my town. She could just keep her distance. "When?"

"Couple of weeks."

I spent a moment scraping meat remains from the bottom of the roasting pot. "So what are you going to do?"

"Deal with her," he said simply. "I'm not going to Flown Raven, of course. It's all been settled. I can't go after the title now even if I wanted to. I'll just have to wait her out."

I dried my hands and pulled out a fresh bottle of wine. I uncorked it, and poured a glass for each of us. "I'll distract her while she's here." I gave him a glass.

"You damn well will not!" he snapped. "She's a perfect bitch." I choked on my wine at that. Well, at least she was perfect about it. But then, she was a Karish. "She'll show you no respect at all. She'll be appalling to you."

"I can handle that, Taro."

He had a glass of wine in his hands so he sipped it, sniffing the bouquet out of habit, but I didn't think he actually tasted it. "No, you can't, Lee. You don't know what it's like. What she's like." And, on cue, he started pacing. "You're used to being treated with a certain amount of civility. You're a Shield. People are naturally respectful. But Her Grace doesn't have any respect for anyone who isn't Landed, and for few people who are. She thinks there's no reason to waste manners on those she doesn't admire." And he paused in his pacing to drain half his glass. "She'll be horrible," he said. "She'll insult you to your face and act shocked if you dare to reciprocate. And she always knows the perfect thing to say to make you feel stupid and small and unworthy."

How would he know this, if he hasn't seen her in seventeen years?

There were the letters, though. At times, he had offered to let me read them. I'd always refused, because their contents were none of my business. Perhaps that had been a mistake.

He leaned back against the counter, one arm crossed over his chest, his other hand holding his wine glass near his lips. "So tell me about this Erik," he ordered, the previous subject swept off the table. And it was an order. Sometimes his lineage influenced his behavior. He couldn't help it.

"Who?"

"This too good looking non-Triple S solicitor that has your mother seeing wedding letters."

Oh. Erin. "I told you I wasn't interested."

"Aye, and you were lying."

"I was not!" I objected, offended. I *wasn't* interested in Erin. What, my mother could drool all over the Captain and it means nothing, but I have a civilized conversation with a man and I must be in love with him?

"Oh, please! You were blushing!"

I was *not*. I never blushed.

"And your legendary self-assurance was notable for its absence." The smile widened into a malicious grin. "What's wrong with this one?"

I resented the implications of that question. "Nothing's wrong with this—with him."

"So he's not planning anyone's murder?"

I grit my teeth at that, biting down a sudden spurt of anger. Bastard. Why the hell did he think I was being so careful, making so many rules? I learned from my mistakes, I did. But of course he couldn't understand the concept of careful, he who slept with every living thing on two legs.

He looked repentant. He raised a hand to touch my shoulder and I avoided it. "I'm sorry, Lee."

Huh. Well, that was irrelevant. I shouldn't be letting myself get upset. I smoothed out my eyebrows and nodded.

Too quickly for evasion, Karish grabbed the back of my neck and leaned down, putting his forehead against mine. "Don't do that," he said. "I just said something stupid and hurtful. I'd rather you admit you're angry with me and yell."

I repressed a sigh. I'd forgotten how annoying Karish could be. He insisted on wearing his emotions on his skin and thought everyone else should be the same way. Well, that was his privilege. He was a Source. I was a Shield. Different standards applied.

What the hell. I sighed anyway. "Welcome home, Taro."

Chapter Three

So maybe High Scape wasn't such a great place to live after all. It was big, the buildings were ugly, it was noisy and crowded. And it was the only city currently experiencing these weather abnormalities. Tilting Ark, only a few leagues down the Fish Free River, was enjoying lovely summer warmth. Which was good for us insane residents of High Scape, because it meant food was growing somewhere and was available to those who had the money for it, but it was annoying all the same. And odd. Because why was this happening to us and no one else? It made no sense. I hated things that didn't make sense.

I wasn't the only one. For the first time since I'd moved to High Scape, there had been called a formal meeting of all of High Scape's Pairs. It was being held in the Stall, a shortened form of the name Paranoia Stall bestowed on the one-room shack by a former Source. It had been built just outside the city limits, and it was where the Pair on duty sat and performed its watch, calming whatever natural events threatened to shake High Scape apart. I didn't know why any meeting had to be held there in the first place; it was so far out of everyone's way.

Walking in deep snow was hard work, I had to raise my feet so high and I could never be completely confident about my balance. I envied Karish his extra inches. He wouldn't reach the Stall exhausted and flustered.

"Hey! Source!"

Karish's arm tensed under my hand. We halted and turned.

A woman was charging up the street after us, trying to hold her homespun skirts over the snow with work-hardened hands. A farmer, I thought. An unhappy one. People's heads turned as they watched her pass. "When are you going to do something about this?" she demanded.

No explanations needed about to what "this" pertained. Karish held out his free hand, palm up. "We can't do anything about the snow, ma'am," he answered in a gentle tone.

"Why the hell not?" She halted before him, holding herself up to her full, considerable height. "This is what you're trained for, isn't it? Why you spend years being coddled in those schools of yours. Why you have everything handed to you your whole life without having to pay for it. Nor work for it hardly."

Nor hardly work? We risked our lives every time we channeled. Even the regulars knew that.

"This is very different from a hurricane or an erupting volcano, ma'am," I said in a voice that was low and, hopefully, soothing. "The world goes about creating these things in very different ways, and the truth is, we *aren't* trained for things like snow."

But the farmer wasn't interested in hearing logical explanations. She was angry, and she only wanted to vent. "Our crops are ruined," she hissed. "We'll have nothing to sell come harvest. We'll have nothing to eat next winter. What do you plan to do about that?"

I hesitated, because what could I say to that? We couldn't do anything about the weather. That was the simple truth.

And everyone knew it. No one had ever expected Pairs to regulate average weather. And there was nothing we could do about dead crops or unpaid mortgages or ruined occupations. "I am sorry." A weak answer, made all the worse by the audience—yes, some people had stopped to watch and listen—that was witness to it.

"Sorry won't feed my children," she spat. She glared at Karish. "While you've been off cavorting with the Empress instead of watching your post, our livestock has been freezing to death. You've ruined us. Be proud, Lord Shintaro." And she turned on her heel and stalked away.

Karish looked ready to call her back. I squeezed his arm to stop him. No one else said anything, but they looked at us. Little surreptitious glances, muttered comments to companions, a few scowls.

Karish didn't look as shocked by the incident as I felt. "Has anything like that happened to you before?" I asked him.

His only answer was a shrug. That meant something had happened. And he hadn't told me about it. He should have.

"You shouldn't have to put up with that sort of thing," I said.

"But I don't, do I? I have my Shield to protect me."

There was an edge to his voice. He didn't like my stepping in as I had. Too bad. That was my job. We headed on to the Stall in silence.

Arriving there we found it uncharacteristically crowded. In my memory, there had only ever been four people in it at a time. The Pair on duty and the Pair relieving them. This time, there were six Pairs. La Monte and his Shield Hammad hadn't arrived yet, and I wasn't sure how they were going to squeeze in. There were only four chairs for the single small table. Those who stood had to lean against walls that were lined with shelving units or were otherwise obstructed by pieces of cheap art. And there was the ancient stove taking up a good chunk of space. Not too comfortable.

Six Pairs. Karish and myself, of course, the youngest of

all the Pairs, but we had been in High Scape the longest, so we were called the Veteran Pair. Source Claire Firth and Shield Dee Stone, two wiry ladies in their fifties who always entertained me by tormenting Karish. They thought he was cute, sexy in a coltish half-grown way that amused them to no end. Source Kyna Riley and Shield Giles Sabatos, both in their thirties and both wonderfully casual about their duties, though they always performed them adequately. Their current self-imposed project was collecting a list of Source and Shield jokes. They were threatening to print a book from it. Source Franklin Wilberforce, who was a pandering sycophant to whichever person in the room was most powerful at the moment, and Shield Mont Ladin, who seemed to have no personality at all. Source Vera Rayne and Shield Lauren Garrighan were a circuit Pair, and their usual routine was to travel from site to site and fill in when the permanent Pair was for some reason unable to function. They'd been in High Scape, though, for almost a year, and the Triple S council seemed to be in no hurry to replace them. And Source Derek Beatrice and Shield Elata Benedict, who despised each other so much they seemed to poison the air around them and taint anyone else in their presence.

"Taro!" Wilberforce squealed. Yes, he actually squealed. A middle-aged man with years of experience behind him, reduced to an adolescent at the sight of Karish. Every time they met. Watching him was embarrassing. I wished I could believe it had something to do with sex. That Wilberforce was in love, or something, with Karish. While that caused my imagination to go in directions I'd rather it didn't, at least I could understand it. But this had nothing to do with affection and everything to do with currying favor. "I do hope you're settling in well after your imperial adventures."

Karish could be the consummate actor, when he felt like it. He didn't wince or gag as Wilberforce oozed all over him. His face was perfectly straight as he said, "It was touch and go there. Going from the excitement of verbally skewering courtiers, whose heels were a shade too high to be fashionable, to the boredom of guarding the largest city in the world from disaster is very hard on the nerves."

From Wilberforce's expression it appeared that he was feeling a little suspicious. Possibly he knew he was being made fun of. Just because he was a bootlicker didn't mean he had to be stupid.

Riley snorted. "I'm sure you'll have plenty to keep you on your toes," she said. "What with having to dodge the Risto Reaper and all."

Karish knew of the disappearances of the aristocrats. I'd made a point of telling him, only to learn I wasn't the only one to do so. He'd been a little annoyed.

He was annoyed now, too. "Perhaps the news hasn't reached here yet," he said, knowing full well that it had, "but I'm not a lord anymore. I never was a lord. The title was honorary."

"Ah, but that's what these sort are looking for," said Garrighan. "Moneyless ristos with empty titles. Better watch your back."

I glared at him. Taunting someone with the warning that they might be the next victim of a serial killer was disgusting.

Chris La Monte came in then, with his Shield, Fehvor Hammad, apparently unaware of the tension that had developed in the Stall. I was glad to see the older Source, which was unusual for me. I didn't like La Monte. He was a decent enough sort, and a good responsible Source, but he thought age should buy him not only respect but reverence. I didn't do reverence. However, his arrival meant we could get this meeting started, and the sooner it started, the sooner it would be over and the sooner I could go somewhere more comfortable.

"Chris!" Wilberforce gushed, exactly as he had with Karish. He liked to watch all avenues. La Monte was a force to be reckoned with because of his age, Karish because of

his fame. Not that Wilberforce thought either of them could
actually do anything for him, advance his own reputation or
anything like that. I got the feeling he was just one of those
people who felt compelled to abase themselves before those
they perceived as their superiors.

"Franklin," said La Monte. I didn't think the older
Source felt any special glow as a result of Wilberforce's so-
licitude. He merely thought it was his due.

"Did we miss anything?" Hammad asked, stamping his
feet and scattering snow everywhere.

"We would never start without Chris," Wilberforce assured him. "After all, he's the reason we're here."

"All right then," said La Monte, clapping his hands together. "Shintaro, can I assume Dunleavy's been keeping
you apprised of the situation here?"

I felt Karish tense beside me. "Are you implying Lee
might be dilatory in her responsibilities?" he asked testily.

La Monte's eyebrows rose in surprise. An emotion I had
to admit to sharing. Where had that come from? "Of course
not, Shintaro. It was primarily a sort of introduction to the
meeting."

"Please consider the introduction made."

Strange. It wasn't like Karish to be rude.

La Monte hesitated, probably recovering from the
shock of being shown such disrespect. Then he said, "Just
so we're all clear, I'll remind everyone that High Scape is
suffering from highly unseasonable weather—"

Garrighan snickered.

"—as well as a complete lack of natural events, which
has been lasting for the past several months."

"Excuse me?" I asked.

The others looked at me with confusion. "You know
that," said Riley.

"How could I possibly? I haven't been on the roster for
months."

"We've been talking about it at the house," Riley
protested.

"You know Dunleavy," Garrighan commented. "If you're not talking to her, she's not listening."

Prat.

"There have been no events for the past several months," Sabatos told me with mock solemnity.

"I got that. Thanks." Quite a change from the year before, when High Scape was known as one of the most volatile sites in the world, and I could expect a few events on every watch.

"And this requires a meeting, why?" Garrighan asked, sounding bored. "I'm particularly interested in the location, when the house would be warmer and handier."

"I want no one to overhear us. No one will come out here."

Zaire. I hadn't been aware La Monte had been inflicted with melodrama.

"The regulars expect us to do something about the weather. They think we are neglecting our duty."

How unfortunate for them. I think I should be the next Empress. How unfortunate for me.

"There's nothing we can do about the weather," said Riley, stating the bloody obvious, but apparently it was necessary under the circumstances.

"The regulars don't understand that," said La Monte. I shifted my shoulders. There was that particular patronizing tone in his voice that was just . . . aggravating.

Garrighan tsked with impatience. "There's nothing we can do about that, either."

"Maybe if we got something official from the Triple S council," Wilberforce suggested. "Some kind of document explaining that this kind of phenomenon is beyond our abilities to address. We could get a few copies and post them in appropriate places. That might make the regulars settle down."

That was actually a good idea.

"Only if they can read," was Beatrice's dry contribution. An unnecessary cheap shot, I thought. And anyway, once a few saw the notices, word of mouth would cover the rest.

"Won't that make it appear that the Triple S council is evading responsibility as well?" Benedict asked.

"Better them than us," Beatrice retorted, as expected, for one partner in that Pair could not say one thing without the other advocating the opposite.

"They *are* us," La Monte snapped. "I don't know that I care for the idea of passing responsibility to some distant institution most regulars have no direct contact with."

"We don't have responsibility," Sabatos pointed out. "How can we pass it?"

Here was a radical idea. I was almost afraid to bring it up. "We could actually try to do something about it." One, two, three . . .

Garrighan barked with laughter. He was awfully emotive for a Shield. "Do something about the weather? Are you serious?"

Yes. Always, apparently. "Has anyone tried to do anything?"

"Don't, Lee," Karish ordered in an undertone.

Don't what? "I mean, if we don't even try we can't know there's nothing we can do." It seemed simple enough to me.

"Leave it, Lee!" His tone was louder and sharper that time, and no one could pretend they didn't hear it.

What was his problem? It was a good idea. We could all experiment with our abilities and see what we came up with. What harm could possibly come from that?

"What is your idea, then, La Monte?" I asked, for of course the reason he'd called the meeting was to dazzle us with the brilliance of his solution to the problem.

La Monte clasped his hands behind his back. "The best course of action is to let everyone know we're working on it." He paced a few steps, which was all the limited space allowed him. "Every time anyone asks us about what we're doing—"

Or accuses us of being lazy parasites.

"—we assure them that we are studying the situation and will soon have things under control."

Incredible. "Tell them we're working on it?" I asked him. "When we're actually doing nothing? You want us to lie to them?"

"It's in their best interest."

"How?" It was in our best interest, maybe, and only for the short term, but no one could reasonably claim it was in theirs.

Though La Monte seemed ready to try. "It will reassure them, make them feel safe and secure again. It will raise their opinion of us. And when this passes, they will feel we have earned their respect and support, that we have done our job. Everything will return to normal."

I stared at him. I couldn't believe what I was hearing. What a bad idea. And from the quality of the silence in the room, I wasn't the only one who thought so. Even Wilberforce was looking a little uncertain.

"What if this doesn't pass?" Sabatos asked. "What if this cold snap stretches on for months?"

Not exactly the point or the central problem with the whole plan, but it was definitely one big glaring glitch. I was glad someone other than me had pointed it out.

Because La Monte didn't like having his opinions questioned. Not by anyone. He didn't lose his temper—at least, I'd never seen him lose it—but his nostrils twitched and his face kind of went taut, and one got the impression that if you touched one more nerve he just might explode. And that would be messy. "As this is an entirely new phenomenon to us, we will say, it will of course require a great deal of study and then the most delicate handling." Oh aye, he was angry. He was speaking slowly and his tone was very, very calm. "It will pass in due time. There is no doubt about that."

Of course there was doubt about it. We had no idea where this weather was coming from or what was causing it. We had no idea how long it was going to be hanging about. To claim otherwise, to make plans as if we did, was sheer idiocy. And it was a stupid, stupid idea.

Why lie? So people were a little unimpressed with the Triple S right then. It was unpleasant but not something to get into a panic about. There was no reason to concoct a ridiculous lie that was almost certain to blow up in our faces at some later date. Someone would be sure to figure out that we had lied about our handling, or not, of the snow. Then we'd see a real loss of confidence and respect. A permanent one. We'd be branded liars. That sterling reputation for always being truthful would be gone.

But most of the others were nodding in agreement, and no one seemed prepared to challenge the idea any further. They weren't thrilled about it, I could see that, but they were going to follow along.

So what was I going to do? I couldn't lie to people about this sort of thing. It was wrong and stupid and it would make a greater mess of things in the end. But if I denied the story that everyone else was using, it would annoy all my colleagues. All to no purpose. Regulars were unlikely to believe one sole Shield over all the other Triple S members in the site, and they might even be angry with me for darkening their false hopes. Er, optimism. Not a happy result.

One thing was certain, if I were to state my insistence on my position right at that moment, La Monte would feel his so-called authority was being challenged, and he would dig his heels in. No one would stand with me against La Monte. He was one of the squeakiest wheels I'd ever met and knew how to be insistently disagreeable.

If, however, I got ahold of people one or two at a time, I had a better chance of convincing them this was an atrocious idea. Better yet, if I could convince Karish this was an atrocious idea, I could leave convincing the others to him. Karish could, I was quite sure, convince anyone of anything.

All I needed was a little time.

"Excuse me, sir." Ugh. That sounded a little too submissive. La Monte didn't seem to find anything amiss, though, and he nodded at me with more favor than he had demonstrated just a few moments earlier. "I would feel much more comfortable about this if the opinion of the Triple S council were solicited." And here was hoping he hadn't already done so. "For all we know, the council has already decided on a way to address this problem. We don't want to be seen as acting in opposition to their wishes."

Again, he wasn't thrilled with the objection, but the change in tone and manner worked wonders. "You're right," he admitted. "If they've already starting putting out an explanation for this cold snap, we could really foul the course if we say something different." He nodded resolutely. "Fehvor will write to the Triple S. We will wait until we have received word back from the council."

Riley, a Source and therefore not required to maintain the level of control that I was, rolled her eyes at his posturing. "Aye aye, captain." She saluted him. With the wrong hand. "Is your head heavy?"

I could tell by the tone that her response was meant to be a clever retort, but the meaning was lost on me. La Monte understood, though, if the glower he shot at Riley were any indication, and some of the other Sources snickered.

"Can we go now?" Beatrice whined.

"Yes, yes," Karish said. "Any further business to discuss?" He barely hesitated before adding, "No? Good. We're off then." He grabbed my hand.

"Wait, Taro." Wilberforce latched onto Karish's other arm. "Some of us are going for drinks to the Giant Nickle. We were wondering if you'd like to join us."

In my mind's eye I saw Karish, distaste curling his lip, delicately removing Wilberforce's hand from his person. He didn't, though. "Sorry, old chap, but we promised Lee's mother we'd head right to the Lion after the meeting," he lied. "She's cooking for us. It has become one of the rules of my life never to pass up the opportunity to enjoy anything cooked by Holder Teshia Mallorough." He yanked open the door. "Later, then," he said, all breezy and bright.

"Aye, I've got to—" said Stone, rising from her seat, but Karish pulled me outside before I could watch anyone else take their leave. He then set such a quick pace that it was a good thing I'd resumed my bench dancing while he was gone, else I'd be breathless in moments.

"Zaire, Taro, what's the rush?"

"Excuse me, *sir*?" I took a good look at Karish's face and saw he was a shade away from laughter. "How evil is the thought rattling around in your head?"

"Evil? Eech! Could we be more melodramatic? Please?"

"Talk, Lee."

And I understood the reason for the quick pace. He wanted to be out of earshot of the other Pairs, who were traveling the same way. Fair enough. So did I. "I am not going to tell people we're working on it when we aren't."

"Ah."

I was disappointed. "You are?" I would have wagered money that Karish had more honor than that.

"It does no harm, and it'll make the regulars feel better."

"It's a lie."

"A harmless lie."

I didn't know that there was any such thing. "Let's forget things like honesty and responsibility and other such old-fashioned customs." For the moment. "Speaking out of pure self-interest, it's too easy for people to figure out we're lying."

He held out his hands, palms out. "How can they find out if none of us tell them?"

"If this cold snap drags on they'll figure it out."

He shrugged. "It'll end, Lee. Everything does."

I paused a moment. There was something about his tone . . . like there was a message underneath his words, something that had nothing to do with the weather. I wasn't receiving it, though, and right then I didn't want to be sidetracked from the current issue. "While I'm always ready to debate the philosophical aspect of the existence of a slice of bread—" Well, no, not really. Who cared whether a falling tree made noise if there was no one there to hear it? "—some things take longer to end than others. What if this cold snap decides not to end for another year or two?"

"It won't take that long," he said.

Probably not, but, "It might."

"It won't," he insisted.

It never failed to astound me, how thoroughly someone could believe something just because he wanted to. "And even if it does, we still say we're working on it?"

"Aye."

I couldn't help feeling frustrated. "Are you even thinking about this at all?"

He sighed. "What else are we supposed to do, Lee?" he asked with impatience. "People are scared and they're looking for someone to blame. And in case you haven't noticed, we're their chosen targets. And we shouldn't be. This has nothing to do with us, but we're the ones they're blaming. If we tell them we're trying out a few theories, they'll feel better, and they'll leave us alone. And even if we don't turn up any answers and this thing drags on a while, they'll be disappointed and unimpressed, but they'll think we tried. That's better then letting them think we couldn't be bothered."

"But we're not trying. We're not bothered. That's my point." I let my foot stray from the path that had been broken in the snow by our earlier trek, and I nearly stumbled.

Karish grabbed my arm to help me balance. "Because there's nothing that we can actually do, Lee."

"We don't know that."

"Of course we do. Sources can't affect the weather."

"I bet most Sources say they can't heal people, either, or create natural disasters instead of only channeling them away."

One thing about Karish, he could stiffen up beautifully.

A strict aristocratic upbringing gave him excellent posture and admirable poise, something he tried to hide when he was feeling petulant. But when he wanted to, he could draw his head up and his shoulders back, every line of his body firming into a barrier of either intimidation or resistance, whichever the circumstance required. At times I could imagine seeing the rod that was no doubt tied to his back when he was a child.

Karish didn't like to talk about his ability to ease pain and to call natural disasters at a whim. Or even think about it. That was what drilled it through my admittedly thick skull that Karish wasn't the glory hound I'd assumed he had to be when I'd first heard of him. He had these unprecedented abilities and if he had his way, no one, not even me, would know about them.

"Regulating the weather is beyond my expertise," he informed me.

Ooh, the aristocratic accent was out in full force. He'd rolled each "r" for nearly a full second, I'd swear to it. "How do you know until you try?"

"Because I'm not some all-powerful protagonist in a ridiculous drama who acquires some new unheard of ability with each new improbable situation," he snapped.

I was impressed. "You get real articulate when you're upset." I wished I could do that. I tended to start stuttering when I was really angry.

I fancied I saw steam rising from his ears. "I'm not saying you can do anything and everything you set your mind to, Taro. I'm rather glad you can't, because then you'd just be impossible." Another glare, and I resisted the urge to tell him he was beautiful when he was angry. "All I'm saying is that you've already proven Source abilities are not as limited as everyone thinks. Maybe this is something you or one of the others can do something about."

Karish stopped abruptly. "We are *not* telling the others."

He looked back towards the Stall, and so did I. He had nothing to worry about; we'd left the others far behind.

I linked my arm through his and got him moving again. "Then if we can't tell the others, you'll just have to do all the experimenting yourself."

He jerked his arm free. "Are you threatening me?"

I frowned. "What?" Where had that come from?

"If I don't do what you want, you're going to tell the others about . . . what I can do?"

My mouth dropped open. "Karish!" How the hell could he think I was blackmailing him, that I ever would? Bastard!

Instantly, he knew he had gone too far, if his expression were any indication. He held up his hands in a gesture of contrition. "I'm sorry, Lee, but that's what it sounded like."

Like hell it did. Maybe to a complete idiot. Maybe to someone who rarely used his brain to do his thinking.

I pressed my lips together, took a breath, and said, "If we can't tell the others, then obviously you are the only one who can experiment." Good, good. Words even, tone mild.

He just looked at me for a moment, then smiled ruefully. "You'll feel much better if you smack me a good one, you know."

If he weren't careful he'd find himself sporting a few bruises on that pretty face. "Will you see if there's anything you can do?"

Now he felt guilty. I could tell. And if that made him more open to my completely reasonable suggestions, well, good for me. "On one condition."

Oh, aye. "Which is?"

"If the Triple S council agrees with Chris that we should tell the regulars we're working on it, you'll toe the party line, all right?"

"Toe the party line?"

"You'll say what everyone else was saying."

He almost never bothered to explain his weird expressions. This must be important to him. "All right." I didn't like it, but I wasn't the only one doing something she didn't like, so it was fair enough.

"It's not like it'll still be a lie. We will be working on it, after all."

Sometimes I could be such an idiot. I grinned at him, relieved. "You're brilliant."

"And *so* good looking." And all was forgiven.

Chapter Four

There was nothing I enjoyed so much as dancing the benches. Nothing. Not even sex. It was so exhilarating, so freeing. It required every ounce of strength I had, and every scrap of attention. I couldn't worry about what anyone thought of me, or how I was doing. And it was something I was really, really good at.

I expected to get beaten eventually. I was better than the average regular and even the good regulars, purely by benefit of having been trained in bench dancing from a very early age at the Shield Academy. All Shields were, and if they were at all interested in the sport, they left the Academy with a high level of expertise.

Still, I couldn't dedicate the hours a day that professionals, and those who aspired to be professional, could spend. So yes, I would ultimately be beaten in almost any tournament, unless the professionals were having a bad day. Or weren't entered.

But I didn't dance to win. I danced to do my best. I danced to clear my head of responsibilities and worries. I danced because it consumed me while I was doing it, and

I was left loose and wrung out in the very best sense once I was finished.

I stood in my bare feet on the two cool wooden benches, one foot solidly planted on each narrow plank. I was wearing my favorite dancing clothes, trousers and a shirt of a loose, light green fabric. My opponent was a gangly young fellow who was shivering in the chill air. An easy mark.

The four stalkers knelt in the dancing sand, picking up the ends of the two bars we would be leaping over. They moved the bars low and slow, as was appropriate for the first round. Jumping over them was ridiculously easy.

And then, I enacted that saying about hubris.

Because I fell off the benches.

I fell off the benches!

The very first round. I wasn't caught by the bars, which was the acceptable way to lose. No, I simply fell off. As I hadn't since the year I'd started to learn. And what was worse, there was no reason for it. I had no excuse. We'd been at the easy stage. And I'd tumbled hard, my face barely missing the bench I'd expected to step on. How humiliating.

And everyone knew I was a Shield. I was wearing the white braid, after all. And knowing I was a Shield, everyone expected better of me. Including me.

I also proved myself a liar, because I did blush. I could feel it. Damn it.

The sand, though cleared of snow, was spikey and hard and unpleasant to lie on. Besides, people were starting to give me looks, wondering why I wasn't on my feet.

No one snickered. I had to give them that.

I stood up. I smiled as I shook the hand of my radiant opponent. I glanced down at the benches and saw they were the regulation distance apart. Not that I really suspected that one of the benches had moved. I just couldn't understand what had happened.

I hadn't even had a chance to work up a sweat.

I didn't grumble as I wanted to when I went to the edge of

the sands and pulled on my stockings and boots. I couldn't deny feeling glum, though. What was wrong with me?

"That was kind of quick."

I twisted up with surprise. Risa's brother was bundled up to ward off the cold, and looking at me with a slightly satirical expression.

I really shouldn't have cared that a near stranger had witnessed my disgrace. "Are you here to watch someone or was it just my misfortune that you were walking by and saw that?"

He sat down beside me. "Risa told me you'd be dancing today, and recommended that I watch. She said you were very good."

I couldn't miss the emphasis he put on the word "said."

Immediately, he seemed to realize that. At least, his eyes widened and he hurried to add, "I'm terribly sorry. That didn't come out at all as I planned."

"I thought you solicitors enjoyed a gift with words."

"The written, not the spoken. That's barristers you're thinking of."

Was there something in his tone suggesting I should have known that? Or was I just hearing things that weren't there because I was in a bad mood?

And why was I in such a bad mood? It was just a stupid dancing tournament. "As you saw, today wasn't a good day to watch. I seem to be experiencing some kind of difficulty."

He frowned. "Are you injured or ill?"

"Neither. Just clumsy."

"Maybe it's the cold. It can't be conducive to any sort of athletics."

I wished I could blame it on the cold.

"So I imagine you now have some unanticipated time on your hands."

That was a dangerous question to answer. "I guess you could say so." I hoped he wasn't going to ask me to help shovel out a walk or something.

"Will you join me for a drink? I've found a tavern that sells excellent mulled wine. It's not far from here."

I had to admit I was kind of impressed that he didn't care that I was dressed in my old shapeless clothes, and that he didn't suggest I change first. He was comfortable enough to be seen with me in public. I wouldn't have expected that from someone who looked as . . . appropriate . . . as Erin seemed to be. "I would like that. Thank you."

My boots laced and my torso wrapped, we started down the street. "Though the invitation loses a little something when I can't buy the drink for you."

"You can if you like. The law says I have to be supplied without charge, but nothing prevents us from paying if we have the money. Taro sometimes pays for things."

Erin looked surprised. "He receives an allowance?"

"An allowance?"

"From his family."

"Zaire, no. He plays cards. And bets on horses. Dogs, too, I think."

Erin's mouth tightened before he said, "You mean he gambles."

"Aye."

We were at the tavern then. It was crowded. There was no seating available, so Erin and I stood crushed into a corner, where we were quickly supplied with large tankards of mulled wine. "What's wrong with gambling?"

"I've seen too many families destroyed by it," he answered grimly.

I was shocked. "How?"

"People wager their family fortunes and then lose them."

"Why?"

"What do you mean why? They bet on the wrong horse. They're dealt the wrong cards."

"No, why would anyone wager their family fortune? There's always an excellent chance they'll lose it all. It's stupid."

"It's not that simple. Gambling does something to people. It makes them crazy, and they make decisions they wouldn't normally make."

"It does this to all people?"

"Well, no."

"So it's the fault of the person, not the activity."

"No. It's much more than that."

I shrugged. I wasn't going to argue about it. But I couldn't imagine risking all my money on a horse, and it was so easy to avoid doing it. Just don't do it. Don't make the bet. Don't play cards. Or, stop before you risk losing more than you can afford. It seemed to me that blaming gambling for losing your money was like drinking too much and blaming the alcohol for being drunk. Just stop.

I took my first taste of the mulled wine. Rich flavor filled my mouth. I usually didn't like hot wine—it often just tasted sour—but this was gorgeous. I'd have to take better note of the location when I left.

Erin stared down at his tankard, suddenly appearing ill at ease. I imagined it was an uncharacteristic look for him. "You have a great deal of influence over Risa."

That was news to me, but he stated it as though it were an established fact. "I don't think so."

"She talks about you a lot."

"Oh." How very uncomfortable.

"She feels you are much wiser than your years would normally dictate."

"I see."

"In fact," he suddenly chuckled, "she sometimes complains that you are a little too sensible."

So it seemed she and Karish had something in common.

Erin sobered. "She seems really, well, not herself. Have you noticed?"

"I'm afraid not." Should I have noticed? Was I being too self-absorbed again? "She seems as she always has to me. But you know her much better than I do."

"I'm not sure I do. There's almost twenty years between

us. I'd left our mother's home when she was very young, just a small child. Since she's grown we've seen each other more, but . . ." He waved a hand as though physically cutting off his words. "It doesn't matter. It just seems to me that there's a carelessness about her now. It worries me."

"The way she's spending money?" Because he wasn't the only one to mention it, and I wasn't a complete idiot. Usually.

"That's part of it. But it's her work, too. She seems to feel driven to work as long as possible, and she seems to be trying to find the most dangerous routes."

That wasn't something I'd noticed or heard about, but I didn't see Risa every day. Still, "I'm not sure what I can do about any of that."

"Talk to her?"

"About what, exactly?" Tell her not to spend money? What did I know about that? Not to take on dangerous assignments? That was the very nature of her job. How could she tell her captain she would take only the safe routes?

"Just that she should, you know, calm down. Be more like you."

I nearly choked on my wine. "Are you mad? Sit her down for a lecture on how she should act like me? How arrogant is that?"

"I don't expect you to say it exactly like that. Shields are supposed to be diplomatic, aren't they?"

I didn't think there was enough diplomacy in the world to make that message palatable to anyone. But Erin still looked uncomfortable, and I didn't want to give him the impression that I didn't care. I did care. I just didn't think there was anything I could, or should, do. "If a good opportunity comes up to say something, I will. That's the best I can promise."

His shoulders lowered in his relief. I had to like someone who showed such concern for a sibling. "I feel your promises are worth a great deal."

Oh, no, that didn't make me feel uncomfortable. "Just because I talk to her doesn't mean I'll have any sway over her."

"Perhaps not. But it can't hurt."

How very optimistic of him. And here, I had thought, solicitors were supposed to be cynical.

Chapter Five

"You promised." I wasn't whining. I was merely stating facts. We had just started our watch. It was getting dark. It was quiet. We had all the makings of an unadulterated, boring evening. The perfect opportunity for experimentation.

He dragged his hands through his hair. "I'm not backing out. I just don't think we should be doing this now."

"What do you mean? Why not?"

He appeared surprised. "We're on watch, Lee." He gestured at the rustic interior of the Stall. "We're supposed to be concentrating."

I raised an eyebrow. Taro Karish, the wild Stallion of the Triple S, playing by the book? Was he serious? "Aye, we're supposed to be concentrating on the forces. And we will be. Much more than we ever do when we're playing cards. Besides, nothing has been happening for months."

"All the more reason to be particularly diligent. We're overdue. There's probably something massive brewing."

All right, this was just too strange. Aye, Karish was very responsible. Yes, he always did his work and did it well. But when there was no cause for alarm he saw no reason to waste his time with excessive attention to duty. At least, he never had before. "Are you getting old or something?" I demanded with the intention to be flippant. Then my brain caught up with my tongue and I clapped my hand over my mouth. Oops.

He looked stunned. "What?"

"You're almost thirty, aren't you?" When was his birthday, anyway?

He leaned back in his chair and crossed his arms, shock sliding into offence. "I am twenty-nine," he told me, carefully enunciating his words.

"That's what I said. Twenty-nine is almost thirty."

"And that's not old."

Really? How else did one explain his sudden stodgy adherence to rules? He was supposed to be wild and rebellious. It was written somewhere.

But pointing out to him that he was old was hardly tactful. Shame on me. Yet it would be an interesting process to watch. The stunning—he had quickly regained his youthful glow and weight upon returning to High Scape—adored, reckless young man having to settle down into middle-age maturity. It had to be awful for a beautiful person, with so much attention focussed on their appearance, watching their youth slip away. A downside to being gorgeous, who would have figured it? I wondered how he would deal with it. Would he accept it with good grace or fight it with every example of denial under the sun?

Of course, knowing Karish, he would probably only improve with age. Take on some element of dignity that drove people of all ages wild. Aye, that was what would happen. Damned lucky bugger.

"We have seven hours of uninterrupted time," I said, bringing us back to a subject I hoped was less touchy. "With no one likely to walk in on us. It's the perfect opportunity and we'd be derelict if we let it slide."

He rolled his eyes. "Fine, all right. But it's a waste of time."

"It certainly will be if you go into it with that attitude."
All right, don't nag. Getting irritated wouldn't accomplish
anything. Changing his perspective might. "You can already
do things other Sources can't." It was interesting to watch a
grown man squirm. "There's no reason to think it's impossible for you to do something about this before you've even
tried."

"All right, all right," he snapped with impatience. "Let's
get on with this."

Try again. "Nothing will be accomplished if you don't
open your mind to it."

He pulled in a long sigh. I could see the tension easing
from his frame, his shoulders lowering. Good boy. "I'll
concede the possibility."

Ooh. Formality. And he did it so well. "So—" Now
what did we do? I had no idea.

And he could tell. He smirked. Then he took pity on me.
"I'll just try to feel something. See if anything's going on."

"Good start."

"Ready?"

"Of course."

The smirk faded into the slightest curl of the lip. "Of
course," he murmured.

Little adjustments, like small pushes in the air, signalled
the lowering of Karish's internal shields, the natural walls
with which he protected himself from the forces of the
world. It was not a physical sensation. More mental, I supposed, though that wasn't quite right either. Fortunately I
was never asked to really explain it. Centuries' worth of
historians hadn't been able to figure it out, or describe it.
No reason why I should be able to.

Sources never lowered their internal shields unless
they felt a disaster brewing. They never thought to. Probably they didn't think they could. And perhaps many of
them couldn't. Karish could, and possibly that was one of
the things that made him so different from many other
Sources.

As his shields lowered, I erected my own around him, so only the forces he was inviting in actually came in. The others tried to rush in, too. It was my job to keep them off, keep them from crushing and killing him. At the same time I made sure the forces Karish *was* channeling didn't drive his blood into such a huge rush that it burst his heart and his brain and killed him.

It had been many months since we'd done this, Karish channeling and I shielding him. It suddenly felt like forever. I hadn't realized how much I'd missed it. It wasn't nearly as exciting as when we were dealing with an actual disaster, but it still felt good. And wasn't good such a weak word? Feeling Karish's blood flow through his veins as I could never feel my own, being able to slow it down, it gave me a strange feeling of power.

And through him, there were the forces, the rushing of the earth and sky. I couldn't touch them myself, not directly. I could work them only through Karish. When he wasn't channeling I was as blind to the forces as any regular. But when he channeled, a whole other world was revealed to me. A strange world of pressures and colors and impressions that were impossible to grab and define. And I didn't know how Karish restrained himself from diving into it all the time. If I were a Source I would walk around with my shields down all the time and just feel everything.

Of course, speaking as his partner, I was glad he didn't. That would be a nightmare to shield.

Hey, Dunleavy, try concentrating.

So I did. And it struck me. "Something's wrong," I said.

"Everything seems normal to me."

"No, there's a difference." But I wasn't sure where or what or how.

He pulled his internal shields back up, and I lowered mine. It was a little difficult to channel and talk at the same time.

"Neither of us know what High Scape feels like when things are normal, Lee. All the disasters we dealt with were caused by Creol. And now nothing's been happening for months."

He had a point. Creol, the same Source who had had Karish abducted the previous year, had also been able to manipulate the forces in order to cause natural events. His plan had been to destroy High Scape with a natural event, and he had spent years practising to do it. So High Scape had experienced an unusually high frequency of natural events, and had acquired seven Pairs to keep it calm.

No one had known what was going on. Karish and I had figured it out. And I had manipulated Creol's shields while he was channeling, resulting in his death.

I usually tried very hard not to think about that.

Still, "There's something off, and it's not like when Creol was up to his stunts."

"Well, I didn't feel anything."

There was a finality about his tone that I didn't like. "So what? That's it?"

Karish raised his hands in a gesture of inquiry. "What can I do if I can't feel anything? I don't have anything to work with. Any place to start."

"You barely even looked," I accused him. This was a big problem. It wouldn't be solved in an instant. It wouldn't even be understood if all one spared was a glance.

He sighed. "All right."

So we tried again. And to give him credit, he waited longer. While it was work for me it was no day in the sun for him, either, having all that power funneling through him.

I could feel it again, that oddness, though I couldn't pinpoint it at all. "There it is again. Can you feel it?" A part of me was frustrated that I couldn't just reach out a hand and show him.

"I feel nothing," he answered. "Well, no, that's not quite right. I'm not you, after all. Let's just say I feel nothing out of the ordinary."

And what had I done to deserve that shot? Prat. "It's there."

"What's there?"

Well, if I could tell him that, the problem would be solved, wouldn't it? "It's just off, somewhere in there."

He rolled his eyes. "That helps a lot. Thanks."

"Like listening to an orchestra, and it's a good symphony, but the second bassoon is flat." Aye, that nailed it.

But not, however, according to Karish. "Care to use a different analogy for the tone-deaf partner in this Pair?"

Picky, picky. "Like looking at a painting, and while red was a good choice, the artist used orange red instead of blue red and so the whole picture looks off." See? Right there. Only don't look with your eyes. Look with your mind.

Karish let his hand fall to the table, flesh slapping against wood. "For Zaire's sake, Lee!"

"What?" Was he claiming to be colorblind, too?

He snapped his shields back into place. As they weren't actual physical entities, he shouldn't have been able to raise or lower them with any kind of variety, but if *my* shields had been fingers, I would have yanked them back and sucked on their stinging tips. "What's wrong with you today?" Sometimes his artistic moods were so tiring.

"There's nothing out there, Lee," he snapped.

"So, what, you think I'm lying?"

Karish, being an intelligent lad, stepped around that. His voice slid into a tone of annoying, condescending patience. "I think you're very anxious to find a solution and are therefore seeing things that aren't there."

Ah. Delusional. So much better. "There is something there, Taro."

"Then why can't I feel it?"

"I don't know." Maybe he didn't want to see anything. Maybe he didn't want anything to be wrong. And that was understandable. The last time things had been unnatural it had resulted in a series of nightmares for Karish. To come home to learn things were once more odd was probably more than he needed to hear, especially with the other things going on in his life. So he agreed to a search of the forces to shut me up, but saw nothing because he didn't want to see anything.

I couldn't very well tell him any of that, though. He would feel insulted. "All right, then."

He raised an eyebrow. "All right?"

"Aye."

"That's it?"

"What else is there?"

"Oh, no, no, no. I'm not buying that. No way would you just drop everything so easily. Tell me what's going on in that dense, mysterious brain of yours."

I thought about that. Dense was definitely an insult, yet mysterious was alluring and therefore flattering. I wondered which I was supposed to feel. "Nothing more than usual." I was wondering if I might have better luck with another Source, one who wasn't experiencing some kind of mental block. Except none of the other Sources in High Scape were as talented as Karish. And my bond with Karish impaired my ability to work with other Sources. What I gained in working with a more openminded Source might be lost through the diminished talent and compatibility. "We'll try it again next watch."

Karish groaned. "Lovely."

"If you want me to claim we're working on it, we'd better be working on it." He was the one who said it first, he was the one who had made the deal, and I was going to make him stick to it.

"I *knew* that was going to come back on me." He dug a coin out of his purse and spun it on the table.

"Because you're such a bright boy."

"Shut up, Lee."

"And in such a fine mood, too." Should I ask him, should I not? Should I borrow the coin? Ah, what the hell. "What is wrong with you?"

Hands through the hair again. "Her Grace is here."

Oh. All was forgiven. "When?"

"Yesterday."

"How did she even know you were back here and not in Erstwhile?"

"I don't know. Magic. I don't care." His shoulders slumped.

"Where is she staying?"

"The Imperial," he said, naming a boarding house like the one my mother was staying at, only for the risto crowd.

"You don't actually have to see her, if you don't want to."

A short exhalation through his nose, a sound of disgust. "I have to see her."

Find me the law that said that. "No, you don't."

The muscles along his jaw clenched. "Leave it, Lee."

Fine. Make yourself miserable. I only have to work with you while you do it.

I watched Karish wander over to the wall and poke around the shelves. He came up with a deck of cards. "Want to cheat at slider?"

I didn't bother to protest the accusation. No need to get too predictable. "Can you afford to fall any further into debt? You already owe me your first six born."

"I guess I'll have to figure out some way to work it off." He winked.

I rolled my eyes.

The rest of the watch passed without incident. No surprises there. I spent some time wondering if High Scape had turned into a cold site. It had been known to happen. Sites constantly rattled by natural events suddenly went still, for decades, while sites that had been calm suddenly went hot. Maybe Creol had been the only reason High Scape had ever been hot in the first place.

Firth and Stone came to relieve us, something I always looked forward to. I loved Firth.

"Karish, my beautiful, my one, my only," she crowed, as she always did.

Karish, who had risen to his feet as the ladies entered, scooped up Firth's hand. As he always did. "Claire, my lovely," he said in a voice as smooth as sanded wood. "It is a treasure to see you, as always."

"You liar," she retorted. "You're such a tease."

That was a little blunter than usual. Fun to see Karish gape like a fish, though. "I never am," he protested.

"Sure you are, lad. All heat and promises and just when you get a girl all worked up you slither out of it."

Karish blushed. I cackled. Stone smirked.

Granted, I wouldn't want a man as old as Firth drooling all over me, but Karish asked for it. He was something of a slut and wore the reputation almost proudly. From what I understood, Firth was a slut, too, and she'd had many more years to practise it. She knew how to make the elegant, confident, suave Lord Shintaro Karish blush in a way no one else could, and it delighted me every time I saw it. He should have learned to back off by then. On the other hand, he might have forgotten after all that time spent away from High Scape. For certain he beat a hasty retreat out of there, taking me with him.

"Rrrrr," Karish growled, once I closed the door behind us. "You have too much fun with her."

Hey, it wasn't my fault. He'd started it the year before by oozing all over Firth when they met. "I have nothing to do with it."

"No, you just sit back and laugh." He sounded almost bitter about it.

"Poor boy." My feigned sympathy couldn't have sounded more false. "Can dish it out but you can't take it."

He appeared scandalized. "I never behave like that." He pointed a thumb back over his shoulder at the Stall.

"No, you're a little more subtle, but give it time."

He huffed. "I will never act that way."

"All right." We'd wait and see. When his looks began to fade a little. In twenty years or so.

"Brat." He took my hand, and we trudged through the snow back towards the city. "Come out for a drink with me?"

"Sure."

His hand squeezed mine a little with his surprise. "Really?"

We'd never gone out for a drink together before. "Aye."

He smiled. "Good girl."

"Aye, you'd think so." Karish was a real fan of debauchery. Not that that was where I was headed. I'd just watch him for a while. From what I'd heard, he put on quite a show when he was enjoying himself in a tavern.

"Lord Shintaro!"

He jumped. I didn't. Score for me. I did want to scowl at the interloper, though. But I didn't, because Karish was doing it for me. "You've got the wrong number," he snapped.

The man halted his jog and stared at Karish, nonplussed.

I looked up and stared at Karish, nonplussed.

"Lord Shintaro Karish?" the man tried again.

Karish gave up on the not-a-lord issue. "What do you want?"

The tone was not at all friendly, but the man bowed. "William Smith, at your service." I thought that if he truly wanted to be polite, he might pull his scarf away from his face a little so we could get a good look at him. It wasn't that cold. "I am a member of the Raiborn, and we're recruiting members. We were hoping you might be interested in joining us."

Karish's fine black brows drew together in a frown. "Uh, what?"

I stifled a giggle. Good retort.

"A club, my lord. A kind of gentlemen's club."

"What kind of gentlemen's club recruits members on the street?" Karish demanded with scorn.

"Our kind of club, my lord."

As statements of the obvious went, the delivery of that one had admirable panache.

"Didn't one of you people already send me a letter inviting me to this club of yours?"

"We very well may have. You are exactly the kind of—"

"And if I recall I sent you a response saying no thanks."

That didn't slow the man down for a moment. "It was no doubt an open invitation, my lord. Should you change your mind."

"Well, I haven't," Karish declared with exquisite hauteur. "And I won't. I don't like gentlemen's clubs. They always let in the wrong sort."

"I can assure you, my lord, we seek out only the—"

"Leave now." Karish pulled me away and started us down the street.

Listen to him. So used to being invited into exclusive high society clubs that the very invitations themselves irritated him. Must be nice to be so sought after.

"My lord!"

"Don't call us," Karish muttered.

"Maybe we'll have a better opportunity to speak another time, my lord!" the man shouted after us. Didn't follow us, though. Smart man.

"What was that about?" I asked.

"You heard him."

"But your refusal was a little harsh." And not like Karish. Karish, in my experience, was usually quite polite.

"He came up to me on the *street*."

"Aye, I wouldn't have thought that was the way they did it."

"It's not. At least, I've never had anyone ask me like that before."

"So you have been asked to a gentlemen's club before?" He really did live in a different world. One I couldn't understand. Which, considering I was his partner, was rather sad.

He shrugged. "I was Lord Westsea's younger brother. Then people thought I was going to be Lord Westsea myself."

"And you turned them down?" I would have joined, out of curiosity if nothing else.

He snorted. "Why would I want to lock myself away with a collection of self-important asses who obviously have no real appreciation for women?" Ah, but think of all the fun he could have had with the men. "Besides, I'm not married. What do I need a gentlemen's club for?"

The thought of Karish married was enough to make me choke on nothing but air and saliva. Good thing I was a Shield, with unsurpassed control over my reactions. Else I might laugh.

Karish was looking down at me. "What? No derogatory comments?"

"I have nothing to say."

"You always have something to say. You just choose not to." Happy with that little comment, he released my hand and tucked it into the crook of his arm.

Damn all perceptive men.

Chapter Six

Music came pouring out through the windows and the door. A fiddle racing over octaves. A pipe emitting a plaintive haunting tone even as it danced over arpeggios. And a flat drum with a rolling syncopated beat. My heart sped up and I bit my lower lip. Images clashed in my mind. Waves crashing against rocks. A window shattering in the intense heat of fire. Standing at the edge of a cliff and wanting to dive over just to feel the air rushing over my skin as I fell. I pulled back on Karish's arm. "Not in there."

Karish had been leading me. He had picked this tavern. He turned back to me, a corner of his mouth turned up in a dangerous smile. Dangerous to me, anyway. His eyes were glowing. "Do you like this music?"

Was he insane? "Of course." A person would have to be dead not to like this music. It was glorious. It lit the air. It moved.

"Do you want to go in? Not—" he cut off my answer with a raised hand, "should you go in. But do you want to? If you had nothing at all to worry about, would you go in?"

There was a bit of a breeze winding its way through the

night. It played with his hair. One dark strand was flutter-ing along his cheek. I wanted to brush it back. Then I wanted to sink my hands into that black mass.

My blood was practically dancing through my veins. My heart was pounding so hard I felt the pulse in my throat. My muscles were tense with the effort it took not to start running or jumping around like an idiot.

I licked my dry lips and nodded.

"You trust me?"

I nodded again, because I wasn't sure I could speak coherently.

"I won't let you do anything you regret. I promise."

The smart thing to do was to refuse to go in. To insist we go somewhere else. Or to let Karish go in alone while I went home. Gods, the music . . .

"So what do you say?"

He wanted so much for me to go in with him, I could tell. He'd be disappointed if I refused. I could feel it even through the music that was filling my head and scrambling my thoughts.

I'm stupid. I'm so stupid. "Aye." Was that breathless voice coming from me?

The smile widened into a grin. Karish chuckled and opened the door. The music, of course, got louder, enough to make me dizzy. I crowded in closer to Karish, my free hand clutching his arm. A part of me screamed that this was a very bad idea. The rest of me beat that single part into silence.

The tavern was dark and filled with people, loud chat-tering people, all the bodies creating waves of heat. The dim candlelight slid over cheekbones and jaw lines and fin-gers and wrists, glancing off dark eyes and flashes of teeth. I could smell sweat and perfume and beer and the musty scent of winter clothes recently pulled out of storage.

And then, all of a sudden, the music stopped. Protests rose up. My heart didn't slow down, though, and for a few moments I couldn't hear the words being loudly spoken from the corner where the music had been coming from.

People were turning to look at us.

"It's all right," Karish said at high volume. "It's fine. Keep playing."

I couldn't see the musicians. I was too short, damn it. And I couldn't hear anything else because that glorious music was still swinging around in my head.

"It'll be all right. Lee doesn't get violent with music." He faltered a little there. Usually I didn't get violent with music. It had, unfortunately, been known to happen. It depended on the music, and the circumstances. But that music, and those circumstances, weren't likely to arise in a tavern. "I won't be leaving her alone. I promise you there'll be no broken mugs or chairs." And, as though to demonstrate how seriously he took his promise, he put an arm around my shoulders. "Please keep playing. I'd like Lee to hear it."

I was still hearing it. It felt good. Really good.

But I could tell when it started up again. It felt even better. Smoothing over my face, filling my blood with light, bursting out through my muscles. It wrapped around me and held me apart from everything around me. I could see, but my mind didn't understand what I was seeing. I wasn't hearing the music but experiencing it inside my head. And the head became nothing more than an enthralling glow against my flesh. The removal of my cloak from my shoulders sent smooth material sliding over my skin. I started shivering.

Then there was movement. Circular, gliding movement. Movement running with my blood, flowing with it, pushing it faster, lifting my feet, curling me through the warm darkness around me.

Dancing. I loved dancing.

I loved Karish. He felt so good. Long slim muscles lining strong limbs. Smooth skin over elegant fingers. His hair was so soft. Gentle light gleamed in his dark eyes. And his smile, such a beautiful velvet smile. I could look at him forever, touch him forever.

Dance forever. The movement. Feeling the muscles work. Experiencing the shift in balance. Trusting your body to know what to do and just letting it. I could do it for hours.

Sometimes the music softened a little, and I could think. It would change into something more gentle, more stately, the steps less acrobatic and more precisely timed, set into specific patterns as partners faced each other and clapped their hands and slid from side to side. I was able to see a little better, watch Karish as he played the gentleman's role in the dance and admire how well he knew the steps, how well he moved. I would have thought the elegance would lose its impact over time, as I saw it almost every day, but I knew then that the unconscious grace of my Source's manner of movement would never cease to rouse my envy.

What was it like to know you always looked perfect? What was it like to know every single thing you did was done well?

Or maybe he didn't know. Maybe he didn't think about it at all. Maybe it was so much a part of what he was that he didn't think any more about it than I thought about the shape of my eyebrows, or the length of my toes.

And I wondered how someone who couldn't sing and claimed no interest in music was able to dance so well. Then the music would rise up again, and the ability to think about anything at all slipped away.

After a while, Karish tried to pull me away from the dancers. I didn't like that, and I resisted. If I stopped dancing my blood would explode out of my veins and spatter everyone, and that would be bad.

"I'm thirsty," he shouted through the music.

"So drink," I said. "I'll dance." Who needed a partner? I was just jumping around like an idiot, anyway.

"No." He headed towards the tables, his grip firm on my hand. "Be a good girl and have some beer."

Beer. Mmmmm. My throat suddenly closed in, rough

and dry. Drinking something seemed like a good idea, and
I moved more willingly. I could always dance after.

Through the haze in my head I saw the occupants of a
nearby table clear away. They looked up and saw us coming and with no hesitation or even discussion among them,
moved away. I opened my mouth to protest. That wasn't
right.

"Leave it," Karish told me. "They feel better about it
this way."

Really? I'd be annoyed, having to make way for someone else like that. But they'd already disappeared into the
crowd, and no one else seemed to find anything odd about
it. I couldn't see any dark looks or discontented mutters.

And to be honest, right then, I really didn't care that
much. I was happy enough to have a seat at a table.

I closed my eyes, letting the notes and the rhythms of
the music flow through me. Another gentle piece, a little
mournful. Beautiful, but disturbing, about lost hopes and
opportunities carelessly tossed aside, and it made me uncomfortable. It made me think. Images and memories I
preferred to repress flashed through my mind. I clutched
the sides of the table, pulling in a deep breath that had
nothing to do with recovering from the dancing. Jumping
around in a tavern when everyone else was doing the same
was one thing. Disintegrating into tears and being the only
one doing it was not acceptable.

Warm hands peeled my fingers from the table. "Don't
try to control yourself," Karish chided me. "That's my job."

Well, no, it wasn't, strictly speaking. His job was to
make sure I didn't hurt anyone, or sleep with anyone, or
damage any of the furniture. "Not much fun for you." And
I didn't like the idea of him doing it.

"Aye, it is." His grin was impish.

Oh, that made me feel so much better.

The beer, when it came, was ice cold and so, so smooth,
spicy flavor bursting over my tongue and flowing down my

throat. Very good. I drained it in short order, and a full mug quickly replaced the empty one. I raised it to my lips.

Karish started laughing at me. "Slow down, girl!" he cried. "You'll make yourself drunk."

And what was so wrong with that? "So?"

"So, is that your plan?"

I hadn't thought about it before, but "Sure!" Everyone else did, and they seemed to enjoy it.

He was grinning. "Have you ever been drunk before?"

Of course not. "What kind of question is that? I'm twenty-two years old."

A brilliantly evasive answer which, unfortunately, failed to divert him. "Have you?" he persisted.

"I'll have you know I get drunk all the time. It's a regular thing."

"You do not."

"Are you going to nag at me all night?"

"Far be it for me to be the voice of reason."

He sounded so all-knowing that it aggravated me to no end. I couldn't help it. I had to stick my tongue out at him again. Because I couldn't think of anything suitably cutting to say.

He started laughing. Threw back his head and howled like I was the most hysterical thing he'd ever seen. I thought, for a moment, of asking him just what he thought was so funny, but realized I really didn't need to know. He was enjoying himself. That was good enough for me, even if it were at my expense. There were worse things.

I finished my beer with no more comments from the man who thought he was my mother. And then we danced. And drank some more. And danced some more. And drank some more.

And it all got a little fuzzy after that.

The next time I could think again, and then not well, it was morning—or some time like it. I opened my eyes, cursed the evil blades of sunlight, and closed them again.

I tried to ascertain my situation. I was in bed, my own. Alone, dressed in my nightgown and lacking any recollection of how I'd gotten there. My tongue was coated with thick fur, my throat was sticky, my stomach stretched and gurgled, and I wished my head would just carry on and explode so I wouldn't have to feel anything anymore.

Then the bed started swinging and spinning.

In my mind I could hear Karish laughing, the bastard.

What a stupid thing to do.

I was still sitting there, and still miserable, when an aggravating Karish pounded on the door and taunted me, telling me I'd feel better if I ate something. The wicked liar. At the thought of food my stomach tried to curl into an impenetrable fist.

But when Riley knocked on my door to tell me my mother had arrived, I knew there was nothing for it but to get out of bed. I washed my face. Dressed. Opened the door.

The aroma of food wafted in.

Close the door. Swallow. Lean my forehead against the door.

Could I die now?

Well, no, not now. After a moment. After I rested for a bit, I'd go back to bed. And die.

Knowing my mother, she wouldn't let me die. She'd just come to my room and berate me for still being in bed.

I opened the door again.

I never before would have described the smell of frying bacon as a stench. And I had to walk through it all the way to the kitchen.

My mother was there. She was causing the stench. She was grinning as she watched me. She knew what I was feeling and she thought it was hilarious. "Sit down."

I was happy enough to rest my wobbly legs.

Mother placed in front of me a plate of glaring yellow and rusty red. "It seems you had a very good time with Taro last night."

The plate had good timing. It provided an excuse for

covering half my face with my hands, ostensibly to ward off the smell. Oh my gods. The whole night was not, unfortunately, lost to me. I could remember drinking. Every moment I was off the dance floor I was drinking. No intelligent conversation of any kind.

And the dancing. Oh, Zaire, that was the worst. Because—ah, I hated even thinking about it. It hadn't really been dancing at all. More like writhing. Against Karish. Body pressed to his, arms linked around his neck. No doubt he believed my behavior was the result of repressed yearning and the last thing I needed was for him to know I lusted after him. Damn it. Why couldn't my memory block have extended over to that?

Thankfully, it had only been Karish. I hadn't danced with anyone else. I didn't think. I couldn't recall. But even if I didn't, dancing like that with Karish was more than bad enough.

Had there been anyone else I knew there? Had they seen us? What were they thinking?

Not that appearing hung over before one's mother didn't have a humiliation all its own.

"Eat, Lee."

"Uh—" I'd really rather not, thanks anyway.

"It'll make you feel better. Listen to your mother. The voice of experience."

I looked up at her at that. Her face was completely blank. She couldn't repress the twinkle in her eyes though.

I stuck a tiny piece of egg on my fork and brought it to my mouth, trying not to smell it. I put the egg on my tongue, prepared for another slosh from my stomach.

I swallowed. Nothing unpleasant happened. And it tasted really good. My next bite was more substantial.

My mother snickered and tucked into her own plate.

I did start to feel better. So my mother was right. Why did I feel irked rather than gratified by that? It made no sense.

"So," said my mother. "Taro told me his mother is in town."

"So he said."

"So I'm going to invite her to the Lion to dinner," my mother announced gaily. "A dinner for the four of us."

There was something perversely amusing about the idea of forcing the superior Dowager Duchess of Westsea to spend an evening in our non-aristocratic company. "What does Taro think of that idea?"

"Well, he didn't really like the idea, but he agreed to pass along the invitation. I think it's only appropriate that we all get to know each other, especially when we're so fortunate as to be in High Scape at the same time. It's almost like we're family, after all."

What was she up to? Because she did not think of the Dowager as family, and she'd never before given any hint of interest in meeting her.

Still, I was glad she was doing it. It was probably the only chance I would have to meet Karish's mother. He seemed anxious to keep us separated.

After breakfast I felt well enough to move without wincing, and even to work on some reports for the council. I wasn't in any shape to bench dance, though, and I felt strangely toxic. I didn't think I'd be drinking again for a good long while. If ever.

The blizzard struck later that afternoon.

Chapter Seven

I'd never been so cold. The frigid air tingled and scraped against my skin. I had to keep blinking strangely aching eyes. My breath rasped in my throat. My feet hurt. I'd made the mistake of stomping them once, in an attempt to warm them up, and it had felt like something very fragile within them—bones, maybe?—had sharply shattered.

Beside me, I heard Karish's teeth rattling. I could see his breath streaming out like smoke. For once he was keeping his hands strictly to himself. His arms were tightly crossed as he tried to control his shivering. The other Sources in the Stall were in just as bad a state, hunched over and stiff with cold, their Shields quiet and withdrawn as they all struggled with a level of discomfort none of them had ever before experienced.

The fire blazing in the stove looked real pretty, though.

"We will tell the regulars we have a plan," La Monte said through chattering teeth. No attempts at an appropriate introduction this time. Just straight to the point. Bless the man.

"We've had an answer back from the council?" Riley asked.

"No," La Monte snapped. "But I've had a brick narrowly miss my head and a horde of non-apologetic regulars telling me to get off my ass to do something." He paused, so we could all be shocked by his news and his manner of relaying it. "So I told them we were working on it. I'm not going to wait until the council puts together a commission that will look into the matter and give us a report in a couple of years. The regulars looked ready to throw ropes over tree branches. I had to say something and telling them I was waiting to hear back from the council wasn't going to cut it." He clapped his hands together to warm them. I thought of bones shattering. "They weren't terribly impressed with my answer but at least they left without stoning me."

All right, I supposed there wasn't much I could say against that. A brick at his head! What was that about? It certainly wasn't a rational or productive response to circumstances. What was that like, calmly walking down the street, minding your own business, to find your peace broken by a projectile flying at your head? La Monte was obviously rattled to be using something other than the pristine language that was his habit, and I couldn't blame him.

"Anything to say, Dunleavy?" he asked me archly, the prat.

Well then, yes, I did. "What are we going to say when nothing happens?" Because, while I understood La Monte's use of the lie, the problems with the lie still existed. "When whatever we're supposed to be doing doesn't work?"

"There was alliteration happening all over the place in that sentence," Karish muttered.

"This will pass," La Monte announced in a calm, resonating voice. All he needed was a mountaintop.

"You keep saying that and it keeps getting worse." I knew I sounded like a nag, but it was true. We had just descended into all new levels of cold, hadn't we?

"It will pass. All things do."

Lord. "What if the regulars acquire better aim before that happens?"

La Monte set his jaw. "They won't. They wouldn't dare."

I would wager that had someone asked him, a week earlier, if a regular would ever throw a brick in his general direction, he would have said they wouldn't dare.

"Now, Dunleavy, I know you're anxious to contribute and prove your worth," Wilberforce interjected in a voice I assumed was supposed to sound soothing and patient. "But wisdom as profound as Chris's can come only with time and experience. Believe me, you will get there, some day."

Blank face, blank face, blank face, and above all ignore the giggling—yes, the giggling—coming from Karish's chest and throat. "One can only hope."

La Monte, being more perceptive than Wilberforce, shot me a hard look.

All right, here goes. "Perhaps we should try actually doing something. Now that we've actually told them we are."

Karish's posture shifted beside me. An ice-cold hand wrapped around mine and squeezed. I glanced up at him. I wasn't going to give away his secret. He would, though, if he didn't stop being so paranoid.

Hammad started snickering. "I was never that young."

"Haven't we already been through this?" Garrighan drawled.

"What's the harm in trying?"

"It's not what we do," said Hammad.

"But we're telling the regulars that it is." Didn't they see the long-term repercussions of telling them that? Could they really be that blind? It was so obvious.

"It's a necessary fiction."

"Also known as a bald-faced lie."

"Dunleavy, we are not having this discussion again," La Monte snapped. "You have made your feelings quite clear. And apparently the injury I've suffered hasn't changed them."

Ah, guilt. I recognized the emotion. I knew what it was. I'd even experienced it from time to time. But had La Monte managed to inspire it within me with his heavy-handed attempt at emotional manipulation? Not at all.

"If you feel compelled to disturb everyone with your speculations about what might be happening," La Monte continued, "and rile people up with pretensions of an ability to solve every problem, then by all means be my guest. But we," and he glanced about at all the others, none of whom appeared prepared to contradict him, "know what we're going to be doing."

He did everything but cross his arms and nod and say "So there." What a bastard. Speculations. Pretensions. Like he knew what the hell he was talking about. Getting a brick thrown at him didn't make him right.

But there was no point in saying any of that, because everyone else agreed with him, or at least planned to follow his lead, and the horse was most sincerely dead.

So I tilted my head in acknowledgement. "So sorry to have bored you all," I said coolly. I didn't understand it, though. Why didn't any of them even want to try?

"Ya done it now," Karish said, but I didn't know to whom, nor in reference to what.

"I've got somewhere to be," Rayne announced. "I'm not on duty, there's no reason for me to be out here risking black fingers."

"Hear hear," said Stone, pulling her cloak about her more tightly and shifting her feet, ready to go outside.

I didn't sigh. I didn't clench my teeth. It was to be expected. There was no reason for any of them to listen to me. I was the youngest, the least experienced. And it wasn't as though I had a real plan or idea.

Or, apparently, any powers of persuasion.

Beatrice and Benedict were on duty, and so remained in the Stall. The rest of us trudged back over the snow-covered plain. No one spoke. It was too cold to speak. We just hurried along as quickly as the deep snow allowed us.

Once we passed the city's ring road the Pairs split off in different directions. Karish stuck with me. I supposed he thought to walk me home. How entirely unnecessary of him.

"What could I say to them?" he asked me all out of the blue.

Caught up in my own thoughts, I let myself frown. I thought about what he had said. I turned the words around, took them apart, examined each one individually, put them back together and studied the whole, then said, "What?"

"At the Stall, when you were talking about trying to do something about the weather. I couldn't tell them about what we were trying. There really wasn't anything to say."

"Ah." I didn't want to talk about it.

"I mean, there's nothing to report yet. And I'm sorry, but I don't want them finding out about . . . things unless we have something real to tell them."

"Fine." It was done. There was no point in hashing it out.

"Damn it, Lee!" he snapped.

I looked up at him. What was his problem now?

He did a weird sort of step and slide thing that had him suddenly in front of me, facing me, and I had to stop. "Will you just admit you're angry?"

Talking about beating dead animals. "I have nothing to be angry about." Not with him, anyway. And it was too cold to stay angry with La Monte.

"You're telling me you don't think I failed you or something by not speaking up back there?"

Actually, I hadn't thought about it. "I am perfectly capable of speaking for myself." And perfectly used to being summarily dismissed. Really. That was the lot of the Shield. Sure, it would have been nice if Karish had said something. They would have listened to him, and thought about what he said, at least for a moment. But most likely they would have eventually chosen the same path regardless. So the fact that he decided not to throw in his lot with the losing side, well there was no point in getting upset about it. And, anyway, I would never dream of

expecting Karish to speak when he didn't care to, just to
support me.

"I could have drawn lines by your spine."

More mental dissection was required to translate that,
but the fact that I could pleased me. Then I rolled my eyes.
"You might have noticed it's a bit chilly today."

"You're angry, Lee."

I had to admit I was starting to get there. I hated it when
people told me how I felt. I shrugged. "Fine. I'm angry.
Can we go somewhere inside now?"

"Damn it, Lee." He couldn't drive his hands into his
hair because both his hands and his head were wrapped. He
tried, though. It almost made me smile.

I waited a moment, thinking he planned to continue, but
apparently he could think of nothing more to say. "You get
irritated when I say I'm not angry and you get irritated
when I say I am angry. I can't win."

"Because you're just saying whatever you think will
shut me up," he accused me.

"Aye, but it's not working."

"Argh!" was his response, and he charged on down the
street.

And I started laughing at his antics. He was so excitable. Sometimes it was exhausting just listening to him,
but there was also something exhilarating about it. Karish
seemed so unconcerned with whether people knew what
he was feeling. After years of being told how distasteful it
was to impose one's strong emotions on others, it was re-
freshing to be with someone who wasn't similarly con-
strained.

"I said nothing funny, Lee."

Now he was frowning, a little line appearing between
his eyebrows. I walked up to him and touched it with the tip
of my finger. "You're so handsome when you're annoyed."

He backed away from my finger. "I'm serious, Lee."

"That's my job." And he didn't do serious well. It made
him all melodramatic. "Can we go in now?"

He scowled. "You don't deserve it."

"What, going in?"

"Going to the hospital."

I thought about that and tried to figure out how visiting a hospital would be a treat. "Huh?"

"Come on." He took my hand and started leading me down the street.

We did indeed end up at the Western Center Hospital. One I'd been to many times. And it looked like a disaster had struck. It was busier than I'd remembered ever seeing it before. The rooms were filled and people were lying in cots in the corridors. The staff looked harried, moving from one patient to another without much of a pause. A couple glanced up when we came in and, after quickly deciding we didn't need any help, ignored us.

I pulled the wraps from my hands and head with relief. The hospital was warm and I was happy enough to be inside. I glanced around and after a few moments I realized most of the patients were very old, or very young.

"Frostbite," Karish told me. "I'd heard, because of the strange weather, a lot of people have been getting frostbite. Bad enough to need amputations." I grimaced. "Some have been getting heart pains from shifting snow. Others are getting sick in their lungs. I can't do anything for that last group, though."

I looked up at him quickly. He didn't return my gaze, concentrating on a child wrapped up in a cot. Clutching a toy to her chest and staring at the wall, she appeared to be alone. "Ah," I said. And I smiled, because I'd realized why we'd come.

"Good afternoon, little one," Karish said to the child, kneeling by the cot, his voice dropping into a low, soothing tone.

She was perhaps six years old, though I was no good at judging the ages of children. She was tiny, and it was hard to believe that her body could contain all the organs necessary for survival. It seemed obscene to me that such a fragile little person had been left unattended in this dark and grim corridor. When she turned her head from the wall her eyes were dark and red with tears. "Who are you?" she asked in a soft, trembling voice.

"I'm Taro. This is Lee. What's your name?"

"Keeva," she answered solemnly. "Do you know my Da?"

"No." Karish stroked back her dark hair with a light hand. "Is he here?"

"He's at the shop. He couldn't keep me at home." The coat of tears over her eyes thickened. "I wouldn't have been any trouble." She sniffed and rubbed her nose. Her hand was wrapped in gauzy white cloth.

"I'm sure he wasn't worried about your being trouble to him," Karish assured her. "But he can't take care of you when you're injured. He doesn't know how. A person can't know how to take care of a shop and be a healer, all at the same time." He bent down to kiss her forehead, an action I thought was a little presumptuous but one she seemed to have no trouble with. Could sway all ages, he could. "But I know it's hard to be away from home."

He glanced at me, and after a moment I felt his internal shields lower.

This was different from when he was channeling events. Then, I could sort of feel the forces through him, or at least I could perceive them. When he healed people, I was aware of him drawing forces in, but I couldn't see them myself. I couldn't feel anything but him.

"I had to leave home when I was very young," Karish said, still stroking back the girl's hair. "Lee left home when she was four."

It was a little difficult to concentrate on the girl's face while I was shielding Karish, but I saw her look at the black braid on Karish's left shoulder, and the white braid on mine. "That's different," she said. "You belong to Triple S."

We did, sort of, belong to the Triple S. In a way. I didn't like the choice of words, though.

"Doesn't make it any easier to leave home," Karish

chided her gently. "And you'll be here only a little while. Then you get to go back to your Da again."

"I miss Maxie," she muttered, the bright eyes dimming as the tension of pain left her frostbitten extremities.

"Is she your sister?"

"Yes," she said, her eyelids lowering. "No," she corrected herself. "She died. She was really really little. Ma died, too." Her voice was starting to slur.

Her words sobered me. So young to deal with death. Too young, I thought, to be so matter of fact about it. I didn't know what I'd do if a member of my family died.

This was not the time to think about such things.

"I'm sorry to hear about that," Karish said in a soft voice. "You must miss them both."

"Uh-huh." The eyes were closed. A long slow breath.

Karish lifted his hand from her hair, his internal shields shifting back in to place.

"Well done," I murmured.

Maybe someday I would tell him how proud I was of him, that he could do such things. Some day when he was willing to listen. I was moved to tuck a lock of his dark hair behind his ear.

"What the hell?" a sharp voice shouted out.

Keeva was startled out of her sleep. Karish and I turned, looking to the cause of the disturbance.

Except, apparently, it was us. A man wearing the sturdy dark garments of a fisher strode up the corridor, reached out and grabbed Karish's arm, pulling him close. Karish's eyes widened in surprise and he arched back from the man, but he made no real effort to free himself.

"Got nerve, so you do, showing up in here," the fisher snarled into Karish's face. "Prancing around your victims instead of working out there where you belong, doing your job."

"Sir," Karish said, and that was all he was able to get out.

The fisher shifted his grip, bunching his fists in the front of Karish's cloak. "Fish stock is down, you know that? My

nets have been empty for weeks. We found my—" His voice
cut off, moisture rising in his eyes. He cleared his throat.
"We found my son dead, curled up by the house. He got
caught out in the blizzard. He almost made it home. He
couldn't find the door. And we never heard him." He shook
Karish once, hard. "How dare you walk among us now?"

Karish laid his hands on the man's wrists. I wasn't sure
whether he was trying to stop the man from shaking him
again or to provide some kind of comfort. "Sir, I am so
sorry, really, but . . ."

"Why did you let him come in here?" the fisher demanded of me. He shoved Karish away, and Karish nearly
lost his balance as he tried not to step into another cot behind him. "Take him out of here."

He was grieving. He was facing destitution. No doubt he
could barely think straight. But helping the injured feel better was something Karish could do. In trying to lay unde-
served responsibility on Karish, the fisher was preventing
him from performing the good he could do. He shouldn't be
able to deny the others a respite from pain. "We are here to
see people, sir," I told him, keeping my voice mild and
level. "Please know I am very sorry for your loss, but—"

"Get him out of here!" the fisher roared.

I was aware of the others. Patients, visitors, one member of the staff, all watching us. They showed no intention
of interfering. "Sir, there's nothing we can do right now."

"Lee." A warning from Karish.

Oh, that's right. I'd forgotten about the lie.

"Nothing you can do!" the fisher echoed with in-
credulity. "Then what the hell are we keeping you for? And
in right fine style, too." His gaze raked over me, from head
to foot and back again. "Better clothes than I've got, and
I've worked hard every day of my life. And now, when we
really need you, you're useless."

What was I supposed to say? They never taught me
how to deal with this sort of thing in the academy. No one
ever warned me there would come a time when the regulars

would accuse me, all out of the blue, of not doing my job. Worse, of being some kind of societal parasite.

It was dealing with the farmer all over again. "Sir," I said. "Please understand. This kind of thing, the snow, the blizzard, it's not something we were trained to deal with."

"Not something—" he practically exploded.

"But we're working on it!" I said hastily, and without really thinking about it. Until after the words were out of my mouth, and then I had to work to keep the grimace off my face. Because there, I'd done it, even though I'd been hoping to avoid it. "We're looking into it. We're trying to see what we can do. But it's going to take time."

I heard people speaking around us then. I couldn't decipher the exact words, I didn't know whether they had been reassured by what I'd said or not. But it didn't feel like anyone was impressed.

"Time," the fisher muttered through his teeth, tone dripping with disgust. "Aye, and what is time to me? I've already lost everything."

I couldn't even imagine what that felt like. "We are sorry, sir. Really." Words were useless. Hollow. But there was nothing else I could do.

He pulled in a deep breath, making an effort to calm himself down. A man of dignity, who knew there was no point in haranguing us further. He nodded at Karish. "Get him out of here."

He had no right to give me such an order, but our continued presence wouldn't benefit anyone anymore. The damage had been done. I grabbed Karish's arm. I resisted the urge to repeat my sympathies to the fisher. That would only make him angry, and it wouldn't do anything to make me feel better, either. But it was a hard instinct to fight.

Karish showed some reluctance over leaving, but after a couple of discrete tugs he was following me.

People watched us leave, silently. I could feel their attention. A dark weight that seemed to press up against me and made me wish I could just disappear.

I didn't understand it. No matter how rationally I took it apart, how objectively I looked at the phenomenon, I couldn't understand the abrupt change of opinion. A month earlier Karish was admired and adored by everyone. Now people were blaming him for all of their problems. It didn't make sense. And it wasn't right. How could people be so damned fickle? Even when things were going so badly, how could someone just reach out blindly, grab the first person they encountered, and pile blame on them?

High Scape had three other major hospitals. We went to each one. No one kicked us out of any of those, but they watched us. Watched Karish. Long looks. Whispers. What is he doing here? Why isn't he doing something about this? How dare he come around here eyeing his victims like a lord looking over his livestock and deciding where culling was needed?

Karish heard. The man wasn't deaf. But he acted as though he didn't. He spoke quietly with those patients who would talk to him. Sometimes he merely asked them their names and about their families. Sometimes he gently flirted with them, unerring in determining which patients would be offended and which could be made to smile with the attention. Under the cover of touching their hand or shoulder or "accidentally" brushing against them while straightening their blankets, he channeled some of their pain and eased them into sleep. And possibly, for all we knew, accelerated their healing a little.

Then, late at night, when we left the last hospital, Karish let his head fall back and breathed out in a long tired sigh.

I clapped him on the back. "You all right?"

"Just lovely."

Oh, no, that didn't ring with insincerity. "If you're not meeting up with someone"—and how likely was that?—"why don't you walk me to the Lion and let my mother fuss over you?" Because I didn't want him to be alone. A part of me always worried about what he might get up to, when he was distressed and alone. His judgment seemed to get a little . . . skewed . . . when he was upset.

He chuckled, but it was a weak, weary sound. "I love your mother."

Well, of course. "And she adores you. More than me." A sad fact of life. I considered being jealous. "Come, Taro. I'm serious. You look exhausted. And the Lion is closer." And it had gotten even colder, though I wouldn't have thought that was possible. I could feel these strange prickles over my nose and cheeks.

"I am exhausted," he said, "which is why I'm going home and getting some sleep. So I can be in top form tomorrow while we sit in the Stall and do nothing for seven hours."

"Well, not quite nothing," I reminded him.

He sighed. "Oh, aye. I'd forgotten. While we sit in the Stall and do something futile for seven hours."

"Taro . . ." I needed him to think there was actually a point to it. If he didn't believe in it he wouldn't be able to accomplish anything.

"I know, I know. I'm sorry." He tried to rub the back of his neck under his cloak.

I felt tempted to run my fingers through his hair. Which was odd, because I couldn't even see his hair. Good thing we were once more all bundled up, so I couldn't make a fool of myself no matter how much I wanted to. But he seemed to like it when I did it. And he just looked so tired. He'd put up with a lot that day, bending his abilities in unnatural ways, while working under the weight of disapproval and hostility. And he'd stuck with it for hours, when he didn't have to, when no one had asked him to. Perhaps it was his way of making up for being unable to do anything about the weather. Or maybe he was just that decent.

"I'm sorry you had to lie to that fisher," Karish muttered.

So was I. I was committed to the story now, and there

was no backing out of it. I was going to have nightmares about everyone finding out that we'd been blowing windless. But it was done. "I didn't have to lie. I wasn't lying. We are working on it, remember? This was part of the deal."

He looked at me. "You felt you were lying to him, and with you that's all that counts."

I shrugged. "Then I'll just have to get over my delicate sensibilities, won't I? And you'll have to figure out some way to fix things."

He grunted. "Lucky me."

I almost winced. That had been careless, and thoughtless, and stupid. Let's just pile a bit more pressure on him, shall we?

I widened my eyes at him, though the effect may have been ruined by the scarves wrapped around my face. "But Taro," I said in a lilting voice, "You're my hero."

He groaned.

I swallowed down a laugh. "You're everyone's hero."

"Shut up, Lee."

"The Darling of the Triple S."

"That wasn't my fault!"

That made me pause for a moment. That wasn't his fault? What exactly did that mean? "The hope of High Scape."

"Will you stop?"

"Defeater of the evil Stevan Creol and favorite of the Empress Constia." I was kind of getting into this. He squirmed so well.

"I swear if you don't stop I'll . . ."

"What?" I challenged him.

"Do something you don't like," he muttered.

As threats went, that was a little weak. "Like what?

From the way his eyes crinkled up I knew he was grinning behind the wraps around his face. And didn't that send a thread of alarm through me? "I am walking you to the Lion," he told me. "Where I will turn you over to your mother. Let her deal with her impossible, wayward, disrespectful child." And once more he had me by the hand and was leading me down the street.

As punishments went, that was rather disappointing.

Chapter Eight

Shopping. With my mother. Ugh.

It had been a good idea. In theory. Because, as life or circumstance or fate would have it, Her Grace, Dowager Duchess of Westsea had agreed to eat dinner at my mother's boarding house. I couldn't have been more surprised. I had simply accepted it as a fact of life that there was no way the Dowager Duchess of Westsea would step foot into such plebeian company without being carried in after being drugged or beaten into unconsciousness.

With Karish's teeth-clenched delivery of the acceptance had come a wave of complete shock that nearly matched my own. He hadn't anticipated the possibility of her saying yes, either.

I had no idea what else had happened at their little meeting, but the way Karish refused to talk about it told me it had not been fun. I began to think that this might be as bad an idea as Karish had warned it would be. I might have enjoyed watching the Duchess mince her way through an evening with her social inferiors, but I didn't want to see Karish being tied in knots.

The invitation had been delivered and accepted, however. There was nothing to be done to change that.

That meant I needed something to wear. My mother had declared my wardrobe inadequate for dining with a duchess, and I had to agree with her. Therefore, shopping. For clothes. With my mother.

Ugh.

I had envisioned arranging for one outfit and then going home. Because, while I liked nice clothes well enough, I hated shopping.

Silly me.

"But look at this fabric, Lee. I mean, just feel it."

I couldn't be more bored. Really. And I'd been bored, in my life. Certain classes at the academy came to mind, where I'd been tempted to pound my head against my table until my skull cracked because it would break the monotony and possibly get me out of the room for a while. This was worse. At least in class I had been able to let my mind wander a bit and think of more exciting things. My mother expected me to pay attention to her, and respond when her voice rose that slight amount at the end of her sentences. "I've felt dozens of fabrics this morning, Mother. They all feel the same to me." All right, big lie. Even I could feel the difference between linen and silk. But I was desperate to get out of there.

She looked shocked, like I'd said something dreadful. "If you'd been raised at home you would never dare utter such a thing, even if it were true, which it wouldn't have been."

"But I wasn't raised at home," I reminded her, and I knew I sounded really, really patient. "I was raised in the academy. And I am not a trader or a holder. I am a Shield. And as a Shield, I do not need a limitless wardrobe, nor to spend so much time shopping for one."

"This material is of excellent quality, and it's perfect for your coloring."

The way I was starting to feel, I wouldn't have cared if

the material were threaded with real gold and woven by the Empress herself. "I don't want it, Mother."

"And it's not too heavy. Your skin will be able to breathe."

I wasn't even sure what that meant. Skin, breathing? "No, Mother."

She turned to the attendant. "Perhaps half a bolt."

All right. That was going too far. Completely ignoring my wishes, pretending I hadn't said anything at all. No. So I spoke to the attendant, too. "Make sure she pays for anything she takes, because I won't be using it."

"Dunleavy!" She looked stunned. Like I was the one acting inappropriately.

And I left the shop. I wondered if I could possibly get away from her before I said something one of us would regret. I was surprised at how irritated I felt. I was too old to be reacting so emotionally about something so trivial.

I heard her running up behind me. "Dunleavy Mallorough! That kind of behavior was completely unacceptable!"

I didn't turn around. Let her catch up if she was so desperate to talk to me. "And ignoring what I said, what I wanted, that's good breeding?"

"You need more clothes, Lee."

"That's my decision to make, and I've decided my clothes are fine."

I felt her hand on my elbow. I couldn't help tensing up. I was not in the mood to be touched.

"You haven't been out of the academy very long," she said.

"So?" What did that have to do with anything?

"Well, maybe you haven't had enough time to learn what society expects of you. I'm just trying to—"

Oh, no, no, no. How dared she? "For one thing, Mother, all society has a right to expect from me is that I fulfil my duties as a Shield. For another, I was living in a school, with professors and other students. I was not living alone in a cave."

"An academic setting isn't the best environment for teaching social skills."

"What?" That was all I could say, because . . . what?

"I mean, look at you, Lee. No idea what to wear. And you're so withdrawn all the time. You can't sit in social situations and not speak for hours. It's rude."

When had I ever done that? "Unlike spilling out a person's flaws to their face without being asked." Not that I thought they were flaws. A disregard for work-a-day clothes and keeping my mouth shut when I had nothing to say was not the sort of thing to irritate a rational person.

My mother sighed. "Lee, I'm not trying to . . . I'm just worried about you. All right? You were so young when we had to admit you to the school."

What did that have to do with anything? "Kaaren and Mika and Dias weren't much older when they started boarding," I reminded her.

"Yes, but they were able to come home for the holidays, and learn our ways and know us. We were lucky if we got to see you once a year."

Well, aye, that was the way it had to be. So, what, she didn't like the way I had turned out, thought I'd become some sort of freak because I hadn't benefited from her superior influence? "So sorry to be a disappointment to you, Mother." And did that sound bitter. Calm down.

"I'm not saying you're a disappointment, Lee," she retorted with impatience.

"Of course you are." I crossed the street with a fine disregard for the carriages driving down it. I was the way I was, and there was no turning back. If my character was not to her liking, there was nothing to be done about it.

I'd hoped that would be the end of it. My mother, unfortunately, didn't know when to let things rest. She scrambled across the street after me. "I'm saying you weren't given the same opportunities to see the world as your siblings were. As anyone has. And now that you're out in it, maybe you don't know how to see it. How to go about in it."

Of all the condescending . . . "Mother, the reason I
don't have more stylish clothes is because they take too
long to purchase, make, put on, take off, and clean. I am
aware that most of my clothes are plain and not stylish. I
just don't care. And if you don't like it, don't look." I
couldn't believe I was being forced to explain myself because of my clothes. My clothes!

Mother reached for my hand and I neatly avoided her.
"Don't be like that, Lee."

"We weren't completely cut off from the rest of the
world, Mother." She'd visited the academy. She knew that.
"We were aware of things like fashion. I just never cared.
Dragging me into an endless string of shops and treating
me like a child in front of the shop assistants won't change
that."

"I wasn't treating you like a child," she protested.

I had nothing to say to that. I was right and she was
wrong. If she didn't want to admit that, well, it didn't matter and didn't change anything.

Mother sighed again. "All right, Lee. No more. I won't
discuss your clothing anymore."

Uh-huh. I'd heard that before.

"Oh, except—"

All right. I let myself glare at her. She deserved it.

"Classic Lines, Lee. It's new. I just heard about it the
other day."

Unclench teeth. "Mother." I was tired. My feet hurt. I
wanted to go home.

"No, no, I guarantee it will be worth your time." She
smirked at me. "It's supposed to cater exclusively to aristocrats. If you don't find anything you like we can make fun
of the pretentious sales assistants."

Now there was an evil gleam in her eyes that was hard
to resist.

I rolled my own eyes.

"Good girl."

I let my mother drag me into the shop. I had no spine.

The shop, to me, looked like all the others we had visited that day. The same fabrics. The same styles. The furniture, flowers and refreshments were finer, but the shop had the same stifling overstuffed feeling that all places attempting to sell goods had. An artificial environment that couldn't help being uncomfortable no matter how plump the cushions on the chairs were. The only unusual thing about the shop was the sales assistant, a young woman with an odd head covering, some kind of dense white cloth that folded low over her forehead and covered her ears and draped down her back. I thought I might have to take back my claim of being aware of fashion, as I couldn't remember seeing anything like that head gear before.

As usual, the mercenary gleam in the sales assistant's eyes faded as soon as she saw the white braid on my left shoulder and realized she would be getting no cash for anything I took out of the shop. She rallied admirably, though. "Good afternoon, ladies," she greeted us with feigned warmth. "I wasn't aware any of our Shields were quality."

Huh. Quality. What a ridiculous term. "You were mistaken. We are all of very high quality. If you are referring to aristocratic status though, then no, I haven't that."

"I see," the woman said, her tone cooling. She shifted her posture so she was facing my mother. "My lady—"

Mother raised her chin. "I am not an aristocrat," she announced proudly.

"Then I must ask you to leave. We cater to an aristocratic clientele."

My mother tilted her head, looking as arrogant as any High Landed. "Well, you're catering to us, now."

"I'm afraid not, ma'am. Please leave."

I felt my eyebrows fly up. How breathtakingly rude.

"My daughter is a Shield," said my mother. "You cannot refuse to serve her. That is the law."

"True." The woman crossed her arms. "But the service I provide isn't legally required to be pleasant."

That woman really didn't want to serve us. It was

bizarre. If I chose to report her she could be fined, and her licence could be taken away. I could even have her arrested. Did she know that?

My mother, losing her hauteur in a hurry, suddenly looked ready to spit. "We will tell people about this."

"Not anyone who is a patron of this establishment," the woman sneered.

Mother drew herself up to her full unimpressive height. "As a matter of fact—"

"No, Mother," I interrupted loudly, desperately. No way was I going to let her tell this complete stranger we would be dining with the Dowager Duchess of Westsea. Or perhaps she was going to tell her my Source was Shintaro Karish, son of said Dowager Duchess of Westsea. Either way, if she didn't shut up she was getting wrestled to the floor with a stocking stuffed in her mouth. "You've committed one of the cardinal sins of haggling. Trying to sell an item you know nothing about."

That snapped my mother out of the staring contest she'd engaged in with the sales assistant. "What?"

"We're leaving." I looked at the sales assistant. "But I'm taking your chocolate wafers." Karish loved them, and there was a great big silver bowl of them on the refreshment table. I could carry a great many of them in my handkerchief.

There was a stack of business cards on the table as well. I picked one up, thinking this woman definitely deserved to have Her Grace inflicted on her. Except a quick glance showed me the card wasn't for the shop.

Raiborn Ladies' Society.

The name triggered a memory.

"Dunleavy?" my mother said, waiting by the exit and impatient about it.

Was it normal for a ladies society to recruit in a shop?

I stuck the card in my pocket and took a half dozen chocolate wafers.

Mother was still fuming as we stepped back onto the

street. "Jumped up little fishmonger," she muttered. "How could a shop assistant think herself superior to a holder?"

I was struggling to wrap up the wafers without handling them too much. "She never found out you were a holder," I reminded her. "And when did you turn into an elitist?"

"That sort of behavior is reprehensible."

"It certainly is, but it's her own business she's hurting." Rude people often got what they deserved in the end, I found, though they never seemed to connect their misery with their own actions. It was almost enough to make me think there was some kind of method to existence after all.

"I suppose you're right," my mother said reluctantly. "And only a fool bases their entire business on aristocratic clientele. They're the best for paying their bills and—oh, Zaire!"

"What?" I looked down the street, expecting to see a mishap. "What's wrong?"

"I hadn't noticed it was so late." She started walking faster.

Frowning, I sped up with her. "What difference does it make?" I asked. "Do you have plans tonight?" It would be kind of nice if she did. I wouldn't mind having the evening to myself. Take a bath. Read a book. Go to bed early.

"Just to treat my daughter to a properly cooked meal."

"Oh." Well, that was a good choice, too.

"And I just hate getting dinner started late. It means you eat too late. That's not good for sleeping."

I raised an eyebrow. "How very maternal of you." I couldn't remember anyone ever caring when I ate once I was older than fourteen or so.

My mother's boarding house was designed along similar lines as the Triple S house, only grander. Not nearly as expensive as the Imperial, where Karish's mother was staying, it was still beyond the purse of the average person. On the main floor was located a large dining room where all the guests could eat, three sitting rooms, and a private room comprised of a sitting area and a dining area, to be reserved for private parties. That was where we would be dining with Karish and his mother.

The guests stayed on the second floor, in large bed-chambers, each with a water closet for bathing. Mother's suite was furnished entirely in shades of green. It was a nice enough room, everything matching and nothing over-done, but it was striving for homelike and hitting artificial.

The first hint that something was going on, was learning that Mother wanted to eat in the private dining room that evening.

The second was when she bullied me into wearing one of my new gowns, one she consented to my requisition de-spite it being premade and off the shelf, because, as she said, it suited me so very well.

Still, I didn't step wise to the plan until after we had been served appetizers and wine in the private dining room. There was a knock on the door. One of the serving maids answered.

And Erin walked in.

My mother was a dead woman.

I plastered a smile on my face. "Erin! Come in!" A dead woman. A dead, dead, dead, dead woman. I was going to kill her. Slowly. A lot.

Erin grinned, and I had to admit that my heart did skip a beat. "Dunleavy, you look lovely!"

"Thank you, Erin. I'm so glad you could come." My mother was taller than I, but I could reach her throat. That was all I really needed.

"Holder Mallorough, I'm so glad you could join us this evening!"

I looked at my mother.

Who refused to look at me. "Oh, no. I was only keeping Lee company while she waited. I have an engagement with the Yings, and I'm going to be late."

I gaped at her, the significance of her words hitting me hard. Then I shut my mouth. Because I had to be wrong. She wouldn't dare.

She rose from the table and crossed the room to stand by Erin. "I must say you are looking particularly handsome tonight, Erin."

"Thank you, ma'am."

"It is so nice to see young people who know how to dress."

Then she looked at me.

"Have a good evening."

She did dare. She was going to leave. She'd set this dinner up, without telling me, and now she was deserting me. I couldn't believe it.

Erin opened the door for her. She stepped out. I sat in my chair and wallowed in the moment of feeling stunned.

A long, drawn-out painful death.

"Care for a glass of wine?" I asked Erin.

"Is there any red?"

"Of course." The maid moved to the sideboard. "No, that's all right. You can go now. I'll serve us." The young woman looked uncertain at the order. I wondered if I should mention that she wouldn't get a tip from me. That would probably help her make up her mind. "I'm really not used to being waited on. Please."

She curtsied and vacated the room.

"Please have a seat." What was I going to do with this man? The plan had been to stay away from him. It was a good plan. A simple plan. A plan I'd had every intention of following through on. It was in everyone's best interest.

Not that there was anything wrong with Erin. He was handsome and sophisticated and charming. But there was something about him that made me grit my teeth, and that gave me a headache.

Damn that woman. And all right, so I couldn't actually strangle her. I wasn't sure I was strong enough. But we had to have a talk. A long screaming serious one. No more soft shoes.

"I admit to being surprised when I got your note," Erin said, having sprawled on a settee. "I was starting to think you were avoiding me." And he smiled, a smile that managed to express the belief he had been foolish while at the same time suggesting he wasn't entirely sure he was wrong.

Damn it, Mother! He'd been getting the hint. "It has become a pretty difficult time for us, right now." I gave him his glass of wine and sat in the chair across from him. "The Pairs, I mean. What with this bizarre weather and everyone expecting us to get rid of it . . . Well, it's a little tense."

He sipped at his wine. "One of the hardest things I had to learn about being a solicitor was how to leave the work at the office. Don't worry, you'll learn it, too."

I had a glass of wine, too. Used the bury-your-nose-in-your-drink-to-hide-your-expression trick. I wasn't going to say anything, but I couldn't believe he thought being a solicitor was comparable to being a Shield. I couldn't *leave my work at the office.* "How is work going for you? How is the Bill working out?" Hey, it was something to say, right?

"Ah, no real progress is being made. Trying to find wording everyone will agree with, that expresses the purpose of the Bill but still has a possibility of being passed. It's a nightmare. And it's all a waste of time."

"Really? Why?" The process certainly seemed cumbersome, all those solicitors working on it. Wouldn't it be more efficient to have one person write a draft and then maybe a bunch of them polishing it up? But then, what did I know about it?

"Because even if we get it through, even if we establish a quota, no one really cares."

I raised my eyebrows at him. "No one really cares?" Was he serious? "People are furious about this."

He nodded. "They are. They'll fight for it tooth and nail. Or they'll fight against it tooth and nail. And let's say the Bill passes, and the merchants get their quota. What will happen? Nothing. Because they'll still be a minority in the council. And minorities have no power, not on their own. The only way they'll be able get anything done is by winning over the aristocrats, and they won't be able to win over the aristocrats because they won't know the game. They won't know the rules, and the aristocrats don't want them to know them. As soon as the merchants do learn the rules, the aristocrats will change them, and it's going to be a huge waste of everyone's time. Because the aristocrats don't believe the merchants should be making laws for people they owe no traditional obligations to. So all the merchants will be able to do is run after the wave, trying to learn moves and make contacts that are out of date. They'll spend all their time running and none learning about whatever political issues are bounding about at the time."

I'd never considered any of that. I hadn't really thought about any of it, beyond the most superficial contemplation. The merchants wanted to be in the council. Representation for all was good. End of story. I never thought about whether it would actually work. Though, come to think of it, Karish had said he didn't think it would accomplish anything, and I'd promptly forgotten. That was kind of bad, wasn't it? Such a thorough lack of interest in politics.

And yet, even knowing that, I still didn't care.

"If this is all for nothing, why are they even bothering?"

"Well," he conceded with a shrug, "It's a first step. Probably. Hopefully. In a very long journey. Maybe. I don't know that it's the right step, though. And really, it's not something I care terribly much about. Let the aristocrats spend their days mulling through incomprehensible bills if they wish. Better them than us, I say. I'd wager a lot of people would say the same, if they thought about it a little. I don't think anyone has, though. I get the feeling the merchants are so desperate to get in only because they've been told they can't."

"Hm." I smiled.

"You disagree?"

"No." Didn't agree either. That wasn't what I was thinking about. "I was just reminded of earlier today. Mother wanted to see what a shop purporting to cater solely to the High Landed was like. We were kicked out."

He looked stunned. "You were kicked out?"

"With brisk efficiency."

"They can't do that. It's against the law."

"So what am I going to do? Sue them?"

"It's a criminal matter. You can have them arrested."

What a ridiculous idea. Getting someone arrested because they wouldn't let me shop in their stores. "I don't care about it, Erin. Let them keep their exclusive shops. I can find all I need elsewhere." But my own words triggered a memory, and my mind veered off in another direction. "Do you know anything about those aristocratic clubs? The gentlemen's clubs and the ladies societies?"

He smiled a little, probably amused by my sudden shift in topics. But they were all connected in my head, really. "I've heard of them, of course," he said. "Never been to one or anything. Why?"

"A member of one came up to Karish when we were walking back from the stall and offered him a place. Or a membership. Whatever they're called."

He frowned. "They tried to recruit him on the street?"

"That was his reaction, too."

"I've never heard of it being done like that." He rubbed his chin as he thought about it. "From what I understand, one member nominates someone to some kind of committee and they vote on it. But it's like a sponsorship, and the reputation of the person who nominates the initiate rests on the behavior of the initiate. It's not something they do for strangers."

"The person doing the recruiting said they were new. That the club was new, I mean. But the very odd thing about it is that in this aristocratic shop Mother and I went to, there were cards for a ladies society that had the same name as the club that was trying to recruit Karish. Are these things usually connected? I mean, like brother and sister clubs or something like that?"

Erin swirled the wine around in his glass. "I've never heard of it, but that doesn't mean much. I never really paid attention to that sort of thing. I only know what I do because a colleague of mine was involved in a trial concerning the murder of a member of Black's in Erstwhile. The murderer turned out to be a member of the club, too. What's the name of these clubs?"

"The Raiborn Society or club."

"That's an odd name," he told me. "I've never heard of them. They're certainly not among the established prestigious clubs. If they're new, though, they may be desperate for members, and that might be why they're recruiting in the street and in that shop."

It still sounded strange to me. Wouldn't a new club, trying to get established, be even more careful to observe formal procedure, not less? "That may explain why they were trying to recruit Karish. He's not an aristocrat anymore."

"Ah, but he's a lord of the people, isn't he?" Erin said sarcastically. "The people love him, regardless of his rank."

That was what I used to think, too. Until a week or so ago. They didn't seem to be loving him too much right then, though.

"So tell me," said Erin, "How long did it take your Karish to accept this honor?"

I frowned. I definitely didn't like his tone. "He refused."

Why did that surprise him? "You're kidding. Why?"

"Why wouldn't he?" I didn't understand the appeal of those kinds of clubs myself. They seemed to dictate who the members could associate with. Why would anyone volunteer to have that kind of control imposed on them?

"It's pretty much his only chance to interact with his own class. None of the other Triple S members in High Scape are High Landed and Karish was probably dropped by all of his friends once he made it clear he wasn't taking the title."

I opened my mouth to deny that and closed it as I realized I really had no idea. I was rather ignorant about Karish's social life—hadn't I once decided to do something about that? But if Karish had been experiencing any social isolation due to his new status I'd seen nothing of it. Which could mean nothing had changed for him, but could also mean I was just blind as usual. Damn it.

Of course, he'd just spent months in the Empress' court, but I knew he hadn't enjoyed it. He'd said it was because everyone there was useless and superficial and because he wasn't able to work, but maybe he'd been ostracized. And what were the chances of him telling me the truth if I asked him? None. Unless I got him drunk first.

To Erin I said, "I've never noticed in Karish a craving to be among his own class. He said he wasn't interested in being in a gentlemen's club." I shrugged.

"Huh. More likely he wasn't interested in joining that club. It wouldn't give him the cache of the older clubs."

I wasn't going to tell him that Karish had been offered membership in other clubs. It was none of Erin's business. "I don't think that's it," I said, and I let my voice be as flat as it wanted to be.

Erin held up his hands in a gesture that was meant to pacify. "Hey, I'm not saying anything against Shintaro Karish. I barely know him. But he is by blood an aristocrat, and that sort have priorities that are different from the rest of us."

"Fortunately for all, the Triple S had more of an influence on Karish than did the members of the aristocratic class." Although I didn't know if that was actually true. He'd been so old when his family finally realized what he was and shipped him off to the Source academy. And he would have had time to study for only a handful of years before being sent out with veteran Pairs to practise what he'd learned. While over half of his life had been dedicated to training by the time I'd met him, one couldn't deny that his aristocratic origins had left their mark. He even sounded like an aristocrat, with the more lyrical pitch to his voice and those rolling *r*'s.

But I wasn't going to delve into the nature of Karish's character with a virtual stranger.

The evening went well. I believed Erin never realized the whole affair had been sprung on me by my evil conniving mother, so at least I was able to fool some people some of the time. And Erin was a charming guest. Witty, well-mannered, surprisingly easy to talk to. I had no objection to looking at his face. He was a beautiful, beautiful man.

But that, of course, was part of the problem. I couldn't help wondering what a man that beautiful was doing spending what spare time a solicitor had with me. I also couldn't help wondering who else he was spending his spare time with. None of my business, but I would never subject myself to being one of many. What I tolerated, was even entertained by, in a friend, I found unforgivable in a lover.

In addition, he seemed to have a tendency to lecture. He really thought he knew everything about everything. And he was always right. He didn't push a point until I admitted he was right. Rather, he just let the discussion end, as though there was no point in going further with it. Because he was right and I just refused to admit it.

So I had another item to add to the long list of reasons why having any kind of relationship with Erin was a bad idea. I didn't like him.

I would tell my mother that, right after Erin left.

And right before I killed her.

Chapter Nine

That night a heat wave hit. A brutally hot, humid heat wave. I woke alone, my mother's maneuvering notwithstanding, drenched with sweat. The room was dark. It was a bad sign when it was hot before the sun was up. I got up and looked through the window, into the densest fog I had ever seen in my life.

Heat was good, in moderation. It was even normal, that time of year. But I knew that degree of heat and humidity was not natural in High Scape. Erstwhile, maybe, but not High Scape. I didn't think anyone was going to be happy with this particular change. This was not what people were looking for.

It was interesting how sheets and pillows could appear to be instruments of torture once the temperature rose high enough. I went to the water closet, where I stripped out of my sodden, heavy nightgown and pumped some nice cool water into a bucket and then into the tub. I soaked in the water for as long as I could without being late. I got up, I toweled off, and moments later a fresh sheen of sweat developed all over my body. I resisted the urge to dive back into the tub, reached into the back of my wardrobe for something light to wear, and cringed as I dragged it over damp flesh.

I'd rather be cold than hot. Any day, any time, any place. And damn it was hot.

I scraped something together for breakfast, but had little appetite. I knocked on Karish's door to see if he was ready to go to the Stall, but he didn't appear to be in. I headed out alone.

Wasn't fog supposed to be cool?

It wasn't so dense I couldn't see where I was going, but I wouldn't have wanted to try sending an arrow anywhere. And the fog gave everything a nice eerie glow, muffling every sound until I couldn't really trust my ears at all. The snow had melted, leaving the roads slick. That didn't keep the usual round of idiots from driving their carriages down the street. There would be some dead people, soon. I ran along as fast as I could, towards the ring road.

I didn't like this, didn't like it at all. There was a strange feel to the air. Like something bad was going to happen. Which was just ridiculous. People couldn't feel that sort of thing ahead of time. I was just letting the thick air and ghostly sounds get to me, imagining things. I was ashamed of myself, letting my emotions slide all over the place like that.

Someone grabbed my arm. It startled me enough to make me almost scream. And that infuriated me. I turned on my assaulter and snarled, "What?"

It was a young woman. Taller than me, of course. Very slim, dressed in a modest, almost drab gown, her light brown hair falling from a precise middle part. I didn't remember ever seeing her before.

"You are Shield Mallorough, aren't you?" she asked.

She was a stranger to me. But she had a sun tattooed in black over her left temple. That meant she was a Reanist. She believed gods existed, that they were responsible for natural disasters, and that all that was needed to appease

the gods and stop the disasters was to sacrifice an aristo-
crat every once in a while. That was all I needed to know.
I yanked my arm free and turned to continue on to the
Stall.

I heard her then, scampering after me. "No, please,
Shield Mallorough. You must listen to me."

I must do nothing of the sort.

"You must bring Lord Shintaro to us."

I hadn't expected her to come right out and make that
particular demand of me. From what I understood they were
usually more circumspect. But perhaps she thought she
didn't need to waste subtlety on me. "He is not Lord Shintaro anymore." Damn it, damn it. What was I doing? Don't
talk. Just keep right on walking. But my mouth opened
again, all of its own accord. "He is now plain Shintaro Karish. Your ordinary everyday peasant. Sorry you wasted your
time, but maybe if you stopped chanting to your gods long
enough to see the light of day you might learn some facts
that are, you know, current."

The sarcasm flew right over her head. Or she ignored it.
Too smoked up to care. "It isn't the name. The title is irrelevant. It's the blood. His blood is pure."

I rolled my eyes. "Lucky him."

She was striding next to me and invading my personal
space. A woman could get hurt doing that. "You must bring
him to us."

I *must* do nothing. "You really think I'm going to try to
get Karish to join one of your cults?" Could she really
think all she had to do was tell me to bring Karish to her
and I would?

"It's your duty."

Well, that was an angle I'd never heard before. "It's my
duty to deliver Karish to you so you can murder him." Why
was I talking to her?

She looked shocked. "Not *murder*," she protested. "We
want to give him to the gods."

"By killing him. Intentionally. And not for the purposes

of self-defence or to put him out of unceasing pain. Sounds an awful lot like murder to me." Logic. You're trying to argue logic with the inherently illogical, Lee. Stop it. Right now.

"It will please the gods, and it will bring tranquility to our turbulent world."

Ech. What had she been reading? "As justifications for murder go, that is less than convincing."

"It is not murder," the Reanist insisted. "Aristocrats have an ancient duty to protect those who serve them. That duty reaches throughout their lives and extends into death, if necessary."

"I'm sure they'd be surprised to hear that." Maybe I would tell the Dowager Duchess.

"Whether they are aware of this duty, whether they wish to carry it out, is irrelevant. It is a duty placed on them by the gods, and they are obliged to serve. And as a Source, Lord Shintaro's duty is doubled. He is sworn to this duty both by birth and by calling. And it is your duty as a Shield to bring him to us."

Bring him to them. Like all I had to do was command him to go to the Ancient Order of Lunatics and he'd willingly go. I had no idea I wielded such power. "How dumb do you think I am?" I just had to ask. "Have you forgotten that when you murder Karish in the name of your religion, I die, too? Or do you merely hope I have?"

"It is your duty, too, to do all you can to keep the world calm."

"I already do."

"Only temporarily. The gods would do it, and do it better than any mortal." Oh, oy. Mortal. "That is their role. It is arrogant of you to attempt to assume it."

"You people are insane," I said bluntly. And stupid. Why was she even in High Scape? All of the Reanists were pretty much exiled to Shina Lake. Wasn't she afraid of being apprehended by the authorities? "You've killed aristocrats before and did it solve anything? No."

Like all illogical people, she had an answer for everything. "The odd one here and there isn't enough. It must be a regular sacrifice, to keep the gods' favor."

Ah. I see. "You're going to run out of aristocrats awfully quickly if you make murdering them a regular occurrence."

"The gods can't demand more if all those who are pure of blood have already gone to their service."

I stared at her. I felt my eyes going wide. I couldn't help it. "You hope to eventually kill all the aristocrats?" I mean, sure, my collective family had sometimes fantasized about a world without the High Landed, but we weren't serious about it. Not serious to the point of wanting to kill all of them.

Although there was a certain final efficiency about it.

Stop that.

"It would finally appease the gods. That much blood will buy us years of stability."

"You're insane." I hated repeating myself that way, but I couldn't help myself. It was so very true. I mean, believing in gods. Our ancestors came to our world on ships that flew in the stars. Even the most uneducated idiot knew that. So what was this idea of gods somehow watching the planet? Where did they come from? And where were they supposed to be? Just floating around up there in the sky, invisible, spying on us?

Creepy.

"I'm late," I told her. "And until those gods of yours decide to watch themselves and do something about keeping the world calm, you'll just have to rely on us mere mortals." Lengthen my stride, try to outdistance her.

She let me go, that time, but she didn't quite give up. "Bring Lord Shintaro to us!"

"Oh, go to hell," I muttered. Maybe I should have stayed at home long enough to brew some coffee. It wasn't a good idea to endure this kind of encounter without fortification. And it might have delayed me long enough so that I wouldn't have met the woman at all. Unless she had been looking for me, waiting for me. I hoped not. That would be too disturbing.

And then I tripped and fell on my face. Looked at the ground and found nothing to trip over. Lovely.

I was in a bad mood. And facing seven hours in a small roasting room. Just glorious.

Karish was at the Stall before me. Firth was there, waiting to be relieved, passing the time by tormenting Karish. "—clings to him," she was commenting as I walked through the door.

She was gesturing at my Source, who was wearing a white cotton shirt unlaced as low as general decency allowed. And yes, in the humidity and with his own sweat, it was pretty much plastered to his body. His hair was kind of frizzing. And he'd kicked off his boots, his bare feet resting on the chair on the opposite side of the table.

It was kind of shocking, actually. I'd seen Karish in various states of undress. But he was always appropriately dressed for the circumstances. It was one of his inbred rules. To see him in the Stall looking like he'd just stumbled out of a bed he'd barely rolled into after a night of debauchery surprised and concerned me.

He was not in a good mood, either. He was slouched in his chair, resting his head on one hand, making no effort to respond to Firth's raillery with even forced politeness. As she finished speaking his expression watched from that of complete disinterest to one of disgust, and he glared at her. I had never seen him do that, not with her, and it wasn't a good sign for me and the rest of our watch. I stifled a groan. I was not in a fit state to be handling a temperamental Source and his death-defying leaps of emotion.

The glare watched to me as I closed the door behind me. "You're late," he said, his voice flat.

"Aye, sorry." If I had told that Reanist "sure, take him!" I probably would have gotten to the Stall on time. "Stone, Firth, good morning."

"Morning, dear," said Firth, holding her braid up off the

back of her neck. Stone nodded her response, shoving the toys she and Firth had used to while away their hours on watch into a bag. "I won't say good morning, though. I can't say it has been for me and I dare say it won't be for you. Himself is in a rare mood."

"All his moods are rare. He's a rare fellow." He was smart, too. I followed his example, kicking my boots off into a corner.

"And he's here," Karish muttered.

"Sorry, Karish. Good morning to you, too."

He snorted. How masculine of him. I exchanged a look with the departing Pair, rolled my eyes, and pumped some water into the kettle.

"Don't you dare light a fire," Karish warned me as I put the kettle on the stove.

"I didn't get any coffee this morning." And I needed coffee. I needed the ritual of drinking something hot so I knew I was out of bed for good and braced to face the day.

"I mean it, Lee. You try lighting that stove and I may just have to kill you."

My hand on the kettle, I looked at him over my shoulder. I supposed he had a point. He did look miserable. I wasn't all that thrilled with the idea of adding the heat of a fire to the close environment of the Stall myself, and he would be feeling the heat more than I. "You owe me, Taro." Making me face a day without coffee. That was just wrong.

He grunted.

Two non-articulate responses in under a half hour. Bad bad sign. "Have you seen your mother recently?" Maybe that was where he'd been that morning.

He straightened in his chair so he could cross his arms and look stern. "I am not talking about it."

I shrugged. "All right." Karish shouldn't be allowed to speak to his mother without supervision. I really didn't know why he was spending so much time with her, anyway.

Since I couldn't have coffee I scooped up a cup of tepid water and found some stale tea biscuits. Delicious. I sat at the table and munched on them, thinking about the Reanist. I wasn't going to tell Karish about her, he was always understandably touchy whenever Reanists were mentioned, but the encounter had made me uneasy. "You're being careful, eh? Not wandering around alone at night?"

He wasn't an idiot. He had some idea what I was talking about. "I am not a lord," he reminded me with impatience. "I never was."

His answer made me think of what Erin had said the night before, that Karish might be experiencing a loss of companionship with his denial of the title. I didn't know how to ask him about it without sounding mother hennish. "We don't know that the title is what's important. I mean, all the people who have gone missing were pretty minor aristocrats. Maybe it's just the bloodlines they're interested in." Like the Reanists.

"Huh. Then I'll be safe. You wouldn't believe the number of whores and horse thieves that litter my family tree."

He was just being difficult. "I only want to make sure you're being careful."

"Don't worry, Lee," he sneered. "I won't get you killed."

I grit my teeth. Spoiled bastard. That wasn't what I'd been thinking about at all. "Zaire, Taro. Please have sex soon. You're becoming impossible."

His mouth dropped open. That improved my own mood just a little. I loved seeing Lord Shintaro Karish stunned. He was so cute.

He closed his mouth with an audible snap. Then his lips curled into the slightest smile. "Any volunteers?"

Aye, I should have known that was coming. I popped a piece of biscuit into my mouth.

He let his head fall back. "It's so damn hot," he muttered. "Maybe this'll shut the regulars up."

"You haven't been getting any brick at the head events, have you?"

He raised his head to look at me. "No." His eyes narrowed. "Have you?"

"No." I was never bothered by regulars when I was alone. I wasn't really bothered when I was with Karish, either. It was all focused on the Sources, it seemed.

"Would you tell me if you had?"

"Of course." No, probably not. He would just get all weirdly protective about it and I didn't need anyone hovering over me.

"Hm," he said, apparently unsure whether to believe me or not. But he let it slide. "I've just been getting comments. Shouts. Accusations."

Why was I getting irritated by this? It wasn't news anymore. "And what do you say?"

"What else?" He shrugged. "We're working on it."

Heh. He was the one who brought it up. "Speaking of which . . ."

He groaned. "No, Lee! Not today."

"Have some water, Taro. It'll perk you right up."

"We've tried every day and we've learned nothing."

"That's why we've got to keep trying, until we learn something."

"Lee," he sighed.

"That was the deal, Taro."

"Argh!"

I chuckled. "You're very . . . ah . . . vocal today, Taro. It's endearing."

He didn't appreciate my most sincerely delivered compliment. "Fine, let's get this done."

"So enthusiastically you dive into your duty, my lord."

"I'm going to smack you."

The mental image of Karish striking anyone in anger was ludicrous. "Promises, promises. Ready."

He straightened in his chair. A little. That was all the warning I got before his internal shields lowered.

As he had complained, we tried this every watch, he lowering his inner shields and just feeling what was out there, letting me see through him. And every time, it seemed I could "see" just a little more clearly. I didn't know what I was seeing, and I hadn't told him about what I considered my progress, because my last attempt to describe what I saw had been so disastrous. I didn't really know how to start putting it into words myself. But the forces, which to me "looked" like huge shapeless waves of overpowering sensation, were developing more subtle elements. Smaller swirls of temperature and color began appearing to me, like threads in a cloth. Each time I saw them, there was more detail, more movement. The last time, I'd almost reached out to touch one of them, though I wasn't sure with what. Not my fingers, of course. So, what? My mind?

This time, what I "saw" shocked me. Not only a subtle elevation in my perception of detail, which was all I had seen before. But change in the detail itself. Great drastic change. Orange blazed into my eyes. Only not in my eyes. Into my brain? Sounded stupid. Sounded bad. The orange was off key.

"Taro!"

"What?" he said, sounding uneasy.

"There! Can you see it?" He had to notice something this time. It was so strong, so obvious.

"See what?"

I clenched my fists. "How can you not see it?"

"I'm not *seeing* anything, Lee," he said impatiently. "There's nothing to look at."

How could he say that? It was there. It was right there. "Are you pretending not to see it?" I demanded.

"Why would I be doing that?"

How was I supposed to know? He'd always been a strange one. Didn't want to know what he could do. Didn't want to find out if he could do anything else. "It's *orange*, Taro. It wasn't before."

"What's orange?" he demanded through his teeth. "What are you looking at?"

"It's right there!" All around us. In the forces right around him. The forces he could touch, he could manipulate. "Will you just look?"

"Damn it, Lee, stop trying to tell me how to do my job!"

What the hell did that have to do with anything? What was wrong with him? Why didn't he just look at it?

I wish we'd done this when we'd first come to High Scape, before all this bizarre weather. It should, I was thinking, be the first thing a Pair did upon coming to a new post. Just take a "look," see what all the colors and shapes were, so they'd notice if there was a change. I mean, all right, fine, neither of us could be sure what High Scape was like when it was normal. We'd never experienced it when it was normal. Creol had been playing with the forces in High Scape long before we showed up. But still, if I had known we could do this sort of thing I would have definitely taken a look, to see how things had changed. Because what I was seeing now, it was different from what I'd seen the day before, and it wasn't normal, either.

Yesterday it had been unseasonably cold. Today it was brutally hot. And now the forces—or at least the details within them—were different. And wrong. I could feel they were wrong, even though I didn't know what they felt like when they right. Why couldn't Karish see the connections? How could he not hear how bad it sounded? The flattened tones scraped against my nerves and made my teeth ring. Surely even a tone-deaf man could feel that?

And man, that orange was ugly. Nothing in life could be that color. Except maybe poison. Aye, it made me think of poison, for some reason. Thick orange sluggish fluid oozing out of a bitterly fatal plant. How could he not see that?

Although even if he could perceive it, I wasn't sure how he could do anything about it. I doubted this could be fixed by channeling. The forces weren't rushing around in the same way as when there was a natural disaster coming. And for some reason I was sure this wouldn't be like healing, either. Both of those were just about letting the forces funnel through the body. This was more like reaching out to the forces and adjusting them, changing how they moved without drawing them in. Kind of like what I did, I realized, when I was steering external forces away from Karish, keeping the forces he was not manipulating from crushing him. I didn't draw those forces into me. I kind of reached through Karish and warded those forces away.

Huh. Interesting. Could this possibly be something I, rather than Karish, could do? Maybe if I reached out, maybe if I just nudged it a little like that . . .

The swirls turned green. The sound skewered into something sharp and piercing. I gasped.

And Karish was immediately asking, "What's wrong?"

"Didn't you feel that?"

A pause. "We're stopping this now," and he snapped up his shields.

I felt a shiver run through me. It was cold.

Karish had seen my reaction. "All right, so what's happening?"

I told him. Because he had asked. But there was no way he was going to believe me. It was too impossible.

Except he did. He hissed in frustration. "Why can't I see any of this?"

How could I respond to that beyond a shrug?

"Have you always been able to see that sort of thing?"

"I don't know," I said. "I never looked before you came back and we started trying." I frowned. "No, that's not quite right. I kind of saw things during the Rushes Creol sent. Images. I could feel and hear things too." A second shiver tried to jolt through me. Bad memories. "But I'm not sure if that's the same thing. The images were much more concrete with Creol, and at the time I thought my brain was just making them up, to help me fight him." And it had hurt like hell. "This is very different, and seems more . . ." I was floundering for words, it was so hard to explain, "more connected to the forces, I guess. Arising from them, rather than being imposed upon them." I shook my head, disgusted with myself. "I'm sorry, I don't know how to explain it. But it never happened before my match, that's certain. And I've never heard of anything like it from anyone else."

He stared at me curiously, dark eyes narrowed, and I suddenly felt I should be pinned on a board somewhere. He reached out, cupping my chin and tilting my face a little to one side.

I couldn't help smiling. "What do you expect to see?"

"I don't know," he confessed. He drew back. "But at least now you know what it's like."

"What what's like?"

"Being able to do things other people can't."

I've always been able to do things other people couldn't. That was all part of a Shield. But I knew that wasn't what he meant. "I'm sure other Shields could do this, too, if they tried." Probably other Sources could, too, if they'd just open their eyes. "I think I did something though."

"What do you mean?"

"I'm not sure. It was orange and flat. I made it green and sharp."

"Oh." He clearly had no real idea what I was saying. That was fine. Neither did I. "Is it supposed to be green and sharp?"

"I don't think so. It still didn't feel right."

"Well," he pulled his damp collar away from his throat, "nothing's changed out here." He leaned his chair back on its hind legs, crossing his bare feet on a corner of the table. I repressed the urge to tickle them.

"That's true." I bunched up my hair and held it off the back of my neck. How big an idiot was I that I hadn't hesitated in my apartment long enough to tie up my hair? But then, I wasn't used to this kind of heat, was I? I'd forgotten how annoying long hair could be.

Karish left the table, poked around the shelves a bit, and came up with a deck of cards. "I didn't feel anything the whole time I was in Erstwhile."

That wasn't a surprised. "Erstwhile is a cold site." There hadn't been an event there in decades.

"And I haven't felt anything here."

"There's been nothing going on here to feel."

"But you're sensing something here, now." He sat back at the table and began shuffling the cards with deft hands.

Ah. I understood. Nothing so petty as jealousy, probably, but perhaps it was difficult for him, used to being able to solve all the problems, finding himself in the position where he could not. "I don't know what it really is or if it means anything."

"Aye, but I'm not *feeling* anything." He shuffled faster.

Hm. "There haven't been any disasters, Taro. What else is a Source supposed to feel?"

He started dealing out the cards. He had an odd habit of dealing. He didn't just toss cards into a pile. He placed them into neat stacks with a snap of each card. "It's just—" He cut himself off, and shrugged. "It's been so long since I've channeled," he said. "I guess it makes me feel strange."

"You mean useless?" I asked dryly. He looked up quickly, frowning in shock, and I raised a hand. "No, no, that wasn't a crack. That's just how I've been feeling." Useless. And oddly disconnected from things.

"Aye. I guess. But it's more than that. It's just," he watched his shoulders. "I guess I'm feeling antsy."

That, I could understand. I hated not being able to do my job. Though I supposed it could be said we were doing our jobs, just by keeping watch. It was stupid and irresponsible and childish to wish for a natural disaster just so I could shield. Really shield. The shielding I did when Karish was healing or during our little experiments lacked all the intensity of shielding during an event. I missed it.

It was like how I felt when I hadn't danced the bars in too long. Like my muscles weren't being properly used. Stiffness and a heavy feeling and the worry that important skills were melting away. I got irritable, which made no sense at all, but there it was.

Karish set the remainder of the deck in the middle of the table. A come-here nod of the head. "Time for you to win my first born."

"First born?" I joined him at the table. "Aren't we down to the eighth by now?"

"So you get to have all my children. Seems like a good deal to me."

I didn't frown as I tried to decide whether that was supposed to be a double-entendre or not. I was a little shaken by the results of our experimentation and I wasn't really up to responding to Karish's teasing. Or thinking about what any of this meant, if it meant anything at all. A mind-numbing game of half-draw sounded good to me right then.

I scooped up my cards. A truly horrendous hand. Good. Maybe I could lose a couple of those kids.

Chapter Ten

Instead of losing children, I gained two more, which Karish found hysterically funny. Fortunate that the debonair card sharp could find entertainment in being continually trounced by his amateur partner. I hoped to sometime play against someone who wasn't Karish. I was pretty sure it was only our bond that gave me some kind of hunch about what kind of hand Karish had. The only way I'd know if I had any talent was if I played against someone else. Only I didn't have any money to make it worth their while.

It started raining during our watch. Hard. I could hear the rain bouncing off the roof. It didn't get any cooler, though. Wet and hot is just a nasty combination.

Uh, sometimes.

It was still raining when Riley and Sabatos came to relieve us. They were good enough to offer to lend us their rain gear, but we refused them. It was too likely it would still be raining once their watch was over, and while it was a crazy idea I couldn't help feeling I might have been responsible for the rain, as I had been playing with the patterns.

No delusions of divinity here.

Of course, about a dozen steps from the Stall I was regretting my nobility, but I refused to go back and ask for the rain gear. I could be petty that way.

And hey, no objection to seeing Karish with his shirt soaked through. It was clingy while in the Stall, but a few drops of rain had it completely plastered to his shoulders, chest, back and stomach. His black hair was slicked close to his head. Rain streamed over his face and throat and clung to his eyelashes. He made a beautiful drowned rat.

Unfortunately, Karish's shirt wasn't the only garment to be quickly soaked through. I couldn't carry off the look with the same panache.

"We'll stop somewhere and get slickers," Karish said, right into my ear. He had to. The rain was that loud.

Well, we'd be soaked, but at least we wouldn't have to march through the city looking one step away from naked. Which I was not going to think about. Karish was walking a couple of steps ahead of me, perhaps intentionally, and wasn't seeing anything. What a gentleman. But thank whim that I avoided light colors for my clothes. My gown was green, not white or yellow or light blue. Just the idea of wearing white under the circumstances—how humiliating.

I was distracted from my mental images of mortification by an awareness that something was wrong. Something was off, or odd. The closer we got to the ring road, the stronger the sensation became.

Oh, enough already. Everything felt odd, all the time. There was no normal.

But there was something happening. Something scraping just at the edge of my awareness, and it made my ears prick up.

No doubt it was just the hot rain pounding holes into the street.

Or maybe the Runner whistles wailing even over the noise of the rain, a plaintive yet piercing note, falling and rising and winding its way through the city air.

I grabbed Karish's arm. He looked back at me, puzzled, and I let him go. I hadn't wanted his attention. I'd just been reassuring myself that my aristocrat was right where he was supposed to be.

"Are the whistles bothering you?" he asked me.

"No, I'm fine."

"Well, let me know." He looked at me for a moment longer, and he smiled. "You're all wet." He pulled on a lock of my drenched hair.

"Imagine that." Shields were allowed to do sarcasm.

He chuckled, stroked my cheek, and took my hand to lead me down the street.

We ran to the first mercantile we could find. A small place I had never been to before. We could barely fit in, packed as it was with people ducking in to get out of the rain. Bitterly complaining people, fuming that if it wasn't one thing it was another.

The people we couldn't help brushing up against fell silent. Then one of them said, "A Pair." Loudly. With disgust. And after a few moments everyone in the shop was wordlessly staring at us. Not pleasantly. Not with admiration.

I raked back my wet hair. I remembered my clothes were drenched and hugging every curve I had. I tried to raise my head and look dignified.

This was not a hospital. There was no one there with a duty to keep order. Anyone could do anything they wanted. It made it all feel so much more alarming.

Alarming? I shouldn't be alarmed. No one was going to do us any harm. As La Monte had said, throwing a brick was a far cry from actually laying hands on a person to do them injury. None of these people wanted to do that. They were just frustrated.

But I didn't want to be there. I was uncomfortable. I shouldn't be uncomfortable. It was only silence. And attention. Nothing dangerous.

Karish's grip on my hand tightened.

"What do *you* want?" the man in the apron—the shop-keeper, I presumed—demanded in a hard, sullen voice. He crossed his arms and scowled.

To turn right around and head back out, to be honest. Why didn't we do that? Because it looked cowardly? Who cared? "Slickers, please, if you've got any left." At least my voice sounded level and calm, like it knew what it was doing.

A woman to my left snorted. "Must be nice," she muttered. But it was a mutter at high volume, if there were such a thing. She wanted everyone in the little shop to hear her. "Get caught in the rain? Don't hurry home. Just pick up another slicker."

"Sure," added the man beside her. "Life's real easy when you don't got to pay for nothing."

The shopkeeper snickered with approval and headed for some shelves filled with folded leather slickers. He tugged out two and threw one at each of us. Threw them. Hard. I caught my bundle automatically, stunned at the treatment. "Don't have braids on them, so sorry," he said without any sincerity whatsoever. "I'm afraid I don't keep Triple S garments in stock. Usually it's a good way to keep your sort out of my shop."

Actually, that was a good idea. I was surprised more shopkeepers didn't think of it.

"Careful, Nate," said one of the others. "Might end up in stocks for an offence like that. Not catering to a Pair."

"I have money," Karish offered. "Not with me right now, but—"

I grabbed his arm to shut him up. Not the thing to say. It made him look guilty, and he had nothing to feel guilty about. I didn't have any other slickers; it was well within our rights to ask for them. But at least he wasn't trying to charm anyone. I had a feeling that wouldn't have gone over well at all.

"Take money from a Source?" the shopkeeper demanded with hostility. "You really do want me to land in the clink, don't you?"

If anyone could land in jail for taking money from a Source in exchange for goods and services, it was news to me. Karish had said before that he sometimes paid for things when he had money. So was the shopkeeper ignorant or lying?

"Of course not," Karish said, assuming a smile. Not a flirtatious smile, thank Zaire, but one that was just as dangerous. Patronizing. Another mood flip, and he was angry and not making much of an effort to hide it. "But as I do have it, it only seems fair to use it to—"

"I know *my* duty!" the shopkeeper snapped. "I don't take money from Sources. Even layabout Sources who do nothing but sit on their asses while the city's being torn apart and who still have the gall to come in here begging."

I could practically see the tension suddenly developing at the small of Karish's back, racing up his spine, spreading through his shoulders and bringing his head up in the most arrogant angle. Lord Shintaro Karish had been released from his backroom of shame and was about to let his presence be known. So warned, I grabbed Karish by the arm and pulled him back towards the door. He, taken by surprise, almost fell with the first step, and flushed in immediate anger.

He couldn't keep his mouth shut, though. "You know nothing of which you speak, you insolent back-scrubbing peasant," he snapped.

I wasn't sure what all that meant but it certainly sounded like an insult. Everyone in the shop stiffened, and I saw a hand or two clench into fists. "Not now, Taro!"

"You useless bastard," the shopkeeper shot back. "Coming in here and making demands and acting all lord of the manor and doing nothing about any—"

Karish flushed. Nothing got to him like being called a lord. "You speak much for one who knows so very very little."

Definitely time to leave. "Now, Taro!" I yanked on the door, I yanked on my Source, and we were back out in the rain.

I could hear shouting from within the shop. People venting, spewing out insults concerning worthless Sources and why had they been kept in the lap of luxury for all those decades anyway? But no one came out.

Karish lunged for the door. I lunged for him. The slickers landed on the ground.

I had no fighting skills whatsoever, but I was heavy and stubborn. "Leave it, Taro."

He shook me off. Not hard. Just freeing himself to grab the door handle. So instead I threw myself at the door. The people in the shop must have heard the thud and wondered what it was about. Or perhaps they didn't care. They still didn't open the door.

Karish grabbed me by the shoulders to try to pull me away, eyes narrowed in a fierce stare. It was shocking. I'd seen him angry. I thought I'd seen him furious. I'd never seen him like this, so intent on doing damage that he couldn't even see what he was doing. I wedged my feet into the two lower corners of the doorway and pressed against the wood and refused to budge. I was not going to let Karish back in there. I didn't care what kind of fighting skills he thought he had, he couldn't win out against a half dozen men.

"Out of the way, Lee!" he snarled.

"We are leaving."

"They have no right to talk to us like that!"

"Keep it down, Karish!" I hissed at him.

"Don't tell me to be quiet! I don't give a damn who hears me!"

No, he didn't. Not right then. He would after every tooth he owned had been punched out of his head, though. I grabbed the collar of his shirt and pulled his face close to mine, and he let me because he still wasn't thinking all that clearly. "Every single person in that shop is primed to lay into us." Actually, probably just him. That seemed to be the way things were going. "We are alone. The Runners are all involved in something else. Don't push them." I flattened my hand on his shoulder, and felt him trembling.

"Don't *push* them!" He jerked out of my grip and paced a few steps away. Which meant he paced a few steps away from the door, and that was good. "Who the hell do they think they are? Blaming us for all this! Accusing us of dereliction of duty!"

"They are scared and," I lowered my voice, "we are all lying to them."

The truth, and reasonable, but if Karish heard the words he wasn't prepared to let them sway him. "I have had it up to *here* with people who haven't got the faintest idea what is going on telling me how easy I have it and that I have done nothing for it!" I wanted to shush him. He wasn't keeping his voice down at all. "You keep telling me to think about it from their side, but why doesn't anyone expect them to think? We're shipped off to school for years, with no choice in the matter, and we aren't allowed to leave. We aren't allowed to leave until they let us out, and until then we are watched and judged and controlled—" he shivered suddenly, such a strong jolt through his body that I could see it. I frowned. "And once we are let out they decide where we live and who we work with and they can change their minds about any of it any time they feel like it."

They, they, they. Who was he talking about? The Triple S? Who was he angry at?

"We risk our lives doing this stuff. And no, we don't get paid for it, so instead we do have to go into shops and restaurants and *beg* for everything we have. We can't buy anything. We can't buy houses or land or accumulate anything that can be left for any children we might have. We can't do anything that isn't within the narrow little boundaries that the whole world has laid out for us and now they expect us to do the impossible and because we naturally can't they think they have the right to violate our safety and insult us in public? Who the *hell* do they think they are?"

He was furious. Really really furious. "Taro—"

"It's not right, Lee! They don't have the right!"

"I know, I know," I said in a low, quiet voice. I reached out for one of his hands. He stopped pacing, but he wouldn't look at me. He was still trembling, his eyebrows drawn together in a fierce frown. "It's what you said, Taro. They don't understand. And you're not going to make them understand by shouting at them. What you will do is really tick them off." I put a hand on the nape of his neck and pulled him down, so that his forehead rested against mine. "I don't want you getting the pretty face of yours—" he stiffened, "broken."

"Damn it, Lee!" He tried to pull away but I had my fingers in his hair and I held him fast.

"Deep breaths, Taro."

"I'm a Source, Lee. I'm allowed to feel whatever the hell I like." But the trembling was easing a little.

"Not when it means risking your face. I'm the one who has to look at it. So breathe. In slow, out slow."

Lips quirked in a sudden smile, eyes gleaming. Wasn't going to ask. Didn't really care. I could see the switch flick, could feel the tension draining from him, and that was all that mattered. I kissed his forehead. "Good boy." It didn't solve the problem, and I wasn't saying he was wrong, but there wasn't anything we could do about it right then. I scooped up the slickers from the street and shoved one at him. "Put this on. Though right now I don't see the point. We're totally soaked." And the slickers had picked up mud from the street. Lovely. "I want to go home and have a bath." A cool one.

"Yes, ma'am." He pulled the slicker over his head, once it was settled on his shoulders pulling up the hood. I followed suit, and was over-heated in a matter of moments. Leather and humidity, what a wonderful combination.

Karish was frowning. "The whistles are still going. That's not normal, is it?"

I listened. I hadn't heard the whistles after leaving the shop, not at first, distracted as I had been with the fear Karish was going to get himself beaten to a bloody mess. But there they were. And I'd never heard the whistles go on for so long. "I don't know."

"I'm not up to any heroics today, Lee." His expression suggested he was expecting opposition from me.

"This from the man ready to fight a half-dozen hot-headed regulars."

"I wasn't going to *fight* them."

"That's what you think."

"No weird stuff, Lee."

What did he think I was going to try to make him do? I didn't even know what was going on. "I just want to go home," I assured him.

"Good."

We headed home, miserable and wet and tense. I started thinking some kind of exotic vacation would be nice.

"You hear that?" I asked him. I wasn't referring to the whistling.

"Aye."

A strange sound, at first barely perceptible over the roar of the rain and the lament of the whistles. A kind of short, repetitive sound. It was familiar to me, for some reason.

It was kind of on our way, anyway, so of course we headed towards it, because we were idiots.

Two people came running towards us from the direction of the noise. One of the young men had blood streaming from a cut on his face, thick enough to be visible in the rain, and they were running as though they were being chased. Only no one was following them.

"What's going on?" Karish called out to them.

Their heads whipped around to look at us. "There's some kind of riot!" the man without the injury shouted back. "Go home! I mean it!" They kept on running and disappeared down a street.

I exchanged a look with Karish. We started running. In the direction opposite to the one they were suggesting.

The noise was getting louder, and I thought I could discern what the sounds were. Voices, shouting. I couldn't hear the exact words. It brought back memories. I suppressed a shudder.

We were almost home. Which gave me a really bad feeling. And then Karish and I skidded to a halt.

"Flaming Zaire!" Karish swore. He took my hand again, and I let him.

I had never seen so many people in one place. Angry, screaming people. Attacking the Triple S house with axes and picks and hammers, pulling off lengths of wood to add to a pile in the middle of the street. A pole rose up from the middle of the pile, from the top of which hung the emblem of the Triple S.

Someone was trying to light it. On fire.

It's raining, you moron.

What the hell was this? Were they insane? Tearing down our emblem? Trying to destroy our house? All because we couldn't fix the weather to their specifications? What was wrong with everyone?

Shoes, human and horse, sticks, rocks, bowls, chunks of wood, were flying through the air. Hitting people. Sputtering torches were waved about. Runners, on horses and on foot, pushed their way into the crowd, clubbing people and dragging them away. It was brutal.

And the Runners didn't seem to be having much of an effect. They dragged off a couple of people at a time, and sometimes they couldn't even manage that much. A captive's comrades would beat off the Runner, sometimes even dragging the Runner off his or her horse.

The noise was painful to hear, dribbling into my brain and stirring it around until I couldn't think. I swallowed and found myself clutching Karish's arm with my free hand. "Let's get out of here."

"Wait a moment." He tapped the shoulder of a chap standing near him. The man swung around, a fist raised. Karish backed off immediately, hands held up in surrender. "I'm just wondering what's going on."

The gossip will reach us tomorrow, Karish!

The man relaxed, grinning. And if his grin was manic, well, that was just one more thing to be nervous about. "Those Triple S whores," he announced gaily. "Sent 'em a clear message, we did."

I saw Karish swallow hard. "What about the Pairs?"

The man lost his good humor, taking on an expression of disgust. "Scampered away like the rats they are, didn't they?

"You didn't manage to catch any of them?"

"Not a one."

Thank Zaire. At least no one was getting hurt.

But what they were doing, it felt bad enough. That had become my home. I had been learning to relax there. I had been thinking of my suite as *my* suite. I knew where almost everything was in the kitchen. I'd even picked up some decorative stitch work and had it framed and hung in the common room.

I could see one of my shirts in that pile of wood. They'd were going through the interior of the house, throwing personal items out the window.

I didn't understand. I really really didn't. How could they hate us so much? All of a sudden? It was crazy. They'd all gone crazy. And they were scaring the hell out of me. I pulled at Karish's sleeve. "Come on, Karish. Let's go." Though I had no idea where.

The man's eyes narrowed. He looked more closely at Karish's face, looked at me, then looked back to Karish. "Karish?" he echoed, his voice flat and cold.

Hell. Me and my enormous mouth. Where did my brain go while I wasn't looking?

"Hey!" he shouted to someone.

We started running. At least Karish wasn't going to try the aggressive male role this time.

"We've got one of them here!"

Oh gods, oh gods, oh gods. Tears pressed at the back of my eyes.

Aye, that would accomplish a lot.

And there were steps ringing behind us.

There was nowhere to go. The Runners weren't at their headquarters and they were overwhelmed. We couldn't lead them to a friend's house, and I had a nasty feeling we wouldn't find sanctuary in any of the shops.

I glanced back. I felt my eyes widen. It wasn't two or three people behind us. There was at least a dozen. Some of them had lengths of wood.

Terror clogged my throat. There was no way out of this.

We ran. It was hard. Hampered by the slickers. My skin was too hot, but my blood felt so so cold. Rain flew into my eyes, into my nose and mouth. It was hard to breathe through a throat that felt like it had tightened to closing, into lungs that had turned to ice. I'd had nightmares that had felt exactly like this.

I followed Karish. I hoped he knew where he was going. He took corners like he knew. Or maybe it was all at random. What difference did it make? We had nowhere to go.

Really, really, really had to learn something about weapons. Though even that might not have helped us out right then.

Karish turned to look at me. Look ahead! Looking back slows you down.

He looked at me. In the eye.

That was all the warning I got. Then his Shields dropped.

He was *channeling!* Idiot! Right, fine, this was the first natural disaster to hit us in months. Very exciting. But we weren't on duty, and we were a little busy.

A moment later I realized what he was doing. The forces were running the wrong way. Being pulled in to him, being stirred up, not rushing about us as they naturally did. It had been almost a year since I'd felt him manipulate the forces that way, but I knew what it meant.

He wasn't responding to a natural disaster. He was creating one.

Was he insane?

Were we in that much trouble?

Wasn't this a little drastic?

He was insane. I was insane. The whole world had gone insane.

Shield, shield, shield.

The ground started to shake. I almost lost my footing. Karish fell into the wall next to him. I grabbed at him to pull him upright. My fingers slipped on his slicker.

It was really hard to shield and run at the same time. The fact that the ground was shaking beneath my feet made it a real treat. So we stopped running. Our hunters had stopped running, too.

He was pulling forces into himself. It felt random to me, like running through the streets had been, but I knew nothing about it. I held off the forces he didn't touch, the forces he somehow knew not to touch, and stopped them from rushing into the vacuum Karish created within himself whenever he channelled. And through him I felt the raw power he could control with his mind and sheer strength of will.

Sometimes I envied Karish so much, for what he could do, for his being able to feel the forces that moved the world. Did he have any idea how fortunate he was? Did he have the most remote inkling? And did he ever realize that I was almost sick with the longing to be able to do what he could do? What he had been born being able to do?

I heard him chuckle. How could he be laughing? "What?" I demanded.

"She's fighting me."

"Huh?"

"Kyna. She's trying to channel the forces away from me."

"Does she know it's you?"

"No reason that she should."

Well, he had felt that it was Creol causing the disasters that had been threatening High Scape the year before. And he hadn't told anyone, because it was supposed to be impossible, and he'd known no one would believe him. But what if Riley felt differently? What if she felt that Karish

was responsible for this earthquake, and she started telling
people? That was exactly what he was afraid of, wasn't it?

The stone beneath my feet shifted. Karish reached out to
catch me, though I would have regained my balance on my
own in a moment. "Don't get too enthusiastic," I warned
him.

"If I do it right, it might clear up the riot. Everyone will
get scared and go home."

"One problem at a time, Taro."

He didn't listen to me. Of course not.

The forces roared on, going the wrong way. It was as
though he were pulling them from the sky and directing
them at the ground, where they churned up the soil and tore
stones apart. And we were trying to channel and shield and
keep our balance.

And it was wrong. Unnatural. Not the way we were supposed to do things. It went against years of training.

Yet it felt so good. Handling all that power, doing things
with it no one else could do. Should I be worried? Afraid
that I was liking this too much?

Far beyond the earth moving and the leather of Karish's
slicker and the rain and Karish himself and the forces and
my shields, I could feel Riley. Faint. Like looking at a person through fog, the fog I'd seen that morning. She was
grabbing at the forces, pulling at them, trying to redirect
them, and having no success with it.

I spared a thought to how this was going to shatter her
confidence. And she would never know the true reason why
she'd failed.

"Do something!"

I heard the shout from somewhere. Off to the side.

"Not too long," I said to Karish. Good as it felt, it was
tiring. And dangerous.

"Just a bit longer."

What a mess. How had this happened? Creating a disaster to protect ourselves from our own people. It was crazy.

A particularly violent buckle under my feet. That sent

me to the ground. I hung on to my shields, though. Good for me.

"Lee!"

"I'm fine. Don't fuss."

He slowed the forces down. Imposed his will on them, clamped it around them, pulled them away from the ground. And then he let them go. They screamed back into their natural courses. Karish allowed his internal shields to slip back into place. The ground settled down. It was over.

I scrambled to my feet and we started running, just in case. No one chased us, and after a few streets we had to slow down, but we didn't stop running.

I peeled off to head towards the Lion. It was the only place I could think of to go. Karish followed.

We met no one on the way. Good. I didn't think I could deal with people. We ran into the Lion. Karish slammed the door shut. People inside, somehow ignorant of the chaos happening only a short distance away, stared at us. We ignored them.

It was silent inside the Lion. While before my mind had felt bombarded by all the noise and activity, now it was so quiet it made my ears hurt.

I bent over, my hands on my knees, and tried to breathe into painful lungs and settle the sharp stitch in my side.

Karish pulled his slicker off, then helped me out of mine, draping them both over a nearby chair. Then he grabbed my arm and pulled me into a tight embrace.

He was shaking. I didn't ask him why, if it was a reaction to what had happened outside or if he found the boarding house too cool. Possibly he was hoping I wouldn't notice.

I pressed my cheek against his chest. He felt good. Healthy and alive and solid. I felt my muscles relaxing, the tension draining from my shoulders. How strange it was, even though that was what was supposed to happen. He was like some kind of medication, soothing and warm.

He soon stopped trembling. Poor excitable boy.

"You're right, Lee."

"Aren't I always?" I quipped. "Tell me about what, in particular, this time, so I might gloat." At least I could get out a coherent sentence. Good sign.

He chuckled, a weak sound. "We have to do something about all this."

Finally. "Well, we're trying."

"Aye, but I've been dragging my feet," he confessed. "I didn't think there was anything we could do. Or, if we could, whether we should."

I pulled away enough to look him in the face. "Why shouldn't we?"

He cocked his head to one side, a slow considering gesture. "It's dangerous, what we're thinking of doing," he said. "Manipulating the forces in ways we weren't trained to. That sort of thing, it can have serious repercussions. Dangerous repercussions." He bit his lower lip, something I'd never seen him do before. "I started an earthquake today."

"You've done it before."

"Aye, but at the time I thought I'd never have to do it again. But I have, and I have no idea how much damage I've done. I might have destroyed things. Homes. I might have hurt people." He swallowed. "What if I've killed someone?" he asked in a whisper.

I didn't think that was likely. The earthquake hadn't been that severe. Still, I could appreciate what he was saying. Drawing outside the lines could have frightening consequences. But I didn't know what else we could do. We had to do something. If for no other reason than that the residents of High Scape weren't going to let us do nothing.

Chapter Eleven

The exterior of the house was in pretty bad shape. Every window smashed, the doors ripped off their hinges, and chunks of the siding chopped out. The interior was a mess, with dishes and decorations smashed, tar splashed around here and there, drapes and clothes slashed and torn. The building was still structurally sound, meaning we didn't have to move out, and there were a couple of Runners wandering around nearby, so no more damage would be done. It didn't make me feel any better.

Everyone was shocked by the riot, including, we were told, the people who participated in it. No one knew how it had started, or why. It just happened.

Contributors to the newspaper decried the action as a disgusting descent into violence. Still, one could, apparently, understand the motivation. After all, people's lives were being destroyed, and we were doing nothing. I didn't see that as a reason to start destroying property, but it seemed that I was in the minority.

Six of the seven Pairs stood in the common room, just looking at the mess. Riley actually had enough initiative to make some tentative swipes at cleaning up. I couldn't make myself help. I was too shocked. And unnerved. And a little angry.

They had caused the damage. Let *them* clean it up.

Only I didn't want *them* coming back into my home.

When Karish stood behind me and slipped his arms around my waist and pulled me into him, it was comforting.

"Oh, for Zaire's sake, find a room!" Beatrice snapped at us.

"Aye, the honeymoon should be long over," Ladin added.

Karish's only answer was to rest his chin on the top of my head. I wasn't in the mood, myself, to worry about appearances. I was soothed by Karish's proximity.

"This is bad," Wilberforce said, pacing by the wreckage. "This has to be illegal."

Garrighan looked at him with an expression of disbelief mixed with disdain. "Of course it's illegal," he sneered. "They destroyed a building."

Wilberforce, as always, was resilient to the contempt of the other. "Yes, but this is a Triple S building. Surely that deserves a harsher punishment."

What an odd thing to say. Why should our buildings be treated with any more reverence than any other? Did Wilberforce spread that kind of attitude around? No wonder the regulars hated us.

Besides, they paid for it. One could almost say they owned it, and had the right to tear it down if they wished.

"I think they did us a favor, personally," said Sabatos, nudging a stray board with the toe of his boot. "Wasn't exactly a palace."

"We need it repaired, though," said Riley.

Sabatos shrugged. "So they repair it."

"'They' being regulars," Garrighan reminded him. "Who aren't exactly enchanted with us right now. Don't know if I would want to be spending a lot of time in something they built especially for us."

Wilberforce halted his pacing to give Garrighan a

condescending look. "They wouldn't dare build a defective house for us."

"Uh, considering they tore the first one apart, genius, it's not outside the realm of possibility."

Wilberforce chose not to respond to that. I would have respected him for his maturity if I weren't convinced it were more a case of him not being able to think of anything cutting to say.

"I am thinking the 'we're working on it' approach isn't endearing us to the regulars." Riley picked up a piece of paper, trying and failing to uncrumple it without tearing it.

"Toast to you, Mallorough, you saw that one a mile coming." Garrighan raised his hand in a gesture that I supposed was meant to be celebratory.

Wilberforce was predictably outraged. "Triple S fully supported our telling the regulars what we did."

That wasn't the story I'd heard. Not that they'd said no. Just that they hadn't responded yet.

"Doesn't make it any more of an intelligent idea," said Garrighan.

"I certainly don't remember hearing you say anything like that when Chris first came up with the idea. To his face. When he was present." Wilberforce crossed his arms, his tone snide and challenging.

"Didn't have to. Mallorough already was."

Well, it would have been nice to have some support then. Though I doubted Garrighan throwing in his lot with me would have been enough to change anyone's mind. Garrighan was known for highlighting the dark side of any situation, and I suspected it was usually just for the sake of being contrary.

"And I didn't have a better idea," he continued. "I try not to criticize when I don't have any constructive suggestions."

Rayne looked at Garrighan like she'd never seen her Shield before. "You what?" she demanded.

"Do you have any suggestions now?" Wilberforce challenged him.

Garrighan wasn't intimidated. "Fresh out," he admitted.
I had one, but no one wanted to hear it.

"Well, we've got to do something." Riley dropped the
balled up paper and brushed off her hands. "I think a
lynching party is the next logical step."

Wilberforce gasped. "They wouldn't dare!"

"Not usually, no," said Rayne. "But they're not themselves right now."

"They're all very anxious about what's going to happen
next," Sabatos agreed.

"No, it's more than that. Lauren and I have been at sites
before, when they were going through hard times. This is
something else."

"Like what?"

Rayne shrugged. "I don't know. It just is."

Well, wasn't that lovely?

"We could leave," said Beatrice, who practically
squirmed when we all looked at him. "Well, if our lives are
in danger . . ."

"We can't leave our post," Garrighan stated.

"Especially after that last earthquake," said Riley. "That
was brutal."

Karish's arms tightened around me.

"Yes, dear, we all felt that one," Firth said. She sounded
sort of sympathetic, and sort of annoyed, as though she had
been personally inconvenienced.

"I told you, it was strange," Riley insisted. An argument had been brewing, perhaps. "I've never felt an earthquake like it. When I was channeling, it felt like it was
fighting me."

Garrighan snorted. "Fighting you. Takes a mind to
fight."

I felt awful, standing there knowing we had caused that
damage, knowing Riley was doubting herself, that there
was tension there that didn't need to be there. Wasn't going
to say anything, though.

Neither was Karish.

"So what are we going to do?" Riley asked.

I could give them an idea of where to start. And Karish knew I was tempted. I could feel his arms tightening around my waist in warning.

He needn't have bothered. I was tempted, yes, but I was also reluctant to let the others know, at this stage, that I suspected we could affect the weather. First of all, I wasn't sure that we could. Had I caused that rainstorm? I really didn't know. But I was pretty sure I'd done something. And once I let that knowledge loose, I'd lose all control of it, and there was no telling what the others would do with it.

Was it arrogant for me to believe I could take better care of this ability than any other Shield? Undoubtedly. But I'd seen other people do awfully stupid things. I couldn't quite trust them.

Besides, they probably wouldn't believe me.

Karish and I were on our own.

They'd never taught me anything about this at the Academy.

Chapter Twelve

It was unacceptable, just flat out not allowed, for a Shield to be nervous. Just no excuse for it. Fear was fine, given acceptable circumstances. Love, as long as it didn't turn into obsession or possessiveness, was always to be encouraged. Hatred, while not actually condoned, could sometimes be forgiven, provided one didn't allow it to poison one's thinking.

But there was no excuse for nervousness. A person was nervous due to an exaggerated sense of anticipation of an event that was in no way life threatening. It did not provide one with a sense of determination or a source of strength. It was groundless, it was debilitating, it served no useful purpose and there was no reason for it.

So breathe in, long, slow—no, damn it, no hitches! Start again. Let it all out in a quick huff and then slowly pull it back in: slow, smooth, there, that's better.

So Her Grace the Dowager Duchess of Westsea was an unpleasant woman. That couldn't hurt me. I wasn't a debutant or an aristocrat of uncertain origins or anyone else clambering for the recognition and acceptance of the loftiest circles. What the woman said would have no effect on me. There was no reason for me to feel nervous. As there never was.

Long smooth breath, and then a slight touch up on the eye paint. Long languid dark lines that gave my eyes a nice catlike tilt and made them look a strange pale green. I'd been told more than once that the effect was odd but striking. That seemed like a good combination to me.

It was Karish I was really nervous for, not me. He just got so unbelievably tense when he spoke about his mother. This evening was going to be sheer hell for him, I had no doubt. I don't think my mother really understood that, else she wouldn't have arranged the dinner. And I didn't blame her for that. I'd had no real idea how bad it was going to be for Karish, either. It was only his behavior over the last couple of days that had me thinking this was really a very, very bad idea.

But the plans had all been made, and there was no backing out of it. We could only make the best of it. I was going to be calm. I was going to be gracious. No matter what that woman said or did, I would be the archetype of elegant courtesy. I owed that to Karish.

Besides, maybe it wouldn't be a disaster. The Dowager Duchess was a well-bred woman, after all, and not stupid. What would be the point of antagonizing her son and her son's Shield? Why wouldn't she make the minimal effort to be pleasant and make life easier for all of us? No reason at all. It would be fine. Probably. Possibly.

Long, slow, smooth breath.

"Now *that* is lovely." My mother stood in the doorway of her bedchamber, watching me fidget in front of her mirror.

My mother had put the fear of taxes into the tailors we had descended on only a few days earlier. Everything I had ordered had been delivered that morning. No second fitting, but I didn't have either the time or the patience for such fussing. The gown fit well enough.

In theory. The bodice was tight and the neckline was too

low, in my opinion, but Mother told me it was supposed to look like that. The color was deep green, which I had to admit to liking, and the fabric felt slippery and smooth against my skin, which was nice. Only, I couldn't see myself ever having an occasion to wear such a thing again. I didn't dine with aristocrats much, except Karish, so it seemed kind of a waste to me.

"Now you look as a woman of your rank should," my mother announced with satisfaction.

I frowned at her, puzzled. "A Shield?" Shields didn't have a real rank in the social strata sense of the word.

Mother frowned back. "No, dear. The daughter of a highly rated trader and holder."

"Oh." That.

I tweaked the lock of hair falling over my forehead. My hair was tied up, high off my neck, twisted in the back, in honor of the occasion. It had taken about an hour to fix. I never really liked my hair up when I was trying to look presentable, despite what my mother would have people believe. It was handy to tie it back from the face, simple and secure, but I was aware it didn't suit my features. My face didn't look classic and refined when my hair was pulled back, just rounded and over-exposed.

I sighed at my reflection. Sometimes, though I hated to admit it even to myself, I thought it would be nice to be stunning.

"Stop fiddling, dear."

Excellent advice. I put my hands down by my side and kept them there. "You look lovely, Mother." And she did. As always. A draping light blue gown, simple and elegant. Her hair was also tied up, much like mine, but with silver chains braided in with the brown locks. Sapphires in her ears and a plain silver chain about her throat. She looked so well put together, and so comfortable with herself, as though she dressed so elaborately on a daily basis.

"Thank you, dear." She came in to check herself in the

mirror, briefly touched her hair. "Do you have any questions about this evening?"

"Questions?"

"Yes. About how things should go tonight."

It took me a moment to realize she feared I might not have sufficient knowledge of the manners one should display around a duchess. "No, Mother. No questions."

"Well, good. Then let's go down the dining room. They should be here soon."

That was what I was afraid of. I was sort of hoping the Dowager would be unavoidably, and permanently, detained.

"Do you think I should have gotten a flutist?" Mother asked as we entered the dining room.

"No, Mother."

"I don't know. Music often adds that extra something."

"Pretension?"

"No, dear. Class."

"Ah. Wouldn't know about that. Too late now." Thank Zaire. A musician! "Want to play cards?"

A chiding look from my mother. "Lee."

"What? These sorts of people are never on time, are they? Might as well do something while we wait." Actually, that wasn't fair. Karish was always punctual. Maybe his mother was, too.

Whatever they were in general, they were late that evening. Not monstrously late. Fashionably, I supposed.

When I heard the firm knock on the door, Mother had to grab my arm to keep me from answering it. "Celia," she said, and a maid drifted to the door and opened it. She curtsied, then stood smartly to one side. "Her Grace, the Dowager Duchess of Westsea, and Source Shintaro Karish."

How ridiculous. They were the only two people coming, and we all knew who everyone else was. But the poor girl was expected to announce their names. I didn't roll my eyes but I really, really wanted to.

And Her Grace wasn't happy, either. She actually tilted

her head back so she could look down at the maid as she
removed her stylish evening wrap. "His appropriate title is
His Grace, Lord Westsea."

He had no such title. Even if she thought he would have
it eventually, she couldn't deny that it wasn't, for the time
being, the appropriate manner in which to address him. So
who did she think she was fooling?

I supposed the Dowager Duchess was a beautiful
woman. She looked exactly like Karish. She had the same
fine-boned delicacy, the same slanted dark eyes. Her lightly
golden skin was still smooth, with few lines. Her black hair,
unmarred by so much as a single thread of grey, was elaborately coiled atop her head. Her lean form was draped in a
gown of similar style to my mother's, but black. She wore
a choker of silver, diamonds and onyx with matching earrings and bracelets.

She was poised. She was elegant. She was cold. I
couldn't imagine her laughing. Or being kind. Or just relaxing. So I couldn't find her beautiful.

And the maid was no match for her. The poor girl flushed
and almost dropped the wrap in her attempts to curtsey as
often as possible in the shortest amount of time.

"Source Karish is both accurate and acceptable," Karish
said to Celia with an encouraging smile. But the smile was
brittle. And as he pulled off his cloak he moved not with
his usual fluid grace, but stiffly, precisely, as though too
much physical activity might cause him pain. He was
dressed entirely in black, which was uncommon for him.
Black boots, black trousers, a black waistcoat with sleeves
buttoned to the wrists and a high, stiff collar, likewise completely buttoned. His braid was there, but as it was black,
too, it was easy to miss. I wondered if that was intentional.
His hair was tied back, and unlike me he had the features to
carry off the severe style.

He looked hard and remote. Very much the son of a duke.

He stepped out between his mother and Celia and he
kissed my mother on the cheek. "Good evening, Teshia.

You are lovely, as always." The he looked at me and grinned. It was a bit more natural than his earlier expressions, but not by much. "Lee, you are gorgeous." He took my hand so he could kiss the inside of my wrist, and I ignored the little jolt it sent through me.

I smelled no alcohol on him. I wasn't sure whether that was a good or a bad thing. He needed to relax. "As always?" I asked him, straight-faced.

"But of course," he answered, equally sober. "You are eternally beautiful, Lee. You know that."

What a liar.

"Yes, Shield Mallorough," his mother added. Her attention was on me, now. Lovely. "You are looking very appropriate this evening." Hm. Appropriate. Did that qualify as a compliment? "I wasn't aware you were so adept at style."

"I'm not," I told her. "My mother picked this out."

I heard my Source chuckle and my mother sigh.

"Your Grace, my mother, Holder Teshia Mallorough."

Her Grace tilted her head slightly to one side. "Lady Holder."

Mother curtseyed, and I hated to see it. "Your Grace," she murmured in response. "Please sit down."

The Duchess nodded again, a slight magnanimous gesture that screamed of her lack of desire to be there.

Why *was* she there? Why did she lower herself to socialize with my mother and me? She couldn't have any desire to know us. I doubted Karish would have been able to convince her to come against her wishes, if he'd ever tried to. So she must have come of her own will. She must have had a reason, but I couldn't for the life of me guess what it might be.

We settled into our seats, Karish and I on a sofa and our mothers in separate chairs. Celia arrived with a tray of sherries. My, how genteel.

"I am so pleased we were able to do this," my mother commented, taking a small sip from her glass.

The Dowager Duchess held her glass, but didn't drink from it. "Yes," she said.

"With our children bonded it is no doubt best that we are able to contact and know each other."

The Dowager Duchess raised an eyebrow, Karish in female form. It was a little eerie. "It isn't as though they are married." And wasn't that a good thing for all involved, because she would hate to be the dead body things were done over.

Relax, Lee. Stop reading double meanings into everything. All she had done was state a bare, simple fact. Leave it alone.

"Of course not," my mother agreed. "Bonding is permanent."

Silence. Had that been a joke?

The Dowager's eyebrows were up again. Very mobile, they were. "Among quality people, marriage is permanent."

According to whose perception of reality? Or maybe they defined marriage differently in the upper class.

"No matter how miserable they are," Karish muttered.

"That's right, Shintaro," the Duchess said, her tone shifting to one of mocking congratulations. Look, everyone, my dim child has managed to learn something obvious. "People must honor their commitments, no matter how they feel about them."

"You know what, Your Grace, you're absolutely right." Karish smirked, looking like he thought he'd scored a point. "Once you've made a commitment, you can't just ditch it just because something new comes along."

They weren't really going to spend the whole evening fighting over his rejection of the title, were they?

The Duchess nodded again, still holding the glass in midair with no apparent intention of drinking from it. Looked kind of silly, actually. "Yes, a wise general rule," she said. "But, of course, some commitments are more important than others."

"I couldn't agree more." Karish, though, had different ideas from his mother concerning what was an important commitment.

"Yes, Lee has been telling me how diligent Taro is," my mother chipped in, her voice warm, trying to diffuse the tension that was already starting to build. Karish looked at me, eyebrows raised. I responded with a half shrug. I'd never said as much to my mother, but I didn't mind her claiming I had. "She feels very fortunate to be working with him."

"I have no doubt," the Duchess said dryly.

Wench.

"Does she plan on moving to Flown Raven with Shintaro?"

"Lee is right here, Your Grace," Karish said sharply. "If you have a question about her, ask her."

"Hush, Shintaro. The Lady Holder and I were speaking."

Hush, Shintaro? What was he, four? Even my mother's eyes widened at that. She looked at me, the weight in her gaze signalling me that it was time for me to contribute to the conversation.

Did I have to? And what was I supposed to say? No, we're not going to Flown Raven because your son has refused the title and that's the end of it. It wasn't my place to say that. "I'm afraid we aren't free to leave our posts whenever we wish, Your Grace." There. That was nice and neutral, wasn't it?

Her Grace made no effort to hide her reluctance in addressing me. Guess who was the least significant person in the room? "Shintaro must return home to assume his responsibilities."

"Flown Raven was never my home." His voice tight with anger, Karish surprised me by taking up my hand. I had expected him to restrain himself in front of his mother. "And those responsibilities were never mine."

Her Grace noticed and frowned, and waved her hand dismissively. "Don't be melodramatic, Shintaro."

"Sources are melodramatic by nature, Your Grace. But then, you never concerned yourself with the attributes of Sources, did you?"

"Of course not," the Dowager said. "Why should I trouble myself with the Source and Shield Service?"

Because your son is a member, you stupid twit.

All right, calm down. No reason to let any of it get under your skin. Just breathe. We couldn't all get nasty.

"Your daughter would benefit from a move to Flown Raven," the Duchess continued. To my mother. "Especially with Taro's connections. She would meet the finest people, have access to—"

"We are not going to Flown Raven," Karish snapped.

"Please don't raise your voice to your mother, Taro."

Back off, Mother. Don't you dare presume to chastise Karish.

Taro's grip on my hand tightened, for a moment, before he remembered himself and deliberately relaxed.

"The manners of the younger generation are appalling, are they not?" the Duchess said to my mother.

If they got into some kind of scenario of mature adults versus callow youngsters, things were going to get ugly. Or I was leaving, whichever came first.

But Mother had recovered from temporarily forgetting that Karish was her favorite new pet. "Actually, I usually find Taro's manners impeccable." No mention of me, but, ah well, I wasn't the one under attack.

Still, my mother's behavior was disturbing me. Both of them were talking about Karish as though he weren't there. While I expected it of the Duchess, I was deeply disappointed in my own mother. She knew better.

"Do you?" the Duchess drawled.

She moved to take a sip from her sherry, but stopped herself before her lips touched the glass.

I found it fascinating how much information she'd packed into those two words. She thought her son was an unmannered oaf, but of course my mother couldn't understand that, being an underbred merchant woman and all.

"I find them to be sadly lacking," she went on, "but then, one can't expect much considering the company he's been keeping."

The tension in Karish's thigh jumped up another notch. "Which company might that be?" he asked tightly.

"There is no need to go into that at this time," was the Dowager's response.

"You already have," Karish reminded her. "You brought it up. You can't make a comment like that and then refuse to give any details to back it up. What kind of company are you talking about?" And then he waited for the answer, expecting to be offended by it.

The Dowager sighed, looking pained. That was when she decided it was time to talk to me again. "Please consider it, Shield Mallorough." Her tone was gentle, soft. I didn't trust it. "You would learn so much in Flown Raven. I myself would be willing to teach you about the necessary manners and tastes required of an associate of—"

I was supposed to be feeling flattered by this, wasn't I?

"There is nothing wrong with Lee's manners!" Karish snapped.

"Well, no, not for a common—"

And Karish was suddenly on his feet, across the room and looming over his mother. "Get. Out. Now."

His mother gaped at him, her polish gone. She didn't move.

"Leave this house. Immediately."

No, no, don't do that. It wasn't a lost cause yet. We could still smooth this out.

I had to hand it to the Dowager, she pulled herself back together quickly. "House? This is not a house. Look at this . . . hovel." Her tone couldn't have been more scathing. "This is no fit place for you."

I glanced about. It wasn't *that* bad. Surely not a hovel.

"Really?" Karish stretched his arms wide and slowly turned around. "It's got to be at least half again the size of my room at Flown Raven. And I can come and go whenever I please. Much better than the most luxurious prison."

I frowned in confusion. What an unfortunate time for one of Karish's incomprehensible Source-isms to start cropping up.

The Duchess' lip curled. "Your room was not a prison. Stop exaggerating."

Oh lord, now we were going to hear about arguments stretching back from childhood. This was going to be awful.

"I couldn't leave, could I? The door was locked from the outside, wasn't it? Sounds like a prison to me."

Karish, Karish, rebellious children are locked in their rooms all the time. A common form of punishment. Melodramatics would not earn you any points.

But the Dowager's next words made me feel ashamed for dismissing Karish's anger so readily.

"We couldn't have you wandering around at will."

I stared at her for that. He couldn't be allowed to wander around at will? In his own *house*? Why the hell not?

"Aye," he said bitterly. "Because the gods forbid anyone should talk to me and find out I was insane."

Oh no, oh no. My mother was looking stunned and shocked and disoriented. She didn't know what to do. I'd never told her that Karish's parents had thought he was mentally unbalanced. It looked like she was going to learn all about it now.

"No one thought you were insane," the Dowager said impatiently. "Don't be ridiculous."

"Then why wasn't I allowed to talk to anyone?" Karish demanded, his face flushed. "Except the staff, of course, because they didn't matter to anyone. I wasn't allowed to see my cousins. You wouldn't let me have a tutor. You didn't send me to school. I was eleven years old, and I couldn't even read. Do you have any idea how humiliating that was?"

"The son of the Duke of Westsea does not mingle with inferiors," the Duchess declared, head raised to a lofty angle.

"The son of the Duke of Westsea doesn't need to learn to *read*?" Karish shouted at her incredulously. "Do you have any idea how stupid that is?"

"You were out of control. We couldn't send you to a school where others would . . ." She trailed off.

Others would what? See? Know? What was there to know except that Karish was a Source?

"Out of control! What the hell did I do?"

"Always babbling nonsense." Her words were thick with repugnance. "It was mortifying."

"I was a child! And a Source! That's what we do!"

"How were we to know that?"

"You could have asked!" His voice broke. "Why didn't you just ask? Any doctor would have known what it meant."

Her calm veneer cracked then. "Bring in a doctor to see the imbalanced child I had given birth to?" she cried, appalled. "I wasn't going to let that be known. Nasty little gossips, doctors are."

I couldn't believe this woman. Did she hear herself?

"Your precious reputation," Karish muttered bitterly.

"Reputations are all we have, Shintaro." She'd slipped back into lecture mode. Despite all the emotion screaming through the room, she was able to revert back into the calm, mild tone she'd been initially using. She was just like Karish, flipping from one emotional state to another. Her range of emotions seemed smaller, but the time required for the switch seemed just as brief. "They're more important than wealth or rank, and far more fragile. They are what make or break a person, bring you power, or strip it from you. You don't understand that right now, but you will."

"I am not going to Flown Raven!" he shouted.

"You are. It is your duty to your family."

"The family can go to hell!"

Damned straight. They treat him like dirt his entire life and then expect him to ditch everything to help them out?

Not if I had anything to say about it. And well, I didn't, but I could tie him down if he lost his senses.

The Duchess' eyes narrowed. "Is that the kind of sentiment whoring about with catamites and prostitutes has given you?" she asked coolly.

Had she forgotten that we—my mother and I—were still there? Or were we so insignificant in the grand scheme of things that it didn't matter what was said in front of us, what we knew? Wasn't this the same woman who was so worried about gossip a moment before?

Karish snickered, of all things. "I do not whore about," he said. "I am not my brother." Thank god, since his brother had died as a result of his whoring about. "I am not my father." Well, wasn't that an interesting piece of news. "And I am not you."

Oh.

My.

Two spots of color rose to prominence in the duchess' cheeks. She jumped to her feet. "Apologize to me this instant!" she hissed.

He laughed, a harsh jagged sound laced with unshed tears. "All this bilge about your reputation," he sneered, looking exactly as his mother had when she'd sneered at him. "I know what the right people say about you, Your Grace, and then I know what everyone else says. I know what you really are. And I've spent my whole life being as unlike you as I could possibly be. Because you're just a cold, hypocritical, manipulative fraud and there's no way in hell I will ever apologize to you. For anything."

This would be the time when she would slap him. She didn't. She just stood there, her hands clenched into fists, and fumed. I considered being impressed by her restraint.

My mother was pale, sitting there, staring at them in shock.

I felt I should be doing something. I had no clue what.

"This was obviously a mistake," said Her Grace. "Fetch my wrap."

Celia, who had been standing with her back to the wall and watching the whole affair with undisguised glee, leapt into action. She jumped across the room to the wardrobe, practically yanking the Duchess' wrap free and draping it over her shoulders.

Then Celia left. I frowned at my mother, who mouthed the word "carriage" at me. Oh. Celia was thinking ahead. Good thing someone was.

"Is there no way I can change your mind?" my mother asked, but not with any real sense of sincerity. I didn't think she cared to change the Duchess' mind. She was just going through the motions. Which was ludicrous. No effort had been made by anyone to make this seem like a normal, civil night. Why start now?

Well, this was a nice mess. Hadn't even lasted an hour. I rose to my feet, as my mother did, because the others were standing and it was polite, and I think we were all too stunned to really think about what we were doing.

The Duchess was adjusting her wrap. "Shintaro is rarely able to stay civil for more than a few moments," she told my mother, and I thought, seriously, about smacking her. "I had hoped in the company of others he would remember his upbringing, but . . ." an elegant shrug.

Seemed to me he was remembering his upbringing all too well, and that was the problem.

"I apologize for my son, Lady Holder, Shield Mallorough."

That was it. "How fortunate he has someone to apologize for him," I said, my voice dripping with feigned sweetness. "Too bad there's no one here to apologize for you."

She stared at me, clearly astonished that I would say something like that to her. She looked at my mother, and then Karish, perhaps expecting one of them to either chastise me or beg pardon from her. What she got was silence.

She closed her mouth. "I will see myself to the Imperial," she said to Karish. "I don't care for your presence right now. I do hope you remember how to comport your-self in time for the Prince's ball."

Karish stared back at her, and I could no longer deter-mine what he was feeling. His mask was on, his eyes blank.

She turned to the door, and halted. Celia was still out hunting up a carriage. Normally I would have been content to let her open her own damn doors, but I wanted her out of there. So I jumped forward and yanked the door open.

Without looking at me she swept—yes, swept—out into the corridor. I shut the door behind her, a shade shy of slamming it. Then I turned back into the room, ready to sigh in relief.

Karish was standing near the wall, the fire drained out of him. He was staring off into space, his shoulders slumped.

Things weren't over yet.

My mother walked up behind Karish, laying her hand on his shoulder. He didn't move. "I'm sorry," he whis-pered. "I'm so sorry. I thought I could . . ." His voice choked off.

He had nothing to apologize for.

"It's my fault." She rubbed his back, slow circular movements. "You told me it was a bad idea." She raised her hand to lightly stroke his hair. "I thought I knew better." She rose to her toes to kiss his cheek. "I should have lis-tened to you. I'm so sorry."

"No," he shook his head. "No, no, no. It's me. It's my fault. I'm a grown man. I should be able to . . . I shouldn't . . . damn it!" His voice giving out on him. "I'm sorry. You went to all this trouble. I'm so sorry."

Karish sometimes berated himself, denigrated himself, made fun of himself. Never have I heard his voice so filled with self-loathing. It infuriated me. He should never be made to feel that way.

"It is my fault, for not listening to someone who knew better," my mother told him. "I can be arrogant that way." She smiled at him.

He didn't smile back.

She shot me one of her communicative looks. I nodded.

She kissed him again. "I am going to drop in on the Hunters," she announced.

"No, no. I'll go." Karish started looking around as though he wasn't sure where he was.

"I need to speak with you, Taro," I said. Though I had no idea what I was going to be saying.

He lowered his head, and if anything his shoulders slumped even more. What, he thought I was going to yell at him? Did he really think I was going to be angry at him for any of this?

Mother kissed my cheek. "I'll be late."

"Good night, Mother. Thanks for everything."

She slipped out, closing the door quietly.

Chapter Thirteen

I looked at Karish. He had drifted closer to the wall. His back was to me.

I had no idea what to do. I was sure I had understood only about half of what had happened, what had been said, and I was sure there was a whole lot more that hadn't even been touched on. I was shocked at what I'd heard and wasn't sure I could believe it. I mean, Karish hadn't really been secluded in his room for eleven years, had he? That wasn't possible. There had to be some detail that hadn't been mentioned, that explained it all the way. Because if it were true, Karish should be insane.

What was I going to do? How was I supposed to make him feel better? Was that even possible right now? I didn't know what he needed. And whatever it was, I probably wasn't the one to give it to him. He was no doubt longing to find his friends and drown himself in their company. But I couldn't let him go out like this, looking so shattered. It would be wrong. Cruel.

I could let him know, at least, that I wasn't angry with him, and that I didn't blame him for anything. That he didn't have anything to be ashamed of. That much I could do. And then maybe he wouldn't throw himself into the drink quite so desperately. Maybe he'd avoid making a mistake he'd otherwise make.

I walked to him and put a hand on his back. He jumped at the contact. I wrapped my arms around his waist, pressing my face against his shoulder-blades. He was so tense.

He shuddered, and he choked off a sound trying to escape from his throat.

I tightened my grip. "It's all right."

He leaned his head against the wall, and breathed. An obvious effort to control himself.

That wasn't good. That wasn't him. The one time he had every reason to indulge in a screaming fit, and he was trying to stay calm. "Don't, don't," I whispered. "It's only me. There's no one else here. No one watching."

"I'm sorry," he whispered. "I'm so sorry."

"There is no reason to apologize." As I said them, I knew the words were of no effect. They were the words the situation called for, the words one said when one was being merely polite. They were expected. How could I convince him that I meant them? "No one is angry, Taro." Except maybe his mother, but who cared about her?

He started laughing, laughing into the wall, the same bitter jagged sound as before. "I'm angry," he said. "Why can't I—" He slammed his fist against the wall.

Don't do that. Don't hurt yourself, not over her. "*I'm* sorry," I said. "We shouldn't have done this. We should have listened to you." So stupid. So arrogant. Dismissing his misgivings, because, of course, he was exaggerating. He was a Source, that was what they did. We had been so sure all we had to do was sit down like calm rational adults, and we'd be able to clear up nearly thirty years worth of bitterness with a single conversation. We, who had never met the Dowager and knew nothing about her, had so quickly thought we could handle her better than her own son,

dismissing Karish's concerns without a second thought. I
was sick with self-disgust.

Another hard laugh. "Should have known I would have
behaved like an idiot."

"No." Imitating my mother, I rubbed his back with my
hand. "There's obviously a lot of things going on there that
we know nothing about." And we shouldn't have inter-
fered. How long would it take me to learn that lesson?

Karish was refusing to accept any reassurance. "Doesn't
matter," he said to the wall. "I shouldn't have humiliated
everyone like that. Leave it to me to turn a common event
into a tawdry melodrama." His voice was deep with repugnance, all directed at himself. "All I had to do was get
through one dinner. I couldn't even manage that."

"Your mother wasn't even trying, Taro. It was exactly as
you said. As soon as she stepped through the door she was
needling you." And not us, not much. That had been sur-
prising. I'd been expecting her to pour her disdain all over
us, but her principal target had been her own son. How can-
nibalistic of her.

"You think I would have learned to handle her with a little grace."

"Why should you? She wasn't showing any."

He shook his head, sort of, his face still pressed against
the wall. Enough hiding. I pulled on him. "Come on, sit
down." He resisted a moment, then let me manhandle him
onto the sofa, but he immediately covered his face with his
hands.

I went into the kitchen to grab a bottle of red wine and a
couple of goblets. I sat beside Karish on the sofa and filled
the goblets. Then, I pulled his hands from his face.

He was so pale, his eyes wide and lost. "Taro."

"I couldn't even last an evening, Lee."

"Neither could she." And she was the one who had
walked out, given up, scuppered any chance of turning the
evening around. It was easy enough to stir up chaos and
sweep out with grand dignity. Much harder to stay behind

and deal with the aftermath. "You don't have to do it again."

"That's not the point!"

No, I knew that, but what else was there? I had no doubt that his mother was muttering to herself about how ill mannered we all were and chiding herself for expecting better. While she, she was assuring herself, had conducted herself impeccably. If his mother didn't recognize that there was a problem, it couldn't be fixed. The best thing for him would be to acknowledge that and put it behind him.

I put a goblet in his hand. "Drink. It's your favorite."

For a moment he looked down blankly, as though he didn't recognize the foreign object that had appeared in his hand. I could practically feel him pulling his mind together. "That's what you think," he said with a weak attempt at a smile. "I happened to have discovered the Deep Valley vineyard last week. It's assumed top rank."

Well, aye. "I know that," I said, and I knew I sounded offended.

He looked at me, surprised. Then he took a careful sip. "It is Deep Valley," he said, frowning.

The frown disturbed me. "What, is it a bad year?"

"No," he said quickly. "It's not that. It's just . . ."

I waited a moment for him to continue, but he didn't seem to want to, so I explained, "You spoke of it to Sabatos."

"Yes, but . . ." But what? He didn't say. Just trailed his fingertips down the side of the goblet.

Maybe it unnerved him, that I knew without him telling me. "I listen to you all the time, Taro. And I watch." Ah. Maybe that was the problem. I certainly wouldn't like someone watching me all the time. "It's part of my job. It's practically become my hobby. And hey, you're nice to look at." He didn't react to my joke. Well, it had been pathetic. "Everything I can know about you by observing you, I know."

His mouth bent wryly. "You think so?"

"I know so." I'd better. Else I'd have to say I stared at him all the time just to look at him. Couldn't have that. "I don't know anything about those first eleven years, though." Not the most elegant way to segue into the topic, but I had a feeling he'd avoid it all night if I let him.

He lowered the goblet, resting it on his knee.

Ask a question. One that was easy to answer. That might enable him to start. "Did you really never leave your room?"

He shrugged. "Sometimes I did. Not often. The door was usually locked."

"You were usually locked in your room?"

"Almost always."

"And not for punishment?"

"No. At least, I don't think so."

So it was true, not just an exaggerated accusation thrown out in the middle of a bitter argument. True, the Dowager hadn't denied it, but I pictured her as the sort who believed explaining herself was demeaning. "But why?"

He stared into the wine. That was why I'd given it to him. Not just to loosen his tongue but to give him something to look at when he couldn't bear to look at me. "They didn't want me talking to anyone."

"Just because you sometimes said things that didn't make sense? All children do that." Hell, all people did that. Last I heard, it wasn't a crime.

"Westsea children don't. I guess my brother didn't."

That was a crock. There had to be something more to it than that, though Karish might not know himself. Not that I thought Karish could have done anything worth getting locked in his room for eleven years, but there had to be something more.

"I did have a tutor, actually, for a short while," he said, dipping the tip of his index finger into his wine. "I don't remember him very well. I was quite young. I don't think he liked me much." I imagined Kairsh as a child. He must have been adorable. Mischievous, I had no doubt, but adorable. How could anyone not like him? "I remember him strapping me. I think . . . I think he was the one who decided I must be crazy, and he told my parents. And because my grandfather had lost his wits, they believed the tutor. He was dismissed, and I never got another."

I stroked the back of his hand where it rested on his thigh, and when he raised it I slipped under so we could twine our fingers together. I wondered what would ease the tension practically singing through his muscles. Nothing I could do.

"After that, it was just maids, coming in to dress me and bring me food and clean out the chamber pot." Another dry chuckle. "It was the strangest thing. Even now I don't understand it. They came in four times a day, one for each meal and to dress me in appropriate morning, afternoon and evening attire, and again to prepare me for bed at night. They expected me to mind my manners, and sit up straight, and use the right cutlery. But no one cared that I didn't know how to do anything useful, lace my own boots or write my own name."

Valuing form over substance. Many fell into that trap. "Other than that, you were alone?"

He ducked his head. "Aye," he whispered.

And why did I feel so bad? I wasn't the one who had gone through it. "So what did you do?" Alone, a small child kept in a single room. It was disgusting. How dare they?

"I don't know. I don't remember very well. Time just passed. I had the toys given to me when I was an infant." I heard him swallow. "Sometimes my brother came to visit me."

And the tone of his voice told me that was not a good thing. "What did he do?"

He took a long draught from his goblet. "Played games."

"What kind of games?" No, no, no, don't tell me. I don't want to hear this.

He squirmed a little. He didn't want to tell me. "Nothing terrible."

Terrible enough, if he brought it up. "That's what you say now, as an adult. Is that how it felt to you at the time?"

He looked down at our linked hands, rubbing the side of my palm with his thumb. "He'd come and bring a new toy," he said slowly. I got the feeling he was choosing his words with particular care. "And I'd be so happy he had come to see me, so happy to have someone to talk to. So excited. And then he would give me the toy, and encourage me to play with it." He paused. I didn't want to hear the next part. I clenched my teeth, preparing for it. "And then he would take it from me, and shout at me because I'd ruined it by touching it." I blinked, my heart twisting. "He was so big, so much older than me, he seemed like an adult to me, and he could get so loud. He would smash the toy, a top or a wooden horse or something, under his foot, right in front of me, and then he would leave. And I couldn't understand what I'd done so wrong. I'd only done what he'd told me to."

I hated boys. They were all monsters.

"Then he would come again," Karish went on, "a good while later, and he would tell me he was going to come back the next day, to take me outside. Take me out for a ride on a horse, or to go swimming. I'd never done either, I didn't really understand what they were, but he made them sound so exciting. And it didn't really matter whether they were or not. All that really mattered was that he was going to take me." For a moment his voice lifted, as though he were once more experiencing the excitement he'd felt as a child. "But then, he wouldn't come back." He whirled the wine around in his goblet. "He never came back. Or so it felt. Only he would. Months later. With another toy. Or more promises that he forgot. And sometimes he shouted. Sometimes he lifted me off my feet, shaking me. I hated that, but then . . . it was the only time he ever touched me. The only time anyone but the maids touched me." He pulled in a long breath. "Every time he came, I was so excited. And every time he came, I was so scared." He paused for long moments, just breathing and rubbing my hand. "Because I never knew what to expect. I never knew whether he was going to be angry or kind. I think that's what made it so hard. The unpredictability of it. Of him." I felt him shiver. "But I was overreacting," he said after another pause, trying to make his voice stronger and calmer, but it cracked. "I know that now. He never did me any harm. But you know Sources. Always overreacting to things." He smiled, a pathetic wobbly effort.

As I had often told him. And no doubt countless others as well. And yes, sometimes he did overreact. But this was different. And perhaps this was not the worst story I had ever heard. Perhaps there were people with much grimmer childhoods. But did it matter? This was his experience. And it was cruel enough.

"The academy must have been a shock."

"Huh." He smiled again, more genuine, but sad. "All of a sudden, there was all this activity. I got all these new clothes and a trunk and all this extra attention from the staff. They were giving me all these instructions on how to behave. They cut my hair for the first time that I remembered." He slowly reached back and pulled the tie out of his hair. The dark locks slid down, softening his features. "I thought it meant something. I thought maybe I was old enough to join the family. I thought that was what it all meant, that when you're young you're kept out of everyone's way, but once you're old enough, you're allowed to be with people."

Only instead he'd been bundled into a carriage and sent away. And I remember him telling me that no one had told him why he was being sent away. How much effort would it have taken to explain things to him?

"It was all so exciting. I was leaving my room. I was leaving the house. I was taking a ride in a carriage. It was all so new. And even though it was a servant in the carriage with me, not my brother or father or mother, I thought wherever I was going to be would be with them. I thought maybe it was some kind of vacation or something."

I didn't understand how anyone could be so cavalier about a child's feelings. He was their son. How could he not matter to them?

I didn't want to hear any more. I could imagine it all too well. The exultation any child would feel when they knew they were leaving one stage of their life and entering a new one. And this one, thinking he was finally going to be receiving the time and attention and affection of his family, only to find himself dumped in an unfamiliar place surrounded by strangers, with his family nowhere to be seen. He must have been crushed.

He cleared his throat. "Of course, you know the rest," he said briskly. "It was the academy. I never saw my father or my brother again." He raised my hand to his lips, kissed the back of it. "I don't actually have a memory of my father. I don't know that I've ever met him. I only know what he looks like through portraits. He was . . . very blond." A frown flickered over his features and disappeared.

"People at the academy thought I was so odd." That surprised me, almost as much as the other revelations I'd suffered that night. I'd assumed he'd been adored at the Source academy. "They laughed at the way I spoke, my accent, the way I behaved." Bastards. "I'd never been around so many people before. It was noisy and crowded and I never knew what to do. I had to be told to leave my room, to eat and to go to class. They thought I was impossibly spoiled, because I expected everything to be brought to me." He laughed softly, and I mentally kicked myself for every silk sheet comment I had ever tossed at him. "It was years before I was able to leave my room on my own, on a whim, for no reason, without feeling guilty about it, without worrying someone was going to get angry at me for being out."

I didn't think I had ever been so angry, at so many people, all at once, in my life.

"But people liked me there, I think. Once I learned how to behave."

"Of course they liked you." How could they not? "Not everyone is as blind as your family."

He chuckled. "There's no of course about it, Lee. You don't know what I was like back then. I had trouble paying attention through an entire class. My mind always ended up drifting away." Well, of course it had. He'd never had lessons before, he hadn't known how to keep his mind on one thing for any significant length of time. "I never had anything to say. I scowled all the time."

"You had plenty of reasons to scowl," I interrupted him, though I did have a difficult time imagining him as anything significantly different from the way I knew him.

"No no, not like that, Lee. You've said yourself that people shouldn't be imposing their negative feelings on other people all the time, that we all have a duty to be calm in public. You're right."

Not when you're a child. Not when you're in real pain. I never meant that.

"It was so embarrassing. A teacher noticed me drifting during a class and got sick of it. He said no one was going to put up with my aristocratic airs just because my family never bothered to teach me proper manners, and I'd better shape up or I'd find myself working as an administrator or something after I was Paired. I didn't know what exactly that meant, but from everyone's reaction I knew it wasn't good."

"You have incredible focus now," I murmured, wondering had he'd managed to develop so far from such an unpromising beginning.

He shrugged. "I wanted to be good at something."

It didn't seem to be much of an explanation, it seemed too simple. But not everything had to be complicated. And maybe that was the reason why Lord Shintaro Karish had gone out of his way to learn how to cook and how to fix cracks in the ceiling. After a childhood of not being permitted to do anything, he had wanted to learn to do something, and do it well.

"And I learned to smile."

"You had to learn?"

"Well, no, I guess I just had to learn the effect a smile could have." His voice took on a tone of bemusement. "If I smiled at someone, they would like me."

"I'm sure it wasn't just because of that."

But he didn't seem to hear me. "Someone could be angry at me, could be shouting at me or arguing with me, and sometimes if I just smiled at them, even though it didn't make sense for me to smile right then, it just seemed to stop them, and they'd smile back."

That was because he had a killer smile, which was just bloody unfair.

"There was a skill to it, of course. The timing, what kind of smile, but I learned. Once I learned how to behave with people, they seemed to like me. It was only at the beginning of my time at the academy that things were . . . difficult."

I got the feeling he was trying to reassure me. Instead he was disturbing me. I didn't like what I was hearing. "You don't have to put on an act to get people to like you."

"I know that," he snapped.

I didn't think he did. Not all of him. There was a part of him that believed people only liked him when he smiled, when he laughed, when he, to use words he'd uttered on more than one occasion, played the fool. And I'd had no idea. I was such an idiot. And I didn't think that was something I could fix. At least, not with words. It was something I'd have to think about. Later. "I'm glad to hear it," I said. "Though sometimes I have my doubts. Because it made me crazy when we first met, when everything was a joke and you were always using that smarmy smile—"

"Smarmy!" he protested. I couldn't tell whether he was genuinely offended or not.

I plunged on anyway. Even anger was better than defeatism. "All that play acting kept me from seeing that you were fine and decent and full of all the traits I admire in a person." So fine, from such barren beginnings. I wouldn't have thought it possible. Who had taught him what a person should be?

And unbidden from the back of my mind came a name. Professor Saint-Gerard. An elderly professor from the Source Academy to whom Karish still wrote. It looked like there was someone I needed to thank.

"Careful, Lee, you'll be making me arrogant." And he finally looked at me. He frowned. He put his goblet down on the coffee table and stroked a fingertip below one of my eyes. "You're crying."

I drew away from him sharply. I touched my cheek and felt moisture. Holy hell. When had that happened?

"You pity me," he muttered. "Brilliant."

"Oh, yes, poor boy," I retorted, injecting as much disbelief into my tone as I could. "The celebrated Shintaro Karish, famously talented and adored by all." Though I did pity him. Not for the person he had grown into, but for what he'd had to endure. How could I not feel pity for that?

But I knew better than to tell him that. I was glad he didn't like the idea of being pitied. No one who was balanced did.

"Not adored by you."

Did he honestly believe that? Where had he been? "I do adore you. Just not for your smile." Though it was nice to look at.

So he smiled, the non-smarmy version. He leaned down to kiss my forehead. Then my cheek. Then my mouth. Just a peck.

But then, immediately after, he kissed me on the mouth again. Not a peck. Again, a lingering touch. And I thought he was getting too used to that.

So was I. Bad, bad sign. Too much familiarity was never a good thing. Getting too comfortable when other people touched me encouraged them to take things a step further, and made me lax enough to allow them.

That's what I told myself, anyway.

His lips opened against mine, one of his hands spearing into my hair. I gasped into his mouth, heat flooding through me. Sweet, sweet danger.

Oh, he was in a fine state, his mouth desperate and fervent. It felt good. And gods it was so tempting just to let it go on. A maelstrom of sensation would be just thing to wipe out the turmoil created by the events of the evening.

And create a whole new set of problems. I pulled away. "Not good." The words came out weak and sharp as I tried to slow my rapidly beating heart. Idiot. Moron. Just what were you thinking?

For a moment his eyes were blank. Then they sharpened into focus, and he flushed a brilliant red. "Oh, Zaire! Oh, Lee! I'm so sorry." He disentangled his hand, caught between the desire for haste and a reluctance to rip my hair out of my head.

Once he was free, I nodded. Blank face, blank face. "Perfectly forgivable, under the circumstances." This was so humiliating. I wanted to crawl under the sofa. I couldn't believe I'd been so careless. Did I want to ruin everything?

Calm down.

"It wasn't the circumstances!" he snapped.

I raised an eyebrow. How had I managed to tick him off this time?

He lowered his forehead against mine. "I like your gown," he drawled, anger dissipated as quickly as it had flared up.

"Aye, you would." Please give me some space. I really need it.

He sighed and pulled back. "I should go."

Yes, he should. I didn't think less of him for seeking comfort in sex, but it was not the kind of comfort I could provide. And I, I was ashamed to admit, was too rattled to be of any use to him in my usual capacity. Whatever that was. "Don't do anything stupid."

"Why break a trend?" He rose to his feet.

"Taro," I chided him, standing and catching his hand. "Only I am allowed to insult you."

"Aye, but you've been failing in your duty tonight."

"Yes, I have." I let that woman tear a strip off my Source. I didn't know how I could have done things differently, how I could have participated in events without making things worse, but it galled me that that woman had felt free to come into what was temporarily my mother's home and treat any other guest, whether he was her son or not, in such an appalling fashion.

"Don't start." He rubbed the back of his neck and looked about the living room. "I'm sorry I turned this evening into such a disaster."

"Hey, stop trying to usurp all the credit. We all did our part to make this evening as uncomfortable as possible." He smiled, but it was another sad effort. I pulled his head down and kissed his cheek to show him that all—all—was forgiven. "I mean it, Taro. None of us can be proud of our behavior tonight. Don't be thinking you deserve special punishment. And don't be too wild tonight. All right? Take care."

He looked down at me curiously, but I could see he was relaxing a little. The lines of tension about his form were easing slightly. I wasn't sure why, but it was good to see. "Lee, what do you think I do when I'm not with you?" And he grinned, something closer to his usual self. I could have hugged him.

"I don't think about it," I said. Major lie.

"I don't participate in orgies, you know."

"Of course not." Actually, that was a shocker. I would have bet money that he did. Though, really, I didn't tend to think about it. Much. But what was the point of being the Stallion if you didn't indulge in indiscriminate sex?

"I don't smoke drugs."

"I never thought for a moment that you did." And that was the honest truth.

"I don't get smashed and hijack public carriages and get . . . smashed."

Hell, I never even considered that possibility. People did that? That explained some of the driving I had seen. Was that legal?

He chuckled, the evil bastard. "Take a look in the mirror, gorgeous."

"Huh?"

"Have a good evening, darling. Pass my apologies on to your mother." With a wink and a graceful turn he grabbed up his cloak and was out the door.

I pulled in a long breath and blew it out again. What a hellish evening. Should have known that would happen when it turned out I needed so much work to be considered acceptable. Anything you couldn't do as yourself was likely to blow up in your face.

I never wanted to see that woman again. I didn't want Taro to ever see her, either. But there was still that hassle with the title to be endured.

I swallowed down a spurt of resentment. Why couldn't she just leave him alone? The resentment surged up again.

All right. Calm down. Wouldn't help Karish. Breathe.

Wine. I grabbed up my untouched goblet and drained half of it. Red wine—blech!—but it would do the job, especially as I had eaten so little all day. Already I could feel it easing my nerves and loosening my muscles. Aye, needed more than that. I took the bottle and goblet with me when I went to my mother's bedchamber to change. And I took Karish's advice. I looked in the mirror.

Hideous black tracks had been drawn down my cheeks. The result of tears running through the black eye paint. I looked a complete mess.

What a bastard.

Chapter Fourteen

"He's toothsome."

"Hair's too long. It doesn't suit his face. I like that one."

"Hm. Delicate. You do like the type, don't you? But he's firmly and exclusively playing for the other team."

"Ah."

"Now that one looks good with his hands."

"I'm sure his wife thinks so."

"Hell."

A mug of mulled wine was plunked down in front of me with a thud. Some of the contents splashed over the rim. I didn't even bother glaring at the server. There was no point.

Risa wasn't so passive. "Hey!" she shouted, but the server gave no indication of having heard, though those at nearby tables turned their heads. "Insolent little bag," she muttered.

I shrugged and raised the mug to my lips. Then I paused before taking a sip. I'd heard stories of some of the things some servers did with food and beverages before bringing them to patrons they disliked.

I put the mug to one side, the wine untasted.

"So," said Risa, "Why are you here with me scoping the scenery instead of . . . uh . . . dancing with my gorgeous brother?"

"Mm." This was why I had been a little reluctant to participate in this outing. "Risa, about Erin, there's really nothing there. I mean, he's very nice but . . ."

"He's a pompous ass, aye, I know."

I felt my eyebrows rise and tried to control that. Not exactly what I'd been planning to say. It was true though.

She chuckled. "I know, I know," she said. "I love him, and really, he's a good man where it counts. But he's just got this way about him that makes you want to hurt him. That he knows everything that's worth knowing. And aye, it's aggravating. But I thought, of all the women I know, you could handle him. Your aren't easily ruffled."

I was glad someone thought so.

"Erin is kind of thinking the same way you are," Risa continued.

What, he thought I thought I knew everything? I didn't act like that. Did I?

"You know, that you were nice, but he didn't think there was anything there between you."

Well, that was a relief. Obsessive admirers were overrated.

"He really admires how you think, though. Erin, I mean."

"Does he?" He could have fooled me.

"He says it's very interesting."

Ah. "Interesting." Not to be confused with "good."

"He says it's like you see patterns in ideas or events that the . . . average person doesn't see."

I wondered what word she had been about to use before so hastily substituting "average."

Risa leaned over the small table between us. "I'm telling you this because I know you're worried about

Karish," she said in a hushed voice, "but it goes no further, all right?"

I frowned at her. "We're in a bar."

"Aye, and everyone's too drunk and too noisy to be overhearing anyone else."

I thought that was an optimistic estimate, but it wasn't my secret.

"Erin was telling me about those clubs you were talking about. The gentlemen's club and the ladies' society with the same name. The Raiborn Societies. So I decided to look into it."

Look into what? Maybe it was a little unusual but it couldn't be criminal to have two clubs with the same name. "Aren't you kind of busy right now?"

She shrugged. "Almost every Runner in the city is looking for the aristocrats, with no hope of finding any of them alive. I think we can spare a few hours of my time hunting up a different mystery."

Here was to hoping I never went missing in High Scape. "So what did you find?"

"Turns out the mysteries aren't so disconnected after all." She smirked in triumph. "Every single one of the victims were members of either the Raiborn Gentlemen's Club or the Raiborn Ladies' Society."

Good Zaire. "Why wasn't that discovered before?"

Risa drew back a little. "Half a dozen reasons," she said stiffly. "The clubs are less than a year old. Both of them. Most of us have never heard of them. And none of the victims belonged to any of the established clubs. They're all minor aristocrats, many I've never heard of before, and no one really paid attention to them before they went missing. Why would I, for example, hear the name Lord Thom Derring and think oh! he belongs to that baby new Raiborn club that has nothing to do with the life of any person I know?"

Yes, yes, that all made sense. Sort of. But I would have

thought investigating all their associations would have been standard procedure. Then again, I wasn't a Runner. What did I know?

"Erin told me one of them tried to pick Karish up in the street. Is that true?"

"Aye."

Risa frowned. "It makes no sense for them to ask him to join. He's been totally cast out of the class."

I didn't know that *cast out* was the right way of putting it. He stepped out, of his own initiative. "Maybe it's the blood that's important to these people, not the title or the class."

And Zaire, did that strike a chord. Hard.

"What?" Risa asked.

Which meant my shock had shown up on my face. Damn it. "A Reanist approached me on the street and asked me to bring Karish to them." It was hard not to snarl. Of all the nerve.

Risa nearly choked on her ale. "To be sacrificed?" she demanded.

"Apparently."

"How stupid did he think you were?"

"She tried to persuade me it was my duty, as a Shield." I had to wonder, though, if she had really expected me to agree with her and comply with her demands. No matter how deluded she was, she had to know I thought differently. "She said that my first priority as a Shield should be stopping the disasters altogether, eliminating them before they start I guess, even if that meant handing Karish over and dying myself. I said what you said. That Karish wasn't a lord anymore, was never going to be a lord. She said it didn't matter. It was the blood that counted."

"Alarming parallel," said Risa.

But not one that piqued her interest, I saw. "There's no chance that the Reanists are behind this?"

Risa shrugged again and popped a syrup nut into her mouth. "We looked into it, of course. Standard procedure whenever an aristocrat is murdered or goes missing. But Reanists really don't do as much as people believe they do. It's too hard for them to find a foothold anywhere. Usually, if you're going to plan a murder, you need a place to plan from."

"I've seen Reanists about High Scape. They must be living somewhere."

"In tents. For as long as the owner of the land doesn't know they're there. Then they get kicked off and have to move on." Risa crunched into another syrup nut, then she grimaced, as though its taste were off. "Maybe some desperate or indifferent innkeeper is going to let them rent a room," she continued after swallowing quickly, "if he doesn't fear they'll drive out his other customers. But even in that case, that's not enough room to keep a victim for this long without being discovered."

"You're assuming the victims are being kept instead of killed."

"Well, we haven't been finding any bodies anywhere. That's not necessarily conclusive, but getting rid of a body without being seen and without it, you know, popping up somewhere unexpected, is harder than you might think. To get rid of a series of bodies without being caught requires access to something. A pig farm. Or land to bury them. Or familiar use of the rivers. Which, again, pretty much eliminates the Reanists."

I really, really didn't need lessons on the safe and effective disposal of human bodies. Thanks.

"And before you even get to that, there's the sacrifice itself. They don't just grab their victims and stake them, you know. There's a ritual to it, and the ritual takes space."

"Oh." I'd never thought of that. I'd never really thought of Reanists much at all. I'd studied them in history, at the academy, but that had been about who they were, where they had come from, what they had done, what had happened to them, and a superficial explanation about their beliefs. Like a lot of things I studied, had never expected to come face to face with them. I'd only started worrying about them when my High Landed Source went missing the year before. But I should have figured that a bunch of religious fanatics wouldn't kill their victims with nothing more than the stake through the heart. If they used a stake. That would be really hard. "Do they really stake people?"

"Aye. I think they think metal perverts the body, or something like that."

"But that would be easy to fight off, I think." I was trying to visualize it. Unless the victim were asleep or drugged, or tied down, it would be hard to force a stake into the right place in order for it to kill. Though, no matter how it was done, it had to hurt like hell. What a way to go.

"I guess that's what the ritual is for."

"So what's the ritual? Do you know it?" And did I really want to hear about it? It was bound to be gruesome.

"I've never seen one, but they do tell us about it. So we can recognize it if we come across it." I found myself wondering about the kinds of things Risa had to know about, had to see. Wouldn't want her job. "For one thing," she said, "the space has to be properly laid out." Seeing that I had no intention of drinking my wine, Risa dipped her finger in and drew a square on the table. "There are four points to it, representing the four directions, and the points are supposed to be marked with the four elements."

"The earth, water, fire and air thing?"

"It makes sense, doesn't it? They're trying to control the world, so the ritual area should represent the elements."

"Huh." Didn't seem terribly original to me.

"Now, ideally—from their point of view—there should be enough victims to form a circle within the area, all facing inward." She drew a circle within the square. "The master of the ritual is supposed to be part of the circle, seated at the northern point, which is represented by fire. The master is the Reanist who called the victims to the circle. The other Reanists are to circle around, outside the circle of the victims but still within the sacrificial area."

"All right." Already seemed too complicated.

"Now, it is important that the victims embrace their roles—"

I had to interrupt there. "Embrace being sacrificed?"

"Hey, I didn't make up the rules. I'm just telling you what I've read. And that's what they say. The victims have to be happy to be there."

"What, do they raid an insane asylum?"

Risa just gave me a look and went on. "The victims get a final meal. Has to be meat of the mountain mammal—"

"Meat of the what?"

She shrugged. "Wine of the new moon."

"What's that mean?"

"No idea. And essence of bee and bovine."

"Sounds vile."

"Apparently the gods would be most offended to have unfed victims. They must be well fed, well groomed, superior in mind and body and talent."

"Ah. The whole aristocratic myth." Because, of course, it was a myth. I'd met aristocrats who hadn't been near a bath in months, and had no talent to speak of.

"Apparently so."

"But then, wouldn't they refuse to eat, if they knew that would keep them from being sacrificed?"

"Maybe they don't know. Or maybe they starve them first."

Which took us back to the theory of the Reanists needing a place to keep their victims for a while. Especially if they were collecting them in order to make this circle of theirs. "Still, a meal for a starving person isn't going to make them embrace being sacrificed."

"I don't know. Hunger can make people do strange things."

Well, for one thing, I remembered, it made them very lethargic. Maybe it made them susceptible to suggestion. But they would have to be awfully susceptible to welcome being sacrificed.

"The kicker though, and the reason why we think the Reanists aren't involved in these disappearances, is that the area must be encased in stone. Apparently the Reanists believe there's some kind of invisible airy substance that leaks from the body as it dies, and it just floats away into the sky. Only stone can contain it, and it must be contained in order for the gods to be able to collect it. That's what they really want, the airy stuff. Not the bodies."

So then why was it important for the bodies to be well fed and well groomed? Did they think the state of the body affected the quality of the airy stuff? I'd wager the Reanists came up with that for more practical reasons. Who wanted to be around the unwashed?

Try to focus, Lee. "So this isn't a set up they can throw together in an hour and roll up again when it's time to leave."

"And Reanists can't own property. Not in High Scape, anyway. They can't build something like that here." Risa frowned at her sketch. "Still, maybe I should look into any new construction going on in the city. Just in case."

"Wouldn't hurt. Wouldn't be the first time someone's found a way around a law." Oh, listen to me, the world-weary, experienced one. But hey, I'd read books.

Risa snickered. "Ain't that the truth?" Then she sighed. "It's a horrible time for Crown Prince Gifford to be coming to High Scape. Why in the world doesn't he cancel?"

I raised one finger. "He said he would come." A second finger. "He wants to show his interest in the most valuable city in the world when it's going through hard times." A third finger. "He's not about to be run off by a bunch of cowardly murderers. Or kidnappers."

She scowled. "Aye, aye, aristocratic pride, damn it all to hell. Funny how it never kicks in when someone asks them to work or do anything else useful. But that damned party. Half the aristocrats in the city will be there."

"So will a whole legion of extra security," I reminded

her. "This is Lord Yellows, remember. The richest man in High Scape. With the Crown Prince as the guest of honor. No one's going to be able to breathe without at least three other people knowing about it."

"I can't be too sure about that," Risa muttered. "The Captain offered to have Runners on the property. His Lordship, apparently, was most offended." The last two words were spoken with an attempt at an aristocratic air. "Gave the Captain quite a dressing down. Reminded him that his family had been providing protection for people on his lands for longer than the Runners have been in existence. Was the Captain daring to presume the people carefully chosen and trained by his Lordship were unable to perform their single purpose? Was the Captain daring to suggest his Lordship would be so treasonous as to endanger the life of the Crown Prince? Perhaps the Captain would be better off concentrating his attention on his own duties and solving the problems that were plaguing the Runners instead of interfering in the business of others." She scrubbed at the wine sketch, as though attempting to mop it up. "The Captain was fuming. And so much fun to work with for the rest of the day. I hate stupid people."

I grinned at her. And yes, I was unsympathetic. It was nice to know others were experiencing professional frustrations. Aye, aye, I was petty.

"But we're going to have Runners around the property," said Risa with satisfaction. "At some places we'll have the house in view. And if one of us accidentally wanders onto the grounds, well, horses can be difficult to control."

"Isn't that trespassing?" I asked the solicitor's sister.

"Bah! Don't bother me with trifles."

I chuckled.

The server returned with a drink for Risa. A tall thick glass filled with dark, dark liquid, topped with a creamy beige froth. Risa glared at the server as she set it on the table. "Were you brewing it back there or what?" she demanded.

The server was unapologetic. "Did you want it properly

pulled or what?" And she slipped away before Risa could respond.

I looked at the exotic beverage. "What is it?" I asked.

"It's beer."

I took a closer look. "It doesn't look like any beer I've ever seen."

"That's because it's a new brew. It's called Roofer's Black. Not many people have heard of it. Plus it's—" She cut herself off and took a reverent sip, giving herself a beige moustache. "Mmmmmm."

"Plus it's expensive," I finished for her.

She shot me a hard look and took another long sip.

"So you got that promotion, then?"

She set the glass on the table with a thud that rang of irritation. "No," she snapped. "Anand did. A very worthy Runner."

"I see," I said, and I swore not a hint of disapproval showed up in either my expression or my voice, but Risa found a reason to get angry anyway.

"Shove off, Dunleavy." A third deep gulp from the glass, with an air of defiance.

"I didn't say anything."

"You didn't have to. I know what you're thinking."

"If you know what I'm thinking there's no reason to talk about it." I didn't want to get into an argument over Risa's spending habits.

"Oh, so you think you should be able to sit there in silence and judge me and I should just shut up about it, is that it?"

I sighed. "Are you spoiling for a fight or something?"

"You haven't got a bloody clue," was her heated response. "You have no idea what it's like to want things and know you can't afford to have them. Ever I mean, look at this." She raised her glass. "It's just beer. It happens to be good beer. Why should I have to settle for the watery swill most places serve? Why shouldn't I be able to drink the beer I like? Or wear the clothes I want? Or live where I want to live?"

She'd said all this before, and I sympathized with her. Really. But my sympathy wouldn't keep her out of debtor's prison. "I didn't make the rules, Risa, and I'm not saying they're right or fair. But we still have to live by them."

"*We?*" she echoed incredulously. "*We* don't have to live by them. *I* do. You don't." That was uncomfortably true. "It's all right for you to tut-tut my spending habits while you're dining on beef every night. Try earning your pay for a while."

She didn't mean that the way it sounded. At least, she'd better not. I earned what I had, just not the way most others did.

Noise exploded into my ears, so loud and so sudden I gasped and jerked in my seat, bumping into the table and knocking over the mugs. When I came back down I grabbed the edge of the table and tried to stop my brain from spinning long enough to figure out what the hell had happened.

Drums. Gods be damned evil drums. With pipes. What, was someone marching off to a war somewhere? And if so, could they stop calling to arms and just get moving to wherever they were going? Who played music like that in a tavern? Any moron barkeeper who played such music deserved to have his furniture torn apart.

All right. Had to get out of there. I jumped to my feet again, urged on by the music. I somehow managed to trip over my own chair. I fell against a body.

The body pushed back and I almost lost my footing completely. "Watch where you're going, bitch!"

The music poured through my veins. Without thinking at all I struck out. "Get out of my way!"

Heat exploded along the side of my mouth. I charged, reached out.

I was grabbed from behind, jerked back sharply. Someone was screaming into my ear. I screamed back, with no idea what I was saying. I scrambled against my restraints, scratched at them to no effect.

I screamed again, in outrage, as I was lifted off my feet.
I felt air moving, a curious swooping sensation. I kicked
out, trying to find some footing, and I couldn't. Nothing I
could grab onto would stay still.

One more swoop and then a hard, unpleasant impact.
Solidity against the palms of my hands, my cheek, torso,
the front of my legs. But the world had stopped moving.
That was an improvement.

The din in my head and ears calmed. Just a little, but
enough that I could think. Kind of.

"Dunleavy."

I was lying down. That's it. Lying down. On the street.
No, the sidewalk. The wood was hard and rough and dirty
against my cheek. Didn't smell too wonderful, either. But it
wasn't yet in me to move.

"Dunleavy."

I closed my eyes, trying to think a bit beyond the obvious. *Hey, you*! I thought at a random note. *Stop moving.*

All right, that was weird.

"Dunleavy!"

I supposed I should respond. It was annoying, after all,
to hear one's name incessantly repeated. "Aye."

"What happened?" Risa demanded.

"Hope you don't want details." Because I couldn't give
them. I really had no idea.

"Was that a Shield going berserk?"

Oh. That. I pressed my palms against the sidewalk and
carefully pushed myself into a sitting position. "It was indeed." I could still feel it, the music, in my head, a little,
though my ears told me the actual music being played
within the tavern had changed into something slower, more
soothing.

"I've never seen anything like that before."

"So happy to contribute to your education." I felt it was
safe to open my eyes. I was indeed sitting on the sidewalk.
People walked by and gave me confused looks.

"Now, now, don't get snarky." Risa crouched down

beside me, took my chin in her hand, and gently touched a thumb to the side of my mouth.

I felt a brief flare of slight discomfort, but nothing too bad. "So what did you see happening?" I asked. I didn't want to hear the specifics of my making a fool of myself, but I had to know in case I had to explain myself to someone. Someone like my mother. Or Karish. Or a Runner. Who wasn't Risa.

She released me and sat back on her heels. "You jumped up from the table and fell into the guy seated next to us. He jumped up and shoved you away. You hit him—a nice solid blow, by the way—and he hit back. So I hauled us out of there."

"You picked me up?" How demeaning. She wouldn't have been able to do that if I were possessed of a few more inches. And how it must have looked, me being lifted right off my feet and carried out like a child in a tantrum.

"It was the only way I could get you to move," she said defensively.

I hadn't been accusing her of anything. I noticed for the first time the scrapes and shallow cuts on Risa's hands and wrists. "I didn't do that, did I?" I asked with dread. Turned into a right obnoxious animal, hadn't I?

She glanced at her hands and grinned. "Aye. You're a vicious little thing, aren't you?"

"Sorry." I felt my face flush. Why was it that every time I got violent, which was far too frequently, I ended up attacking one of my friends? Was there something going on deep in the back of my brain that I really didn't want to know about? "Did I do any real damage in there?"

"No, but the barkeep said he was barring you. He can't do that, can he?"

Huh. I'd never been rowdy enough to be barred before. "Not usually, but if a Shield creates a serious disturbance they'll probably make an exception."

"They did it on purpose, though," said Risa. "They were

trying to drive you out with that music. I'm sure of it. I saw
the barkeep talking to the musicians, and they looked right
at you. I thought he was telling them to keep it down, or I
would have said something, but obviously not."

Yes, that was the impression I got, too. That kind of music, no one played it in a tavern. It was practically marching music. I climbed to my feet, brushing off my trousers.
"He has the right to play what music he wants." That was
true, too. "It could be said that I shouldn't have even been
there without my Source."

Risa straighten up from her crouch. "I'd like to see Karish do any better than I did," she objected.

"No, he couldn't have." Probably. I don't know that he
would have been able to carry me out as Risa had. On the
other hand, he might have been able to talk me into a
calmer state and allowed me the dignity of leaving under
my own power. But none of that was really relevant. "And
thank you for acting so quickly." Before I'd done something worse. As it was, I couldn't believe I'd actually struck
a complete stranger. I couldn't even recall what he looked
like. I could meet him again in under an hour and would
have no idea I'd assaulted him.

Damn it. News of that was sure to spread, an unattended
Shield going berserk and attacking another patron. This
was going to do wonders for our relationship with the regulars, it was.

I sighed and brushed dirt off my hands. "I'm not in the
most festive of moods right now," I told Risa. I was disgusted with myself. "But there's no reason for me to ruin
the rest of your evening. I'm going to head home." How pathetic. "Sorry things turned out this way."

"You want me to take you to one of the hospitals?"

"Oh, no." There was no reason for that. All I felt was a
warm tingling about my mouth, no real pain. Besides, the
healer would expect me to tell her what had happened,
which would be just too embarrassing. It was going to be

bad enough explaining myself to people I knew. I wasn't going to add complete strangers to the list.

But Risa was getting that stubborn, immovable-object look about her. "You're bleeding a lot."

I frowned and put careful fingertips to the side of my mouth. They came away bright red. I shrugged. "It doesn't really hurt."

She snorted with exasperation. "So says the Shield. Not exactly reassuring."

Pleased to meet you. I'm the unstoppable force. "I am not going to the hospital, Risa." She would have to carry me. Which, granted, she could do. Probably without breaking a sweat. But I was hoping she would allow me to retain some shred of decorum that evening.

"Fine, but I'm walking you home."

"That's not necessary." Zaire, I already had Karish insisting on squiring me about. It was aggravating. I was fully capable of putting one foot in front of the other, thank you very much.

It was because I was small. They assumed I was helpless. So what if they were actually right, that if stuck in a physical confrontation I would come out the undisputed loser? Did that mean I had to be dogged every step of my life?

"I think it is, Dunleavy," Risa said bluntly. "There's a problem here. The way the servers in there were treating you was scandalous. And so was deliberately driving you out. We've been getting complaints about this sort of thing from all the other Pairs, though to be honest I didn't think it was anything serious. I thought they were just whining because people were a little too distracted with all that's been going on to give them the fast and eager service you Pairs are used to getting."

Ouch.

La Monte getting a brick thrown at his head was whining?

"Because, you know, we hadn't heard anything from you and Karish."

And because of that they decided nothing was really going on? How oddly flattering.

"But I've seen it for myself, and I know it's real. And your braid isn't going to protect you from any harassment right now. In fact, the way things are right now, that braid is an invitation to trouble, not a source of protection." She pursed her lips, lightly touching the braid on my left shoulder. "I don't suppose you could leave off wearing it for a while?"

I was shocked. "You think things are that bad?"

Risa shrugged. "Everyone's acting so strange, Dunleavy," she admitted. "Not just farmers and fishers and people most affected by the weather. Everyone. It's like everyone is getting . . ." she hesitated, looking for a word, "antsy or something. We've been getting a lot more calls. And not for thieving, which I'd kind of suspect. Violence. A lot of assaults. Brawls. Domestic disputes. Not murders, yet, but I think it might be heading that way."

"Good lord." I'd had no idea. Sure, I'd noticed some people were getting irritable. It was perfectly understandable under the circumstances. But I hadn't known the condition was near universal. What was going on?

Well, there were a few things going on. Aristocrats were disappearing. The weather was going crazy and so were the regulars. And High Scape wasn't experiencing any natural events. But none of those things were connected to each other.

Were they?

"So I'm walking you home. No more arguments, all right? I have to go to headquarters and report this, anyway."

"Must you?" Lovely. The whole lot of them, all the Runners at her headquarters, would get to hear in gory detail how I completely lost my head. Wilson, Risa's partner, would love it.

"Yes, I must."

Great. Now she was imitating my diction.

"Let's go."

"Yes, ma'am."

And I found myself childishly relieved to have the company after all. The incident at the tavern was the first time the Triple S anti-sentiment had been directed at me. Like Risa, I'd been too ready to dismiss it all as a minor inconvenience. Now I'd been convinced otherwise.

Chapter Fifteen

The next day I went to the Stall for my watch with Karish.

Firth and Stone were there, of course. Firth looked up at the door when I came in, and then looked disappointed. I wasn't Karish. Hey, I'd be disappointed, too. I supposed it was one of the few times I'd arrived at the Stall before Karish, and now Firth wouldn't get her daily dose of tormenting him. I didn't know how he stood it with such good grace.

"Good afternoon, young one," Stone greeted me, her tone mild. "Have a habit of walking into doors, do you?"

"I got in a fight."

I would have thought it impossible to shock to such . . . uh . . . seasoned women. "You what?" Firth demanded.

"I was in a bar. The barkeep objected to my being there. He had the musicians play some volatile music." I shrugged, trying not to look as embarrassed as I felt. "I got into a fight."

They looked, if possible, even more shocked.

Stone snapped her mouth shut. "Are you saying they deliberately played music to rile you?"

"That's what it seemed like. And I've been banned."

Stone looked grim. "Which place is this?" she demanded. "This will be addressed."

Did it have to be? It was only one little incident. "I was there with a Runner. She said she'd report it."

"And did she?"

"I assume she did. No reason why she wouldn't."

"Is she going to have his license suspended?"

"You think a person should lose his livelihood over something like this?" That was, I thought, a little harsh. Especially as no damage had actually been done.

"He didn't just order you out, Mallorough," Stone said, looking unusually serious. "He used music to force you out. Even the regulars know how unpredictable we can be under the influence of music. You could have been seriously hurt. You could have hurt someone else. It was dangerous."

Still, it seemed to me he shouldn't have to lose his license over it.

"At least give us the name of this place," said Firth. "So we don't go there, and we tell everyone we know not to go there."

That, I could agree with. "The Red Onion."

"Oh," she said. "I'm surprised. I've always loved the service there. And they always have great musicians."

"Great musicians have an expanded repertoire," said Stone. "All the easier to choose something appropriate to make a Shield go berserk."

And I did go berserk. Completely lost control.

"We'll be sure to tell all the others," Firth promised me. "And everyone else we know, too. In a week Mel Opp will find himself working in an empty bar."

I wasn't too sure about that. There were no doubt many who sympathized with the barkeep and all the other business people who were forced to hand over their goods and labor to people who apparently did nothing in return.

Karish arrived for his watch. I wondered if he would be as disappointed as Firth by my uncharacteristically early appearance. Maybe he and Firth had some kind of weird tormenting game going on that I was interfering with.

He was surprised to see me there. And of course he saw the bruise, I could tell by the narrowing of his gaze. But after a moment's hesitation he merely smiled. "Good afternoon, ladies," he said. "Lee, are you skating?"

Firth snickered.

"No." When in doubt, take the words at face value and answer accordingly.

"Well, someone must be." He moved to the stove and checked the embers. "There are buskers on East Cooper Street, Claire."

Firth's eyes lit up. "Really?"

"Jugglers and drummers. Likely looking lads from the Southern Islands."

That sparked my interest. The Southern Islands. I'd read about them in the Academy, but there hadn't been much to read. The Southern Islands had only recently opened up trade with the mainland and little was known about them. People had been living there since the Landing, but they had been separate from us, and from all accounts had developed differently from us. Apparently they didn't have Sources or Shields, neither born there, nor posted. The Southerners just grit their teeth and bore with it.

I'd never met anyone from the Southern Islands. I wished I had known about the buskers. I would have liked to have watched them for awhile, maybe even spoken to one, rather than coming to the Stall early.

Firth's smile, though, quickly skidded into a scowl. "Is that really true?" she asked Karish. "Or are you just saying that to get rid of us faster?"

"A little bit of both," he admitted. But his smile took away the sting, and pretty men were granted leeway the rest of us were not. "They really are there, but they have been there for a while. They may be moving on soon." He reached for the coffee canister.

Karish didn't drink coffee.

"So we should move it, aye?" Stone commented wryly, packing up her papers. "Or Firth should. I'm not going to risk drums."

"Oh, bosh, Dee," said Firth. "I'll keep an eye on you. Besides, you're not as bad as Dunleavy."

"No one's as bad as Mallorough."

Yes, yes, we all knew it. Of all the Shields on the planet I was the weakest when it came to resisting music. I bore evidence of it on my face. Now please go away.

The older Pair left with only a little more teasing. And as soon as the door closed behind them Karish was on me, tilting up my face to get a better look. "What the hell happened?"

So I told him, using the blandest, least emotive language I could think of and knowing it would do no good.

Karish swore. "I'll kill him," he fumed. "I will. We're going back there, Lee, and you're going to point him out."

Aye, and Karish would be snapped like a twig. Or maybe not. I'd never seen Karish fight. Maybe he was good at it. But he looked kind of fragile. "Don't be ridiculous, Karish."

"Look at your face, Lee!"

"Not unless I have to."

He was not pleased by my witticism. "This is no joking matter."

Actually, it probably had been funny to watch, me stumbling around like an idiot. "And getting melodramatic about it will help, how?"

"I'm not being melodramatic." The kettle started whistling. He poured the water into the coffee. "You were assaulted last night."

"I did the assaulting."

"I meant the music."

Oh. An odd way of looking at it, but that was a Source for you. "It's done now."

"It won't be done until that bruise is gone and that cretin is punished."

I sighed. "You've got to learn to let things slide, Taro."

"You let too much slide. Something has to be done about this."

"Something is being done. Risa is reporting it. Firth and Stone are going to do their best to make sure no one ever walks into the Red Onion ever again. So leave it. It's over."

He pulled a mug out from the jumble on a shelf and blew the dust out of it. "Does it hurt?"

"Not really."

"Huh." He poured out the coffee. I watched him with curiosity. My Source had once loftily declared coffee the merchant class' joke on the world, for look at it. Liquefied mud, and people were willing to pay for it. What had made him decide to drink it?

Oh, lord, the effects of coffee on a person who'd never had it before. This was going to be fun.

Only he set it on the table before me.

That set off the bells. What did he want and how much was I going to hate giving it?

He sat in the chair opposite mine, pulling it close under the table. As was his wont when he wasn't thinking about it, he sat ramrod straight, his spine nowhere near the back of the chair.

I took a sip of my coffee and grimaced.

"Did I not make it right?"

It was actually quite awful. Far too strong. "What's this about, anyway?" I hefted the mug.

Karish assumed an expression of offence. "What, I can't do something nice once in a while?"

"You frequently do nice things, but something about this rings of buttering up."

He grinned ruefully. "You know that party Lord Yellows is having for Prince Gifford?"

"Aye."

"And you know I've been invited."

"Aye." Not so cut off from his aristocratic circle after all.

"And you know I can't refuse an invitation commanded in the name of the Prince."

"Aye." Sucker.

Karish's grin turned feral. "I hope you've ordered something appropriate to wear."

I set my mug on the table with a bang, eyes growing wide with alarm. "No!"

"You have to go, Lee."

"I do not!"

"It's your duty."

"In what alternate reality?"

He assumed that air of patience that always made me crazy. "You're my partner."

"Your Triple S partner. Not your social one. Take one of your lovers."

"*One* of my lovers? What, do you think I keep a stable?"

"Take Michael. He'd love it." All the high fashion and good food, Michael would think himself in the best dream.

Karish appeared scandalized. "I'm not sleeping with Michael."

Oh. Not that either of them had ever said they were lovers. I'd just assumed it from their interactions. They were all over each other every time they met, and Karish never called Michael anything but "Michael, my love." Could anyone blame me? "One of the others, then."

"This is fascinating. Who do you recommend? Who else do you think I'm sleeping with?"

The little edge snapping off each of his words warned me to clear off. Karish had always been touchy when it came to talking about his lovers. Which was fine. It was none of my business. "The point is, I'm not going. The place will be crawling with aristocrats."

"Including Her Grace."

"Just another reason to refuse to go."

"An option I don't have."

I glared at him. He learned too fast, that one, and was nowhere near above manipulating people to get what he wanted. "You bastard."

He grinned, knowing he had won. "You can't wear the

gown you wore in Erstwhile, lovely though it was," he said, speaking of the dress I had worn to meet the Empress the previous year. "That's a winter gown."

"I hate you."

"You've left it very late. My fault, actually. I'd originally planned on going alone, else I would have given you more notice. But you'll be able to get a gown in time if you put enough pressure on the tailor and get your name put at the top of the list."

"I really hate you."

"Do you want to practise some small talk?"

"There's a special place for you in hell, you know."

He blew a kiss at me. "You know you think I'm adorable."

Aye. He knew it, too. That's what made him so dangerous. The prat.

But I would have my revenge. "Ready to experiment?"

He groaned. "We're not getting anywhere with that."

"We don't stop working on this until it's fixed. That's the deal."

"What if it doesn't get fixed?"

"But Taro," I widened my eyes at him, "you promised me it would."

"Do you *have* to remember every single thing I say?"

"The sterling words of the beautiful Lord Shintaro Karish."

"Please shut up."

"I will when you do."

I couldn't be sure, and I certainly wasn't going to admit it to anyone, but I suspected I was the cause of the blizzard that hit us that night.

Chapter Sixteen

I arrived at the Lion by order of my mother. Not the first time that had happened, but something about the note, the stiff formality of it, gave me an uneasy feeling. I really didn't want another Erin incident. I had told my mother there was no possibility of anything happening with Erin, but she hadn't shown any inclination to listen to me so far.

He didn't appear to be in the private dining room, but that didn't mean anything. He could be coming by later, as he had before.

"Oh, Lee," my mother said in deep disapproval. She was seated in the settee, sipping a sherry.

I shrugged. "It started raining on the way over." So I was soaked. If Erin was on his way over, he wouldn't be getting "something pretty to look at" that night.

He wouldn't have anyway. Some little demon had prompted me to wear loose brown trousers and a brown shirt, both of which I loved to wear for the sheer comfort of them. I did recognize, however, that they looked hideous and were too big for me.

My mother's gaze flicked over my clothes, but she made no comment. Maybe she was finally learning.

She sent Celia away for towels and a robe and I stood near the door and watched my mother fiddle with the flatware on the table and avoid looking at me.

I decided to just dive in. "Are there going to be any surprise guests tonight, Mother?"

She stopped fiddling long enough to look at me. "If there are, it's not due to my arrangement."

The maid returned. I took a towel from her. "Is something wrong?" What had I done this time?

"You should get out of those wet clothes, Dunleavy," she said.

She'd called me Dunleavy.

I took off my wet clothes and gave them to the maid, quickly drying off and donning the robe.

"So how was your day, dear?"

About to get bad, I had no doubt. "It was all right." I wrapped my head in one of the towels. "Karish expects me to accompany him to that party thing Lord Yellows is holding for Prince Gifford."

"Of course he does."

There was no of course about it. "I have to get my hands on some kind of ball gown. I'm relying on you to help me choose something." That should make her smile, a chance to order clothes for me.

But she didn't smile, or demonstrate any other symptom of enthusiasm. She sat down at the table. "I won't be able to help you, Lee. I'm going back to Seventh Year. I'll be leaving the day after tomorrow."

I frowned and fought the urge to ask her to repeat herself. I'd heard her the first time. "You just got here. I thought you were staying a few months."

Mother fiddled with her fingers, examining the paint on her nails. "You know I love you, Lee, don't you?"

This definitely bad. "Aye."

"And I know you love us."

"Good." I waited. "But . . ."

My mother took a deep breath of her own. "I don't know exactly how to say this, so I'll just say it."

Really, really bad.

"Do you remember when you left for the Academy?"

"No." She knew that.

"You were four."

"Yes."

"You were four. And we packed you up and took you to the Academy. You understood that you would be living there from then on. That you wouldn't be seeing us for a long time." She finally looked up from her fingers, looked at me, and I was surprised to see tears filming her eyes. "You didn't seem upset."

I had no idea how to respond to that. What did it have to do with anything?

"You didn't cry. You didn't cling. You put on your best company manners and politely said good-bye."

Should I be resenting the fact that my mother apparently wished to see me in emotional distress?

"The Head Mistress assured us this was perfectly normal. Shield children don't feel things, express things, as other children do. It didn't mean you didn't love us. We shouldn't take it personally. But it was hard not to. It was hard."

There was no point in becoming angry, but I was. I couldn't help what I did or didn't feel as a child. I didn't even remember.

"Then next time I saw you, it was about two years later. You were only six. But you were so reserved. So well-mannered and . . . distant. You were happy to see us, of course, but not . . . I don't know . . . not as excited as I would have expected a child to be on meeting her family for the first time in years."

That was so unfair. "We are taught . . ."

"Yes, I know," my mother interrupted me with a tone of impatience. "The Head Mistress explained it all to us. It is essential that you learn to keep yourself under control. It is an essential part of your role. It is a threat to yourself and your Source and to everyone you will eventually be protecting, to let your emotions run free. Except no one could tell me why, exactly. Why it was so important for Shields to be so restrained, any more than any other professionals should be while performing their tasks. Or why, if you're naturally less emotional than the average person, it would be so dangerous to let you display what you did feel."

Because that wasn't quite right. It wasn't like the sky would fall if I let it out when I got angry or scared or anything else. It was merely that it was my job to stay calm while I was working, to counteract the impact of a Source who wasn't expected to be calm, ever. It was a matter of balance.

"I understand that it was important for you to learn to be calm and in control," said my mother. "But can you understand how hard it is to have your own child treat you like a mere acquaintance?"

Obviously I could not, being as I was all child-free.

"But it wasn't just that."

There was more? Oh, joy.

"The rules, the values you were being taught, they were so different from what we would have had you learn. Not bad," she said hurriedly, seeing something in my face. Seeing more than I could interpret myself. Because to be honest, I didn't know what the hell I was feeling. "Just different, and nothing of what we would teach. About bartering. About trading. About sizing up your opponents. About how to make a customer feel he's better than you so he doesn't notice how much you're overcharging him. But no one was better than you. Or below you. Because you were outside such considerations."

I frowned, because now I was intellectually confused as well as emotionally. "I wasn't ever going to be a holder or a—"

"That's not the point!" my mother snapped. Then she

sighed, closed her eyes, and rubbed her temples for a few moments. "I knew you were never going to be a holder or a trader. I knew that as soon as I realized what you were." And there was a bitterness in my mother's voice. "I'm not claiming that what I felt made sense. But here was my daughter, my little girl, being taught to believe in things that I would never understand."

But she had three other children who would be learning exactly what she wanted them to know. Kaaren was a holder, Dias and Mika were traders. She had exactly what she wanted in them. The family assets were well looked after. What was wrong with having one child who did something different?

Mother took a sip from her goblet. "From the day we left you at that school," and she said the words—that school—as though they tasted badly on her tongue, "you didn't need us."

And I made no response to that—not that she appeared to be waiting for one—because it was kind of true. I guessed.

"Someone else was teaching you what you needed to know, taking care of you, disciplining you—"

"Kaaren and Mika and Dias all went to Whitewood," I reminded her. Everyone who could afford it sent their children to board away. It was considered normal and healthy not to have children becoming too dependent on their parents. It was the way of things.

"I've already told you it isn't the same," she said sharply. "We got to see them for months out of every year. They knew us, knew what we expected. You treated us like strangers."

I took a sip of wine. This was just all so irrational and so damned unfair. There was nothing I could say. It wasn't like I'd had any control over it. I hadn't made any of the decisions. She was blaming me for things I wasn't responsible for.

"Kaaren and the boys, they need me," my mother went on. "They come to me, they ask me for advice about their

work, and how to smooth over disturbances with their partners and companions. I can't understand your work, and I
know I would be the last person who should advise you
about any aspect about it. But don't you understand? That's
what makes it so hard. It's like you're living in a different
world than the rest of us, with these strange rules and rituals and objectives that I can never be a part of."

Aye, Mother, that's what being a Shield is about. We
don't have a choice in the matter. We have to do a job that
no one else can. But there are no strange rituals involved,
no howling at the moon, no secret handshake. Our objectives are pretty obvious. Keep the planet from being torn
apart. And if you don't like how we're trained you'll have
to take it up with the Triple S council.

"There's nothing I can teach you, Lee. About anything.
You don't care about any of the things I consider important."

"Like clothes," I asked her.

I saw her clench her teeth. "One's clothes reflect one's
character."

Bilge. If that were true, there'd be no such thing as fashion. People would just wear whatever the hell they wanted.
I liked nice clothing well enough, but I didn't care to spend
the time to get it. What did that say about me except that I
didn't care to spend time on clothes? And I'd seen Karish
look the part of a useless mindless lordling. It didn't mean
he was one.

"You seem to resent any input I try to have in your life—"

"Like trying to arrange something between me and Erin
Demaris?" Damn straight, I did. "You thought you had the
right to do that?"

She raised her chin. "Yes," she declared. "That is a par-
ent's role."

"Maybe in—"

"Yes!" she interrupted, loud and harsh, so I shut up,
though I didn't like it. "I was wrong to do so. But that
makes it worse."

What?

"Trying to bring Erin into your life was a disastrous mistake."

Disastrous might have been overstating the case a little. "He is a fine man, Mother, it was just—"

"I know there is nothing wrong with Erin."

Ah. Then that meant there was something wrong with me. It appeared my mother was not yet finished running down my character.

"But it's because I didn't understand what you have with Taro—"

Now it was my turn to interrupt. "I don't have anything with Taro, mother. Not like that." And yes, my tone was sharp. It was one thing for strangers to think I was sleeping with Karish. They had nothing but rumors to work with, and if they thought someone like Karish would settle for someone like me, it was almost a compliment. And while it irked me that the other Pairs thought I had no discipline, I couldn't really blame them. Karish acted like we were lovers, and I didn't do much to stop him. But for my own mother to think so little of me, to think I would so forget my responsibilities that I would have sex with my own Source, that was disappointing.

"I'm not saying you're lovers, Lee. I know you're not."

Oh. Good.

"But you don't believe that's the only kind of connection you can have with a man, do you?"

"Of course not." I was not an idiot. "There is the bond—"

"I'm not talking about your . . . Pair bond."

Zaire, would the woman please stop interrupting me?

"It's not your Pair bond. It has nothing to do with your Pair bond. Well, maybe it does, but that's not it." Mother stopped, pulled in a breath, and started again. "I'm not claiming to know everything about the Triple S, Lee, but I have met a lot of Pairs in my time. I went out of my way to meet them, after we realized what you were. We wanted to know what you were getting into." She frowned in memory.

"Some of the partners despised each other," she said. "The tension in the air was so strong, it seemed to catch me in the throat. I felt like I couldn't breathe. And I worried about you ending up in a Pair like that. It seemed so unhealthy, almost destructive. But most of the Pairs weren't like that. The partners were just friends, or colleagues. They just went about doing their business, and most of the time you wouldn't know there was any connection at all between them. Just two people who worked together and probably didn't think of each other much when they weren't in each other's presence. Just like regulars."

And we didn't appear that way. That, at least, was something I could explain. "I know we seem more . . . wrapped up in each other than a lot of Pairs, Mother. But that's just because of circumstances. All that mess last year, it forced us into each other's company a lot more than most Pairs require. And I know Taro touches me a lot, but it doesn't mean anything. He just—"

"Of course it means something," she said irritably. "It's his way of making sure people are giving him their attention, and that they don't forget he's there."

For a moment I was startled out of my own irritation. "What?"

She rolled her eyes with impatience. "Think about it, Lee. You've said yourself that he flirts with absolutely everyone, that he's always oozing charm and touching people. Why do you think he acts the way he does? I don't know all the details, but he obviously felt isolated and neglected when he was a child, and he hated it. He needs people to know he's there, to remember he's there. He flirts with people because it's sure to get everyone's attention. He hangs on to a least one person in the room because he can be sure at least one person will remember he's present. It's obvious."

Oh, Zaire. I put my hand over my mouth. She was right. It made perfect sense. It was obvious. And I had missed it. While my mother had picked up on it after only a couple of meetings. I had wondered why she had taken to kissing him and stroking him. It didn't seem at all like her.

I felt sick.

"But it's not that, either, Lee," she said, oblivious to or ignoring my reaction. "You're just different with him than you are with anyone else I've seen. You snipe at each other, you tease each other, and you were ready to go for his mother's throat the other night." She reached across the table, grasped one of my hands and held it in both of hers. "I've seen you with a lot of different people over the years, Lee. And never have I seen you so . . . natural with anyone as you are with Taro. You relax a little. Laugh more freely, express anger more easily."

Really? I was sure he would be shocked to hear it.

"And he adores you. You can see it." I didn't squirm, but I wanted to. She was reading more than was there. "Your opinion means the world to him. And he didn't really start to break down the other night until he felt his mother had slighted you too much. And no, I'm not claiming some grand dramatic love. But there is a real, strong connection there, more than with any other Pair I've seen, and I think . . . I don't think any other relationship is going to be able to compete with that. Your Source will always come first with you. Another man will have to be willing to accept that. I doubt many would be."

Karish and I were not freakishly obsessed with each other. "Most Pairs have relationships outside the bond. Riley is married. And Hammad." And dozens of others I couldn't name right then.

"You're not listening, Lee. I'm not talking about other Pairs. I'm talking about yours. I've seen you and Taro. There's something very strong there. And I never should have thought anyone else could break into that. Especially someone Taro didn't approve of."

"Taro has no right to approve or disapprove." He had nothing to do with it, and I would tell him so if he ever thought to interfere.

"If Taro despised a man you were keeping company with, it wouldn't bother you?"

"I don't pass judgment on *his* lovers."

"That's not what I asked you."

I wasn't going to answer the question. It was a stupid question, and the answer was too complicated. Taro had so far despised every man I'd ever met, or so it seemed. Taro had hated Ian on sight, and there was nothing wrong with him. Sure, he was kind of a prat. He'd been sleeping with his Source and trying to pick up Karish right in front of her. But in many ways he had been much like Karish was himself, so it was illogical for Karish to dislike him. Karish had met Aiden once, a fleeting moment, and had had nothing good to say about him thereafter. And all right, during that fleeting moment Aiden had managed to insult Karish, and yes, Aiden had turned out to be . . . well . . . a would-be murderer. Karish hadn't needed anything but Erin's name—which he still found himself unable to pronounce—to start disparaging the man. And yes, Erin had been . . . annoying. But Karish hadn't known any of that at the relevant times. He had just decided to dislike these men to annoy me. That he had been bizarrely right—no, lucky—was nothing more than a weird coincidence.

And if he hated whatever man I ended up with, it would be hell.

I didn't want to think about it. "What does this have to do with anything?"

"The fact that I didn't see it," said my mother. "Or that I didn't understand it. The fact that I tried to contribute something to your life and not only chose badly, but risked something that was essential to you."

What? Karish? Was that what she meant? How had my bond with him been risked? The bond couldn't be broken. By anything.

"But that's your whole life," she continued. "Your whole

life is something I don't understand, and can't contribute to without causing damage."

"My life is not so fragile, Mother." While I didn't care for her attempts at manipulation, I didn't think I'd actually suffered anything because of it.

"Is it not? Maybe not. I don't know. Maybe your bond to Taro isn't so essential to you. Maybe it's so strong nothing can break it. Or maybe it'll shatter if you look at it too hard. *I don't know.* I don't know when I'm taking the wrong step. I don't know your rules of right or wrong and when I might be offending you." She sighed again, suddenly appearing exhausted. "You don't need me for anything, Lee. Not for guidance. Not as an example. Certainly not as a confidant. You haven't talked about anything more profound than the weather since I got here."

"That's an exaggeration and you know it. We've talked about politics and the tension here and—"

"Nothing personal to you," my mother finished for me. "You come here with your face so badly bruised." I touched my face in reaction. I'd forgotten about it. "You didn't think to tell me how that happened, when that happened. Maybe because it really doesn't disturb you, which to me is incomprehensible. Or perhaps because you think I am an *inappropriate* person with whom to discuss these things, which I have to admit is painful."

What, did she expect me to fly into hysterics over it? What possible good would that do?

I didn't understand. What did she want from me?

I was an adult. I had responsibilities. Did she want me to be weak? What good would that do me? Or her? Or anyone? It didn't make sense.

She had no right to do this. No right to come into my life and criticize how I did things. Especially when she was correct in realizing she didn't comprehend the kind of decisions my life required.

And trying to make me feel inadequate because I didn't

share with her every thought I had in my head? What was that about? My thoughts and feelings were my own and I had every right to keep them to myself when I wished. She was wrong to try to make me feel guilty about it.

"I came here to get to know you again, Lee. To try to resume our natural family positions."

Our natural family positions? What did that mean?

"You have been a very considerate hostess, taking good care of your guest. But I should not be a guest to you. I am your mother."

So she was upset because I had treated her too well? "I don't understand," I confessed.

"No. I know. You can't understand. And I don't understand."

And now, after she had been so eloquent, that was all she had to say. "This is why you are leaving?"

She looked frustrated. Like I should have gotten it from all she had said. But what she had said hadn't made sense. "I expected to have a certain place in your life, Lee. But it's been made clear that I don't have it.

What place? A place of authority, or control? She honestly believed she had the right to that? She thought she could swoop in after seventeen years and rewrite everything I had been taught? "I don't understand what you expect from me."

"I know. And I know it's not your fault. Please understand me, Lee, I don't blame you for anything. If it's anyone's fault, it's mine. For expecting too much."

Oh, that was comforting. It was her fault for expecting a dog to speak. "So you're leaving?" That was her solution? Things weren't going exactly as she planned, so she left?

"I don't know what I'm doing here, Lee. I'm not getting to know you. You're not coming to rely on me for anything. And I'm causing problems for you."

Why did I have to rely on her? Why did that have to be part of the equation? "I don't want you to go, Mother."

"Is that the way you really feel? Or is it merely the appropriate thing to say?"

Now that was totally uncalled for. My lying wasn't that out of control.

"It doesn't matter, Lee. It's not your fault. It's not something you've done. Not really. I came here expecting things, things I obviously shouldn't have been expecting. It's completely my doing. But I have to think about this."

"Think about what? What is there to think about?" I didn't know what to say, what I should be saying. What had happened? I really couldn't understand. How could she be upset that I wasn't complaining about my life, that I wasn't asking her questions she didn't know the answers to, that I was handling things on my own? Wasn't that what parents wanted, for their children to be self-sufficient? Wasn't that supposed to be a source of pride for them?

What was I doing that was so wrong?

"I'm not comfortable here, Lee. I need to think about what my place is in your life."

She was my mother. That was her place.

Suddenly, two servers entered the room, bearing armfuls of plates.

"Maybe, in a little while, when you have the time, you can come visit," my mother said. "Maybe with all the family together, it will be easier. You can watch us. See how we are together. Maybe it will help you understand." She rose to her feet, suddenly looking regal and untouchable. "I think I will retire."

She wanted to end things like that? But nothing had been accomplished. "Mother—"

She raised a hand, cutting me off. "Sleep well, Dunleavy." And with an elegant tilt of the head, she left the table and the dining room.

And she had accused me of treating her like a stranger.

Chapter Seventeen

"This is a stupid idea." So said the rational part of me. Most of the rest of me was practically bouncing from the feeling in the air, the excitement and the noise and the activity.

Karish didn't even slow down, mercilessly dragging me along behind him. I had to jog to keep up with his long strides. "Stop complaining, Lee," he said impatiently. "I'll keep you under control."

"Don't you have any friends?" I demanded. I mean, really, we were spending more and more off-roster time together, and it wasn't natural. Aye, his mother was still in High Scape, and while I hadn't told him the real reason why my mother had left he knew it wasn't due to her business interests, and that I wasn't calm about it. So we were both a little tense. I wasn't sure that the best solution was to spend even more time in each other's company. That was just begging for a serious argument to erupt and I didn't think we needed to add those kinds of problems to the mix. If he wanted to have company for the parade, why hadn't he gone with someone he didn't have to watch over?

"Why do you do this every time?" He hurried me across

the street, cutting pretty close to an indifferent—and moving—carriage. "Is it a test?"

"Test of what?" I stepped over a pile of horse remnants,
carefully keeping the green skirt high. One could not dress
practically while attending a parade in honor of the Crown
Prince.

"To see if I'll insist on your coming."

I frowned. "Why would I do that?"

He looked back at me with exasperation. "Never mind."

I shrugged. All right.

"Just trust me."

"Of course." It wasn't like I thought he would let me do
anything stupid. It was just that having to be restrained
while foaming at the mouth lacked a certain dignity. And
guards and Runners might decide to lend a hand.

The parade would be traveling down First Center Road,
from east to west. Following the path of the sun. Earlier the
arrogance implicit in that choice of route had made me
smile. I had since heard, however, that it was an arrogance
that was supposed to be reserved for the ruling monarch,
currently the Empress. For the heir to presume in such a
manner was apparently something the Empress couldn't
afford to let slide. And she wouldn't be well pleased with
High Scape for allowing it. Though how the mayor was
supposed to refuse an order of the Crown Prince was beyond me.

The route had been decorated, of course, and everyone
was dressed in their festival best. But the mood was subdued. People were excited to be seeing the Prince, but they
weren't happy. They'd had a hard summer so far and it
didn't look like it would be getting better any time soon.
No doubt they were hoping for answers from the Prince,
but what could he say? What would he know about the
weather? What could he do to change it? Nothing more
than we could.

We were having no more luck with it. Every time I tried
anything the weather experienced a nice flip, into rain, into

hail, into horrific humidity. Never anything pleasant or useful, and nothing I could predict ahead of time. Karish had said it was a waste of time, and I was beginning to suspect he was right, but I wouldn't let him stop. As long as we continued to claim we were working on it, we would be.

We chose a corner where Way Street crossed First Center. People were already crowded along the street. One of the disadvantages of being short made itself evident. Karish released my hand to blow into his—it was a little nippy—and rose to his tiptoes. But there wasn't anything happening yet.

To be honest, there was a whole other reason why I wasn't keen on being at the parade. I wasn't all that comfortable around regulars anymore. The attack on the Triple S house had scared the hell out of me. And apparently it had scared the hell out of the regulars, too, that they had descended to that level of violence. They'd reverted back to the hostile looks and muttered criticisms, and invitations to leave their places of business. Unpleasant but not dangerous. But I was a bloody coward. Surrounded by regulars wasn't where I wanted to be.

But it was where I was. So I could just stay calm, damn it.

Besides, I was too pessimistic. There was a chance I would actually have a good time. I had never been to a parade before. They had to be fun, or people wouldn't keep having them.

We waited. I heard children complaining of boredom, or being tired or hungry. I heard snatches of conversation. People drooling over Karish. The usual sort of thing. But no one harassed us. I started to relax a little.

I could hear them then. Very faint. Drums and trumpets. I felt a shiver.

I laced my fingers together. I would keep myself under control. I was not going to rely on Karish. I was an adult. It was ridiculous that I couldn't stay calm. Just breathe. Remember who and what you are.

And the drums and trumpets got a little louder.

Karish could hear them then. He looked at me, eyebrows

raised in inquiry. I shook my head. I was all right. He nodded and looked back to the street.

There was a loud explosion, and everyone jumped in alarm. My heart leapt into my throat. It was only some kind of firecracker.

Men came running up the street. Men dressed in rags of bright blue and red and yellow, paint exaggerating their eyes and mouths. They jumped and rolled and spun into hand-flips. My shoulders relaxed.

Following the acrobats were dancers, jugglers, animals and their trainers. A lot of color, a lot of movement. Some of it moved me to laughter, and that felt good. The animals, walking awkwardly on their hind legs and smothered in vests and hats, were disturbing. Watching the contortionists made my back hurt in sympathy.

Wagons were pulled past, gaudily decorated with ribbons and flowers. One wagon carried a scantily clad young couple who flung out candies and coins to the crowd. People scrambled for them. I thought it was pathetic. Then I reminded myself that I had no idea what it was like to lack for money, and if I ever wanted candy I only had to grab some up without thought and without paying for it.

Still, though, so undignified.

Another carriage drew up, bearing the mayor. Four white horses, an open carriage, the mayor seated with her husband. Occasionally she waved at the spectators, but she looked subdued. Almost grim. But then, no one was particularly happy to see her. If I'd thought about it I would have come to the logical conclusion that people were blaming her for their difficulties, too. Only I'd never thought about it.

I could be a self-centred wench when I wanted.

Other wagons slowly drove by. Other dignitaries whom I didn't know. I supposed I should learn who they were, sometime. I was living in the city they ran.

The drums were getting louder. The rat-ta-tat-tat of those annoying military drums. Strangely, while they made me kind of jumpy they didn't seem to influence me to do anything, perhaps because there wasn't really a melody. The trumpets did have a melody, occasionally blaring out something suitably majestic. That didn't move me much, either. How disloyal of me.

Dancers, twisting to mandolins I hadn't been able to hear earlier. The mandolin music was light, pretty. It made me want to dance but it didn't take me over. I felt Karish touch my arm but I refused to look at him, and his hand fell away.

More jugglers, and I thought they were probably the Southerners Karish had mentioned seeing a few days earlier. They were gorgeous, long dark limbs gleaming through flowing red garments, black tattoos slithering over their skin, silver rings hanging from ears and wrists and ankles as they tossed flaming torches and gleaming knives at each other. They were totally insane, and I wondered how many injuries they acquired about the face and shoulders and who knew where else before they learned to handle those tools of destruction so competently.

And then the drums were overpowering everything else. Troops were marching by. Rows of young men and women, draped in chain mail, wearing bulky helmets with the nose guards I always thought looked so awkward and useless. They wore cloaks of black, yellow knotting crossing from right shoulder to left corner hem. The personal guard of Lord Yellows.

Lord Yellows himself followed, surrounded by more members of his guard, riding a black gelding and looking suitably Landed. He didn't nod or wave or smile. He stared straight ahead and appeared very bored. Well, I would be, too, to be honest. Riding at a snail's pace through the city streets with hordes of people staring and screaming at me. I didn't even know why he was part of the parade, except perhaps because he sponsored it.

More guards trailed after him—how many did he have?—and the blare of the trumpets became deafening. The crowds settled down. The man himself approached.

Crown Prince Gifford, riding a huge white gelding, dressed in armor, though as far as I knew he'd never lifted a sword in any battle. A thin, dark man in his early forties. Everyone knew he was desperate to get the throne; not that I could blame him entirely. It had to be awful having nothing to do, having to wait until your mother died before you could take on the role you'd spent your whole life being trained for, and in the meantime not being able to pursue any other goal because it wasn't fitting for your station. A very hard, tiring, useless place to be.

He waved. He smiled. His eyes looked kind of blank. It felt artificial to me.

And then, shouting. From behind. Almost drowned out by the trumpets, but the long wordless howls held out against the brassy notes. I turned around to look and through the crowds saw people running up Way Street, bearing clubs and swords and bricks. "What the hell?"

People parted ahead of them, instinctively drawing out of their way. Some of those running let loose with the bricks. The bricks arced high into the sky, and landed in the general vicinity of the Prince.

And chaos.

There seemed to be a sudden storm of bricks and rocks and sticks. Someone shoved me from behind, and Karish caught me by the shoulders. Horses reared up, people screamed. The members of the Yellows guard drew their swords and split into two groups, one circling around Lord Yellows and the Prince, the other wading into the crowds. People started running. The noise burst into my ears.

I didn't know what to do. Running seemed so cowardly. Staying seemed so suicidal. Would I be a help or a hindrance if I stayed? Would I be abandoning some sort of duty if I left?

Pain exploded in the back of my head, a sharp jolt that seemed to shake my skull, hard. I felt the color slipping from my vision and the sound draining from my ears.

When I could think again—kind of—I was off my feet

and being jolted about in a manner that both my head and my stomach warned me might occasion unfortunate results. "Karish," I said, but my voice came out all whispery and useless, and Karish was too busy yelling at people to get the hell out of his bloody way to hear me.

At least he was cradling me and not carrying me over his shoulder. The latter would have been bad. Very. As it was there was too much noise crashing into my ears and Karish was holding me too tight and my feet kept hitting people. What was happening?

And then there was less crowding, but that only meant Karish felt he had space to run. I was jolted with every footfall, and that was really not fun. I grabbed at his shoulders, trying to stop the bouncing, but my hands weren't working right and all the strength had been sapped from my arms. "Karish."

"Just a bit more, Lee," he said, his words strained with breathlessness. "Just hold on."

He kept turning corners. I wished he'd stop that.

Why was I nauseous, anyway? I hadn't eaten anything odd. Had I?

Don't think about what you had for breakfast. It doesn't matter. Thoughts about food weren't going to do anyone any good right then.

He turned another corner, and then he stopped. Thank Zaire. He swooped down and sat me on the sidewalk, leaning me against the wall. I let my head fall back, which kind of hurt. "Ow."

"Lee," he gasped, his shoulders rising and falling with the effort of breathing. "What happened? You just crumpled all of a sudden."

"Uh, dunno." I was kind of tired. And kind of not. I wasn't sure. "Uh, something hit me on the back of my head, I think."

"Damn it." Then his hands were in my hair which, considering how tightly bound my hair was, wasn't an easy operation. He seemed to be trying to press every curve of the surface of my skull.

"Ouch! Damn it, Karish, what are you doing?"

"Checking for blood. There doesn't seem to be any." He pulled his hands out of my hair and sat back on his heels. "Leave it to you to stick your head out in the path of flying debris."

That, I thought, was a little unfair. "You got injured last time. It's my turn."

"What last time? That makes no sense."

"Hm? It did when I thought it."

"How many fingers am I holding up?"

I stared at his hand. I could see his hand. It was just that all the lovely colored spots moving about in front of my eyes prevented me from counting his fingers.

"All right, I'm taking you to the hospital." He pulled me up by the shoulders.

"I'm not going to hospital," I objected. "I feel fine." Well, fine might have been overstating the case a little, but I wasn't in any pain. I felt kind of numb. Almost like I was floating.

"Like that matters. You Shields don't feel anything someone hasn't spent a day and a half pounding into you first."

The ground moved. Just a bit. Not so much a swaying as that the sidewalk had decided it really didn't want to be touching my feet anymore and so had distanced itself a little. "I'm fine," I insisted. "I just need to lie down for a while. It'll all go away then." Too bad, really. The colors were so pretty and made such interesting shapes. Like clouds twisting and performing just for me.

"And you will lie down," he agreed, wrapping an arm around my waist. He felt good. Safe and solid and warm. "In a hospital."

"All right." I really didn't care. If he wanted to waste the time and effort of taking me to the hospital, that was his fallacy. But, "Hey, you can heal me!"

"Shhh!"

It was too much effort to check if there were any people near enough to have heard me. It would require turning my head.

"It's not healing, and whatever it is I need to be shielded while I do it. By you. I don't think that would work right now."

"You don't need me to shield you." Not to heal. He'd done it without me before. I suspected he really didn't need me to shield him at all, ever. He was just afraid to try it alone.

"Now's really not the time for a foray into your delusional beliefs in my exaggerated abilities."

Even with my mind as clouded as it was, I recognized the warning signs of all the multi-syllabic words. "You have been in an evil mood all morning, Karish."

"My partner just collapsed at my feet. Forgive me if it's made me a little testy." He got us moving. I groaned in complaint. I just wanted to lie down. "And stop calling me Karish, damn it."

Aye, aye, aye, don't get into hysterics over it.

"Karish. Taro. Stop a moment."

"Leave it alone, Lee. I'm taking you to the hospital and that's final."

"Do you *want* me to throw up on you?"

He halted and let me go. Pain shot out from the back of my head, spearing through my brain and reaching down to give my stomach a good hard twist.

Throwing up in a public street. Just the kind of classy, professional image I'd hoped to create for myself. And the act of vomiting made everything hurt, my head and my stomach and my throat. It also drained what little strength I had left. After a few painful moments of retching up nothing but bile I leaned weakly against the wall. "Oh, gods."

Karish rubbed my back, and the pain in my head eased. He carefully pulled me from the wall and wrapped an arm around my shoulders. Ah, that felt good. "I'm sorry," he whispered into my ear. "You scared me." He kissed my temple, twice, hard.

"I'm fine." In fact, I suddenly felt pretty warm and relaxed.

"We won't know that until we get you to hospital. Come on. We'll take it slow."

Yes. Agonizingly slow. That strange disconnected floating sensation grew stronger the whole time, and I found it harder and harder not to trip over my own feet. Karish flagged down a carriage, the fourth he tried to catch. I lasted a couple of blocks and I had to scramble back out to throw up again.

Oh, no, that wasn't humiliating.

So we had to walk to the nearest hospital, and it was pretty crowded by the time we got there. I was so happy to stop moving that I didn't care that I had to sit on the floor. I heard Karish barking orders at someone but couldn't quite understand the words. A fog had drifted into my mind and it made it hard to perceive things.

"Lee?"

"Mm?"

"There are a lot of people from the parade here, Lee. Some of them are in pretty bad shape. We'll have to wait a bit, all right?"

"Mm." I didn't mind. I wasn't too uncomfortable. In a few moments I'd be drifting into a nice warm sleep.

"Forget that, Dunleavy." A hand grabbed my chin and shook my head. Only a little, but it was enough to irritate.

I pushed at his hand. "Stop that."

"Open your eyes."

"They are open." Weren't they?

"Open your eyes and look at me."

"I know what you look like, Taro. Don't worry. I still think you're pretty."

A sigh of annoyance from him. "I've got a mirror. Drink this."

"Hm?"

"It's water."

That seemed like a good idea. In theory. In practice, what goes down must come up. Karish managed to grab a bowl from somewhere just in time, quickwitted lad. And I had thought losing control due to music was humiliating. I hated being sick, being injured. It was such a waste of time.

"All right, so water's out," I heard Karish say.

"Go home, Karish." I didn't want him hanging around while I was being so pathetic.

"What?" The word was sharp. It hurt my ears.

"Go home. Or wherever. You don't need to wait here."

"I'm not leaving you alone here," he snapped.

"I'm in a hospital, Kar—Taro. I'm perfectly fine."

"Just shut up, Lee." He sat beside me and pulled me nice and close. I couldn't help sighing at the pleasure of it. "And keep your eyes open."

"You might have some thought to my pride."

"Right now I couldn't care less about your pride, not when it's making you stupid."

"You do stupid things for pride all the time."

"I'm allowed. I'm a Source. You're a Shield. You're supposed to know better."

"What utter tripe."

"You know, Lee, sometimes your eloquence just overwhelms me."

"Oh, shut up."

And the prat wouldn't let me close my eyes. He was being ridiculously over-cautious. Sleeping for a while would do me no harm. But try telling his Lordship that. He knew everything.

Not that I could really blame him for being paranoid. If I died, so did he. It wasn't pleasant, watching your partner and having no idea how serious their injury was, if it would mean the end of both of your lives.

Besides, it was nice to have him there. I wasn't sure I could remain upright without him. And he was so comfortable to lean against.

It wasn't so very long before a healer could see me. He knelt beside me and touched my forehead.

"Where do I take her?" Karish asked.

"Nowhere yet," the doctor told him, his voice curt. He pulled the pins out of my hair. I felt my hair fall down my shoulders with the ache hair changing directions always gave me. "What happened?"

"She says she was hit in the back of the head. Maybe with one of the stones that were being thrown about. Have you heard what—?"

"Yes, I've heard about the Reanists," the doctor said impatiently, putting his hand on the exact wrong spot on the back of my head.

I grit my teeth and said, "I can feel that."

Karish's mind was going in another direction. "Reanists?"

"That's what they say. Name?"

"Shintaro Karish." Karish asked.

"*Her* name."

"Dun—"

"I'm asking *her.*"

"Dunleavy Mallorough," I said.

"Where do you live?"

"Second building, West Carriage Street."

"What year is it?"

"578."

"All right, she looks fine."

"She looks fine?" Karish echoed him incredulously. "She was throwing up all the way here. She can barely stand on her own."

"She gave her head a jar but there's no damage to the skull and her eyes look fine. Take her home and let her sleep. Wake her every couple of hours and ask her questions to make sure she remembers who she is. If you have trouble waking her or she can't answer the questions, bring her back."

"Why can't she stay here for a while until you're sure she's all right?"

"Because we're filled to the rafters with people suffering from broken bones and severe bleeding," the doctor snapped. "There is nothing wrong with her that time and rest won't cure."

"Told you," I sang.

"I'll have one of the attendants fetch you some daiova leaves. In a few hours make her some tea, let it cool before you let her drink it. She should be able to keep it down. Tomorrow she should be able to eat light food, broth and fruit and the like. Watch her balance for the next few days. Don't let her stand on anything high or off the ground. Definitely no bench dancing." The doctor stood.

"That's it?" Karish demanded.

"Aye." The doctor was moving away.

"Hey!" A pause. "This is unbelievable!" Sounding his most aristocratic. "This is absolutely inexcusable. I'll have that man dismissed."

"Not now, though," I murmured. I was so tired. "I want to go home."

I ended up in a carriage again, this one without extra passengers, and this time my stomach stayed somewhat stable. That was something, at least.

Karish left me in my room to change into a sleeping gown while he fetched me some water to rinse out my mouth. Then I climbed into the bed. Nice big bed with cool clean sheets. I rolled up in the blankets. But when I closed my eyes, the bed started rocking and spinning.

"Here." Karish sat on the edge of the bed, holding out a mug. "Don't swallow the leaf. It's mint."

I could have given him a look for assuming I couldn't recognize mint, but it would require moving my eyes too much. I took a sip of water, swished it through my mouth, and spat it back into the mug. I let Karish take the mug from me. So I had no dignity left. I only had to live with it for another sixty years or so.

"Would you feel better if I lie beside you until you go to sleep?"

I nodded. Carefully. No dignity, no pride.

He stretched out beside me and put an arm around my waist and gathered me close. It felt so-o-o-o nice. Except . . . "You're—"

"What?"

"Nothing." No need to point out that he was shaking. He probably already knew. And I understood. I'd been a wreck, when he'd been injured and no one was sure he was going to live.

He buried his face in my hair. "You're all right," he whispered into my ear. "You're all right."

I laid my hand on top of his. "We're both all right," I said. "We're both going to be fine."

I'd never liked the idea of the bond. It was, I thought, an unnecessary chain. Two professionals shouldn't need it. And it wasn't right, to link the life of one person to another so thoroughly. Neither of us were careless with our safety, but accidents happened. One person shouldn't have to walk around knowing that at any moment they might die because their partner has. It wasn't right.

And yet . . .

At least he couldn't leave. No matter what I did wrong, he couldn't leave.

Chapter Eighteen

Karish spent the night in my suite. It wasn't strictly necessary—I felt better after a couple of hours—but he snapped at me when I suggested he could go. And I had to admit, though not to him, that being taken care of was wonderfully luxurious. Dangerous, though, as it inspired laziness. Late the next morning I was still wearing my sleeping gown. And I was a bad influence on him, as he wore a loose-fitting pair of trousers that had seen better days and an ancient shirt that had been stretched shapeless. We looked like a pair of hags when Risa came calling.

"Well," she said with a smile after Karish had let her in. "This looks cozy."

Please don't start. Risa was one of the few people who believed Karish and I weren't sleeping together. That didn't mean she didn't like teasing us about the possibility. "Good afternoon, Risa," I said. "Is something wrong?"

"I figured I might find you here, Dunleavy, when you weren't scheduled for a watch, but I didn't expect to find the two of you looking so . . . comfortable."

Karish rolled his eyes. "Lee got herself knocked on the

head at the parade." Risa frowned at that and crossed the room to the chair where I was lounging. "I'm staying here until I can be sure she won't sink into delirium and reveal any sacred Triple S secrets."

"Are you all right?" Risa asked me.

I nodded. "Hard head," I said. "How did you know we weren't on watch?"

"Have a seat, Risa," Karish invited. "Can I fix you some tea?"

"Aye, that'd be good." Risa settled on the sofa. "We try to keep track of where the Pairs are," she told me. "Just something we feel it's good to know, in case of emergencies. It's been hard this last year or so, though. You guys have been switching things around so much."

"Ah." That disturbed me, that the Runners were watching us. People weren't supposed to notice us much, weren't supposed to think about what we did. And emergencies? What emergencies? When we were doing our jobs, the regulars weren't even supposed to know there had been an emergency.

"You're going to want to hear this, Karish," Risa said as Karish opened the door to fetch the tea.

"Why?" I asked. "What's happened?"

"The uproar at the parade yesterday, they were Reanists."

"We'd heard that," said Karish, and he left.

"They weren't really trying to kill the Prince, were they?" I couldn't believe even the Reanists could be that stupid. The place had been crawling with guards. The chances of them succeeding had been remote, and the possibility of their escaping afterwards was nonexistent.

"They were indeed," said Risa. "They're all slated for execution next week."

My eyebrows flew up to my hairline, I could feel it. "Not going to bother with the nasty little inconveniences of trials?"

Risa didn't care for that, settling a hard look on me. "They've all confessed," she said. "If you don't know people

who confess don't get trials—'cause what's the point?—
then maybe you should have hung around Erin a little
longer."

I actually hadn't known that. It was alarming. But then
again, she was right. If people confessed to a crime, there
was no point to a trial. Especially when in this case, hun-
dreds of people had seen these people trying to kill the
Prince.

"I have never seen so many people so happy to talk,"
Rise said. "They're incriminating themselves with every
word, and we tell them they'll hang for it, and they don't
care. They're so proud of their mission, they didn't hesitate
to brag about it, even though they failed at it."

"But the Prince? In the middle of a parade?"

"Well, really, it was the only chance they'd get at him.
The rest of his trip he's going to be sequestered at Yellows
Plain. And apparently they believe that if there's a big
enough sacrifice, it will appease their gods indefinitely, and
the world will be peaceful forever. That's what they kept
saying. The big sacrifice will save the world. And their
eyes would start glowing and their faces would get blank
and it was like they were seeing something the rest of us
weren't. It was creepy. Why do religious fanatics always
fall into these final-solution traps? One big nightmarish
event and then everything will be wonderful? I mean, does
anything in real life work that way?"

"I think the whole point of being a Reanist is so you
don't have to deal with real life," I said.

"Well, their lives are going to be getting pretty real, I
tell you. We rounded up every single one of them and
they're getting their necks stretched. In public. We want to
make sure everyone knows no one is getting away with going after the Prince in High Scape. You should go."

I grimaced. The fascination with watching people killed
had always escaped me. "No thanks."

"Suit yourself," Risa shrugged. "But here's the really
big news."

"Bigger than hordes of Reanists trying to kill Prince Gifford?" Karish asked as he re-entered the suite. "I'd wager he wouldn't think so."

"Aye, but you will." Risa tapped me on the knee. "You were right. The Reanists were behind the other disappearances. And the clubs."

"What's this?" said Karish.

"Dunleavy had a theory that the Reanists were behind the abductions of the aristocrats. And she was right."

Huh. Interesting. And this time I hadn't needed to be led to the obvious conclusion by my nose. Maybe I had the makings of a Runner after all.

"They lured in lower status Landed by inviting them into those Raiborn clubs," Risa continued. "Then they'd sacrifice them."

"So they're dead?" I asked.

Risa nodded. "We think so."

"Really?" Karish crossed his arms and glared at me. "She didn't bother telling me any of this."

"You hate it when I hover," I said.

His eyebrows dipped. "Eh?"

"She was worried about you," Risa told him. "You being an aristocrat and all. And one without any real power. You fit the category."

Karish sniffed, unimpressed. "She could try walking down the middle of the yardstick once in a while," he announced. "Excuse me. The kettle's boiling." He gave me a look that told me this was not over and left the suite again.

Risa and I looked at each other for a moment, realized neither of us had any idea what the yardstick comment was about, and shrugged it off.

"What about that ritual space you were talking about?" I asked.

"Do you know about the condemned hospital in the southern quad?"

"I do now."

"It had a stone cellar. It had a pile of dirt, a bucket of water, embers, and a window."

"The window sufficed for air?"

"I guess so. The directions—you know, north-east-west-south—were a bit off, but I guess that doesn't matter so much."

So. The naive young aristocrats, desperate to belong to something, were taken down to a dank cold cellar and ritually sacrificed. How awful. "You got them all?"

"All the Reanists in High Scape. We've sent an envoy to Shina Lake warning them any other Reanists discovered in High Scape will be arrested on sight. That'll hold them there for a while, I think."

"So it's all over?" I just wanted to be sure.

Risa smiled. "It's all over."

A long, slow breath. Thank the gods. Well, no, that wasn't quite right under the circumstances. Thank Zaire. Thank the Runners. Karish wasn't going to wind up missing one night. Good thing, too. I didn't think I could handle that again, the blind, ignorant fear of having him taken by someone and not knowing what was being done to him.

Having an aristocrat for a Source was so inconvenient.

Karish returned bearing a tray. He set it on the coffee table and poured out three cups—mine from a separate pot—with mindless precision that bespoke years of practise. Was that something he had been forced to practice, whiling away the hours locked in his bedroom? But pouring tea with grace was considered a feminine skill, was it not? Yet Karish looked completely natural doing it. Totally un-self conscious.

It was, perhaps, a question his mother could answer. She arrived that afternoon, after Risa had left, and during an argument over whether Karish should stop mothering me or not. When the light knock sounded on the door, Karish sighed with impatience and hauled himself to his feet to answer. Then he'd just stood there in front of the open door. "You're not welcome here," was his cold greeting.

A soft "Don't be ridiculous" from his mother, who was able to move him to the side with a wave of a hand that didn't even touch him. She noticed me as she entered. I was grateful that, at least, I was dressed.

"Please dismiss your little friend, Shintaro. This is family business."

Little friend? Man, did I want to stick my tongue out at her.

The front door slammed. "This is her room." Karish declared. He stepped around her and sat beside me on the sofa, taking up one of my hands and lacing his fingers through mine. "It's customary to greet an acquaintance when you see them."

"It's customary to rise when a duchess enters the room."

Oh. That's right. I'd forgotten. Oops.

"What do you want?" Karish demanded.

"Send the girl away, Shintaro."

I really didn't want to be there, anyway. "Maybe I should—" I started to rise.

He squeezed my hand. Hard.

All right, maybe I shouldn't. I settled back down.

His mother drifted over the floor and alighted into a chair. She waited. There was silence, for a moment. "Are you not going to offer me refreshment?"

"I didn't even offer you a seat."

Her eyes narrowed. "This discourteous manner you've assumed is inexcusable."

"Isn't it just?"

"I've really had enough of it."

"You may leave any time."

I didn't look at him. I carefully kept my eyes trained on the Duchess. Because if I looked at him *she* might perceive that I didn't agree with how he was behaving, and I didn't want to give her any ammunition.

Stay civil, I thought at him. Stay calm. Be polite. It'll make dealing with her so much easier, and you won't be so upset once she leaves.

Her Grace evidently decided to abort the unproductive trail of conversation and try one equally disagreeable. "I spoke to Prince Gifford this morning," she said.

Really? The day after his arrival and, incidentally, an attack on his life, and she managed to get a private audience with him? She really did have influence.

"I explained to him your situation."

I felt Karish freeze beside me.

This sounded bad.

"I have no situation," said Karish, his voice low and cold. "Certainly not one that needs to be brought to the attention of the Crown Prince."

Please, please, *please* let this not be what I thought it was going to be.

"Gifford was very interested in the possibility of your re-attaining your title."

It was exactly what I'd thought it was going to be. Damn woman.

And Karish was on his feet. "Get out!" he shouted, full roar.

The Duchess was unmoved by his choler. "Sit down, Shintaro."

My, she was cocky. If I were her I'd be worrying about being slapped around some.

"How *dare* you discuss my business with the Prince!"

"He said—"

"I don't care what he said! Get out!"

Deep breath. "Taro!" I snapped out, deepening my voice so it would cut through the noise the two of them were making. He whirled at me, stunned I was interfering. I caught his gaze. "We should hear what was said."

"I don't—"

"We should hear—" I repeated firmly, "what was said." I stared at him, wishing our all-powerful mystical bond allowed actual communication.

Karish clenched his jaws and crossed his arms. I didn't

think I'd convinced him of anything, but he trusted me enough to know I wasn't doing this for no reason.

Her Grace interpreted the silence as permission to proceed. If she thought she needed permission. "I informed His Highness of your difficulty."

"I don't have a difficulty!"

Shut up, Karish.

"I told him that when you abjured your title, you had been enduring a very trying time. Newly bonded, hunting down that mad Source, mourning the loss of your brother"—Karish snorted—"it was no wonder you were not quite yourself."

"What did you do, Mother?" he demanded in a voice grown hoarse.

"Really, Shintaro, I don't know why you're acting this way. I told His Highness you were seeking to regain your title and—"

"Oh, gods!" He pushed his hands into his hair. "Oh, gods. You didn't. You didn't really tell him I was hoping to get the title back. Please tell me you didn't."

"Be sensible, Shintaro. How can he assist you if he doesn't know what you want?"

Oh Zaire. Oh hell. I couldn't believe what I was hearing. She was supposed to be adept at political games. She was, at the very least, supposed to possess a basic level of intelligence. What did she think she was doing?

Was she trying to get him killed?

"You stupid *bitch*!"

The Dowager's expression was one of total shock. I couldn't believe it. How could she think he would be anything but horrified to hear this? "Shintaro!"

"I'm going to end up in prison! Or dead! Gods, woman, how could you be so phenomenally stupid? What are you trying to do to me? Once I've given up the title, I can't ask for it back! You know that!"

Shock faded away to be replaced by anger. "You

ungrateful little parasite!" she hissed. "Do you think I want you taking the title? A mad wastrel of no manners and no morals, no education and no discipline? You could not be less worthy, and the idea of you stepping into your brother's shoes disgusts me."

His brother's shoes? That would be the man who slept and gambled his way through life, dying at an early age through a sexually transmitted disease? That brother?

"Then let the title go to my cousin!"

"I will not! You are my son, much may I wish it otherwise. You are your brother's natural heir. You will take the title. That you don't wish it, that it is inconvenient to you, is irrelevant. It will happen. Prince Gifford assures me there is no reason why you can't have the title, as it hasn't passed to your heir yet. He will arrange it."

"The Empress won't allow it." This was said with desperation. I could see he wasn't entirely certain that she wouldn't. Maybe she would. Maybe it would suit some other plans of hers that we knew nothing about.

"The Empress' power is waning. Much like her health. You must learn to watch for these developments, Shintaro. They will be essential for your survival."

She was so sure. She had calmed down from her shock and was passing on political advice. As though it were all a done deal, and all that was left were the formalities.

What if she were right? What if Prince Gifford did manage to saddle Karish with the title?

Damn it. Damn her. Why did she have to interfere? Why couldn't she just leave us alone? What did she care who was the next duke? It wouldn't change her life, her title, her home.

Karish stood there silently for a moment, his hands still clenched in his hair. Then he let his hands fall again, his shoulders slumping. "Get out," he ordered in a quiet voice.

His mother cocked her head to one side, a gesture eerily like her son's, and she studied him for a moment. Then she began gathering up her gloves and purse. "You can be sure

I find our association as distasteful as do you," she said. "I promise you it won't continue once you assume your proper role. Do your part, and we never need have anything to do with each other again."

I hated her. She had to know that she was cruel. She just didn't care. And watching her leave I just wanted to tackle her and pound her head against the floor until her skull cracked open and what few brains she had dribbled out.

That might stain the wood, though.

I waited until the door had closed behind her. I watched Karish rub his face with his hand, trembling with rage and pale with shock. "Taro, come here."

He didn't respond.

"Taro."

"She's going to get me killed," he whispered.

"Or ennobled." He didn't find that funny. Imagine that. "Come here, Taro." He kind of drifted over the floor, as his mother had. When he sat beside me I draped my arms over his shoulders and stroked my finger though his black hair.

"What am I going to do?" he asked, his voice breaking.

"Well," I said, drawing out the word, trying to think. "You told the Empress you didn't want the title. You told the court. You told your mother."

"So?" Karish said after a moment.

"You were honest. You were forthright. Your mother is trying to circumvent your honesty."

"And?"

"You have to act quickly. Before the Prince talks to anyone else about the possibility of reinstating you. If we do anything, it has to be before the Prince has committed himself. Slighting and humiliating him won't help us at all."

"All I'm hearing is negatives here, Lee, and I kind of knew about them already."

"It's time to use guile."

"Guile?"

"Deceit."

He frowned. "I don't like that."

"You'll like being headless even less. I wouldn't care for it myself. I'd miss your mane." I ruffled his hair.

"I don't think I can do guile."

"Of course you can. It's in your blood." He was an aristocrat, after all.

He growled. "What are you suggesting?"

"You go to your mother—"

"Oh, no!"

I grabbed the collar of his shirt before he could jump up and start pacing. "Hear me out, Taro."

"What!" he snapped peevishly.

"You go to your mother tomorrow or the next day. You don't have to be particularly civil, though that would help. You don't have to act like you like her. But you take a page from her book. You stay calm. You tell her that her promising you she won't interfere with your life once you're the duke has put a whole new perspective on things. Complain about the shoddy way the regulars have been treating you over the weather this summer. That people are rude to you, and the shopkeepers don't give you appropriate service. No way at all to behave towards a duke. Tell her being a Source has brought you nothing but danger and inconvenience."

"She's not going to believe I suddenly changed my mind."

"Tell her you were bragging about being disrespectful to her in front of La Monte. And he chastised you about the deference that must be shown to one's mother, and a lady. You came to realize that you were behaving childishly."

He quirked an eyebrow at that. "It's awfully weak, Lee."

"Aye. It is. A good thing, then, that we are dealing with a person who shows a tendency to believe in whatever she wants to believe, regardless of how unrealistic it is. This is exactly what she wants to hear, Taro. Are you going to tell me she won't grab onto it with both hands?"

He didn't say anything to that. He couldn't deny it.

"The first day, you go to her and apologize. Not contritely. Not with any emotional fervor. Merely tell her you recognize that you have been behaving inappropriately, and it will not happen again. Use me, if you like. You could say after she left I started slagging her, and that made you angry. The second day you start complaining about being a Source in High Scape. The rigid schedule, the constant demands on your attention. And having to watch me all the time is a serious inconvenience. At least if you were a duke, you could hire someone to watch me. The third day you admit that she was right and you're feeling guilty for neglecting your family duty. Say you had a fight with one of your lovers, someone you'd been serious about but who wouldn't marry you because you were nothing but a feckless Source and she wanted a normal man with a normal life. The fourth day, you ask her for the password, so you can race back to Flown Raven and tell the family solicitor and attend Lord Yellows' ball as the Duke of Westsea."

"And then what? Because I know you aren't suggesting I actually go to Flown Raven. You would never suggest that." His tone plainly told me that I'd better not ever suggest that.

"You send it to your cousin. Tell her to race to the solicitor and get the title, and send you word when it's done, so you can somehow let it be known to the Prince that the title has been passed. Discreetly, and before he's made any moves about it himself."

"Send the code through the *mail*?"

I couldn't help smirking at that. "How much do you care that the code might fall into the wrong hands?" And a ditch digger becomes the next Duke of Westsea. It would serve his mother right.

He sighed, and I felt some of the tension drain out of him. "It's going to be hard."

"I know. But being honest isn't protecting you. Your mother won't let it. You have to move fast and I can't think of any other way to do this."

"Me, neither," he admitted.

"So you'll have to lie."

"Aye," he said wearily. "Won't be the first time."

"And you'll be able to stay here. With people who care about you. And not just because you're so pretty."

He snickered. Then he groaned. "This is going to be awful."

"Poor boy," I said. And this time I meant it.

Chapter Nineteen

It was a nice gown, especially considering it was a rush job. Tailor Dagong had not been at all pleased to take me on, and was downright temperamental about putting my gown before her other orders. Not that I could blame her. I had no doubt that customers were hellish to deal with, just in general. Ask them to wait even longer than they'd planned for a product and it could only get worse. I was afraid she would make the dress too tight, or make the seams rough, or enact some other form of subtle revenge that I probably wouldn't notice until after I'd been wearing the gown an hour or two. But so far so good. Too much pride in her profession, perhaps, to indulge in such petty punishment.

The gown was well-made, a simple cut that suited my frame as much as any garment could, the sleeves less narrow than the fashion to de-emphasize my too-broad shoulders and a less severe waistline that obscured the fact that my figure was other than hourglass. It was royal blue, as opposed to my usual dark green. It made my hair look really red.

The white braid on my left shoulder was a glaring accent that ruined the whole look, as far as I was concerned. Too bad I couldn't wear white sometimes.

I was not looking forward to this evening. It was not going to be fun. Aristocrats had no use for slip collectors. Being a Shield didn't really increase my value in their eyes. And the only people I'd know would be Karish and his mother. Loved him, wanted to kill her. Balanced, eh? Then there was the Prince. I didn't want to deal with royalty. That sort was barely human.

"I don't want to be late, Lee," Karish called in from my living room.

"We won't be late."

"There'll be a whole line of carriages. It'll take us ages just to get to the front door."

"So we won't be any later than anyone else." What was his rush? Wasn't there a certain cache to being late?

"Come on, Lee. You look gorgeous."

Liar. He hadn't even seen me yet. But I supposed there wasn't any point in stalling any longer. Deep breath in and I went out into the living room. Karish stopped pacing at my entrance.

He looked stunning, of course. A long sleek doublet of dark blue—an unfortunate coincidence—that framed his slim shoulders and lean waist. The high stiff collar was completely buttoned, and I wondered when he'd gotten so modest in his dress. The doublet was decorated with subtle black brocade that blended perfectly with the braid on his left shoulder. Why did Sources get the black, while Shields were stuck with the white? There was so much more that could be done with black.

I didn't like the outfit, though, for all its beauty. It made him look unreachable and hard and rigid. Not like him.

A carriage was waiting for us. The driver wasn't too impressed with the delay, especially as she wasn't going to be getting paid. People were still tense, and still resented us. The weather had tilted in turns from hot to cold, from humid to blasting rain, with only the odd day of reasonable weather sprinkled here and there. The loss of lives and livelihoods continued.

But it really wasn't our fault. Or I hoped it wasn't. I really hoped my experiments weren't just making a bad situation worse.

"So how are you going to handle it?" I asked Karish once the carriage was moving.

"I'm still not sure," he admitted. "The Prince has no reason to love me. Merely bringing the subject up could be interpreted as pursuing the title, if someone wanted to look at things that way."

"You can't afford to wait too long," I warned him. "He'll hate you if he asks the Empress about this and learns the title has already passed. He'll think you made a fool out of him."

"I know that," he said sharply. "Give me time. I only found out myself yesterday."

He had gotten a letter from his cousin, confirming that she had used the code and officially received the title from the solicitor. "When will you tell your mother?" I bit back a grin. I wanted to be there when he told her. Even though I knew it wouldn't be as fun as I found myself imagining it would be. The Dowager would probably just deny the reality of it. Order Karish to go back to the new Duchess of Westsea—what was her name again?—and try to wrest the title back from her. Or she might ask the Prince to interfere again. On the other hand the impossible might happen and she might actually accept that her will had been permanently foiled. And that, I wanted to see.

"I don't think I'll tell her at all," he said. "I think I'll let it be an unpleasant surprise. Let some gossipy hag drip insincere sympathy all over her, condoling with her about her wastrel son's idiocy, and Her Grace will have to actually ask someone what the hell is going on." He chuckled, a brittle flat sound. "Or better yet, she'll nag at the Prince for not acting on his promise, and he'll get to tell her. Oh, I would like to watch that."

That didn't seem like a good idea to me. I mean, yes, there was a certain vengeful appeal about it, but that sort of petty behavior tended to blow up in a person's face. "Are you sure that's how you want to handle it?"

"Yes." He drew out the *s* sound. "This is all her fault, interfering in things that don't concern her. This will teach her to leave me alone."

He was tense beside me, and I decided to drop it. Perhaps he was right. Maybe that sort of social humiliation was what it would take to keep the Dowager out of his life. And, coincidentally, out of mine. I might not like the means but I would certainly appreciate the ends.

As the carriage drew up to the long driveway to Lord Yellows' manor, I began noticing mounted Runners trotting up and down the street. They weren't being particularly discreet, but maybe that was just me. I'd known they were going to be there and why they were there. Maybe no one else noticed them, or thought their presence was standard procedure. Karish didn't comment on them.

The huge crush Karish had predicted did not materialize. We had to wait only a few moments in front of the large manor of Lord Yellows as the carriage before ours disgorged its passengers. Karish helped me down to the sidewalk—such a gentleman—and we started our climb up the obligatory long staircase.

I had never been to Lord Yellows' manor before. It looked much like I would expect a manor to look. One of those huge stone monsters that weren't practical in a region subject to earthquakes. Lots of windows that were no doubt a nightmare to keep clean. Probably hard to heat in the winter. But very pretty.

I wouldn't want to live in it. Even with a horde of servants to take care of it.

I wondered whether the manor at Flown Raven looked like it. If it were bigger. It was probably bigger. The title of Westsea was apparently a powerful and wealthy one. Fortunately, I was unlikely to have to find out for myself.

"It's not too late to back out, is it?" I muttered to Karish.
"Hush." He squeezed my hand.

A servant met us at the door. I was momentarily distracted by his livery which was, frankly, weird. "While the shirt, vest and trousers were normal enough, on his head he was wearing some kind of wimple, worn low over his eyebrows and draping over his ears.

He relieved us of our wraps and escorted us down a long, wide corridor. I tried to be discreet as I examined the portraits and hangings and furniture. I didn't want to look too much like a rube among all these High Landed and their servants.

I didn't like it. Too many things fighting for attention, pictures on the walls and knickknacks covering every flat surface. So busy with stuff I wanted to close my eyes to give them a rest. And probably no fun at all to keep dusted.

We were led through a series of corridors and then into a long narrow room which, I presumed, was the ballroom. Thousands of candles, a good half dozen chandeliers, and yellow walls. All very bright, but not in a warm, comfortable way. It felt . . . prickly.

Which made no sense at all.

There weren't as many people in the ballroom as I'd expected. I'd heard of aristocratic parties where one could barely move across the room, it was so packed. And for a party for the Crown Prince, I would have expected huge crowds. But if there were more than a few dozen people there that night I would be surprised to hear it. And in the large room the gathering was looking particularly scanty. Was that normal?

There were pairs of guards standing at each doorway and at each window. Stoic in their master's livery, their faces nearly covered in odd black helmets, they certainly drained any festive feeling out of the air. Perhaps such precautions were necessary, given the attendance of the Prince, but I couldn't imagine anyone being able to relax and enjoy themselves with those black helmets scowling from every angle.

Of course, relaxation and enjoyment weren't what the party was about. The party was about power plays and prestige and showing off and shoring up, and a bunch of other High Lander priorities I would never understand. Why was I there?

At least it was easy to see everyone. Like Karish's mother, standing near the wall with two other extremely stiff women, holding what I was sure was a scintillating conversation about other people's lack of money and morals while scanning the room for someone interesting to molest. I saw the Dowager notice her son, but her face didn't reveal any emotional reaction to his presence. Karish's attention was directed towards Crown Prince Gifford, who was seated in a huge wooden carved chair that might as well have been a throne. To his right sat Lord Yellows. To his left was his third wife, Princess Jane. Their chairs were on a wooden dais, raising them above us mere mortals.

"Source Karish and Shield Mallorough, Your Highness," the servant announced. A few people turned their heads to look at us.

Karish bowed and I curtseyed.

"Please approach us," the Prince said.

I didn't like his voice. It was a rather high, thin tenor. I doubted he could sing.

I could feel everyone's attention on us as we stepped up closer to the dais and bowed again.

"How are you this fine day, Source Karish?" the Prince asked.

Fine? It was raining. Cold biting rain that wasn't far from sleet.

"Quite well, thank you, Your Highness."

"High Scape has been experiencing some difficulties this summer," the Prince commented.

"Aye, Your Highness."

"We must admit to some surprise that you have not used your special talents to rectify the situation."

Oh damn. As discreet as an elephant. I held down a gasp and wondered if I could glance around without looking like I was glancing around. It felt like there was no one else close enough to hear what the Prince was saying, but I would have liked to make sure by looking at their faces.

On the other hand, Princess Jane and Lord Yellows were hearing every word and didn't appear surprised. Was that because they already knew something, or were they just wearing their High Landed masks?

And what was with that royal "we"? That was a privilege reserved for his mother, the Empress.

I couldn't feel any reaction at all from Karish. "I fear the weather is beyond my abilities, Your Highness," he said calmly.

"Ah. Inconvenient, that."

"Yes, Your Highness," Karish said because, I supposed, he had to say something.

"But, fortunately, such concerns will soon be beneath you."

Here it came. I hadn't expected it to happen out in the open, where others might overhear us. Maybe the Prince didn't care, but I found it odd, since, after all, Karish's alleged pursuit of his title and any assistance the Prince might give him in said pursuit were illegal.

"Your Highness?" said Karish, sounding uncertain.

"Her Grace, the Dowager Duchess of Westsea, has made us aware of your difficulties. We assure you we will address this."

Damn damn damn.

"I fear I don't understand, Your Highness." Karish gave the impression that he was narrowly avoiding stuttering. I was impressed.

The Prince looked irritated. I suspected he'd already spent more time talking to Karish than he'd originally planned. "Come come, my man. You are in no danger. You seek the return of the title you so foolishly abjured."

Again, no reaction from Princess Jane nor Lord Yellows. I found it disturbing. Just who was discussing what about Karish's life?

Karish, however, appeared stunned. "Your Highness," he said after clearing his throat. "I can't imagine—I had no idea . . ." He pulled in a deep breath, as though giving himself time to gather scattered wits. "Your Highness, my cousin, the Lady Fiona of Centerfield, has delivered the code to our family solicitor and has taken the title. She is now the Duchess of Westsea."

The Prince's eyes narrowed.

Karish bowed again, more deeply than before. "Please, Your Majesty—"

I glanced at him. Was that mistake of title intentional?

"My most humble apologies. Please forgive my mother. I cannot imagine how she came to be so egregiously misinformed. It must have been some fault in me. I must have said something that . . ." He broke off, raising his hands helplessly.

The Prince's nostrils flared. "We are not pleased."

Karish bowed for a fourth time, and this time he kept his head down as he spoke. "Please, Your Highness. I beg you mercy. She meant no harm."

To see Karish grovelling before that man was disgusting. I resisted the urge to tug him back up. I kept my eyes on the floor, so no one would see how much this disturbed me.

"If the title has already passed, there is nothing to be done," the Prince declared.

"Yes, Your Highness."

"And you might want to take your mother in hand."

Oh, I really wanted to take a hand to his mother.

"Yes, Your Highness."

"You may rise."

"Thank you, Your Highness." Karish straightened to his full height.

"Enjoy the evening, Source Karish."

"Thank you, Your Highness." Karish linked my arm through his. We bowed once more and left the dais.

That was it? That was it. Thank Zaire.

I wouldn't have to go to Flown Raven. I wouldn't have to not go while my partner did. I wouldn't be taken off the roster again. I wouldn't be made useless and redundant. Who could I kiss for this?

As we walked away from the Prince, Karish turned his head and unerringly found his mother near the other end of the room. So he'd known she was there the whole time. She arched one eyebrow in inquiry. He nodded once. She turned back to her conversation, confident her will had been done.

And the tension flowed from Karish's arm. "It's done!" he hissed into my ear with sudden glee. "Lord, I half wish I could be there when she finds out."

"You could guarantee it if you told her yourself," I reminded him. And the evil side of my nature wished he'd do it right then, in the ballroom, in front of everyone, where she would have to control herself and might actually physically explode from the repressed rage and frustration.

"Ha!" he said rather loudly, drawing attention from others in the vicinity. He showed no signs of caring. "I'll never speak to that woman again. Ever."

"You say that now, Taro—"

"And I mean it."

No doubt he did, but if she summoned him again he would go. Because there would always be a part of him that hoped there was some real connection there. A hope that she would show some recognition that her actions of the past had been wrong, and that there would be some desire on her part to know him as something other than a disgrace or a tool. How could he feel otherwise? She was the only family he had left.

There was no point in saying so, though. He would never admit it. "Can we go, now?"

He laughed, relief ringing out through the sound. "Do you have so little faith in me, my love?" he asked me. "Do you doubt my ability to make this evening a delightful experience for you?"

Delightful? Where had he been? Last I heard we were counting ourselves lucky if we could just get through the evening without stabbing ourselves out of sheer boredom. "Why? Who are you planning on killing?"

"I am shocked," he avowed. "I am appalled. I am hurt. I am currently looking at young Lord Nairn." He indicated a handsome sandy-haired young man standing across the room. "He's engaged to Lady Iona, but sleeping with his valet."

"Karish!" I hissed at him, scandalized. "I have no interest in gossip."

"You're surrounded by the High Landed, Lee. It's time to wear togas."

Karish didn't personally know as many of the people in the room as I would have expected, and those he did know were those I remembered meeting myself in Erstwhile. It made sense, when I thought about it. He didn't actually grow up in aristocratic circles, and I guess he didn't frequent the same kind of establishments or go to the same parties as they did. So he couldn't really tell me many of their intimate secrets. But that was no obstacle. Once he ran out of things to say about the people he knew, he made up stories about the people he didn't. I found those easier to laugh at.

The ballroom never became very full. Only a couple of dozen more people were introduced to the Prince before the musicians began playing the first waltz. "Is it normal to have so few people at an event like this?" I asked Taro as he led me to the middle of the floor. At least I knew the waltz, possibly the only form of ballroom dancing I could perform to aristocratic standards. Hopefully I wouldn't cripple my partner with my newly-discovered levels of clumsiness.

"I'm not sure," he said, curving his arm around my waist and guiding us through the first steps. "I've never been to anything quite like this before. But it seems to me that everyone here is a titleholder. None of the usual hangers on, escorts, untitled Landed. Maybe it's a select crowd because of the Prince."

"Well, then, why were you invited?" Because he'd gotten the invitation before his mother had arrived in High Scape, so it probably hadn't been done at her urging. Unless she had started contacting the Prince about Karish's title before she'd even reached High Scape.

Karish grinned. "I don't know. An oversight on someone's part."

"And why were you allowed to bring me?"

"The invitation didn't forbid us to bring untitled guests. I think we were supposed to gather it from the hints. Too bad I'm so dense, eh?"

I couldn't grin back at him. I was thinking about a few of the hints the Prince had been tossing about. "Do you think Gifford knows what you did in Middle Reach?"

"No one really knows what I did in Middle Reach, except you and I. Have you been talking to the Prince behind my back, Lee?"

"Be serious, Taro."

"Be at ease, Lee. Not everything happens for a reason. Sometimes things just happen. And sometimes people just say things that have no logical connection to anything else. That can happen when you open your mouth more than three times an hour."

Ah, he was being flighty, and determined not to think. It would be impossible to get anything useful out of him. "Is your brain hurting you again?"

He punished me by kissing my forehead, right out there where everyone could see us. And his mother.

True to Karish's word I did, surprisingly enough, enjoy the following hours. He kept me laughing, in a manner I'm sure no one else approved of. They were all being very correct, smiling when required, and if anyone so much as giggled they kept it quiet and short and hid the failure behind a hand. That, in itself, was entertaining.

But I found it odd how little overt attention Karish received from the other guests. In Erstwhile he had been always surrounded by people, sometimes having to plead exhaustion just to get away from the crowd. In Yellows' ballroom, however, he was largely ignored. While many came to exchange brutally civil greetings, no one lingered to chat. I wondered what had changed.

Or maybe it was me, my presence that was keeping them away.

He didn't seem disturbed by it, but sometimes it was hard to know what he was thinking. He didn't seem tense as he spoke with those who wandered by. And as usual he looped his arm over my shoulders without a care as to what others thought. He danced with no one other than me, even staying with me during dances in which I refused to participate. I intercepted some long looks cast his way, but there was a definite distance between Karish and everyone else in that room. And Karish appeared indifferent to it.

Perhaps I was making too much of it. After all, if I went to a ball held by a member of the merchant class, I would probably be equally isolated. I didn't really know any of my economic peers, either. I was as much an outsider to my class as Karish was to his.

But Karish was different.

And despite the fun Karish managed to derive for me, I was happy to hear it when supper was announced. That meant the greater part of the evening was over. We would eat. As soon as manners allowed it, we would go home.

That would be the end of any dealings with the Crown Prince. And then Karish's mother would leave. Life would start sliding back towards normal. I was really looking forward to it.

Chapter Twenty

Precedence had to be observed. Both of us being titleless meant Karish and I were at the end of the long procession leaving the ballroom and heading for the dining room.

"I've heard Lord Yellows completely renovated his dining room for the Prince's visit," said the man in front of us.

"Oh, Zaire," his companion muttered. "My eyes have barely recovered from the ballroom."

Good. So it wasn't just me.

"It wasn't that bad," the man chuckled.

"Oh, please, the man has no taste whatsoever," she said.

"You're just jealous," the man accused her with a laugh. "You wish you had the money to renovate your manor."

"Well, aye, no kidding. You must have been a Runner in a former life."

"Well, you know Yellows. Crazy."

"Please, my boy. The word is eccentric."

Great. We were dining courtesy of a nut. I glared at Karish, who appeared to be concentrating at something farther up the hall. Had he known what Yellows was like before he invited me to this thing?

But entering the dining hall itself waylaid a lot of my apprehension. It looked nothing like the rest of the manor, and it was, in a word, gorgeous.

The floor, the walls, the ceiling were all made of a polished grey stone, with specks of black and grey and white and the odd hint of blue. It had the potential for looking cold, but the roaring fire in the huge fireplace at the other end of the hall sent gold light dancing over the polish and made the whole room feel elegant and magical.

The multitude of plants huddled near the entrance helped cut the severity of the stone. They smelled nice, too. A deep breath made me feel warm and slightly dizzy, like a swallow of strong wine.

All the guards had traveled in from the ballroom, lining the walls, and it appeared there were almost as many guards as there were guests. Surely, that many weren't required?

Maybe Yellows had heard something. Maybe there was something going on. But he would have canceled the party if he suspected the Prince's life was in danger.

"What's wrong?" Karish asked, noticing my frown.

I smoothed out my expression. I was being hysterical and felt no need to let him know. "The scent of the plants disturbs me," I lied.

"Ah," he said, looking back at the entrance and wrinkling his nose.

The tables weren't the usual straight tables I had been expecting. They were curved, two long arcs, one on each side of the room. And because there were so few guests they were seated on only one side of the tables, with their backs to the walls, facing each other across the room. I wanted to get a look at the grain of the tables, wondering how it was possible to make such long tables with such dramatic curves—trees didn't grow that way after all—but the tablecloths obscured everything.

I smirked as I thought how horrified everyone would be if I pulled up the tablecloth to look at the wood. Or crawled down underneath the table.

I was in a strange mood.

Karish and I were seated together, at the end of the table near the door with the plants. I was relieved to be seated with Karish. I had heard that married couples weren't allowed to sit together at such events, and too many people equated the Pair bond with marriage. Lord Yellows, or his housekeeper, apparently didn't.

"Why isn't Lord Yellows married?" I asked Karish as he held out my chair for me.

"Why would I know?"

"I don't know. I just thought all titleholders were married. Like it was practically a law."

Karish's eyes widened as he let himself drop into his own chair, not as graceful as he should have been. "Oh my gods!"

I tensed. "What? What's wrong?"

"That would have been next!" He grabbed my wrist, too tight. "Once she had me all titled up she would have been after me to get married. Oh my gods."

Ah. I looked across the room to the Dowager, who was chatting with her neighbour. She was near the middle of her arc, seated directly in front of a large window, the strong light of the full moon silvering her features. I would have thought, as a former holder of the great Westsea title, she would have been closer to the Crown Prince, but perhaps that "former" was very significant.

I wanted to shiver. The idea of being near the window when the weather was so bad made me feel cold.

"And then it would have been children! Zaire!"

I grinned at him. There he was panicking over what might have been. It was cute. "You don't want children?"

"Not under orders from my mother! That would have taken all the fun out of it!"

"You really think so? You have so little faith in yourself?"

He sniffed, unimpressed with my good humor. Then he shivered. "Damn, it's cold in here. And Yellows would keep the fire to himself."

Lord Yellows and the Crown Prince sat at the far end of the tables, opposite from the entrance. I didn't know how Lord Yellows could bear to sit immediately before the fire. The Prince looked uncomfortable, his face red and shining. "It's not that cold."

"Normal people—you know, people who aren't Shields—find it cold. Everyone's shivering."

I did notice some discreet tugging on clothing as people tried to derive some warmth from flimsy summer fashions. "The water fountain isn't helping." Set into the wall at our backs, though fortunately down by the middle of the room, water flowed from the ceiling and over the stone wall and disappeared into the floor. It was very pretty, though the constant trickling sound was a little irritating.

"At least I can feel a little better about the dinner," said Karish.

I didn't like the sound of that. "What do you mean?" I asked suspiciously.

"Lord Yellows is reputed to be overly concerned with his own health. Apparently it leads to unusual dietary choices."

"Oh lovely. Why didn't you warn me of this before you asked me to come?"

"Because I'm not an idiot, perhaps? Besides, you have ears. I assumed you heard the same rumors I had."

It was almost over, it was almost over, it was almost over.

I realized there was music playing. I noticed a flutist in the far corner. The music was very faint, and even when I was concentrating on it I couldn't really pick out a melody. It would do no harm at that volume, though, so I forgot about it.

As there were no people seated across the table from me, my only options for conversation were Karish on my left and the young man seated to my right. I recognized him as the man who had been joking about the decor with his lady while we were entering the dining room. I was aware that as a person of far inferior rank I was not to speak to him unless he spoke to me first, so I was resigned to an awkward meal of pretending the person to my immediate right didn't exist.

And again, my resignation was premature.

"This hall is something special, isn't it?"

Those words, spoken in a delightfully round bass, were directed towards me. I hid my surprise and looked at the young man. He had a pleasing appearance. Dark hair free of oil, gorgeous green eyes and pale skin. Not the sort to turn heads in the street but still nice to look at.

"I've never been in an aristocratic manor before. I'm not familiar with aristocratic fashion."

"But you spent some time with the Empress in Erstwhile, didn't you?"

I hadn't caught the announcement of his name earlier in the evening. I was always a little uncomfortable when speaking to someone who clearly knew me, when I didn't know him. "I did, but the palace felt much less like a personal home. Even in the bedchambers, I felt like I was in a government building. And the palace was different from this manor."

He glanced beyond me. At Karish, I thought. "Am I—am I *allowed* to talk to you?"

What an odd question. "Of course."

He appeared embarrassed. "I must admit to knowing little about Pairs," he said, "and I hadn't heard that there were any, you know, special rules, but I didn't notice anyone speaking to you in the ballroom. I thought perhaps we weren't supposed to."

Interesting. "I think some"—I was about to say "regulars" but caught myself in time—"people who are unfamiliar with the Triple S don't know how to think of us. I think they believe there *are* all sorts of rules about talking to us. There aren't." Unlike the aristocracy.

"How should I address you?"

"Shield Mallorough if you want to be formal. Dunleavy if you don't."

"Well, Dunleavy, my name is Doran Laidley. It is a pleasure to meet you."

"Yes, quite." I shook the hand he offered.

"I swear, I can't take you anywhere," Karish muttered into my ear.

Oh, please, all we'd done was exchange names. Like I'd ever have anything to do with an aristocrat. Even if he was pretty in a non-intimidating way.

The first course was served with exquisite precision by a virtual horde of young women, all wearing those ridiculous wimples. Poor girls. The dish was a watery fish soup with no seasoning that I could taste. And water. Which was, um, unique.

"Good lord." Doran had lifted a spoonful of the liquid and was letting it dribble back into the bowl. "Maybe he should have moderated the renovations a bit and splashed out for a decent chef."

"I suppose it's . . . er . . . healthy," Karish commented, sipping at the soup with a palpable lack of enthusiasm.

"So are the bath waters at the Ruins," I heard from Doran's other side, his female companion. "Doesn't mean I'd drink those, either."

A glance about the room told me no one was terribly impressed with the offering, though some were concealing their distaste better than others, and everyone was politely eating it. The Crown Prince, I could see, was particularly displeased. Lord Yellows was speaking to him, no doubt extolling the virtues of the soup. The Prince didn't appear to be listening.

"I fear for the rest of the meal," said Karish.

"No one says we actually have to eat it," said Doran. "We should just wait it out and go out after."

That sounded like a good idea. I put my spoon in my bowl and curled my hands in my lap.

"I can't eat so late into the night, Doran," his companion objected. "It's bad for the digestive system."

Doran snickered. "Is this the same woman who dragged

me down to the kitchen at Sevy's house party after the staff had gone to bed and ate half an apple pie?"

If more than four people witnessed the discreet smack she delivered to the back of his head, I would have been surprised to hear it. I looked at her and answered the smile she sent me. I liked her.

She wasn't intimidatingly beautiful, either. She was slight, with thick brown hair and lightly dusty skin, brown eyes with wrinkles around them. Not that she looked at all old; I would say she had only a few years on me, but obviously she allowed herself to smile whenever she felt like it. They made a nice looking couple, I thought.

"Don't be such a stick, Lydia," Doran complained. "Lydia, Dunleavy. I'm Doran. We all know Shintaro Karish. We're all friends now. We'll suffer through this awful meal in stoic camaraderie and reward ourselves with the fine cuisine at The Table. What say you?" And he pushed his bowl away.

I repressed a smirk. Had to admire the take-charge attitude. I looked at Karish and raised an eyebrow.

Karish rolled his eyes before, like Doran, he pushed his bowl away. Then he leaned back in his chair. "Well, Lady Lydia," he said to the young lady, who looked back at him with amusement, "if your lord is the incorrigible flirt my Shield is—"

"*You* are calling *me* a flirt?"

"He's not my lord, I take no responsibility for him."

"—we may find ourselves consoling each other in our misery."

"I fear our means of consoling ourselves might be radically different, Source Karish."

"Really? I feel there is nothing like a good book and a hot mug of tea for soothing ruffled spirits."

Doran hooted derisively. I laughed. Lydia covered her mouth with her hand, but her dark eyes sparkled.

Karish appeared affronted. "If I didn't know better," he said in a voice laced with feigned outrage, "I'd say you were all doubting my word."

The three of us were suddenly re-absorbed in the contemplation of the awful soup.

The next course was a salad. Of sorts. Half a dozen spinach leaves arranged on a plate, with some shredded carrot piled in the center. Dressed with some kind of honey sauce, from the smell of it. Served with more water.

"I'm not even sure how to eat this," Lydia confessed, holding her knife and fork as though she were considering trying to slice up the thin drenched leaves and scoop them on to her fork.

"When in doubt, don't." Doran took her plate and stacked it on top of his own. "Ooh, let's give the servants a heart attack." He took my plate and added it to the pile. "Please forgive my appalling lack of manners, Dunleavy." He reached across me to nab Karish's plate.

Karish was watching the proceedings with a smirk. He appeared to be entertained, but there was a strange air about him. The word that came to mind was resignation, but that was coming out of nowhere, and it couldn't be accurate. Something else was no doubt going on in that head of his.

"I'm hungry, Doran," Lydia complained.

"That's good. Foster that appetite. That way you'll be in the proper frame of mind when we go to The Table, which, I'll have you know, serves the best leek-and-potato soup in the city."

"Yes, yes, Doran. I have eaten there, you know."

I hadn't. How had I missed that one?

"One can't help wondering, though, if Lord Yellows has a death wish," said Karish. "Serving the Prince a meal like this."

I looked up at the Prince again, and I was surprised to find he appeared considerably more relaxed and to be amiably chatting with his host. I guessed he liked the meal after all. And he would be Emperor one day. We were all doomed.

I looked across the room, wondering how the Dowager

Duchess of Westsea was reacting to the insult being delivered to her stomach. And if I was surprised by the Prince, I was stunned by the Dowager. She was, or so it appeared from my angle, leaning against the back of her chair and *smiling*.

Obviously, the world was about to end.

"Is there something wrong with the meal, my lord?" A servant was hovering over Doran. She appeared distraught by the stack of plates before him. "I can bring you all new servings if these are not fresh enough."

"Oh no, my dear woman. Everything looks beautiful. But we're wanting to save ourselves for the main course."

I expected her to nod and leave. She didn't. "His Lordship would be most distressed to learn you didn't partake of the opening courses, my lord."

Were servants supposed to debate with guests like that?

Doran's eyebrows dipped together in irritation. "I'd wager my miniscule fortune that Lord Yellows doesn't even know where his kitchens are," he said. "And it's probably physically impossible for him to actually enter them. The mere thought of it is no doubt enough to make him swoon in well-bred disgust. In other words, he'll never know. So do stop being tiresome and take the plates away. There's a good girl."

She did what she was ordered, with obvious reluctance. Which struck me as odd. I mean, really, who cared?

"They're not eating any of it," I heard her whisper.

I turned in my chair and saw that she was speaking to the nearest guard. Who would care even less than the host. Realizing she had my attention, the servant hurried away. I watched the guard for a moment longer, but he continued to stare into space.

Cheese course next. And the cheese platters looked normal enough. With substantial portions. The other guests fell on them with audible—very audible—delight. But for Lydia, Doran, Karish and I, it had become almost a challenge not to eat anything that was served to us. A test of

our resolve. Besides, I was looking forward to the leek-
and-potato soup that was the best in the city, and I wanted
to be good and starving for it.

This course was served with wine. Karish broke the pact
to take a sniff. Then he grimaced.

"Bad?" I asked him.

He took a careful sip. He jerked his head back, looking as
though he had been struck. He quickly put the goblet on the
table. On the other side of the table, as though he wanted to
get the wine as far away from himself as possible. "Good
gods."

I went nowhere near my goblet. Neither did Lydia. Doran, being male, had to have a taste. His reaction was almost identical to Karish's. "Zaire, that's evil."

But everyone else was drinking it, and seemed to be enjoying it. Even the Prince, who I would have assumed had
access to the best wines in the world.

All right. Everyone was insane. That was the only explanation.

Which made me think of another source of insanity enjoyed by the city, because that was the way my mind
worked. "Doran?"

"Yes?"

"You don't perform in the Hallin Festival, do you?" I'd
been told it was required by law that every able-bodied person perform, but surely that wasn't imposed on the High
Landed.

Then again, who'd made up the law in the first place, eh?

He grinned. "Of course."

Lydia rolled her eyes.

"You're kidding," said Karish.

"What do you do?" I asked Doran.

"Sleight of hand." He picked up one of his unused forks,
held it in his right hand, briefly curled his two hands together and held out his empty right hand, the fork nowhere
in sight.

"Well done," Karish said with admiration.

I grabbed Doran's left hand and pulled the fork from his sleeve.

"Hey!" Doran protested, and Lydia laughed.

Karish chuckled. "Don't be too downhearted, lordling. Misdirection may not work so well on a Shield."

"Well, the circumstances aren't the best." Doran took the fork back and balanced it on his index finger. "You won't be able to catch me out so easily when I'm on stage with costumes and props."

If Lydia had not been a well-bred lady I would have sworn she groaned. "And they get more ridiculous and elaborate with every year," she said dryly. "It took days for the paint he slathered all over my face to finally fade. I couldn't leave the house for a week, nor see anyone. Mother was not pleased." But the look she shot at Doran was fond. She hadn't minded so much, I guessed.

"You do sleight of hand, too?" I asked her.

"No, I play his assistant. Hand him things on stage so the performance goes smoothly, with no gaps in the action and movement. It's the best way to get through a talent show without having an actual talent."

What a brilliant idea. "Don't happen to need any more assistants, do you?" I looked at Doran and hoped desperation was beaming out of my eyes.

"Back off, Shield," Lydia growled. "He's *my* ticket through the Festival."

"And," Karish tugged on my hair. "You're doing something with me."

"We never agreed to that," I protested.

"We're agreeing now."

High-handed bastard. "Neither of us have any talent." Which was a pretty pathetic state of affairs.

"You must be able to do something," said Lydia.

"You'd be stunned by the level of my ineptitude."

"Stop that," Karish snapped.

Doran and Lydia were understandably startled by Karish's swing in mood. There was nothing for it but to let them get used to it. "I can't do anything but shield and dance the bars," I told our new acquaintances. "I can't do anything anyone else would find entertaining. Except make a fool of myself, and I'd rather avoid that if I could."

"Do a scene from a play," Doran suggested.

"I've never acted," I said.

"Neither have I," Karish added.

Not on stage.

"That doesn't matter," Doran was saying. "It's the traditional way of getting through the festival when there is honestly nothing else you can do. Pick a short scene and act it out."

"Ugh!" was Karish's eloquent response.

Well, it was something, I supposed. Though the very idea of standing on a stage in front of a bunch of people stuttering out a string of tortured lines made me want to cringe.

Uproarious laughter coming from up the table. From the Prince, of all people.

"Maybe he has no head for wine," Karish commented.

No, I didn't think that was it. Or it was, at most, only a part of it. Others about the table appeared equally relaxed, speaking loudly, animatedly, gesturing broadly. Spines were resting against the backs of chairs all over the room. The Dowager was smiling again.

And she looked so much like Karish then.

"Maybe the wine is unusually potent," I said. "Would that affect the taste?"

Karish snorted. "It's too new."

"Too new?"

"If it was waved at a bottle between the vat and the glass I'd be surprised."

I frowned, my memory twigging.

"Three weeks," said Doran, eyeing his goblet. "Bet it's three weeks old."

"I'd take that bet, except it would require actually tasting it again to be sure." Karish shuddered. "No amount of money is worth that."

"Hah! Money. Like you have to worry about that."

Karish stiffened at that. "I always honor my gambling debts," he said coolly.

Doran's eyes widened. "Forgive me," he said, with every appearance of sincerity. "I honestly didn't mean to imply anything disrespectful. I only meant that, your being a Source—so how much did you lose in the upset yesterday?"

We all recognized the diversionary tactic for what it was, and Karish's shoulders relaxed. "You mean that vicious stumble in the fourth race?"

Racing. Gambling. Wonderful. I had to admit Karish was good about not boring me to suicide by constantly talking about such things, which were of no interest to me. But I could hardly expect him to restrain himself when he encountered a fellow enthusiast.

I noticed Lydia's avid interest. Make that two fellow enthusiasts. I predicted I would be feeling very ignorant and very stupid soon.

However, before the three could degenerate too far into racing slang the main course was served. Thick round slices of beef covered in gravy and surrounded by steamed vegetables. Mouth-watering commenced immediately. My stomach twisted painfully. "That's it. I'm eating."

"Lee," Karish said with disappointment.

"And I thought Shields were supposed to be so disciplined," Lydia teased.

"Discipline be damned. This smells good and I'm starving." Besides, I loved roast beef. I neatly sliced off a corner and stuck it in my mouth. I bit down, anticipating a rush of flavor.

But my teeth didn't sink through in the manner they were supposed to, and the taste was . . . different. Because I couldn't spit it out I quickly chewed and swallowed. I put down the cutlery.

"What's wrong?" Karish asked me.

"I don't think it's beef." And I *hated* eating something

when I didn't know what it was. My imagination went to bad places.

"Maybe it's ostrich," Lydia suggested.

Karish picked up my cutlery and took a slice from my meat. Like he didn't have his own plate right in front of him. "What, do you feel it's less like cheating if it's from my plate instead of yours?"

He chewed and swallowed and returned the cutlery. "It's goat. Quite good, actually."

"Goat," I said. Things starting clicking in my head.

"Aye."

"Just as well, then." Doran grimaced. "Can't stand goat."

Oh god.

Could I have been any more stupid? If I gave myself a year? And tried really really hard?

Wine of the new moon.

Mountain mammal.

Cheese.

Honey.

Plants would be in soil. Earth. Fireplace. Waterfall. Window for air. Everyone seated in a circle. Of a sort. In a stone room. It couldn't have been more obvious if there'd been a sign saying SITE OF RITUAL SACRIFICE hanging over the door.

Everyone was an aristocrat, except me. Almost everyone had a title. Risa had mentioned a belief that one big sacrifice would still the planet for a good long while. Maybe indefinitely. The Reanist who'd stopped me in the street had told me killing off one aristocrat at a time wouldn't accomplish anything.

Yet they had been killing them off one at a time. Or at least taking them. Why would they bother if they were just going to have this big party and kill everyone. Why not just invite them to the party with everyone else?

A test run? Proof killing aristocrats would work? There hadn't been an event for months. Not, of course, that that meant anything. Of course killing aristocrats didn't actually calm the world. Not in a geophysical sense, anyway. But someone could probably point to the coincidence and make a convincing argument.

Except no one who wasn't a member of the Triple S knew there had been no events.

This was Lord Yellows' home. He had served the food. He was High Landed. He'd have to be involved, if the Reanists were planning something that evening, but why would he be? Did he have his own reasons for wanting the Crown Prince dead? Surely he couldn't be foolish enough to believe he would get away with it.

On the other hand, if we were all dead, who knew what story he could tell?

What could I do? Who was involved with this? The guards? The servants?

But the Reanists had all been captured at the parade. Risa had said they were.

Everyone working for Yellows had their heads covered.

What was I going to do?

How could I have been so thrice-damned stupid?

But maybe I was wrong. Maybe it was all a coincidence. Everyone said Yellows was eccentric. Maybe he'd stumbled on a description of the Reanist sacrificial rituals and thought they were charming. I could be about to make a huge public fool of myself.

Better humiliated than dead.

Of course, I might not be killed. Not yet. My bad merchant blood might taint the rest. Just one more reason to be grateful for not being an aristocrat.

Stop rambling.

What the hell was I going to do?

I put a hand on Karish's shoulder and subtly pulled him closer. "We have to get everyone out of here," I whispered. "I think this is a Reanist ritual." Damn it. What an idiotic way to put it. It demanded doubt.

He stared at me, and I could tell he was wondering

whether I'd been nipping at the wine without him noticing.
"You what?" he demanded. But he kept his voice low.
Good boy.

"Trust me." I didn't have time to explain it all. We had
to think of a way to get everyone out of the manor, or at
least out of the room, without alerting whoever was responsible for this.

Karish studied me a few moments more before nodding.

I wasn't relieved. He didn't try to talk me out of it, didn't
think the idea was beyond the realm of possibility. Hell.

He looked up towards the Prince.

I could hear movement behind me. I could see guards
moving around behind the guests at the other table.

Something slipped before my face and around my
throat, squeezing tight, cutting off air. I opened my mouth
and no sound came out.

Chapter Twenty-one

Colors streaked before my eyes as the pressure cut into my throat. Panic flared as I tried to draw a breath and couldn't. I grabbed at the cord wrapped around my throat, forcing my fingers between my skin and the abrasive material. I couldn't pull it away. All it did was bite into my fingers. It hurt. The colors were swirling into black. I couldn't think at all.

And then the cord was gone, the lack of it almost stung, and I could breathe again. I slumped over the table, my hand landing in a plate of meat and gravy, and I pulled in huge gasps of air. I shrank away from the cacophony roaring in my ears, the blood pounding in my head and air scraping through my larynx. Movement, movement, too much to feel.

People were screaming.

Did they *have* to do that?

Still panting, rubbing the stinging skin on my throat, I opened my eyes. It took a few moments for my vision to slide back into focus, and even once it did it was hard to understand what I was seeing.

It was chaos. People were running around. Tables were being knocked over. Not two long tables after all, but sectionals, and people were falling into them and pushing them over, spilling dishes and food and wine over the floor. And then someone would run through the mess on the floor and slip and fall.

Some of them were wearing ridiculously high heels. I hadn't noticed before. My shoes were nice and flat. I could run if I had to. The advantages of having no sense of style.

No one made it to the doors.

The guards were attacking the guests. Some had come up behind with cords, like they had with me. But they weren't throttling them to death. High above a seated, choking victim, the guard would hold a stake, an actual pointed wooden stake, and in a hard quick arc would bring it down and thrust it into the victim's heart.

At least, that was the plan. Only the victims were squirming around too much, some managing to slip out of their chairs and away from the cords. Or the guards, who were not professional guards at all, didn't have the strength to bring the stake down hard enough, to force it deeply enough into the chest. Or they didn't know precisely where the heart was. And guests with quicker wits than I were grabbing up utensils from the tables, knives and forks or anything handy, and shoving them into the faces of their attackers, knocking them unconscious with heavy platters or the center pieces decorating the tables.

I heard the triumphant shout as one of the guards found his target. With one hard thrust he plunged into the chest of an older man. My whole body spasmed in shock as I envisioned the brutal wood piercing soft flesh, shredding the delicate organ. Blood spurted out. The guard laughed ecstatically, eyes gleaming. Words were chanted, a short phrase I couldn't decipher over the din.

I felt sick. What a way to die.

I tried to stand and found I couldn't move my chair back. I looked down and saw the body of the guard who had been standing behind me, now crumpled on the floor by my chair, a cord loosely tangled in one of his hands. Meat, gravy, and the shattered remains of a plate littered the area about his head. I shoved harder, panic surging back. I couldn't move the damn chair. I had to get out. I couldn't move like this. I was an easy target.

Karish was still seated, struggling awkwardly with a guard who was crouching over him and trying to stick a stake in him. I imagined Karish had spared a moment dispatching the guard who'd attacked me and left himself vulnerable. This second guard hadn't used a cord on him but had gone straight for the stake. Karish had grabbed the guard's wrist and was holding the stake away—he was stronger than he looked—but trapped against the table there wasn't anything more he could do to defend himself.

It appeared that the guards had really been relying on their victims being pliant. Few of them were having much success. But they didn't need to worry. The servants started to lend a hand, dropping their trays and jugs and rushing in to hold people still.

Who the hell was behind all this?

I grabbed a knife from the table. It wasn't sharp but it would have to do.

The guard struggling with Karish was wearing armor. I didn't know anything about fighting. I couldn't think where . . . Oh.

I took a deep breath and shoved the knife into the side of the guard's exposed neck, forcing it through the layers of resistance, swallowing down the revulsion that welled up in my own throat. I heard something snap, and an awful gurgling sound, and blood started pouring out over the knife and my hand and into Karish's face.

I blinked away sudden tears.

The guard jerked away from Karish, grabbing at the knife protruding from his throat. He stumbled over a body on the floor behind him, falling. He arched and writhed as he choked on his blood. I couldn't bear to watch him die.

Karish put his hands under the table and deliberately shoved it away. It skidded a few feet over the stone floor before tipping over. Why hadn't I thought of that? Karish jumped to his feet, blood spattered all over his clothes and the side of his face. His skin was pale, his eyes wide with shock. But he was alive.

Doran was fighting with a footman. Seriously fighting, with real brutal bare-knuckle competence. It looked like he'd already dispatched one of the guards and he had taken the stake from him.

Lydia was lying on the floor, curled up in pain, a stake protruding from just below her right breast. I grimaced in sympathy and took a step towards her, but I would have to get too close to Doran to get to her and I knew nothing about medicine anyway. I looked to Karish, but he was staring at the head of the table, mouth dropping open.

Lord Yellows was struggling with Prince Gifford. It was hard to tell who was trying to kill who. Their tables had been shoved away, and two guards lay unmoving on floor. So did Princess Jane. The two men were engaged in a knife fight, dancing around each other, thrusting and parrying, a bizarre example of art in the graceless chaos erupting around them.

After a moment I realized Lord Yellows was bearing a stake, not a knife. That answered that.

Lord Yellows was behind all this? But he was an aristocrat. It didn't make sense.

Act now, think later, Lee.

But act how. They appeared incompetent, but I was beginning to think they'd done something to the food to make us weak and slow, and we were hampered by our finery. All they needed was time, and eventually they'd get us all.

I had no idea what to do.

Then I was flying off my feet and landing on my face on the stone floor with a bone-crunching thud. Smacked my head good and hard, too. It was the serving girl, the one who'd noticed we weren't eating. She'd tackled me. Presumptuous little bitch.

Fear tasted sour in the mouth, but anger ... ah, anger was fun.

I was able to turn over a little on the floor as the servant crawled up onto me, a stake in one hand. The floor was hard and bruising against my hip. I couldn't get free, couldn't crawl away.

She was holding the stake wrong, surely. Clutched in her fist, which meant she had to raise it fairly high to get any kind of momentum and power behind it. This gave me plenty of time to grab her wrist and hold the stake off. It was hard though. Most of my strength was in my legs, from the bar dancing.

If only I could get a chance to kick her. Then I'd do some damage.

The drape of her wimple was getting in my face. I took a moment to reach out with my spare hand and rip the whole thing off her head. And there was the sun tattoo on her temple. Damn it, but sometimes I hated being right. Were all these people, all the guards and the servants, Re-anists? Where'd they all come from? Risa had been sure they'd all be arrested or forced out of High Scape.

Risa! Relief roared through me. The Runners. They were out there, watching the grounds! Or were they still? The party had started hours ago, with no apparent disturbances. And the Runners were no doubting thinking any danger would be from an external attack. They could be riding around out there thinking all was just dainty and delicate within. I had to get their attention.

What was I supposed to do with this woman?

I could use my legs after all, to flip us over. She shouted in outrage. I slapped her, which shut her up but otherwise served no useful purpose. Having spent years watching boys fight on the academy grounds, I curled my hand into a fist and punched her in the nose.

Zaire, that hurt, shoving bones in my fingers in directions they were never meant to go.

But it hurt her, too, so all right then. I grabbed her stake and stood up. I thought about kicking her, for knocking me over and being a part of all this, but it seemed so petty. She was curling up a little, blood seeping out from the fingers curved over her nose. She screamed insults at me, but they weren't particularly creative, and they were easily ignored. She was out of the game. That was all that mattered right then.

I looked around, not knowing what to do next. Karish was still on his feet, fighting another guard. I guessed he'd endured his fair share of schoolyard tumbles, because he seemed to be managing all right. Not exactly the stereotypical gentleman boxer, though. His style seemed to involve a lot of grabbing whatever came to hand and throwing it at his opponent, or using it as a club. But hey, whatever worked.

I heard shattering. A glass had been thrown against a window. That made me think. The ritual space. Maybe if we changed the space. Rendered it an inappropriate place to hold the ritual. Would they stop because, according to their rules, there was no point to killing anyone without a viable space, or would they continue fighting out of spite?

It couldn't hurt. But how to do it?

I couldn't begin to imagine how to stop the waterfall from flowing. I didn't even know how it worked. Maybe I could shove something into the passage where the water came through, but I couldn't reach the ceiling. Unless I stood on a chair. But it would be too easy to knock me down. And maybe it would alert the Reanists to my plan.

The fire was burning too hot and too large to dowse with whatever water might be available on the tables, or to smother with tablecloths. Besides, I'd have to cross the whole length of the room to reach it. I doubted I'd make it that far.

The pots for the plants were huge and appeared to be made of stone. They were too heavy for me to shift.

Smashing the windows would accomplish nothing. There would still be air out there.

But hey, it might attract the attention of the Runners. If they were still out there. A glass hadn't managed to break it a pane, but maybe a platter would? I grabbed up a platter and threw it at the nearest window. The platter shattered, the window didn't. Damn it.

And out of nowhere I felt those subtle shifts, tickling the back of my mind. I looked at Karish, and he'd clobbered his guard and for the moment was standing free. Apparently he'd decided it was time to whip out another earthquake. A handy weapon to have, I was beginning to think.

Much of the fighting stopped as people freaked over the experience of having the floor slanting beneath their feet. Not all of it, though. Some of the guards and servants lost their footing and clambered back up and tried again.

I wasn't sure how long Karish could keep the shaking up. I couldn't imagine the control it required, to maintain the movement without letting it get too strong. And more of the Reanists might have time to get over their shock and resume their assault. All that effort and all it did was buy us some time. Which was good. It was a good idea. It just needed some adjustments.

I wasn't exactly used to walking through an earthquake myself, though the way my life had been going I actually did have more experience at it than the average person. I was able to make my way back over to Karish. I had an idea. A really stupid one.

"Karish!" I grabbed the front of his doublet and yanked on it to get his attention. "Can you blow off the roof?" That would get everyone's attention.

He looked down at me. The shuddering of the floor died down quite a bit. "What?" he asked.

"A cyclone. Blow off the roof." The ritual required an enclosed place of stone. With no roof the people's essence or whatever would escape. And the Runners couldn't possibly miss that level of destruction. They'd come running.

Karish started swearing. I didn't blame him.

"You expect me to spin up a cyclone inside of a room?" Karish demanded after a few moments.

It sounded so asinine when he said it like that, but it couldn't be that impossible, could it? "I expect you to try."

Karish resumed swearing. I punched him in the arm. I didn't care how good he sounded when he did that, it was not the time.

The shaking stopped. For a moment nothing happened, and in the silence I could hear harsh breathing and pained moans. Then someone started crying, and the Reanists began waving their stakes around again.

And then I felt it, a wind curling about my feet. It was cold, icy, and I almost shivered. At first it played about the floor, tickling ankles and flowing over hems. In a few moments, though, it was stronger, moving faster, and creeping higher.

The wind spread out, weakening as it rose but strong enough to push the goblets off those tables that still stood. Serviettes flew into people's faces, hair escaped from pins and ties. And I did shiver as the chill climbed up my legs and wrapped around my torso.

Reanists and victims alike looked about, searching for the source of the unusual droughts. Someone started screaming. The wind seem to carry the sound about the room, twisting it and hollowing it out, until it was an eerie wail circling within the walls.

"They're coming!" One of the guards dropped his stake and pulled off his helmet. His eyes glittered, his face twisting into an expression of vacant ecstasy. He looked up at the ceiling and raised his hands. "The gods are coming! They're pleased with us!" He grinned, white and wide, and laughed. There were murmurs from the other guards and the servants. They all started pulling off their head gear and raising their hands to the ceiling, demonstrating the same delight.

Oh, good Zaire. Could they be any more ludicrous? But good for us. It kept them preoccupied. Maybe we should start charging them. Who was still standing?

The wind grew stronger and higher.

A plate shattered against the wall. Those nearest ducked away, one not fast enough. He shouted out in pain, clutching a hand to his eyes. This was going to get messy. Messier.

And the wind got stronger.

Tables scraped over the floor, were picked up by the wind, were set rolling. Smashing crockery. Candles blown over and blown out. Sparks flew out of the fireplace and landed on a tapestry. The wind blew out any fire that might have started.

I didn't know if whatever was happening was a cyclone, but it was certainly destructive. My hair was whipping about my eyes, obscuring my vision. I tried to hold it back from face, but it took both hands and tendrils kept fluttering loose.

The guards and servants were still standing around with hands and faces uplifted, like a goggle of proper gits. Lord Yellows was standing in a similar posture, only his eyes were closed and he appeared to be muttering something. Praying? From the expression on his face he was pretty happy about the way things were turning out. The guests were huddling on the floor, arms curled over their heads. Maybe I should try that.

The Reanists were vulnerable, distracted as they were. It was the perfect opportunity to overpower them. I couldn't. I was shielding. No one else seemed to think of it. This was killing me.

A flying chair took out one of the guards. Neat.

A gust of wind whipped my feet out from under me. Not so neat. Once again my head met the floor.

Don't drop the shields!

Fortunately, I had some experience with holding on to my shields while the world was going insane. Zaire, my life.

And then the wind was pushing me across the floor. I scrambled against the stones, tried to catch a corner with my fingers, but they were too smooth. I couldn't stop myself.

And all the while I had to hold onto the shields. I had to keep my shields up. If I didn't Karish would be crushed by the forces he wasn't manipulating and that would be the bad ending of a lovely evening.

I wondered if I was getting at all hysterical.

I rolled into someone's legs and felt them fall. I kept going until I hit a wall. That hurt.

But I didn't drop my shields.

I couldn't see Karish. A table was blocking my view of him and I was glad enough to have it there. Crockery, cutlery, candlesticks were flying about. So were tables and chairs. No one was on their feet anymore, not even the Reanists.

Would they stop screaming?

The roof could go any time. Please. Now would be good. Or the cure would kill us all.

Instead, the windows shattered, glass flying out into the night with sharp loud cracks. At least they went out. My mind flashed me an image of huge shards of glass showering down on us and impaling us, blood spurting everywhere.

Stop that.

And then the wind stopped. Karish's shields fell back into place. I withdrew mine. I raised my head.

The roof was still firmly in place. Had he given up? Was it too hard?

We'd failed. Damn. What were we going to do now?

People were crying. Like that would accomplish anything. But it seemed that no one had resumed killing yet. That was a plus. But it was so dark in the room, only the moonlight offering any illumination.

I climbed to my feet, wincing at the sharp pain jolting through my left knee. It had been the first part of my body to make contact with the wall. "Taro?" I looked over the room. What a mess.

I heard whistling. The high unnatural piercing whistling used by the Runners to call all the members to the site of a crime. Oh, thank Zaire, the Runners were coming. The windows must have done it. We weren't going to die. Who could I hug?

Someone was laughing. It was a chilling sound, under the circumstances. And familiar. I followed the laughter to its source.

"Blow off the roof," Karish chuckled from where he lay prone on the floor. He had a cut on his forehead. It was bleeding, adding to the blood from the guard that had dried on his face. "Like the kind of force that would require wouldn't kill everyone in the room first. It's made of stone!"

I knelt beside him, looking for other injuries. "Oh, shut up!" It wasn't as though he'd thought of it at the time, either. And the effort had accomplished something, hadn't it? That was all that mattered.

But perhaps I was congratulating myself too soon. "Keep going!" Lord Yellows shouted, having found his feet. "It wasn't the gods! It was just—" He cut himself off, because he didn't know what it had been. "Continue the ritual! We have to finish what we've started or they'll be even angrier!"

Temperamental creatures, these gods of his. I stood again, so I could run, if I had to.

"Yellows, have you gone mad?" Prince Gifford demanded. He was back on his feet, too, crouched in a fighting stance, his knife still in his hand. His fine clothes torn, blood trickling from his lip, something having sliced open his left cheek, he was alive and furious. "This is treason!"

"It is our duty!" Lord Yellows kicked away some debris cluttering up his feet. "We are the rulers of this world, we are the vanguard," he announced, the power of the rhetoric diluted by the fact that he appeared to be looking for something on the floor. "It is our duty to pacify the gods for the safety of our people. Where's that damn stake?"

Very noble and all, but I didn't remember seeing anyone trying to stake him.

Prince Gifford was staring at him, stunned. "You are

mad," he breathed, the words echoing through the stone room.

"No!" Lord Yellows exclaimed, giving up on his quest for the stake. "No! I have seen the truth. And it is a hard truth. I didn't want to believe it, either. I don't deny that. But the gods resent our being on this world. They resent the damage we have done to it."

Damage? What damage?

"That's why they punish us by destroying our cities, our homes. They are angry with us. We have abused their gifts."

"Forgive us, Pillars of Might!" one Reanist cried. Her words were echoed by several of the others.

"But we can appease them," Yellows ranted on. "We can purchase their favor. With the blood of the High Landed. That's all they ask. Please, sire." Lord Yellows implored the Prince, hands outstretched, as though he actually believed he could convince his prince to agree to die. "There are so few of you, and with your lives we can purchase peace and prosperity for all people in this world." Ugh, alliteration. Someone kill him. "Isn't your life worth that?"

I heard shouting from outside. The Runners were dividing up the entrances. Hurry people.

Lord Yellows heard them too. He started speaking faster. "I know what you believe," he said to the prince. "You believe it is merely the way the world is, all this chaos and destruction, and that all you need are the Sources to keep it quiet. But the Sources are an abomination."

"Hey!" Karish protested, but weakly. He was still sitting on the floor. I looked down at him with concern.

"They interfere with the work of the gods. They only make the gods more angry. And their effects are only temporary. There will be no lasting tranquility until the High Landed do our duty and give ourselves to the gods."

Oh. So Lord Yellows was planning to sacrifice himself, too. For some reason that made it all the more disturbing. Offering to throw away your life for something so vague and improbable, something so fantastic with no proof of its actual reality. How could one put so little value on one's own life?

Prince Gifford appeared disgusted. Imagine that. No matter what else anyone had to say about him, there was no denying that the man was sane. "Superstitious nonsense," he spat.

Doors were slamming open somewhere in the building. Hurry hurry hurry. Or were they indulging in a summer stroll?

Lord Yellows looked right at Karish. "You know it is truth," he said to my Source. "Since we started giving High Landed blood to the gods, the world has been at peace. Hasn't it?"

Karish didn't respond. I don't think he quite got the significance of the question. I did, though, and I felt my own eyes widening in shock.

Pairs that were doing their jobs properly dealt with disasters long before regulars could perceive the threat of a disturbance. We should be able to be threatened daily, hourly, without the regulars of High Scape having a clue anything was going on. And none of us had the habit of telling regulars whether there had been any events that day, or none. The regulars were not supposed to know what was going on.

So how come Lord Yellows did? How did he know, why did he feel certain, that there had been no events in months? How could he know that?

"Continue the ritual!" the lord ordered.

And he actually stamped his foot, like a child.

My attention was caught by something behind him. It made me grin. Hah! Sucker! "The fire's out!" I shouted loudly, both to point out that the wind had indeed put out the fire, and to attract the attention of any nearby Runners.

Lord Yellows spun towards the empty fireplace. "Light the fire!" He looked for something with which to start the fire again, but all the candles in the room had been blown out. Some of the Reanists, perhaps believing a completed ritual space was not so essential, raised their stakes again. Others appeared to be losing heart altogether.

The doors to the dining room swung open, hitting the walls with a bang. The first group of Runners ran in, lead by Captain Wong. The captain mother had found so charming at Risa's party. I wondered if it would be terribly inappropriate to run up and hug him.

"Arrest them!" the Prince shouted.

"Who, Your Highness?" a Runner shouted back.

"All of them!"

Well, I hadn't been expecting that.

Chapter Twenty-two

Our arrest was only temporary, just long enough to sort out who were the raving Reanists and who were the victims.

Doran came out of the experience with nothing more than a few scrapes and bruises. Lydia, we were told, was badly injured but would probably survive. Her Grace walked out under her own power. Mother and son made no attempt to speak to each other.

And the Prince, before sweeping out of the ballroom, informed my Source that the both of us were expected to attend upon him the next morning.

So that's where we were. Sitting in the front room of the suite in the Imperial, to which the Prince had moved from Lord Yellows' manor. I was dressed in my morning best. Karish was sitting beside me. He had flattened my hand on his leg, laid his own over the top of it. He was soberly dressed in black, every lace tied. He sat so correctly on his chair, spine straight with a good handspan of air between it and the chair. Expressionless mask firmly in place, but his eyes were blank, as though his mind were a million miles away.

Under my hand, his thigh was hard with tension.

"You are not going to be Doran's assistant," he said suddenly.

"What?"

"Lydia is unlikely to be in form to play Doran's assistant for the Hallin Festival. You will not take her place. You are mine."

Well, yes sir. Talk about a million miles away. "Taro, you have a thousand different people you can ask to perform with you." And it wasn't healthy, all this togetherness. We'd start hating each other. Or worse.

"Yes, but I like them too much to humiliate them with my incompetence." And he threw a tense smile at me in case I thought he was serious.

Still, I said, "Thanks a lot."

"You've already seen me at my worst. I see no reason to spread that kind of knowledge around."

"At least, not until you're on stage." With me, perhaps, to attract most of the crowd's derision.

"Precisely."

"I love logic in a man."

He squeezed my hand.

A staid elderly lady entered the room, her face blank enough to do a Shield proud. "His Highness will see you now."

About bloody time.

We followed the woman from the foyer through a sitting room and into, to my surprise, the bedchamber. His Highness was still in bed. In a dressing gown, his hair brushed and oiled, some cosmetics and cologne applied, but in bed. And eating from a breakfast—or lunch—tray.

I did understand that it was considered acceptable for royalty to receive guests while still in bed. Some people even considered it an honor. I didn't. It was rude. How much effort did it take to climb out of bed and pull on a pair of trousers, for Zaire's sake? Where was the man's pride?

There were eight servants in the room. They stood by the walls, posture stiff, waiting to be told what to do. I would find that sort of thing—people just hanging around watching me—irritating, but I guessed the Prince liked it.

Karish bowed, I curtsied. We waited as the Prince spread cheese on a slice of hardbread. "Lord Yellows is going to be executed for treason," he told us, sounding almost bored about the whole thing, "among other charges. He'll have a trial, of course, but there is no doubt how things will turn out. Many of the guests at last night's . . ." here he paused, looking for an appropriate word, "event have indicated a willingness to testify. It is unlikely you will need to come to Erstwhile to participate."

I hadn't even considered the possibility of that, but thank Zaire. That would have been a nightmare, participating as a witness in a trial. I'd heard about that sort of thing, that barristers took pride in making the witnesses cry through the sheer act of brutal questioning.

"It is unfortunate and disheartening to see one of our most powerful Landed fall under the influence of madness," the Prince spoke through his mouthful of bread and cheese. "We can't understand how the Reanists acquired such a firm hold over him. Can you imagine? He was to be sacrificed along with the rest of us. And he knew it." The Prince shook his head. "We have been informed, Source Karish, that you inspired him." The Prince dunked his cheese-covered hardbread in his coffee. Ugh. "When you disappeared last year, and no one had the slightest idea where you'd gone. And you'd just left of your own free will. You didn't mean to disappear. Or so," tap tap tap of the bread against the rim of the coffee cup, "Yellows believed."

I didn't glance at Karish. I kept my eyes trained on the Prince, eyebrows raised slightly in inquiry, as though I had no idea what he could possibly be talking about.

But, damn.

"His reasoning was that if you could be impossible to

find without putting any effort into it, other aristocrats could be easily hidden with a little care and planning."

I'd hoped to get through this interview without speaking, but I just had to ask. "Was Yellows really behind the disappearances of the aristocrats this summer?" I wasn't sure why I didn't want to believe it. It was no worse than what he had done the night before. But if he had arranged the disappearances, and had had those people sacrificed, it almost lent credence to his claim that it was working, that he knew there had been no events over the past few months, and his actions were somehow responsible for it. And that didn't bear thinking of.

Because what if sacrificing aristocrats did, in some way, calm the world down? And what if someone else found out about it?

"He was," said the Crown Prince. "He had formed those clubs. You know, those ridiculous little social clubs. Invited third drawer Landed to join on the condition that his participation be kept a secret. The little fools were so thrilled to be invited—" Oh, the disdain. So easy for him, the Crown Prince, to denigrate the need of those less prominent to be recognized, to belong to something, "that they rushed to join. And now they're dead. Or so Lord Yellows boasts."

So, what about that basement ritual space that the Runners had found, the condemned hospital? Unless that had merely been the place the Reanists had used while Yellows was renovating his dining hall. Or had it had no connection at all and was just some weird coincidence?

"The food was drugged, at the dinner. So was the wine. So we would all be happy to be sacrificed. I understand neither of you ate or drank anything. This is true?"

"Yes, Your Highness."

"Why didn't you?"

Karish hesitated a moment before answering, "We didn't like it."

Damn, did that sound childish. It probably saved our lives, though.

"When they noticed this, they realized it might be enough to ruin the entire plan. They panicked and pushed into the next step before the rest of us were ready to be subdued."

There you go.

"Is it true?" the Prince was asking.

"Your Highness?" said Karish.

"His claim, that there have been no," the Prince made a vague gesture with his hand, "earthquakes or tornadoes or what have you threatening. Since he's started sacrificing aristocrats."

My fault. I shouldn't have been thinking about it, as apparently the Prince could read minds.

Karish cocked his head to one side. "The axis holds fast," he assured Gifford.

"Ah," said the Prince, the lack of comprehension beaming from his eyes. He looked at me.

I shrugged. No ideas here, mate. "There have been events, Your Highness." The ones Karish had caused, but events all the same. So not, technically, a lie.

The Prince mused on that a moment, then apparently decided to put aside that line of questioning. "We did not call you here to discuss Yellows." He dropped the remainder of his bread into his coffee cup. A servant jumped forward and took his tray away. "You could have learned about that sort of thing well enough from the news circulars and gossip. No." He wiped his hands with a serviette. "We are presently much more interested in the intriguing activities in which you were engaged at Yellows Plain last night."

Ah hell.

"We have heard interesting rumors of you, Source Karish," said His Highness. "Rumors of strange doings in Middle Reach. Of some ability to actually bring earthquakes and such."

We were in so much trouble.

"Your Highness," Karish said, looking shocked. Well

done, Taro. "Forgive me, but that is an ability Creol had. Creol could cause earthquakes at a whim. It's an unprecedented talent. I had never heard of it before. And yes, at the time I claimed to be able to do the same thing, but that was only . . ." He was talking too fast, damn it. Rambling. Sounding guilty of something.

"We are aware," the Prince interrupted him, "of the story you told our noble mother."

And he didn't believe it any more than his mother had. Wonderful. The one thing the warring royals had to agree on had to be the opinion that we were liars. How scary would they be if they decided to work together on something?

"We are not sure what, precisely, happened at Yellow Plains," the Prince said, "but we do know there was an earthquake, and that . . . wind. And that you were there."

And that was a reason to suspect Karish of nefarious deeds? Brilliant logic.

Karish, having recaptured his tongue, bowed his head. "I can offer no explanation, Your Highness."

I watched my Source, and marvelled at his calm. He was the target of all these questions, lucky fellow, and he was handling it with admirable panache. I was the one grinding my teeth with tension.

"Can you not?" Gifford steepled his fingers together. "Perhaps you can explain your hospital tours, then."

"My—my what, Your Highness?"

This was ridiculous. That had been ages ago. Was he being watched? And since when? This was bad.

"We have heard rumors of you going to hospitals and visiting the patients. Tending to them, as it were."

Karish's expression was on of perfect innocent confusion. "When I have friends in one of the hospitals, I visit them," he said, sounding diffident and uncertain, as though he couldn't for the life of him understand what the Prince was suggesting.

"Oh, this is not simply about visiting friends. Not according to the stories We have heard. And such stories they are, Source Karish. Of the blind being made to see, the cripped to walk, the dead to live."

The last shreds of that cool demeanour I'd been so admiring fell away as Karish's mouth dropped open in shock. "Your Highness?"

And his voice actually squeaked. I almost winced to hear it.

"They say you're some sort of miracle healer, Source Karish. You walk up to a complete stranger, lay your hands on him, and drag him back from the brink of death."

Ah damn. I'd always hated hyperbole. It was always causing trouble.

"My—Your Highness! No! I can do nothing like that!" There was no doubting the sincerity of that denial.

Only the Prince did. "You are suggesting that Our most reliable sources of information are liars?"

Karish assumed an expression of bemusement. "These are rumors, Your Highness," he said, mild and calm once more, utterly reasonable. "I've had the most ridiculous things said about me, and this is just another. I can't heal people."

No one could prove he healed people. No one would get it from me. Bastards. He does something decent and kind and he gets all this grief from it. Why couldn't people just leave him alone?

"You are denying these rumors?"

"Most wholeheartedly, Your Highness."

"And you had nothing to do with whatever happened at Yellows Plain last night?"

"Certainly not, Your Highness," Karish answered. "I have no connection with the Reanists, I promise you."

That wasn't what the Prince had meant, and everyone in the room knew it.

My stomach was clenching into a nice tight knot. I wished I hadn't eaten breakfast because it was beginning to feel like there wasn't room for it down there. If I thought about it very hard I could keep my breathing slow and even. In, out, in, out.

Why was this happening? Why was I getting caught up in this sort of thing? This wasn't supposed to be my life. I was too ordinary for it. I'd just wanted to do my job. Be a Shield, live my life, not hurt anyone. What was this dangerous, secretive mire I was finding myself in the middle of?

Maybe we should tell everyone. Tell the Prince, tell the Triple S council, tell everyone. Get it all out in the open. Secrets that were shared by everyone, that were out in the open, were no longer secrets, and no longer dangerous.

But we'd already lied. To the Empress, to the Prince, to the council. Everyone. Could we dig ourselves out so late in the game?

And Karish was *so* afraid of telling anyone. And if dealing with Karish's mother had taught me anything, it had taught me that when Karish got hysterical about something, he had an excellent reason for it.

"And what about you, Shield Mallorough?"

Oh hell. I had thought I was going to get away with being a piece of furniture. "Yes, Your Highness?"

"What is your explanation for the events in Middle Reach and Yellows Plain?"

I suddenly wanted to swallow. My throat felt so tight, I was afraid of what my voice would sound like once I spoke.

No matter what I thought, there was no way I was going to contradict Karish about this matter in front of anyone. I didn't know that Karish wasn't right to be wary. And once there appeared to be any disparity between our stories, the game would be over, replaced by a nightmare. Relieving my conscience by telling the truth, without Karish's concurrence, would make us both look suspicious. It would land both of us in serious, serious trouble that we wouldn't be able to get out of, because no one would believe us anymore.

Not that they should. We were, after all, lying.

And so, "I'm sorry, Your Highness, but I don't know what you're looking for." Voice didn't sound too bad. Even and clear. I'd believe me.

"The truth," he snapped, his patience finally thinning.

"Of course." When in doubt, act like an idiot. "*I* didn't start any earthquakes in Middle Reach."

"No one thinks you did, girl!"

"Then I'm afraid I don't understand your question, Your Highness."

"No, of course you don't!" The Prince rubbed at his reddening face. "You would have me believe these are all just coincidences. All these rumors and events are inexplicable fantasies with no basis in fact. The both of you treat me like a fool." He glared at us, eyes flicking from one to the other. "You don't appear to understand how dangerous that is."

I had a feeling it was a bad sign when Prince Gifford forgot to use the royal plural. "Your Highness," I said. "We mean you no disrespect. We honestly can't tell you what you want to know." Because we were terrified of what the consequences would be.

"I don't like the way you speak, Shield Mallorough," was his blunt response. "I've never found that monotone you Shields seem driven to assume at all attractive, and you choose the words you use with too much care, words that are subject to several interpretations. It makes you sound slippery."

All right, then. Time to shut up and hope I didn't just sink our boat.

I felt Karish watch beside me. "It's a Shield's task to take care with her words." The accent strengthened as his voice acquired an edge. "They are all trained to do so. I thought everyone knew that." Shut up, shut up, shut up, Karish. "Perhaps if Your Highness were more informed about the responsibilities of Shields and Sources, you would not find our behavior so disquieting."

While it was all chivalrous and noble and whatnot for him to defend me, *this was not the time*! And this certainly wasn't the manner. One did not chide the Crown Prince for being ignorant. I really wanted to gouge Karish in the ribs for that one.

And the Prince plainly wasn't pleased. His face turned a darker hue of crimson, and for a moment I thought he was going to start yelling. But he didn't. He pulled in a deep breath through his nose and visibly grabbed control of himself. It was a little uncomfortable to watch, quivering rage hauled back and stomped into invisibility.

But his voice shook a little when he spoke. "You may be correct, Source Karish," he said. "We do find ourselves lacking in specific information about the Triple S. We hear that they stop all of these natural disasters that our world is apparently heir to, and of course we are well aware of the enormous levels of revenue sent to the academies and the council, but we never think anything beyond that." That was good. That was the way we liked it. "But it is clear that We should rectify that error. It appears to Us that We might be . . . underutilizing you."

That

sounded

bad.

"Underutilizing, Your Highness?"

I'm glad Karish asked. I'd been dying to. Sort of. A part of me had been. Another part of me had been thinking ignorance was bliss.

"Perhaps *you* can't honestly explain these unusual events. But perhaps your council can."

Ah hell. Damn, damn, damn. The council was already suspicious of us. What were they going to think—or do—if the Crown Prince went to them with whatever wild speculations he dreamed up? Just . . . hell.

"Yes, Source Karish, that's an excellent idea," the Prince said with growing enthusiasm and blatant malice. "We have been remiss, ignoring the needs and interests of the Triple S as we have. For centuries the family have done nothing but hand over a small fortune and leave you to it. But it has been made clear to us that the Triple S might benefit from some . . . supervision."

Oh. Hell.

"Obviously, Our next step must be Shidonee's Gap, so We can discuss such matters with the council. No doubt, in their collective wisdom and experience, they can answer questions you cannot." He looked beyond us to a servant who had been lurking behind us. No words were spoken, but I heard the clinking of glass. "Leave now."

It took us a moment to start moving. I was too stunned.

As soon as we were outside the apartment and the door had closed behind us, I looked up to say something to Karish. I wasn't sure what, exactly, but I had no doubt it would be stupid and useless. So it was just as well that I was pre-empted by the arrival of a servant. One of the Dowager's, I realized.

"Source Karish," she said, her voice hard with the unimpressed arrogance of a person who had spent her life waiting on someone truly unworthy. "The Dowager Duchess of Westsea requests your attendance."

Karish scowled. "Couldn't care less."

"Now, my lord."

That startled me. Was she allowed to talk to him that way?

Karish's face flushed. "Go to hell."

Oh, no, he wasn't at the end of his tether or anything.

The servant was still unimpressed. "I am instructed to follow you until you concede," she told him. "If that means following you to your home or to the home of someone else and knocking on the door until dawn, then that's what I will do."

And she didn't appear disturbed by playing such a humiliating role. I wondered what other kinds of weird tasks the Dowager had demanded of her.

"Oh, for gods' sake." Karish wanted to shove his hands in his hair but it was too tightly bound. "Why can't the woman just leave?"

Yes, why couldn't she? She either thought Karish was safely strapped down as the next duke, or knew it was impossible and too late to do anything about it. Now that her presence was of no more use one way or the other, why couldn't she just leave and resume the disinterest she had had for Karish during almost three decades?

Karish was going to talk to her. I knew he would. "Go on ahead, Lee," he said.

I'd planned on going with him. Moral support. "But—"

"Her Grace has no desire for the Shield," the servant informed Karish.

"She doesn't do much for me, either." But I wanted to go with Karish. I wanted to be there to remind him that there were sane people who knew his worth.

"Lee, please." He was serious, resolute, all those irritating grown-up things that more often than not just got in the way. "I don't want you to come with me. And I don't want you to linger around here waiting for me. I want you to go home. All right?"

If that was what he truly wanted. It was none of my business, after all, and I'd already seen more of his family life than I'd any right to. It was just . . . "Are you sure?"

"Yes, I'll be fine." He ducked down to kiss my cheek. "I'll see you at the Stall."

Another watch with him all wound up after breathing the same air as his mother. Joy. "All right." I patted his chest. He knew best.

She'd just better not do anything to him.

I watched him follow the servant down the hall. I thought about waiting for him anyway, but I dismissed that idea. If he came out of that interview in a foul mood I might be the last person he needed to see. So I would leave him alone.

I went home. And thought about how disastrous the meeting with the Prince had been. Not as bad as it could have been, I supposed. I was still breathing. And not in jail. All good. But he'd been throwing around ominous hints and I didn't have the least idea what was going to happen next. I hated that.

I didn't want to think about it. There was no point in it, not until I knew what was going to happen. Besides, I'd never be able to sleep if I didn't calm down. Karish and I had a watch during the darkside, never my favorite time slot, and I needed to get some sleep before I went to the Stall. I changed into the trousers and shirt my mother hated so much and heated up some stew I'd picked up the day before.

I heard a knock the entrance to the house. I couldn't have been more surprised when I opened the door to Doran.

My shock must have been plastered on my face, for he stepped back diffidently. "Is it not proper to visit a Shield in her home?" he asked.

"Of course not. I mean, yes, it's fine." Very good, Lee. Excellent impression of a rambling idiot. "Please, come in." What was he doing there? How had he gotten my address? "How is Lydia?"

"Furious that she didn't make a better show of it at Yellows Plain," he said with a tired smile. "She always thought if something dangerous happened she'd be able to handle herself."

"It was a mess. I don't think anyone really handled themselves as well as they would have liked."

"She'll be fine in time, though."

"Good. I'm glad to hear it. Please, have a seat." I scanned the room for articles of clothing or dishes that weren't supposed to be there. All looked clear. "Can I get you a drink? Some wine?"

With the efficiency of movement that was apparently bred—or maybe beaten—into the majority of aristocrats, Doran took his place on the sofa. "Wine would be good."

"Red or white?" Oh, I wasn't supposed to ask that. I was supposed to know what wine was suitable for the time of day. How horribly classless.

But he didn't smile at me. "Red please."

I nodded and took off to the kitchen, which gave me a few moments of respite as I poured the wine. I wasn't prepared to be dealing with unfamiliar people right then. My mind had been set to going to bed and avoiding thinking for the next few hours.

And I looked awful.

Like that had anything to do with anything.

I brought the wine to the living room, handing a glass to Doran and sitting down in the chair opposite the sofa.

"I've just sent a letter off to Lydia's fiancé, telling him what happened last night," said Doran. "She's going to kill me." But from the way he grinned, he wasn't too worried about it.

Oh. I'd assumed the two of them were some kind of couple. "Why wouldn't she want him to know?"

"He gets all militant and protective of her," Doran chuckled. "Begins to treat her like glass. He hasn't known her as long as I have. He hasn't seen the bloody noses she's earned, or watched her fall out of trees and whatnot and shake it off. Some part of him thinks she's done nothing more than sit on a sofa and read her whole life. It makes Lydia insane. But he has a right to know."

"He was brave enough to refuse an invitation to last night's party?" From what I understood of such thing, the refusal of a Prince's invitation meant the end of acceptance in any social circle within the High Landed.

"No, he's not Landed. He's merchant. He didn't get an invitation, lucky beggar. He's out inspecting his property somewhere." Doran waved a hand back over his shoulder. I wasn't sure whether he was indicating the direction in which the property of Lydia's fiancé lay, or merely suggesting that the man was out of town, or swatting away a fly. "Lydia couldn't convince him to come back to escort her. But he'll come racing back as soon as he gets my letter. He adores her."

Well, good for her, good for him. But why was he telling me?

He sipped the wine and appeared to be surprised. "This is very good!" he exclaimed.

My, how polite. I'll be sure to pass your compliments on to Karish.

"It just so happens I'm going to be out an assistant for

the Hallin Festival. Unless I can find some sympathetic young woman willing to take Lydia's place."

"Ah." Damn it. The perfect opportunity to get through the festival with minimal humiliation and I had to let it pass. "Karish has threatened me with punishments most gruesome should I desert him in this trial."

"How ungenerous of him. I would have thought Shintaro would have been able to find any number of willing victims."

"I have no doubt, but he probably doesn't want any of them watching him go through the embarrassing steps of learning a new skill."

He grinned back. "Then I shall forgive him for dominating you for such a purpose."

"That's right kind of you." And now what? I was so bad with small talk.

Doran sobered quickly. "About you and Shintaro—"

Ah. Here it came.

"—what were you doing last night?"

Not quite what I was expecting. "I'm sorry. I don't understand."

"That wind in Yellows dining room, you two did that."

How completely unbelievable. Now the average regular was starting to suspect something. "We can't manipulate the wind, Doran."

He frowned. "But you can control things like cyclones, can't you? That's wind."

I was irrationally irritated at the man for his making me lie, but I kept it out of my voice. "That's different," I said. "It feels different." It used different forces. But I wasn't sure either of us were up to a long lecture about the skills of Sources. "Just trust me on this." Yes, Doran, trust me while I'm lying through my teeth.

I felt awful.

"All right, then. If you say so."

"I do."

"But you have to admit, that was a pretty wild night."

"That is one word for it."

"From what I hear, a lot of wild things happen around you."

I raised an eyebrow at him. "And what, precisely, does that mean?"

He was undaunted by my cool tone. "Just that interesting things seem to happen wherever you are."

Who had he been talking to? And what had they been saying? "I think there has been some gross exaggeration going on."

"If you say so," he said, but his eyes were shining. "So, do you ever watch the races?"

"Not without getting really drunk first."

He laughed.

He stayed almost an hour. It took only a fraction of that time for me to realize we had nothing at all in common. But we had fun denigrating each other's preferences, and I found myself enjoying his company.

And, frighteningly enough, he wasn't caught by my list of restrictions. I never crossed off poor aristocrats. Hm.

I went to bed as soon as he left. I couldn't sleep, though. I was thinking about the Prince. And Lord Yellows. And Karish.

So I was awake when, several hours later, there was another knock on the door. And this time it was Karish. He leaned against the door and he smelled of smoke and liquor.

"I'm sorry," he said as soon as I opened the door. His words weren't slurred, but he sounded tired.

"For what?" I took his hand and pulled him inside, closing the door behind him.

"I shouldn't be here." But even as he spoke he was slipping his arms around me and hugging me tightly.

Very tightly. I put my hand on the back of his head. "What happened?"

"She knows." I felt him pull in a deep breath. "She's leaving."

Hooray for that. "Do you want to talk about it?"

"No."

I stroked his hair. She was leaving. This was a good thing. "Are you going to be all right?"

"Yes," he said. "I'm sorry. I shouldn't have come." But he didn't move.

"You're always welcome here, Taro."

A sound that might have been a chuckle under other circumstances. "Always?"

"Well," I smiled, "I might not always appreciate your timing, but you'll always be welcome." With no dazzling show necessary.

I pulled on the front of his shirt. "Come on. Let's sit down."

He resisted for a moment—what, he thought I was going to let him go back out there alone?—but then he followed me to the sofa. I sat down first and he sprawled the length of the sofa, his feet hanging off the end, putting his head in my lap. I ran my fingers through his hair, savouring the immediate calming affects of his proximity, and we waited until it was time to go to the Stall.

Epilogue

I stepped down off the stage, pretending to need to watch my feet so I wouldn't trip, but actually doing my best to avoid the eyes of anyone in the stunned, politely applauding audience. After the most humiliating experience of my life I wanted to slither away as quickly as possible and not see any of these people for at least a month, if then. But a part of me was angry, that I'd had to do something so unsuited to my temperament, and that these people had expected so much of Karish and me simply because it was Karish and me.

The crowd had been at least four times as large as that of most other amateur performers. Because everyone who had heard of Karish, and didn't have friends and family to support on other stages in the same time slot, were curious to know what the Stallion of the Triple S would do on stage. Damn Karish. Damn my being bonded to him. I didn't deserve such notoriety.

And he'd chosen the damn poem, too. Some nonsensical rambling thing that neither of us understood and the audience didn't appreciate, despite a flawless delivery. I wanted to know what ancient tome my Source had dug that poem out of, so I could burn it. I wanted to know whose good idea it was to teach that man to read in the first place. Really, why wasn't it enough for him to channel and look pretty? That was more than most people had.

But at least no one was throwing anything at us.

A month earlier, we might not have been so spared, and things were still a little tense. I still overheard the odd uncomplimentary comment. But things were better. Normal summer weather had finally descended upon High Scape, with comfortably hot days and fine, misted evenings.

Events had finally started occurring again. Not that the events were inherently good, of course, but to be useful again was a relief. The first time I had to shield Karish through an actual event, it had been a divine release. And after, it had felt like things were finally getting back to normal. Whatever normal meant.

La Monte and Wilberforce had been unbearable, each in their unique idiosyncratic ways. Not only had the Triple S finally responded to La Monte's inquiry with the assurance that we should claim to be working on the weather problem while we—and they—actually did nothing, but the problem had apparently fixed itself. Just as La Monte had predicted it would. I didn't know which was worse, La Monte's smug aura of superiority or Wilberforce's constant promises that when we were as experienced as La Monte we would know what we were doing, too.

I wasn't going to tell them what I suspected. That the Reanists had been sacrificing aristocrats, and that the sacrificed had been preventing the events. That I suspected there was also a connection to the weather—the events weren't happening as they were supposed to, so the pressure events released came out in the weather—and the behavior of the regulars. I had no evidence of any of it, except that all of the changes had happened contemporaneously.

I had also found that I could and did effect the weather

myself, but only once it had calmed down on its own could
I control the nature of that effect. I could, if I chose, stop
the rain. Or start it. But once the weather had become sea-
sonal, I saw no reason to play with it.

It was an interesting thing to know, that I could do it, but
of no real use.

So the weather was what it was supposed to be, but the
changes had come too late for most to recover their lost
crops or other earnings. People had gone bankrupt. People
had died. The damage was done.

Yet some had managed to recover something. Some had
planted late variety seedlings. Some had been forced to
find other ways of making money and had experienced an
amount of success at it. People willing to travel to nearby
villages and cities to pick up supplies continued to make a
fortune. And Prince Gifford had promised and delivered
grains from the royal stores. No one was going to starve
over the winter.

Then there were the executions. I was horrified to acknowledge that the hanging of the Reanists appeared to
provide people with some kind of perverse thrill or release.

The first batch from the parade, Risa had told me, had
been throwaways. Expected to fail, they were meant to address any rumors the Prince might have been hearing concerning an attempt on his life by posing as whatever threat
the Prince had been told to anticipate. The protection provided by Lord Yellows' guards was meant to encourage
Gifford's trust and reliance on his host.

The residents of High Scape resented that their city had
been used to attempt an assassination on the Crown Prince.
They really resented learning that Reanists had been living
among them without anyone doing anything about it. Having every single one of them executed made the High Scap-
ers feel vindicated.

These successes seemed enough to take the edge off
everyone's anger. At least enough that I didn't have to worry
about being spat at on the street. Not enough, however, for

them not to enjoy watching us make complete fools of ourselves on stage.

Next year, I didn't care what it took, I was going to be away from High Scape during the Hallin Festival. If it meant temporarily abandoning my post, or even being relieved of it, I was never doing this again.

I got off the stage, I kept my head down, and I walked, resolute in achieving my escape. I was thinking ahead to putting my feet up in my flat and drowning my sorrows in a cask of wine. Then I was grabbed by the arm and almost whirled off my feet.

"Oh no you don't," Risa grinned down at me, her brother a pace behind her. "It is shockingly ill-mannered of you to deprive the spectators of your presence after such a fine performance. I'm sure they are all longing to tell—"

"Shut up, Risa," I snapped at her. Of course she had been there to see it. Despite my refusing to tell her the location and time of our performance. Despite my forbidding her to come should she manage to find out. "When are you going up again? I want to be sure to be there to watch and mock." And laugh.

"I went yesterday," she informed me smugly.

She—what? She went yesterday? "You told me you were going on the last day."

"I lied." She smiled. A superior curve of the lips that had me debating the merits of slugging her. On the one hand, she deserved it. On the other, she was much bigger than me. "I didn't want you coming and heckling me."

Wench. Refusing to tell was one thing. Lying about it, that was just wrong. I wished I'd thought of it. "But you felt perfectly comfortable coming here to heckle me?"

"Sure." She shrugged. "I'm a commoner. A regular. A member of the lower orders. I'm not expected to know better. But you are, being a responsible Shield and all. You're supposed to be above publicly humiliating others. You should be thanking me, for helping you stick to your standards."

What complete bosh. I had no standards.

"Besides," Erin added, "You would have nothing to heckle Risa for. She's an excellent tumbler."

Another reason I'd wanted to avoid Risa right then. I'd left things with Erin kind of hanging. True, Risa had said he wasn't terribly interested in continuing things with me, but I felt there should have been some kind of ritual closing of the possibility, a shared glass of wine or an argument.

On the other hand, Erin didn't appear to be feeling awkward right then, so why should I? "I suppose you've already done yours, too?" I demanded.

He grinned. "Nothing gets people laughing harder than mimicking politicians."

Damn. I would have liked to have seen that. I could have used a laugh.

"But," he said, frowning a little. "What are oysters? And how can they wear shoes if they haven't any feet?"

I waved my hands in front of my face in a negative gesture. "I don't know what any of it means," I admitted. "Karish claims he doesn't either, though he's the one who found it. I don't even know who wrote it. Karish says it's very old. I think an early Source wrote it to torment all generations who come after. And I'm going to do my best to burn it out of my memory. Liquor is good for that, isn't it?"

"Come to my place tonight," Risa suggested. "I'm having a little party for Erin. He's leaving tomorrow."

I looked at him with surprise. "You're leaving already? The Bill's drafted then?"

He shuffled his feet, suddenly serious. "We've been told the Empress' health has taken a turn for the worse," he said. "And she's anxious to get this Bill shoved through before she dies."

I felt my mouth drop open before I hastily pulled it shut. "It's that serious?"

He shrugged. "That's what they say. The last week has been sheer hell, trying to get all the important bits on parchment. That's been done and most of us have been ordered home. There're three solicitors still working on it, polishing it as much as they can. I think the idea is to get it through and then do the fine-tuning after it's passed."

I whistled. "The Prince must be thrilled with that."

Ah, the Prince, the Prince, I'd promised myself I wouldn't think of him. At all, if I could help it. Since he left High Scape I'd been waiting for something to happen. For summons to Erstwhile. For the Runners to show up to arrest me. For the Triple S council to order us back to Shidonee's Gap. Something.

But nothing had happened. Which was good. But I didn't know if that meant there was nothing to worry about, or that the different parties involved were just taking their time deciding what to do. All I could do was wait and hope it was all coming to nothing. Very hard on the nerves.

I frowned as a new worrisome thought disrupted the others. I looked at Risa. "This is none of my business," I said, "but should you really be throwing one of your extravagant parties right now?" I've heard of people who were bankrupt going out with a bang, but I didn't want to see Risa following down that path of folly.

She grinned, apparently unoffended by my inquisitive question that I had no business asking. "Got a loan," she announced. "Erin arranged it."

"Not so you could blow it all on frivolous tripe," Erin muttered.

She glared at her brother. "Don't start," she warned him in a hard voice. "I'm not a child. I'll use my money as I like."

It was on the tip of my tongue, the suggestion that now that she had gotten this break she should use it to start clearing up her debts, not squander it on insubstantial amusements. But I didn't want to resurrect our earlier argument. And Risa was right. I had no idea how frustrating it could be to want something and not be able to afford it. To know you would never be able to afford it.

Everyone did stupid things every once in a while. I'd

indulged in some masterpieces. Just look at my fiasco on stage.

Risa's gaze left her brother and she made a deliberate effort to resume her earlier carefree air. "So are you coming?" she asked me.

"Aye, and bring your mother," Erin added. "She's brilliant."

Risa nudged him in the ribs and he glanced at her with surprise.

"My mother went home," I told him.

"Oh. Sorry. I was under the impression that she was here for a good while."

"She felt she had to get back home."

I had received a letter from her the other day, thanking me for my hospitality and congratulating me on High Scape's improved circumstances. Telling me that it looked like Dias was developing serious interest in an appropriate girl. Enthusing about the profit margins of the last quarter. In other words, it was a letter identical in tone and general content to all the other letters she had ever sent me. No mention was made of why she had left early. No attempt was made to continue the discussion she'd left with. No hint was given that we ever would.

I didn't know how to respond to the letter. So I had decided not to, for a while.

I pulled in a quick breath of surprise as an arm curled around my waist from behind. Then I realized who it was. "Trying to ditch me?" a voice spoke into my ear.

I tried to jerk away, though not too hard, because I didn't want to make a scene, so Karish didn't let me go. "I'm not speaking to you," I told him. "That poem was a disaster."

"Ah, they're all a bunch of city sackers," he said dismissively. "What do they know?"

"Bad poetry when they hear it."

"In time those who achieve real wisdom will look back on this day and appreciate that poem for the artwork that it is."

Erin snorted.

"I'm having a small get-together tonight, Karish," Risa said. "It's a going-away party for Erin. I've just asked Dunleavy. Would you like to come?"

I didn't look up at Karish; it would be too uncomfortable from my current position, but I imagined him cocking his head in that gracious way of his. "We can't attend," he said formally. "We have a watch in the Stall this evening. But thank you for the kind invitation."

Risa's gaze watched to me and I nodded. "I was going to tell you but I got side-tracked." And I was relieved not to be going. I wouldn't have felt comfortable drinking Risa's wine and eating her food and knowing she couldn't afford to be serving it.

Someone on the stage started singing. Really really badly. So completely off-key I couldn't believe he wasn't doing it on purpose. He had to be. No one could be that bad by accident. I clapped my hands over my ears without thinking. Erin and Risa, who'd had their backs to the stage, glanced over their shoulders with grimaces of disgust. Didn't the man know he was risking a barrage of fruit?

"What's wrong?" Karish asked.

I looked up at him then. And saw he was serious. He honestly couldn't hear it. For a brief moment I thought how wonderful it must be to be tone-deaf.

"Let's get out of here," said Erin.

"Wait wait wait!" a voice called from the side, and Doran of all people jogged up to us.

Karish's arm tightened to an almost uncomfortable degree before loosening again.

"What are *you* doing here?" I demanded with an appalling lack of manners. It was just, did everyone I know show up to watch my humiliation? He was another person who'd asked when I was performing, and another person I'd refused to tell.

He smiled without repentance. "I wanted to see your show."

I held back a sigh and gave into the hints Risa was giving me with her steady, unsubtle stare. "Doran, this is Solicitor Erin Demaris and Runner Risa Demaris, his sister. Erin and Risa, this is Lord—" I stumbled, realizing I didn't know Doran's proper title, "—Doran Laidley?"

"Lord Stoneridge, if you want to get pompous about it," he said easily. "Old title, little chunk of land you couldn't grow potatoes on, no cash. No excessive pride, here."

"Do you work, then?" Erin asked.

Doran, if he had felt like it, could have expressed horror and indignation at the thought. Instead he shrugged. "I've been known to carve the odd trinket or two. Little statuettes. Miniature profiles. Toys even. People have been willing to pay a few coins for them." And then he put his index finger to his lips, a parody of a request for secrecy.

And once again I had to squash down the envy I felt for people who could do things with their hands. "How's Lydia?" She had, of course, left the hospital, and I had visited her at her home, but she was requiring a long convalescence.

"Getting over the fever, finally. But still quite weak and finding it infuriating. And Ivan—her fiancé—is simply driving her mad with his hovering." He grinned. "It's fun to watch."

"You have no sympathy for the poor woman? Hardhearted man."

"I have sympathy for us right now." He winced at the stage. "That guy is simply awful. Do you think he's working out some latent anger?"

"Think I should arrest him?" Risa asked with a mischievous gleam in her eye. "Disturbing the peace or something. Inflicting emotional distress on the public."

"Voluntary assumption of risk," said Erin. "Everyone knows going in that they might see something awful." And he looked at me with amusement, the prat.

"Aye, but he can't use that defence until he shows up in court. In the meantime I'll have him arrested and silent. A short-term solution is all I'm looking for right now."

While Erin explained to Risa the difference between a tort and a crime, Doran touched my arm to get my attention. "They're holding a bench-dancing competition on West Baker Street," he said. "It's just a little one. Most people are still watching the performances. But I thought you might like to indulge in something you're good at. You know, after—" he waved at the stage, "—that. And I've never seen you dance."

There was no reason why he should. "I'm not dressed for it."

"Please. For me."

I let myself roll my eyes.

Doran glanced at Karish's arm, still around me waist. "My lord, please. Use your influence. This will be good for her."

"You overestimate my influence," Karish said over my head. "But you should go, Lee. For my sake if nothing else. You've been impossible this last little while."

I twisted around to glare up at him.

He grinned back.

I was surrounded by men who thought they were just too clever.

But what the hell. I had nothing else to do. "We'll have to go by the house so I can change."

"We've got time if we rent a carriage."

Karish withdrew his arm. "Don't sprain an ankle." He leaned down to kiss my cheek.

"I'm never going to forgive you for today, you know."

He winked at me. "You'd forgive me anything."

Aye, probably, more fool I. But I was so happy to have the old Karish back, the easy-going relaxed Karish, that I wasn't up to pretending I was seriously angry with him.

We said good day to Risa and Erin, whose discussion had degenerated into some kind of practical versus theoretical legal argument. Karish slipped away with a wave. Doran offered me his arm and as I was wearing those obnoxious skirts over uneven ground, I took it.

"May I call you Lee, too?" he asked.

I hesitated. Few people called me Lee. My family. A couple of old lovers. Karish, from the day we met and without bothering to ask permission. Shields were usually called by their family name by those within the Triple S. Dunleavy, from a regular, was acceptable. Lee, though, assumed a sort of familiarity I wasn't usually comfortable with.

Perhaps I needed to get over. "Sure," I said. Besides, I liked him.

So did Karish, it seemed, though that wasn't as much of a relief as I would have expected. And that was foolish.

He seemed a nice, normal person. Easygoing, nondazzling, with a calm, regular life. And I could use a little of that. No more weird adventures.

RESENTING
THE HERO
by Moira J. Moore

The ties that bind sometimes strangle...

In a realm beset by natural disasters, only the
bonded Pairs—Source and Shield—make the land
habitable and keep the citizenry safe.
But can Dunleavy Mallorough and Lord Shintaro
Karish put aside their differences to defeat
something even more unnatural than their reluctant
affections for each other?

0-441-01388-0

Available wherever books are sold or at
penguin.com

Penguin Group (USA) Online

What will you be reading tomorrow?

Tom Clancy, Patricia Cornwell, W.E.B. Griffin,
Nora Roberts, William Gibson, Robin Cook,
Brian Jacques, Catherine Coulter, Stephen King,
Dean Koontz, Ken Follett, Clive Cussler,
Eric Jerome Dickey, John Sandford,
Terry McMillan, Sue Monk Kidd, Amy Tan,
John Berendt…

You'll find them all at
penguin.com

Read excerpts and newsletters,
find tour schedules and reading group guides,
and enter contests.

Subscribe to Penguin Group (USA) newsletters
and get an exclusive inside look
at exciting new titles and the authors you love
long before everyone else does.

PENGUIN GROUP (USA)
us.penguingroup.com